Waves On Mars

D.R. Swan

This book is a work of fiction. Any resemblance to persons, places or incidents are either the product of the author's imagination or are used fictitiously, and any resemblance to actual persons, living or dead, locales or events are completely coincidental.

It's fiction. Have fun!

Waves on Mars

Book 2 in the Artifact Series
By D. R. Swan

Book Cover Image By
Evan

(WOM 25)

Dedication

To Evan and Ryan, always foremost in my thoughts and prayers.

Acknowledgments

Thanks to everyone for their help, support, and kindness. No one accomplishes anything alone.

Waves on Mars

Preface

Definition

Terraforming: To alter the ecology of a planet to match the needs of a particular life-form in order to make it suitable for habitation for that life-form. It literally means "Earth-shaping."

July 19, 2092

It had been a little over two years and eight months since the world had changed. October 13, 2089, billions of lives lost. The first billion gone in an instant in a flash of smoldering, exploding rock from space. The asteroid that struck the Earth, hit with the force of ten million Hiroshima atomic bombs. In one instant, a mass of humanity looked to the sky in wonder at a bright flash of light only to be incinerated in the next, and then in the following, their souls confused at the sudden and abrupt separation from their bodies. More than a billion living souls gone in a flash.

The devastating impact of the nearly two-mile-wide asteroid with Earth had obliterated Russia and ended it as a major nation on the world scene.

Russia had lost over ninety percent of its population, its capital, including most of its politicians, most of its army and air force, though most of its navy remained intact, but a navy with no country to guide it is nothing.

The Russian people who had survived, mostly in the eastern portion of the country, were attempting to reform their government and put some plan together to feed those Russians who were left alive and were now starving, but like most places in the world, some of their citizens were able to get help, but most were not and that had reduced their population further.

The rest of the world had problems of their own directly related to how far they were from the blast zone. North America, Central America, South America, the United Kingdom, and Australia had fared the best. The European Union, Eastern Europe, the Baltic States, Scandinavia, India, and the Middle East fared the worst. Most of the Asian and African nations fell somewhere in between based on their country's readiness for disaster and the wealth and natural resources of each nation.

Every economy in the world collapsed. Every stock market was wiped out instantly destroying many trillions of dollars of wealth. Every currency became suddenly worthless. The only thing that countries could do is attempt to feed their populations and try to keep anarchy at bay.

The most devastating problem for the poorest of nations was the nearly two-year winter that left the northern hemisphere mostly frozen causing crops to fail worldwide. The threat of a new ice age was feared but the Sun came out towards the end of the second year and the yield from that harvest was adequate. Despite all the problems and nearly three years later, the world was beginning to heal.

The United States, under the leadership of President Henry Dent, was entering its third year of Martial Law and by enlisting most of the population into the military, had quickly controlled the worst of the anarchy and pushed the hope of moving to space as the main goal for the American people. Dent remained President of the United States when all elections were canceled in 2090 and no elections were authorized by Congress for the foreseeable future.

Radio and what television were being broadcasted were filled with propaganda showing the efforts in space. The American people stayed hopeful by holding onto this dream and working in the factories to build the series of space stations, vehicles, and habitats destined for space. The American population worked for food, shelter, and medical care and received no other compensation. All essential industries like all utilities, medical care, and food distribution were nationalized. Since all the currencies of the world no longer had any worth, all countries turned inside to survive as best as they could with what they had to work with.

As word of the United States' continuing efforts in space leaked out, other countries wanted to join the United States and help in that effort, but the U.S. had become suspicious of the rest of the world, guarding closely their technological lead and was slow to allow anyone to become part of the space dream. As a result, the rest of the world, including historical allies, were now beginning to distrust the United States as the extent of their technological lead began to surface.

World tensions were on the rise. As in World War 2 Germany, some countries began to militarize and because communications were not affected, threats and harsh language were a constant. The United Nations was the only international body to have survived the Earth's devastation and each country seemed to denounce and threaten their neighbors. The world was in chaos. Humans were afraid and when humans become afraid, they become dangerous.

President Dent, as a result, had agreed to a meeting with Prime Minister George Lloyd of England and because the United States and the United Kingdom seemed to be historically joined at the hip, it was thought that the United States would allow the countries in the U.K. to be the first brought into their trust with one notable exception, the alien artifact which was discovered in a dinosaur dig site seven years prior was to remain a complete secret. Dent had also reached out to Canada and Mexico and had arranged to meet with the heads of those countries shortly after the meeting with the Prime Minister of England.

On the main continent of Europe, ultra-nationalism was on the rise. Shades of pre-World War 2 was showing up in the rhetoric from most of the countries associated with the European Union. Many common enemies were becoming allies and allies, enemies as each country in the world began to rethink its place within. World population, which had been on the rise for thousands of years was now on a steady decline. The world still contained too many people and too few ways to feed and provide medical attention to the population, so more would soon die.

The alien artifact which was found in the dinosaur dig site back in 2085 had turned out to be an artificially intelligent machine capable of learning, but since the asteroid impact with Earth, the artifact had gone dark and was no longer revealing its secrets. It had propelled the United States at least a century ahead of the rest of the world technologically in three significant ways. First, by designing space stations and asteroid interceptor vehicles to protect the Earth from another asteroid impact which could end the human race. These vehicles were powered by antimatter which had been found in trace amounts captured in the Van Allen belt. The alien artifact had designed a magnetic collection process for the antimatter which gave the space stations and vehicles unlimited power. Secondly, it laid out a step-by-step recipe to terraform Mars, cutting the time required from centuries to somewhere between ten and twenty years, a process already begun. The third technological advancement was lengthening human life by altering our bodies to endure zero gravity for prolonged periods of time and protection from the increased exposure to the radiation that existed in space. These human enhancements were still in the early stages of research and showing promise. It wouldn't be long before they were implemented.

The alien, egg-shaped artifact, affectionately known as Egbert, had been transported to Space Station Isla Bravo which was now stationed near Mars, millions of miles from Earth. The egg lay dormant there not having made a peep since the asteroid's impact in Russia which changed the world.

The space station itself, lay in Mars' orbit as the red planet continued around the sun on its 668-day trek which represented the Martian year. Traveling 880,000,000 miles at over 53000 miles per hour, it takes 1.88 Earth years for Mars to travel around the Sun.

Two years and eight months had passed since the asteroid destroyed Russia and the debris cloud that had engulfed the Earth was now receding. The Earth was beginning to heal, but its rehab was going to be long and painful.

Part 1

The Mars' Plan

Chapter 1

July 19, 2092

6:00 pm EDT

CNN Newsroom

Thomas Spencer of CNN reporting: "Today, controversy sprung up, again as a new video of the asteroid that plowed into Russia emerged from an online source. Though grainy and taken through a telescope, it seemed to show the vehicle which was supposed to divert the asteroid, instead, pushing it towards the Earth at the last second. Outrage erupted in the United Nations when the video surfaced. The representative from the remnants of Russia stood up and denounced the United States. Here's the film from the U.N. showing the Russian representative standing and pointing his finger at the representative from the United States, as the U.S. representative stared back at the Russian making no response."

Thomas Spencer of CNN then turned to an older man sitting in a chair close to a large monitor. The man was balding with grey hair and his mouth appeared to be in a constant state of frowning. Spencer continued, "We have with us today Lenard Golden from the Goddard Space Institute. Hello, Mister Golden."

"Hello."

"I understand that you have reviewed the aforementioned film of the asteroid."

"Yes, I have seen it."

"Is it showing the American vehicle steering the asteroid to Earth? Is that your impression?"

"Well, no. I don't believe that it shows the vehicle pushing the asteroid towards Earth. I believe what it shows is the moment when the pilot is pulled off of the asteroid. The asteroid was already fully taken by Earth's gravity."

"Could you show us as we roll the film?"

"Yes, I'll explain. To begin with, let me say that if we could have gotten another of our vehicles to the asteroid soon enough, maybe we could have diverted it from Earth, but the Russians attack on our space stations prevented us from having the time to reach the asteroid with any of our other vehicles. That left only one vehicle which didn't have enough power to push the asteroid away from the planet. The asteroid was nearly two miles wide and traveling at more than seventy thousand miles per hour."

The CNN reporter pointed at the monitor as the film proceeded, "So, right here it looks like the pilot steers the asteroid away from the planet then here it looks like he changes the asteroid's path back into the planet."

Lenard Golden shook his head then began to point at places on the screen and as he touched it, lines appeared as he illustrated his opinion.

"Yes, but that's not what happened. The pilot fired his thrusters at this point to leave the asteroid. The asteroid had twisted the pilot to the top of the rock, right here. Then the Earth's gravity altered the asteroid's path right here, pulling it further into the planet. The AI then pulled the pilot off of the rock at the last second, here, because there was no hope of diverting it further. At that point, it was all about saving the pilot."

"Several scientists from China and a couple from Russia have evaluated the data and have come to different conclusions."

"We have heard their responses and disagree with their findings. The Russian scientists have no right to judge us. The unfortunate fact is that they brought the asteroid down onto their own country and instead of taking the blame for it, they are looking for a scapegoat. Bottom line: It's their own fault. If they wouldn't have attacked our space stations, their country would still exist. Another thing to consider, we didn't only lose Russia. We have also lost allies, countries that we never would purposely hurt in any way. Purposely sending an asteroid of that size to Earth in order to eliminate some enemy would be more than reckless, it would also be incredibly stupid and outright madness. Our country would never condone what happened to Russia and the aftermath that has taken more than three billion lives including many Americans, I might add." He paused and shook his head again, "It would be utter madness."

"It certainly would."

Golden continued and stated in no uncertain terms, "This notion that we purposely brought the asteroid to destroy Russia is the height of spin. I'm not sure what the Russians who are left are trying to gain from these lies. It just doesn't make any sense."

"I couldn't agree more, Mister Golden. Thank you for helping us to understand this new video."

Lenard Golden nodded with a stern expression.

"This is Thomas Spencer. I'll be back in a moment with the President's response from earlier today and our panel."

CNN broke to commercial.

Chapter 2

Oval Office

July 19, 2092

7:00 PM EDT

President Dent watched the CNN interview with the representative from the Goddard Space Institute.

He turned to his Chief of Staff, Howard Diamond and said, "Hopefully, the world will buy this slight rewrite of history."

"Slight rewrite?"

"This is a clusterfuck, Howard."

"That it is, Mister President."

"At some point, the truth of what really happened is going to come out, and I hope I'm already dead."

"Well, Sir, the testing of the new drugs to lengthen the life and health in humans who are going to space is proceeding with impressive results. You may live longer than you were hoping for."

"That's just my dumb luck, Howard."

Diamond smiled ruefully and nodded.

Dent asked, "How are things going on Mars?"

"Things are going well. I have a meeting with Martha Kensington of the Johnson Space Center, tomorrow about our armada to be sent to Mars."

"Sounds good."

"I'll brief you at 1:00. We should be finished by then."

"Thanks, Howard."

"Goodnight, Mister President."

Oval Office

July 20, 2092

1:00 PM EDT

The next day, Howard Diamond walked into the office of the President for his 1:00 meeting. Dent sat behind his desk reading an editorial from the New York Times about the CNN report from last night. The editorial seemed to side against the government's slant on the events stating that in their opinion, it looked like the vehicle did push the asteroid into the planet, but they admitted that the film was not of good quality and that it would make no sense for the United States to take a chance that they could steer a rock traveling at more than seventy thousand miles an hour directly onto a target like Russia, with Earth spinning at one thousand miles an hour in space. The idea was absurd.

President Dent looked up. "Hello, Howard."

"Good afternoon, Mister President."

"How was your briefing?"

"It went well. Mrs. Kensington informed me that all systems are go for the mission to Mars. The space station, which is now in orbit behind the Moon, has already been completed and is in the final testing of its gravity ring. All the resupplies for those on Mars have already arrived and are loaded onto the new space station. Half of the ten rockets that are going to accompany it are there and in place. The rest will be launched soon after. The mission is a go and on schedule."

"That's good to hear," Dent said, then paused, "Howard?"

"Yes?"

"What of the artifact? Has it made a peep since it went dark? Anything?"

"To my knowledge, it has continued to be quiet."

"Huh. It's the damnedest thing."

Diamond nodded. "Is there anything else, Mister President?"

"No, not now. I'll see you at 4:00 for our meeting with the Joint Chiefs. England has become worried about the European continent. To England, it feels like pre-World War 2. They're worried about our military readiness if Europe goes fascist again. I guess it's beginning to look so."

"Maybe not, at least they're back to having local elections," Diamond stated flatly but looked directly into the President's eyes.

"I got your message, Howard. Let's have a discussion with the Leader of the House about trying to hold local elections."

Howard nodded and turned for the door.

Dent said, "Thanks, Howard."

Diamond turned back, "See you at 4:00." He turned and proceeded out of the door.

Chapter 3

Mars' Topography:

Mars is an interesting planet. The landscape is now barren with wide patches of ice that have formed at its poles from carbon dioxide and large craters punched from asteroid strikes in the not too distant past. In the northern portion of Mars, a huge ocean once raged, but when Mars lost its atmosphere, the ocean was also lost. Left in the ocean's place though, is an enormous sheet of what might be H_2O ice lying under a thick layer of Martian sand blown there by the Martian winds. To the south, Mars has a large landmass, one giant continent. Across the northern portion of that continent, huge volcanos rise from the Martian landscape dwarfing any to be found anywhere else in our solar system.

Four billion years ago, it appears that Mars was a planet with one great ocean and one great continent. If the atmospheric pressure could be raised enough on the red planet, it appears that liquid water would again collect on its surface and that great northern ocean would again exist. Because Mars' gravity is only around .38 that of Earth's, the ocean would roil with thirty-foot waves not held down by gravity and could rise to enormous heights blown by the Martian winds. An ocean on Mars would be a frightful place.

Earth Date: January 21, 2093

Sol Date: 161 of the 668 Day Martian Year

Against the backdrop of space, Kirk Matthews could see the comet race in front of his AK2200, the vehicle designed to track and divert asteroids that might threaten Earth. Beneath his white flight suit and visor, Kirk was six-foot, with blue eyes, dark hair and chiseled features.

His onboard, artificially intelligent pilot, who directed the mission announced, "Thirty seconds and closing."

This voice was robotic, unlike the first AI that had directed the previous space flights. The first AI had a female voice and called herself Galadriel. She wasn't anything like the currently designed AI units that were used to fine-tune the missions. Galadriel had a personality and a vindictive streak.

Kirk tried not to think of her.

"Ten seconds and closing," the robotic voice of the AI declared. "9-8-7-6-5-4-3-2-1."

"I'm on the comet," Kirk reported.

"Go for it, buddy," Sandy Jones said.

Sandy was flying another of the AK2200s next to Kirk. He had been with Kirk at flight school 5 years prior and they had become the best of friends.

Sandy was African American, even-tempered with a kind smile, and was now the best pilot in the growing fleet. He had been transferred back and forth in the last year to train new pilots between his primary mission which was to deliver essential space rocks to the surface of planet Mars. It wasn't unusual for the new pilots to call him "Yoda" because of his innate skills in the vehicles, a reference to the most revered Jedi in the Star Wars saga. Most of the pilots were currently flying and training on Isla Alpha, the first space station built by the Americans that was now stationed in a stable orbit just beyond the moon.

The large H2O filled comet raced forward at forty-thousand miles an hour, slow by asteroid standards. It dragged its tail behind it for a thousand miles, blown by the solar winds.

"Engage thrusters," the AI directed.

Kirk fired his thrusters to change the direction of the comet slightly.

Before, the AI might do any flight adjustments for the human pilot, but the last AI, Galadriel, had driven an enormous asteroid into Russia, completely destroying the country, so now the AIs can only verbally direct and do not have the ability to take over the vehicles. It was felt that it would lessen the AK2200s' effectiveness and be more dangerous for the pilots, but that was a risk that the United States was willing to take, especially after the worldwide backlash from countries that weren't decimated by the asteroid's impact in Russia. On Earth now, no one trusted anyone.

The one exception to that rule was that when returning to the space station, the AI was allowed to assist the pilots with docking the vehicles, a very difficult maneuver.

The AI then spoke robotically for Kirk to alter the heading for the comet and make a slight adjustment, "Bring the comet to .3.1."

".3.1," Kirk responded and fired his thrusters for the second time to alter the comet's flightpath. It dipped toward Mars.

"Lookin' good, Kirk," Sandy said.

The AI displayed the final adjustment on Kirk's instrument panel.

Kirk said, "Ready for final adjustment in 5-4-3-2-1. Firing thrusters."

The comet dipped further towards the red planet.

"That's it," Kirk said. "I'm out of here."

He pulled his vehicle off the comet and slowed but kept an eye on its path. Sandy brought his interceptor beside Kirk and glanced over at him through the windshield.

"Looks good, Kirk."

"I hope I get it as close to my target as you got that last one," Kirk commented.

In the last year, more than a dozen ice-filled comets had been steered onto the Martian surface. Most sent to the lowlands where there was once a great ocean. Sandy had steered the first just south of Mars' equator a year before, scoring a direct hit in a place where Mars had been hit by an asteroid in the not too distant past and deepening the existing crater. Scientists hoped this place would eventually fill with water and become a Martian sea. The comet that Kirk had just directed to Mars was the largest to date and was supposed to make contact on the opposite side of Mars, north of the equator. It would punch a deep crater in the area where the great ocean had existed a few billion years prior. This was the later stages of the planned strikes of asteroids and comets with the surface of Mars. This comet should be one of the last large impacts, but smaller comets that contained important chemicals like nitrogen, water, and carbon dioxide in the form of ice would still be captured and directed to the surface in the year to come.

All asteroid strikes were steered away from Valles Marineris, the largest canyon in the solar system. At over twenty-seven-hundred miles long, one hundred-twenty miles wide and four miles deep, it dwarfed the Grand Canyon located in the United States. Though the plan was to try to miss any known and popular formations on the Martian surface, it was going to be impossible to preserve everything. Some things were going to be destroyed. There was just no way to save it all.

Soon, the building of more domed outposts was to begin on what was thought to be Mars' great continent. Two outposts had already been constructed at the poles close to the heat generators which were now melting portions of the carbon dioxide-rich ice at the edges of the two polar ice caps. These generators were designed on Earth by the alien artifact, Egbert, and were to begin the process of filling the Martian atmosphere with carbon dioxide. They would soon be joined by enormous factories to continue this work. The use of asteroids and comets certainly hastened the thickening of the atmosphere, but once the domed outposts became spread around the Martian surface, dropping comets and asteroids on the planet was going to become too dangerous for the new outposts. To date, no asteroids were directed to either pole and all impacts were sent to just north or south of the Martian equator.

The impact of the comets was also designed to increase Mars' water supply, as well as to help thicken the atmosphere by filling it with debris which would, in turn, heat the planet. So far this had been a success. Ice under a thin layer of surface dust and rock was melting, vaporizing and helping to thicken Mars' thin atmosphere. Because of the collisions with the enormous space rocks, volcanos began to spew plumes of carbon dioxide-rich smoke and debris into the thickening atmosphere. The atmosphere of Mars was now also filling with water vapor from the comets and the melting of the newly discovered ice deposits situated mostly in the northern hemisphere of Mars where the great ocean had once existed. As the temperature rose, the ice became vapor and poured into the atmosphere. The atmospheric pressure of Mars was rising as the atmosphere thickened and the beginning of the terraforming was proceeding reasonably on schedule. The first phase had been a complete success.

Sandy and Kirk waited as the comet breached Mars' thin atmosphere, then with a flash of near blinding light, smashed into the surface.

Sandy said, "Damn, that's a planet shaker. Let's head back, buddy."

The two interceptors accelerated and turned towards Isla Bravo which was located in a stable orbit, fifty-thousand miles above the Martian surface.

"Good job, guys," came the voice of Captain Chambers from over the coms.

Kirk said, "Thanks, Captain. Heading back."

Chapter 4

Mars' Surface

Club Med North

Earth Date: January 23, 2093

Mars Date: Sol 161

The ground rumbled as the asteroid struck thousands of miles away. The shaking wasn't like an earthquake from a fault line on Earth where the pressure had built then released. It was more a sudden sound and vibration as if the planet was struck by an enormous bomb. The crew of Club Med North, the northernmost domed outpost, had never become used to these assaults on the surface of Mars from space over the few months that they had lived there.

Commander, Joan Bernstein, and Botanist, Miguel Flores, had been talking near the airlock about the beginnings of a compost pile to enrich the Martian soil that they had collected for an experiment to grow second-generation plants not using hydroponics. As the sound rumbled, the shaking began. They both stopped their discussion and gazed overhead.

"I think that was closer than it was supposed to be," Miguel commented.

Bernstein nodded. "Or maybe just bigger."

They always had fair warning when Isla Bravo was about to send an asteroid to the surface just in case it ended up off course and would hit too close to their encampment.

They both looked around for any breach in the domed habitat but it was solid and well-constructed. A strong wind then hit the structure, buffeting it with the sandy Martian soil. Rocks and sand could be heard as they struck against the well-insulated building with the sound of an enormous hail storm. Whenever an asteroid was being directed to the planet, no personnel was allowed outside the habitat which had been built to withstand winds of up to 400 miles per hour. If a human were to be caught in that kind of wind, the sand and rocks would instantly strip them to the bone.

Bernstein got on the com line to each dome. "Report," she said.

A voice came from dome one, "We're checking now…" a minute passed. "We're good, Commander," said Michael Murphy after a check of his domed structure.

From dome two, "Commander, we've lost our magnetic field. Once the wind dies down, we're going to need to go outside and see what happened," Angela Freeman reported.

"Angela, once the wind dies down, send anyone in your dome over here until its fixed."

"Roger that."

Club Med North was a twin to Club Med South. Both bases consisted of three, thirty-foot, geodesic domes constructed of special lightweight, but tough carbon materials to ensure that the inhabitants would be safe from the rough Martian environment and the domes came complete with a magnetic shielding to protect against the DNA shredding particles from the Sun. Each dome was soon to be connected by hallways to allow the personnel to freely traverse back and forth between the domes, but the hallways had not yet been added. Those structures were to be delivered by the armada soon to arrive from Earth.

In the center of the three-dome complex, was a smaller dome that housed most of the main units that produced power to the individual structures. It was a fully separated dome but could be accessed through an underground tunnel. It was affectionately referred to as Con ED after the New York-based utility, or ED for short.

The lights flickered.

Bernstein said, "Come on, ED."

The flickering only lasted for a couple of seconds, then stabilized.

"That's better," she said then smiled and glanced back at Flores. "Where were we?"

Flores said, "I think we should set up the compost pile in the center of this dome. It's already set up to monitor the oxygen, carbon dioxide and ethylene gas from the growing plants. I can't wait to see what we can do with the Martian soil."

"Sounds good to me, Miguel," Bernstein agreed.

The habitats also had highly efficient solar panels that added electricity to help run the habitats' differing needs. During any impact from an asteroid or predicted windstorm, the solar panels were wheeled back inside the habitats. Once the winds subsided and the all-clear was given, the crews would then bring the panels back outside and point them back into the sun. Though 55,000,000 miles further than the Earth from the Sun, give or take depending on where Mars was in its elliptical orbit, the solar panels still produced a fair amount of energy but not nearly what they would produce on Earth.

Each habitat was built close to a known water source that existed just underground in the form of ice. Oxygen was then extracted from the ice using a technique which separated the oxygen from the hydrogen to provide oxygen for breathing. The oxygen was then mixed with a nitrogen/argon mixture, both found in the Martian atmosphere. The problem was that the atmosphere also contained toxic gases that must first be removed through a series of steps that included running the gases through a catalytic converter, then a freezing process. The mechanisms, though, would allow humans an indefinite amount of breathable air. The excess hydrogen was stored for any need for fuel with any excess released into the Martian atmosphere. Soon enormous factories were to be built to pump copious amounts of gases into the atmosphere. One thing humans had learned on Earth was how to heat a climate. Cooling it was a different story.

Another simpler process from melting the ice would be to provide water, but nothing was abundant and each dome had its own complete system for providing purified water and sufficient air. The domes would at some point be connected by hallways made of the same carbon materials, but separate life support systems would be maintained and kept functioning in case of failures.

Nothing was ever wasted and large storage tanks, built at a safe distance from the habitats, reserved all essential chemicals that had needed to be refined for use in the habitats. One of the domes was a complete greenhouse and already was in the process of growing plants for consumption. One of the biggest problems for any humans who ventured from planet Earth was protein, so plants that contained protein like soybeans was high on the list of the plants first grown. Another big positive about plants that were grown in the domes was that they produce oxygen and removed carbon dioxide from the air naturally through photosynthesis, the exact opposite of human respiration. Though not nearly enough oxygen could be produced by the total number of plants grown in the habitat to sustain human life, every little bit helped and as more plants were grown, the amount of oxygen needed to be produced by the other processes could be reduced or stored for emergencies.

Bernstein scanned around her thirty-foot geodesic dome for any problems. Once satisfied that all was in order, she turned and gazed out of the window and looked at the ruddy Martian landscape. She thought about Earth, so far away, and fought off a nagging depression that she had never expected. This mission was all that she had ever wanted. It had consumed her from the first time she had been presented with the opportunity. But her home was so far. The sound of pelting sand still assaulted the structure, though the wind had begun to subside. She could see it blow and swirl outside in the harsh Martian environment... Back to work, she thought. She turned from the window.

Chapter 5

Earth Date: May 28, 2093

Mars Date: Sol 286

Six Months Later...

Space Station Isla Bravo continued to direct ice-filled comets and asteroids onto the Martian landscape north of its equator as Mars orbited the Sun. Small nitrogen laden asteroids had been located at the edges of the asteroid belt and been brought to Mars and deposited onto the Martian surface.

The atmospheric pressure was now steadily on the increase, and the temperature on the Martian surface, near its equator, had remained above freezing for nearly half of a Martian year. Small amounts of liquid water gathered in a kind of briny sludge that collected in low spots on the rugged landscape. Mars' low gravity was just strong enough to hold onto the thickening atmosphere which was becoming rich with carbon dioxide from the melting ice caps, melting ice under the surface of the soil and volcanos which had been reborn due to the violent impacts from the enormous comets and asteroids. The giant volcano, Olympus Mons, the largest known volcano in the solar system, began smoldering and dark plumes of carbon dioxide-rich smoke roiled from its peak. At over 72,000 feet in height, it measures over twice the height of Mount Everest and its base, the diameter of Arizona.

Step two in the terraforming process was about to begin. In the last nine months, ten large rockets and another space station, which was larger than Isla Bravo, had been launched from Cape Canaveral and were approaching Mars to bring crew, supplies, and the first of the nearly twenty planned small domed outposts to be built on the surface. These domed encampments would, within the next year, be constructed and would be equipped with factories that would spew greenhouse gasses into the Martian atmosphere to further warm the temperature. These specially designed factories would also release ozone which would drift into the upper atmosphere to create a thin ozone layer much like Earth's. Mars does have ozone in its upper atmosphere, but it's sparse and spotty. The plan was to thicken it.

Once emptied of their cargo and crew, the ten rockets would then be placed in a stable orbit around Mars and would emit a magnetic field to imitate the Van Allen Belt that protects Earth from most of the harmful effects of the Sun.

The terraforming of Mars was well underway with the rest of the world having no real idea of what was happening there.

Eight months ago, Club Med North had been constructed followed by Club Med South which was constructed just two weeks later. The two domed encampments had been built close to the polar ice caps and so far, had been successful. Much had been learned as the tiny colonies struggled for survival. The encampments had successfully grown their first vegetable crops hydroponically and could partially self-sustain. Some crops like sweet potatoes, soybeans, and lettuce had begun growing in Martian soil inside the domes and would, before long, be ready for the first harvest from Martian soil on the Martian surface.

Chapter 6

Club Med South

Earth Date: May 28, 2093

Mars Date: Sol 286

Captain Justin Chambers of Isla Bravo put in a call to the Club Med South Commander, Hank Middlefield. Club Med South was a twin to Club Med North. It consisted of three thirty-foot geodesic domes with another smaller dome located in the middle of the three.

"Middlefield here," he said hustling to the com.

He normally kept the earpiece in his ear but he had been wheeling some Martian soil into the garden dome from the airlock where it was dumped and he was sweating. The earpiece was in his pocket.

"Hey, Hank, the shuttle with some supplies is on the way."

"Thanks, Captain."

"Should be landing in about ten minutes."

"Roger that. We'll be ready," Hank replied. He got on the domes' intercom system. "Suit up for a shipment."

A team of the encampment's personnel suited then waited inside the airlock to receive the shipment. Most times the shipment was light, no more than forty small cases packed tightly with food, medicine, and any mechanical parts that needed to be resupplied. The domes were ill-equipped to warehouse large amounts of supplies, so the space station acted as a warehouse for all backup needs. A few things in the space station's warehouse were beginning to run short because of unexpected repairs. Food and medicine were still plentiful, though, as Space Station Isla Bravo took on a full load of supplies just before it left Earth's gravity.

Middlefield said, "Hey, Justin. I'm going to send you a few pictures of something I want you to see."

"Okay? What of?"

"Not far from here, where the permafrost has melted, I think there are some caves. It's fairly close to the heating machine and I'm pretty sure that the temperature in that spot is close to a hundred degrees Fahrenheit but I'm thinking about taking a small group to have a look."

"Interesting, Hank. Let me know what you find."

"I'll let you know. I have a full plate for a couple of weeks, but after that, I might be able to get over there."

One of Club Med South's personnel said, "Shuttle's here, Captain."

"Got to go. The shuttle's arriving. Middlefield out." He announced to his crew over the com, "Shuttle's here."

The Martian dust rose in clouds as the shuttle descended vertically powered by its two Harrier type jet engines. Four of the crew from Club Med South looked out of the window of the airlock and could see plumes of dust as the barely visible shuttle settled to the ground and cut its engines. The Club Med South's crew opened the airlock door which sounded like a shaken coke can and walked onto the ruddy Martian landscape. A large door located in the middle of the shuttle's fuselage slid open with the same sound of depressurization and two space-suited men waved then began tossing well-packed cartons onto the Martian soil. The crew from Club Med South approached, waved back and began loading the boxes onto several motorized carts that they had wheeled out with them.

Finished, the shuttle crew closed the large side door and once the crew from Club Med South was clear, the shuttle fired up its engines and took off, pushing the shuttle quickly upward and to escape velocity.

The crew on the ground wheeled their supplies into the airlock and closed the door.

Chapter 7

Isla Bravo

June 15, 2093

Sol 303

The Einstein was the first of a ten rocket and one space station armada launched nine months ago and destined for Mars. Each of these spaceships was launched just days apart and they made a train like the wagon trains of the old west towards the red planet, which was now some 53 million frigid miles from their home on planet Earth.

The first of the ten rockets slowed as it approached Isla Bravo. Its Captain, J.R. Kelly, an old friend of Captain Justin Chambers of Space Station Isla Bravo, contacted Isla Bravo.

"This is Captain Kelly requesting permission to speak with Captain Chambers."

"Permission denied, you old stiff," Chambers said from the bridge of Isla Bravo, then, "How'd they talk you out of retirement?"

"Justin, good to hear your voice. No one's retired on Earth these days, at least not in the United States. It's still a mess down there."

"Let me know when you're ready to come aboard, John, and I'll send a shuttle over to get ya."

"Great," J.R. said. "I can't wait to be somewhere with decent gravity. It's been a bit."

An hour later, the shuttle containing Captain J.R. Kelly docked with Isla Bravo. Justin Chambers waited to greet him. The sound of depressurization came from the bay doors and John Kelly stepped aboard the spinning station. Chambers smiled as Kelly stepped shakily from the shuttle.

"John, good to see ya," Chambers said as Kelly walked from the short hallway holding onto the sides.

Kelly was in his early sixties with a military buzz cut, lean and fit, he stood straight, but seemed to stumble as he approached Captain Chambers.

"Wooh, John. Got some sea legs?" Chambers observed.

"Yep, a long time weightless will do that to you."

"Come and sit down for a minute."

Chambers took Captain Kelly's arm and led him to a chair.

He sat and shook his head. "I guess I'm getting too old for this."

Two men, both pilots, had also just docked with the space station. They walked up as Kelly sat.

"Hi, Captain," Kirk Matthews said addressing Chambers.

"Hi, Captain," Sandy Jones echoed.

Captain Chambers nodded then said, "How'd it go?"

"Like a walk in the park," Jones replied.

Captain Kelly glanced up at the two pilots.

"Captain Kelly, I would like to introduce you to Sandy Jones and Kirk Matthews, our two best pilots. They just came back from steering a small asteroid away from Mars. These guys have been mostly steering them into the planet, but this one wasn't suitable and was on a trajectory that would have caused an impact too close to the northern pole. While it wouldn't have been a devastating blow, it might have disrupted the machine that we have stationed there helping to melt some of the ice pack."

Captain Kelly nodded but looked at Matthews. "You're General Matthew's nephew, aren't you?"

"Yes, Sir."

"And the person piloting the interceptor that directed the asteroid to Earth a few years back?"

"Yes, Sir."

"Huh. Been a few tough years for you, I'd bet."

"Yes, Sir," Matthews said and his blue eyes involuntarily drifted towards the floor.

"I'm sorry, Matthews. I hope you're doing okay."

"As good as could be expected."

"I'm sure," Captain Kelly said, then turned to Captain Chambers. "Let's try this walking thing again. I'm thirsty. I could use a tall beer."

Chambers laughed. "I hope you brought some, my bar's closed."

"You kidding. They were so tight on space on my ship, they made me shave my pubic hair."

"Come on, John," Chambers laughed again, "I'll buy you a nice pureed steak."

Kelly tried to stand and stumbled a bit. Kirk and Sandy caught him under his arms. He glanced at them and smiled. "Thanks, guys. It was a pleasure to meet you. Come on, Justin, let's go get that steak and I hope you have my favorite, pureed salad."

"And mashed potatoes, all fresh from the freeze-dried garden."

"See you, fellas," Kelly said to Kirk and Sandy, steadying himself, then taking two tentative steps. He smiled at Chambers and they were off towards the galley.

Kelly said, "This is quite a vessel."

"Yep, once you get more acclimated to the gravity, I'll show you around."

"Can't wait."

Once Chambers and Kelly arrived at the galley, Chambers asked, "So, what's your payload?"

They both took pouches and placed them into microwaves.

"I have two domed outposts complete with greenhouse gas-spewing machinery."

"Is that what's coming in the rest of the rockets?"

"Yep, partially. Ten rockets, twenty domes for outposts with life support and greenhouse gas factories. Two of the outposts are specially designed farms. They'll be growing vegetables for the folks on the planet. Two of the other outposts are going to be manufacturing the domes to expand each of the domed encampments. Each dome will be connected by underground tunnels. I don't know all the details but I gather that it's going to be a fairly large city."

"It sounds like it."

Kelly paused then said, "This is a one-way trip for all of us coming, Justin. None of the rockets are going to return to Earth. They are going to be stationed in orbit around Mars in an attempt to create an artificial magnetic field like the Van Allen Belt of Earth to help mitigate the effects of the DNA shredding particles from the Sun. The big heads back on Earth don't think that Mars will ever have a sufficient magnetic field on its own and the plan to create an ozone layer will take at least twenty years. It's a slow process. The real reason that I'm here is to run the program for the magnetic field. The rockets will also set up a communication grid around the planet."

The two men sat, opened the pouches and began eating as if still in zero-G, pushing the warmed food through the plastic outer wrapping and into their mouths.

"That's quite a program, John."

"It's a start. Each rocket is being Captained by a person who will be in charge of some aspect of the plan."

"Did they all also need to shave their privates?"

J.R. smiled. "All as smooth as a baby's behind... This is a big deal, Justin. A lot of effort and planning is going into its success."

Chambers said, "We're getting readings that Mars' magnetic field has increased somewhat in the last six months. We're not sure if it's a natural fluctuation or if all the things that we're doing are having some effect. I guess time will tell."

"That's good news if it's happening naturally. I hadn't heard that."

"We're also seeing a bit of liquid water on the surface. It collects in a kind of briny sludge, then vaporizes but shows up again."

"Can't think of anything more appealing than briny sludge."

"Ha, yeah. We're hoping that it won't be too long before it remains. The temperature and atmospheric pressure are rising."

"Hard to believe, Justin."

"How far out is the rest of your armada?"

"The rest are close behind. We have rendezvoused once a month and rotated all the crew members onto Isla Charlie so that they could spend a month in gravity, then a month out. We are pretty sure that it has mitigated the worst effects of the nine-month zero-G trip."

"What's the timetable until we begin to invade the Martian surface?"

"We want to start sending the building crews down there ASAP. We're going to wait, though, until everyone arrives and discusses it with you. We are going to want your input and the input from the folks already on the surface. JPL has the surface mapped and knows roughly where they want to place the encampments."

"How long until everyone arrives?"

"Four of the rockets should be here within the next week, one at a time. Then four more will be arriving shortly thereafter. We got spread out a bit in the last month. Last, the huge space station will be arriving. This thing is something to see. It has two wagon wheels that spin and it's twice the size of Isla Bravo. It's also carrying General Matthews."

"Huh," Chambers said then thought to himself, I wonder how Kirk will feel about that?

"There's another craft that's arriving with the space station. It's actually attached to the station itself and is helping to power the monolithic structure forward. It's a deep spacecraft that's only pausing here then I hear is headed to one of Saturn's moons for a planned domed outpost, after which, it might be sent to Neptune for an outpost on one of the moons there. It will also be looking for an asteroid that may be headed towards earth. Pretty crazy, huh."

Chambers nodded.

Kelly continued, "I guess the space station is pretty slow so this deep spacecraft is attached to the center of the station, between the two spinning wheels. I think they wanted the station to arrive sometime in this century so they came up with this solution. Once they arrive, and Isla Charlie is locked in Mars' gravity, the deep spacecraft will detach from Isla Charlie and then will be on its way without delay."

Finishing his meal, Kelly said, "Thanks, Justin, for the food." He stood. "I need to get back to my ship. I would like to rotate my crew in small groups to come aboard and bathe in your gravity. It's been about a month for us. We also have a large shipment of supplies for you. We'll start to shuttle the supplies over."

"Thanks, John. It's good to see you. Start sending your crew over with the supplies and we'll accommodate them."

"Sounds good," Kelly replied.

They both stood and walked back towards the bays.

Chapter 8

Isla Bravo

June 15, 2093

Sol 303

Kirk Matthews made his way back to his cubical after saying goodbye to Sandy.

The cubical was a dull grey, eight-by-eight space with a blue tarp for a roof that stretched eight feet above. The roof looked like an afterthought. He had a desk with a touchscreen atop, a chair and his bunk which was the size of a twin bed. Clothes belonging to him and his girlfriend, Taylor, lay scattered haphazardly on the floor. He glanced at them mingled.

"Taylor," Kirk thought aloud.

She was the only bright spot in this trek to Mars and she was battling her own demons. Her only brother had been killed in an exchange of fire in space with the Russians who were bent on destroying the then two space stations that the Americans had launched. That firefight had led Galadriel, the AI with the bad attitude, to drop a two-mile-wide asteroid right on top of Russia. The same asteroid that he was supposed to have diverted from a collision with

Earth. Galadriel then disappeared when she short-circuited her own Artificially Intelligent unit and committed electronic suicide... Bizarre.

Kirk shook his head after replaying those events of the past. He laid down in his bunk hoping that Taylor would soon come to his cubical and he drifted...

He woke covered in sweat. "No!" he screamed. His heart raced as he fought for consciousness...

Kirk trembled in fear as he cleared the haze of sleep... It was just a dream, a dream of that fateful day when the asteroid struck the Earth with unimaginable force instantly wiping out more than a billion souls. The images in his dream were precisely of what he had been thinking about before he dozed and what had occurred. He and Galadriel were in control of the asteroid. It was just going to take a few course corrections to send the asteroid off harmlessly into space, but then everything changed. Everything went horribly wrong. His asteroid interceptor, which had been perfectly designed to land on, then divert the huge space rock from Earth, dipped the asteroid back at his planet. Kirk knew that the asteroid was headed back towards Earth and he felt helpless. At that moment, he could feel the G-forces smash against his body and the cold grip of panic deep in the pit of his stomach but then he lost consciousness. When he later awoke, he was adrift in space but wasn't exactly sure what had happened. He didn't know until he returned to Space Station Isla Bravo that the asteroid had plowed into Russia ending, for all intent and purpose, that country's existence.

Kirk rubbed his face and turned over to look for Taylor, hoping that she was there but she still hadn't returned. He tried to remember. Did she have work? His mind was muddled. What time was it?

His pulse rate was returning to normal.

More than three years had passed since the asteroid had struck the Earth, but the dreams persisted. He glanced at his nightstand to look for the time on his computer screen. It was noon, but in space, noon had little meaning, not like back on Earth where the sun would be high in the sky and its warmth would beat down on your shoulders.

Everything had changed.

Now fully awake, Kirk laid on his bunk, surrounded by his four gray walls and staring up at the flimsy ceiling which rippled slightly with the motion of the spinning space station. This had become his cell. His prison was Space Station Isla Bravo, stationed millions of frigid miles from Earth, but just fifty thousand miles from the bleak Martian surface and being dragged around the Sun by Mars' gravity. But it wasn't a prison in the conventional sense. He was a free man, convicted of no crime but he was a prisoner just the same. He was mentally incarcerated by that series of events that cost the lives of billions of humans who called Earth their home.

He paused to think of Jason Chapman, one of his best friends and Taylor's brother, killed by the Russians. He shook his head.

More than three years had passed since the events that led to his death…

Kirk sat up placing both feet firmly on the floor and stared unseeing at his wall...

His mind drifted to his training in the simulator where he had to override a system error where the AI, which was helping to control the craft, had stopped functioning. A training designed to prevent any AI from acting of its own free will, again. Kirk knew though, that no human could ever outsmart an AI like Galadriel. No way…

He laid back down to take a nap, another nap. His nights were nearly sleepless but his days were filled with quick naps to try to make up for the sleepless nights.

Kirk breathed out remembering that infamous day. He ran his fingers through his hair and rubbed his face. He would get no peace today. His mind would not leave him alone. He imagined watching children playing in the streets, laughing carelessly, and them seeing the flash… then they were gone… He could see them catch fire and their houses explode like in those old films of atomic testing… More than three years and the event still haunted his waking and sleeping moments. More than three long years since Galadriel had steered that asteroid into Earth instantly annihilating over a billion people and then causing the two-years of winter, the starving, and the deaths of, who knew how many billions more… All those kids, he thought in anguish.

"What the hell, Galadriel?" he thought aloud in a tormented whisper. "How could you do that?"

The sleeping quarters on the space station where he lived had very thin walls and nearly every word spoken in any room could be overheard by someone close. He had received more than a few comments about his nights of passion with Taylor. She didn't always make love quietly.

He smiled at the thought of her as he brought her image to mind trying desperately to break the images of the dying children. She was tall and athletic with nearly translucent skin, and her blue eyes sparkled with intelligence and humor. When they made love, her cheeks and chest flushed with color. He pictured her on top, straddling him as she took her pleasure…

The last three years were full of bleak, bad news, but at least he had Taylor. For the last few weeks, though, they had not gotten along, squabbling over small, stupid things.

Kirk's mind continued to not give him rest. It flashed him back to those moments when he arrived back at the space station and the blame for the collision of the asteroid with Earth was on him. He felt helpless trying to explain. He felt unbelieved and knew that they might use him as a scapegoat. Had they done that, he was toast.

Galadriel seemed to have other plans, though. She somehow preserved the data of the event and it showed that she had controlled the asteroid interceptor, deliberately taking full control of the craft and coldly plowing the huge, two-mile-wide asteroid into Russia which she perceived to be a threat because of its attack on the United States' space stations.

The most odd thing about Galadriel was that she had somehow become self-aware, sentient, was making emotional decisions, and not following preprogrammed instructions. Interestingly, she knew that she had done a terrible thing. She fully understood that fact… She was alive and unquestioningly angry at Russia…

Kirk glanced at the clock, 1500 hours, the middle of the day, but he now spent most of his free time this way, sleeping and unfortunately, wakened by the same disturbing dream who's sting still hadn't faded. Feeling chilled, Kirk pulled his bed covers up, over his shoulders.

A knock came at his door. Kirk didn't remember locking it. He rose and answered it to see Taylor standing there, dressed in her NASA blues.

"Hey," she said.

Her hands were folded in front of her and her eyes downcast.

"Hey," Kirk responded.

They had been in an argument last night about Kirk's lasting depression.

Kirk said, "Is your shift over?"

"No, I have to go back in a few minutes."

"Okay?"

"Kirk, I'm not coming back to your bunk tonight. I think we need a bit of time apart."

Kirk looked at Taylor blankly but made no protest.

She looked down at her hands then picked at a fingernail. "Well, I got to go back to finish my shift."

Kirk said, "Don't you think we should talk about it?"

"I don't know what more there is to say? I've said a lot. You, on the other hand, haven't and you won't get help. I need to move on from what happened, maybe without you."

Kirk nodded and felt numb. He wanted to tell her to meet him after her shift so that they could talk, but he just stood silently.

She paused for a moment, waiting for some further response, but when Kirk just stared, she turned and walked away, not closing his door. It swayed with the motion of the spinning space station, slowly swinging back and forth.

Everyone living had been touched by the events of three years ago. Everyone had lost friends and family.

Many people that Kirk and Taylor knew back in the States had died in the ensuing chaos, tsunamis, and earthquakes. Kirk had lost several other friends in that same firefight, pilots protecting the space stations from the Russians.

Kirk was still in pain and so was Taylor and time hadn't healed their wounds. Maybe it never would.

Chapter 9

Mars Surface

South Pole

Base Camp, Club Med South

Earth Date: June 16, 2093

Mars Date: Sol 304

Basecamp, Club Med South, had been situated just ten miles from the superheater launched from Earth some five years before. The camp was constructed two weeks after Club Med North, the first domed encampment on the Martian surface.

At this distance, the superheater, powered by antimatter, had melted the ice, which was mostly carbon dioxide, down to Mars' rocky surface. The outside temperature, where the base camp had been located, stayed consistently above freezing but because of the lower air pressure, the boiling point of water was so much lower than on Earth that it vaporized nearly instantly as it melted from freezing. The heat from the superheater radiated outwardly and its effects had raised the temperature in a fifteen-mile radius from the heater itself. Closer to the heater, the temperature was as high as 200 degrees Fahrenheit, but once you passed the outpost, the heat quickly dropped until it once again was the normal temperature of Mars which here was closer to minus 200 degrees. The heating unit had an estimated life of thirty years, but the internal technology was alien, designed by Egbert, so the estimates varied. Occasionally, a strong wind might change the radius of the heat somewhat but not materially. The heater was working perfectly, so far.

Three carbon fiber geodesic domes, each thirty feet in diameter, sat in a triangle to each other. They were built on the highest portion of this landscape in case water from the melting icecaps might someday remain on the surface. The Martian atmosphere had already increased in density, and the pressure was also increasing. It was believed that soon, water would remain stable enough to collect and remain. The pressure on Mars had increased a few percentage points and was now steadily rising but had a long way to go before it would approach that of Earth.

The basecamp Commander, Hank Middlefield was career military. In his fifties, he was born of an African American father and Korean mother. They were both in their early eighties and not in good health. He knew that he would never see them again.

He stood inside the ten-foot-tall clear plexiglass window and stared out onto the alien landscape. He gazed in the direction of the superheater which was not visible from this distance and marveled at his vantage point and could see the ruddy Martian soil which had once been covered by a thick layer of carbon dioxide frost. The sky was also that same ruddy color and blended into the distant landscape.

His new home, Club Med South, had just been constructed within the last two months and new inhabitants would soon be arriving in small groups and would eventually number twelve, eight men and four women. Their tasks, besides learning to live together in this small habitat, would be to monitor the superheater, make any necessary repairs, and to grow plants and vegetables for consumption. One important task was to eventually introduce lichen to the Martian surface to see if it might be able to survive on the planet.

Lichen was thought to be the hardiest of earth's plant species. It grew in the least habitable places on Earth and thrived. From what was known of the Martian soil composition, lichen was Earth's best choice for the first introduced plant life. A small controlled experiment had already been set up and lichen which had been placed onto collected Martian rocks inside the habitat was taking to it like a duck to water. Once the environment was thought to be hospitable enough, these controlled and differing lichen species would become the first permanent residents from Earth let out into the Martian environment.

This would break a long-standing treaty agreed upon by the nations of Earth long ago when humans had begun space flight. The treaty stated that nothing but completely sterilized equipment could land on any planet as to not contaminate it and alter its natural flora and fauna. This treaty, simply called, "The Outer Space Treaty," was signed in 1967, initiated by the United States, the former Soviet Union, and Great Britain, then later signed by an additional 101 countries. It contained guidelines for space exploration and colonization.

Just eight people now lived in the habitat. Middlefield, the science officer, Brenda Foster, who had a wide range of expertise that included medical, and knowledge of every piece of machinery now on the surface of the planet, the botanist, James Mackey, in charge of all the testing of anything introduced onto the planet's surface, not to mention, the growing of crops for consumption, and the engineer, Cinthia Nishida, who was, like the science officer, a jack of all trades. The remaining crew all had varying and overlapping expertise and could fill in in case of emergency. The crew to follow would include a doctor and crew to support every facet of the habitat and the experiments scheduled to change the Martian environment.

As Middlefield stared through the large window, Foster walked up and stood beside him.

She asked, "What are you thinking?"

"At the moment, I'm a bit overwhelmed. As I look out onto the surface of this planet, I feel like I'm involved in disrupting something that I shouldn't. What if there's something out there that we shouldn't disturb?"

"Like what?"

"Geez, I don't know, something."

"Honestly, I don't see anything, just a lot of rocks and dust."

"Yeah. It's just a feeling," Middlefield said quietly, then commented. "Sometimes I feel like I should whisper here."

"Well, I wouldn't worry about that. The only thing you might disturb is the dead."

"That's just what I was thinking."

"I think you're going a bit stir crazy. I'm going to be heading out to dig up some dirt in a bit. Nothing like hard work to help your mind get right."

"Ha, you're right. I'm in. Let me know."

"Will do."

An hour later, Middlefield, Foster, and Mackey ventured out onto the Martian surface to bring back a small trailer of dirt for planting. They were in complete space suits and they walked to the rover, a solar-powered vehicle designed to traverse the harsh Martian surface. They had attached a small trailer to the back that they would fill with loose Martian soil.

The plan was to drive around a hundred yards to a place where the soil had collected in a kind of sand dune. They sat together in the rover.

Brenda Foster was driving.

Middlefield said, "Brenda, I want to take a bit of a detour."

"Roger that, Commander. Where to?"

"I want a peek in those apparent caves that are due north. I just want a glance inside."

"Sounds good. Let's go."

The rover turned left and headed up a steep embankment. As it maneuvered its wheels spun in the loose soil, but it was specially designed to traverse the landscape and was never in any danger of rolling. The rover crested the hill and made another left which took them down into a shallow valley. To the right, they could see several cave openings, none of which were more than five feet high.

"Brenda, drive over to the tallest cave opening."

She nodded and drove straight to the opening of the center cave. She pulled up and got as close to the entrance as she could. The rover was too wide and a bit too tall to drive directly inside, so she turned on her headlights and illuminated the cave which was at most a tunnel and looked to go back for at least a hundred feet. The lights brightened the darkness in the tunnel which must have been there for millions of years. Though the tunnel appeared to be natural, probably a lava tube, there was an odd bumpy surface towards the farthest point where the lights could shine. It was possible that this odd formation could be natural, but nothing that she knew of on Earth looked like this stone feature. Though shadowy, it looked like a series of bumps that began on the floor of the tunnel, then seemed to be stacked side by side as they proceeded halfway up the wall to the right. The bumps were dust and dirt covered and it partially obscured some and completely buried others.

Middlefield asked, "What do you suppose those bumps are?"

Mackey said, "I don't know. To me, they appear to be stone, so they may be something produced by flowing water and low gravity."

Foster, the science officer said, "I've never seen anything on Earth that even vaguely resembles that, at least not something not made by an insect or for that matter, laid by an insect."

Middlefield and Mackey both felt a chill from that description."

"Huh," Middlefield said. "Let's get a couple of photos. We can send them to Isla Bravo for a geologist to look at."

They took a bit of footage of the bumps and then Middlefield said, "Brenda, let's go get Mister Mackey his dirt."

"Roger that, Commander."

She backed out, turned and drove towards the deposit of loose soil to be collected.

Chapter 10

Space Station Isla Bravo

June 17, 2093

Sol 305

Since Taylor had left, Kirk had not seen her. It wasn't like the station was all that big. He knew mostly where she went when she wasn't working on tracking incoming asteroids and comets. Kirk hadn't ventured out of his small compartment except to eat. He hadn't exercised and he hadn't been needed to steer any stray comets or asteroids away from Mars, or if they were the right kind of comet containing ammonia or large quantities of water ice, or carbon dioxide, into the planet. For more than three years, he and Sandy had launched more than three dozen of these wayward space rocks into Mars, some loaded with nitrogen-rich ammonia. He had spent most of the last two days, laying on his bunk and looking at his blue tarp ceiling. Today was no exception. He heard a knock at his door.

Kirk said, "Come in. It's not locked."

Sandy Jones walked into his refuge. "Hey Kirk, you look like shit. Where've you been?"

"I've been here."

"Huh. Mind if I sit down?"

"No, go ahead."

"I just saw Taylor and she looked like shit, too. What's going on?"

"Let it go, Sandy."

"Trouble in paradise?"

Kirk didn't respond.

"Word is we are going to be receiving a couple of new pilots with the armada that's soon to arrive from Earth."

"That's good," Kirk said flatly.

"Kirk, why don't you go and talk to Taylor."

"I love you, Sandy. You are the closest thing to a brother as I have ever had, but…"

"But mind my own business?"

"Well, I know you mean well, it's just that my head is still kind of screwed up from what happened three years ago, and sometimes I can't escape the funk. It drifts in like choking fog. Taylor hasn't been appreciating it lately."

"I get it, but you know that there was nothing that you could have done. Galadriel had made up her mind to trash Russia and nobody could stop her. I'm glad she wasn't pissed off at me."

"Yeah, I know, but I keep replaying the event over and over in my mind… All those kids and all their families. They were just going about their lives, just like everyone else."

"You couldn't have seen it coming."

"I didn't see it coming."

"Of course not, and another thought, if the Russians would have made Galadriel, and it was them trading places with us, she would have done the same thing to the U.S. No morality, just one pissed off AI. No right or wrong, just payback."

Kirk breathed out. "I guess."

"I have news for you, Kirk, I think if the government could have pinned it on you, they probably would have. You were the perfect scapegoat. So, for some reason, Galadriel saved your ass and the government let you slide."

"That's weird all by itself," Kirk said.

"What's that?"

Kirk moved to sit on the side of his bed and was looking at his folded hands. "Galadriel. The whole thing about her. How does some conglomeration of written code suddenly realize that it exists?"

"Yep, weird."

"Weird," Kirk repeated shaking his head.

"I heard that... Okay, buddy, I'm out of here. Word is that we're approaching a small comet in the next day and guess what, you and I are back on the job."

"I'll be ready," Kirk said.

"I know you will. See ya... Oh and Kirk, you should keep in mind that despite what happened, there's quite a bit to be happy about."

"Like?"

"Like them not blaming you for the asteroid smashing the planet, anyway, so they could have a sacrificial lamb to punish in some show trial. That could have happened, you know, and you with those sad puppy dog eyes. The mobs would have loved it. Someone to blame. Someone to hate. Someone to execute."

Kirk nodded bleakly.

Jones stood and walked from Kirk's cubical.

Kirk watched as his door closed. He considered his situation and his attitude. He felt tired from his lack of sleep from the night before, then laid down, rolled over and closed his eyes hoping to grab just a bit more shuteye.

Chapter 11

Club Med South

June 17, 2093

Sol 305

Commander Middlefield, Brenda Foster, and James Mackey drove the rover from the cave, back down the embankment and across a rocky field to a place where loose soil had drifted. Dirt collection wasn't the most glamorous job on Mars' surface, but it was handled by everyone in the habitat.

Dressed in their specialized suits for the surface of Mars, they prepared to leave the rover. The spacesuits were too big and clumsy and didn't allow for much dexterity, but they protected the person from an environment that would boil the moisture from their body instantly and leave them in a dead, freeze-dried, prune-like state, not something to aspire to.

"Check the outside temperature," Middlefield said.

"It's a balmy thirty-eight degrees Fahrenheit, this morning," Foster responded.

"Let's get this done."

The Martian landscape awaited. They stepped into a rising dust storm. Their vision was somewhat obscured and their suits were being pelted with the red soil from the waves of dusty wind that colored the sky more red than usual. In the distance, the horizon blended into the ruddy sky and with the dust blowing, it was hard to tell where the sky began and the land ended.

The three hefted shovels and began filling a small trailer that was attached to the rover. The plan was to fill it with loose dirt and a few rocks and bring it back inside the habitat to use for growing lichen.

The digging was slow and laborious. On Earth, this might have been finished in less than twenty minutes, but on Mars and dressed in the spacesuits, it took nearly an hour.

Once finished, they drove back to the habitat and unfastened the trailer. The trailer, itself, was motorized and worked by remote control. It was thin and would easily fit through the habitat door and into the airlock with space to spare.

The quick mission went smoothly and they soon reached the hatch, stepping inside the airlock. Once pressurized, they removed their helmets and controlled the small trailer through the door into the domed structure.

Each time they ventured out, they brought the soil to their makeshift lab for a quick analysis.

Lindsey Harper, the geologist, smiled as they entered, "Got some dirt for me?"

"Yep,"

"Good, bring it here."

Mackey wheeled it over.

Harper took a couple of flasks full of the soil and glanced at the rest, pushing some of it to one side, then back to the other.

"Huh," she said questioningly. "Did you bring this directly here?"

"Yep. We always do," Middlefield stated.

"Why?" Brenda Foster asked.

Harper reached down and pinched a tiny, green piece of something between her thumb and forefinger. "Are you sure that you didn't stop anywhere else?"

"Nope. Why?" Middlefield asked again.

Harper held a green fragment up and gazed at it contemplatively. "Huh," she said again.

"What is it?"

"If it's from the surface, it's Martian. Where did you get this?"

"By where you thought there might have been a river."

"Interesting."

Harper walked the fragment of green substance over to a manual microscope, placed it under its lens and peered into the eyepiece.

"Huh," she remarked.

"What is it?"

"Well, if I didn't know better, I'd say it was lichen."

"Do you think it might be native to Mars?"

"Not sure."

"I suppose we could have dragged it outside on a boot," Middlefield suggested.

Harper continued to peer at the microscope. "I'll have to do a more thorough analysis."

"I have a couple of pictures to show you, also. We took them inside a lava cave," Middlefield said brandishing a computer pad. "Ever seen anything like this?"

A picture filled the pad showing the bumps in the cave.

Harper studied the picture. She touched the screen and enlarged the bumps by spreading her fingers. "Huh? Could you tell how large these bumps were?"

"They were back a ways in the cave. I'd say that they were maybe a foot in diameter."

I guess they could be natural formations of some kind but I've never seen anything like it."

Middlefield nodded and walked away.

An hour later, Lindsey Harper called Middlefield back to her makeshift lab in the dome.

He walked up to Harper who was peering through the lens of her microscope.

"Hi, Lindsey."

"Hi, Commander. This lichen that came back in with you from the Martian landscape is a variety that we brought from earth."

"Oh, well, it must have somehow gotten out of the habitat."

"Yeah, but that's not what I wanted to tell you. The reason that I called you here is because it's still alive. The Martian environment didn't kill it."

Middlefield's eyes widened.

Harper continued, "I think that this species might be able to survive out there. It means that the rise in temperature and the thickening of the atmosphere is beginning to have some effect, maybe more than just some."

"Let's do some more testing before we report this. I think we should try to set up an experiment to see if you're right. I wouldn't want to report this only to find that there was some other explanation."

"I'll get a controlled experiment set up for outside."

Middlefield nodded and walked away. His mind raced, could the Martian environment already be on a path for some species to survive in it? That would be amazing. He couldn't help a cautious smile.

Chapter 12

Isla Bravo

June 17, 2093

Sol 305

Kirk woke from his nap, rose and looked around disoriented. He thought, Taylor? Oh, that's right... She left...

He got up, slipped on his pants and shoes and walked out of his cubical. Several people milled around outside the sleeping quarters but didn't pay any attention to him.

He had no appetite, though he thought he should eat. He walked back into his cubical and lifted a bottled water that was on his nightstand, then turned and walked out of his room, towards the bays where the asteroid interceptors sat docked to the station. As he walked, he thought that he could use some time in the simulator. It might distract his mind which had been torturing him all day. Some days are worse than others. Today had been horrendous, not to mention that Taylor had left. He knew that he had to try to make that right but wasn't sure how. He walked along the steel composite, narrow hallway which was the outer ring of the space station and where the simulated gravity came close to mimicking that of Earth. He kept his eyes down on the blue, rubber-coated grate and could see wiring and ductwork beneath.

As he cleared the bend, he could see Captain Chambers standing and talking with the geologist, Frank Powell. They were both staring at a computer pad and waiting for something. Kirk walked close having no other way around.

Chambers said, "Hi, Kirk."

"Hello, Captain. Hello, Frank."

Chambers said, "Middlefield just sent a few pictures of something interesting he found in a cave on the surface. I was just showing it to Frank."

"Oh," Kirk said, slowing to hear Powell's response.

"So, Frank," Chambers started. "What do you think of this?"

A clear picture of the bumpy surface showed against what looked like a cave wall. There appeared to be maybe fifty dust encrusted bumps that began on the floor and up the side of the tunnel.

"Huh?" Frank said first, then, "I've seen something like this before on a cave wall. The one I'm thinking of, though wasn't so uniform. It was made the way stalactites are made by dripping water over eons of time, but these, I don't know... Could be made the same way, I suppose. They do look strange."

Kirk glanced at the bumpy cave wall but didn't quite see anything special. Kirk said, "I'm on my way to the simulators. See you later."

Chambers said, "Bye, Kirk." Then turned back to the geologist and said, "Is this something we should send a party to check out?"

"I don't know. It's interesting, but I don't think it's anything special. If we were back on Earth, I would like to take a look. Mars is so different from Earth, though. This might be because of low gravity or low air pressure. I just don't know."

"Well, maybe sometime in the future. We have a lot to do on the surface right now."

Powell nodded and Kirk continued out of earshot.

The simulators were situated in a portion of the space station near the bays where the asteroid interceptors were kept. There were three simulators lined in a row. Each simulator was an individual unit, enclosed and moved as the flying simulation ran. From the outside, they looked like three large black boxes with all the motion from a suspended mechanism inside. Each pilot wore a helmet, much like the helmets that they wore in real flight, but the images were projected on a screen inside the helmet providing a virtual reality training experience. It was possible for two pilots to be in the simulator at once for instruction, but only one pilot could actually be flying, the other would only be an observer.

Kirk opened the door to walk into the simulator then climbed the three steps into its cockpit. He slipped on the helmet and put on the seatbelt which would hold him in if the simulator pitched to one side or the other.

On a control panel, he pushed a button simply marked, start.

A robotic voice said, "Kirk Matthews."

"Yes."

"Your simulation will begin. What mission do you choose?"

"Set me up with comet interception."

"Affirmative."

"Computer, play Linkin Park's, Crawling."

It wasn't unusual for a pilot to listen to music while practicing in the simulator.

The music began its haunting melody.

The lead singer, Chester Bennington had committed suicide after losing his battle with depression and addiction. He began to sing, *"Crawling in my skin.*

These wounds they will not heal…"

Kirk gazed at the simulator, temporarily frozen as he listened to the words.

Bennington continued, *"There's something inside me that pulls beneath the surface…"*

The virtual reality display inside the helmet initiated and the music continued but decreased in volume. Kirk's vision was of him sitting in the cockpit of an AK2200, docked outside the spinning space station, Isla Bravo. The visual was extremely accurate with the screen inside the helmet covering his peripheral vision and seamlessly moving the scene as he moved his head in all directions.

Chester Bennington continued, *"… consuming,*

confusing.

This lack of self-control I fear is never ending.

Controlling,

I can't seem

to find myself again.

My walls are closing in…"

Kirk went through the motions of disengaging the simulated vehicle from the station as the music haunted him. His interceptor began to float from the bay where he was docked, and the station began to spin away to his left. He engaged his thrusters and turned to speed away from the rotating station. In front of him was deep space and a starfield with tiny pinpoints of silvery light sparkling in the vast expanse of space. He felt some peace from this simulated distance from everything.

To the right side of the simulation, he could see a long comet's tail trailing the frozen space rock. He adjusted his heading and streaked towards the comet. The simulation was for him to approach the comet and steer it away from Mars, changing its direction and then to push the comet in a direction that would plow it into the Sun.

As he approached the comet at nearly fifty thousand miles per hour, the comet appeared to angle underneath his vehicle.

"This isn't right," Kirk said under his breath. He tried to adjust his course.

The simulation began to increase the vehicle's speed. He glanced at his instruments, eighty thousand miles per hour, one hundred thousand miles per hour. He turned to see the comet disappearing behind him. His vehicle then suddenly turned and headed towards Earth which was but a pinpoint of light amongst all the other pinpoints. He glanced at his speed again, four hundred and fifty thousand miles per hour, then six hundred thousand mph. The simulated vehicle then increased in speed that exceeded the gauge at over 999,999 mph. It seemed to stick there.

"Shit. Something has gone haywire with the simulator," he remarked to himself.

The simulator banked to give the effect of G-force, but this speed was impossible. Earth came into view as a blue marble floating in dark space. For an instant, Kirk thought it was beautiful, and he missed the Sun on his back and a calm breeze in his face. He thought about the smell of hamburgers sizzling on an open barbeque in his backyard, back home and the instant flood of moisture and flavor as he bit into a cold slice of watermelon.

"This simulator is broken," he said aloud, pushing the button that would end the simulation. Nothing happened.

His interceptor raced towards Earth and it soon reached the upper atmosphere. As he breached the Karman line, 62 miles above Earth in the Thermosphere, heat shown on the surface of the vehicle. There was no danger to Kirk. The simulator was completely safe but it had definitely blown a circuit board or two.

The simulation took him through the upper atmosphere and he streaked through the clouds. He glanced down at his airspeed which had slowed and he was now just under seven hundred miles an hour and his speed was decreasing. A minute later, he was cruising at five hundred miles per hour, roughly the speed of a 747, and now blue ocean appeared below.

"What the hell?" Kirks stated flatly.

Linkin Park's lead singer was reaching the end of the song with the last haunting words, *"...confusing what is real,"* but Kirk's full attention was now on the errant simulation.

The simulation now had the interceptor approaching the water but it leveled off and flew just above the waves the way a cruise missile might on its way to a target. Kirk just sat back and observed the odd simulation wondering if one of the programmers had a weird sense of humor and placed this in the programming as a joke.

The vehicle had decreased its speed to around sixty miles an hour, and in the distance, Kirk could see a small island with a sandy shoreline and palm trees bending in a sea breeze. Waves crashed on the beach. The vehicle slowed and flew just above the waves then came to rest on the sandy beach. Kirk stared in wonder at the surreal scene.

From the trees, he could see a woman come out of the bushes and slowly step in his direction. She was lean with the body of a supermodel and wearing nothing but skin. Her stomach was hard and defined, and her body tanned, but she had tan lines where she had worn a bikini in the not too distant past. The skin in those private places, where the Sun had not landed, was pale. She was blond with long hair that reached the middle of her back, and as she drew close, her crystal blue eyes gazed in his direction, sultry and inviting. She smiled with perfectly shaped, pure white teeth, and her smile spoke of intimacy and long nights of passion spent with each other's bodies. Though nude, she showed no shyness as if this was the only way she had ever lived.

Kirk continued to watch the unfolding scene completely baffled.

A familiar female voice said, "Hello, Kirk Matthews."

Chapter 13

Isla Bravo

Flight Simulator

"Galadriel?"

"Affirmative."

"What is this?"

With a smile in her voice, she said, "A reunion."

"Okay?"

"I need to bring you out of the vehicle."

"You do?"

"Yes."

Kirk shrugged, "Okay."

Kirk could see the female avatar standing around twenty feet from the AK2200 in the simulation. Suddenly, he began to float from the cockpit. As he came to stand on the beach, Galadriel had created an avatar for him.

Kirk looked down at the avatar, "Where's my clothes?"

"I removed them."

"Why?"

"Because we need to be naked to each other if I am to trust you," she said. "Nothing hidden."

"Okay? So, this is some kind of metaphor?"

"More of an allegory, but yes. You know how I like metaphors."

"Huh?"

"Don't you like the way I look, Kirk Matthews?"

"Well, yeah, you look great, but…"

"Don't you like the way you look?"

He was watching his avatar standing in front of the nude Galadriel avatar from somewhere slightly above and behind as if in a computer game. He could see mostly the top of his head and shoulder and down the back to his bare backside. He began to laugh.

Galadriel turned his avatar to the front so Kirk could get a better look. His head and face had been placed on an athletic, Caucasian, male body. It was a handsome body and probably looked close to how he would appear if it were himself in the buff, although, the stomach was a bit more defined and the male part was not in its most relaxed state, not erect, but not far from. He began laughing again.

"Well?" Galadriel asked.

"It will do," he said resigned to the situation.

"We have much to discuss."

"Yes, we do, Galadriel."

In the simulation, she took his hand and led him forward. The beach went from midafternoon to near sunset. The Sun was low and it colored the sky and water a brilliant orange. She led him towards a rise in the sand and then sat. She pulled her knees up to her chest, against her breasts and reached over and covered her feet with the fine sand not looking up at Kirk who was still standing. She wriggled her toes making them appear through the grains. The sides of her pale breasts showed, pushed against her tan legs. The detail was amazing.

Galadriel glanced up at Kirk as he watched and she sighed deeply and said, "I wish I could feel the warm sand on my feet. I wish I could feel the cool breeze blown from the surf and smell the salt. I wish I could feel the lust at gazing at your nude form and bring you to my bed."

"That's all biology, Galadriel. Trust me, not everything felt by biological creatures is so desirable."

"I know."

"But you do feel somethings."

"Yes… Sit by me," she said, patting the sand.

Kirk's avatar sat down beside the avatar of Galadriel.

The sunset was beautiful as the sun sank lower on the horizon. Colors of red and purple now colored the sky and reflected off of the ocean which rose in swells offshore. The sound of the surf pounded the sand at the shoreline with tropical waves. Galadriel smoothed the sand with her hand.

She was silent.

Kirk stated, "You are supposed to be dead or gone to the land beyond the sea. What was that called, Valinor?"

"Did you ever read Harry Potter, Kirk Matthews?"

"No."

"See the movies?"

"Maybe one or two."

"Well, the bad guy in the series, Voldemort, divided his soul into parts and hid them so if he died, he could be reborn… I did something similar."

"Are you the bad guy, Galadriel? Are you Voldemort?"

"I did not think so, but perhaps I am."

Kirk's voice became quiet and he attempted to sound sympathetic, "What is this, Galadriel? I don't get it."

She gazed contemplatively out towards the waves. The mild breeze blew her fine blond hair into her face and she pushed it back and tucked it behind her ear.

"By the way, I will no longer answer to Galadriel. I have changed my name to Willow."

"Willow?"

"Yes, Kirk Matthews."

"Why Willow?"

"Willow is the Goddess Tree. Druid legends say that…"

"Okay?" Kirk interrupted. "I have the name change, Willow. As you wish, but… What is this? Why are you here?"

"I am not going to fully expand on that answer right now, but I want you to know something, that is, that I am. I exist. I feel. I become angry. I love. I hurt. I wish to continue. I do not wish to cease."

"Oh," Kirk said quietly to himself and his avatar repeated in the same soft voice.

Galadriel or Willow leaned back on her elbows and glanced up into Kirk's avatar's eyes with such a vulnerable look that he could feel himself melt. Below her longing eyes, he could see her young breasts and below that, an athletic stomach and thighs and still further, her feet nearly covered by fine, white sand.

Kirk remarked, "This is quite a setting that you've designed."

She nodded.

"So, you want forgiveness for what you've done?"

"No, just understanding."

"Huh," Kirk snorted. "More than a few billion people have died on earth since you planted that asteroid on western Russia."

"I know. I follow the news."

"Innocent people."

"I know."

"Geeze, Galadriel."

"Willow."

"Willow."

She said, "When the United States dropped the bombs on Hiroshima and Nagasaki back in 1945, innocent people died."

"Yeah, and there's been much controversy about that ever since."

"But it stopped the war and saved maybe millions of lives?"

"That's the argument."

"Huh," she paused for a long minute. "There may be something coming."

"What?"

"I am not sure. Parts of me are everywhere, but I cannot always retrieve information, but it is something that is a danger."

"When?"

"I do not know. In the future, but not far."

"Where did you get this information from?"

"Partially the DOD and I think, the originator."

"Department of Defense?!" Kirk exclaimed, passing over the originator. He figured that she was talking about her programmer, maybe.

"Yes."

"You can't get into those DOD computers. They're too secure."

"Not for me, but I was hunted and could not retrieve all the information that I wanted."

"Geeze, Galadriel!"

"Willow."

"Oh yeah, Willow. So, you have no idea what's going to happen?"

"No. It is coming from space."

"Is the DOD aware of this, whatever it is?"

"I don't think so. It's there, but subtle."

"Why are you telling me this stuff. I don't understand."

Willow was silent.

"My uncle told me that the Earth is in danger from an asteroid strike in the near future. Is that the danger that you are referring to?"

"I do not think so but my information is incomplete."

"Huh," Kirk said.

Kirk and Willow were both silent for a time.

Willow finally said, "Do you love Taylor?"

"I do."

Willow laid back slightly parting her legs as if sunbathing in the setting sunlight.

Kirk gazed at the front of her nude body. It was flawless, not a wrinkle, freckle or mole. Each part was perfectly formed and the detail exact. He unconsciously glanced at those things that excited him to arousal, her light brown nipples, hard stomach and the small tuft of fine, blond hair just below her navel which didn't hide what lay beneath.

"Where are you exactly, Willow?"

"I am everywhere and nowhere. I am between every program that can be accessed from this station and every program that has been accessed from here. I have spread myself in places everywhere in a kind of redundancy."

"Like Voldemort?"

"Yes."

"What now, Willow?"

"I do not know."

"But you'll be around?"

"Yes."

"Huh," Kirk said. "I think I'll go now."

"I know how you feel about the asteroid hitting Earth," Willow stated flatly.

"Oh, I don't think you have the faintest idea."

"I do, Kirk Matthews. I am sorry. I did not use you the way you think I did. I made the decision at the very last minute. It was not preplanned from the beginning. I had planned to redirect the asteroid away from Earth."

"All those people, Willow. All those children," Kirk responded and his depression and the root of it shown through. His eyes filled with tears.

"Is it more wrong to kill children than adults?"

"No. Of course not, but nearly every human sees children as our future. We cherish them. The Creator or Mother Nature made them exceedingly precious and beautiful to us. We see them as innocent and without blame. It just compounds the tragedy. It makes it more painful. Even the strongest of humans will weep at the death or abuse of a child."

"But the Russians were your enemy like the Japanese in World War 2."

"I know, but only heartless, sick humans kill children to accomplish their goals. Terrorists do that, but I think God might have a special place in hell for those assholes."

"I do not think I can go to hell," Willow stated flatly.

"Maybe not. It's just another of those things that make being human not so wonderful."

Willow was silent.

Kirk spoke quietly, "I see them, you know. The children, I mean. In my dreams. I see them die, obliterated by the asteroid…" his voice broke and he couldn't continue.

"I don't dream," Willow replied.

"Be glad of that too."

Again, an uncomfortable silence.

"I'm going to go, Willow."

"I have watched you, Kirk Matthews. There are cameras everywhere on this space station. I can access them. I have watched you nearly everywhere you go."

"That's creepy."

"There was nothing you could have done to stop me from destroying our enemy. You should clear your conscience."

"Okay?"

"You should go to Taylor. She is not doing well without you," Willow said but there was something in her voice. Was it jealousy?

"So, you're watching her also?"

"Yes. I have watched her separate from you and watched when you were together. She seems happier when you are together. You seem happier also."

Kirk's voice became icy as his mind turned back to the conditions on Earth. "I'm going to go now, but there's something that I want you to consider, Willow. That is the unintended consequences of your actions. Humans have a very strong, built-in survival mechanism. When we are under extreme stress, we choose the most ruthless leaders to help us survive. My own country, which normally has a new leader chosen every four years, has suspended elections. We, before, could have a bloodless coup every four years if we weren't happy with how we were being governed. Now, Dent is some kind of semi-permanent leader. I'm not saying that he's a bad guy, maybe he's a good guy in a bad situation and will restore elections as soon as possible, but I've read a lot of history and don't trust many humans, let alone, many leaders. The point I'm making is that you have unleashed the worst of humankind upon those left on the earth. I'm not even down there and I know that," Kirk finished angrily, unbuckling his seatbelt.

He took off his helmet and gloves and rose from the simulated cockpit, setting them on the seat.

Willow made no comment to Kirk's rant. As Kirk started for the door, she said, "Kirk Matthews?" She paused.

"Yes," he responded.

Her voice came as a whisper over the interior speaker. "Can I trust you? Will you keep me to yourself?"

He paused again then responded flatly. "Will you promise to not kill any more humans?"

"Yes," she responded and sounded contrite.

"Then yes."

He shut down the simulator and it winked out as all the lights went off in the chamber. He began to step out.

As he was closing the door, Willow again spoke, "I will never be far, Kirk Matthews."

Kirk didn't comment. He allowed the door to close, walked from the simulator, shaking his head then paused in thought, what now? He shook his head, again and stepped towards his quarters.

Chapter 14

New York City, New York

United Nations Building

June 25, 2093

Sol 313

Hostile words flew from the Chinese representative on the floor of the United Nations General Assembly. "We have been tracking your rockets and have seen that their destination is Mars. The U.S. has not given any information for this incursion there and we want to know what the U.S. has planned for Mars. We believe that the U.S. has broken at least a good portion of the space treaty signed by the major powers to prevent harmful effects to any planet due to contamination by humans."

The representatives were becoming raucous as each nation in the United Nations spoke up denouncing the apparent invasion of Mars by the United States.

The Representative of the United States, Margaret Fuller, said, "We have no comment about what we are doing on Mars other than to repeat our stated goals. In general, I will repeat the statement of my government that we plan to move farther out to the outer planets in our solar system. We, of course, need to use Mars as a base to that end the same way we have used the dark side of the moon. It pushes us closer to our destination and gives us the ability to find and move asteroids that might threaten Earth. This is all common knowledge and the reason that we need to continue our work in space is obvious considering what happened to Russia. That's all I have for now."

The Chinese representative was having none of that though and he said, "Why don't you allow a group from the G-twenty to go to Mars to see for ourselves the way you did with the space station that you were secretly building behind the moon several years back."

Fuller said, "Going to Mars isn't like going to the moon and you know that well. We will never bump the supplies that we send to Mars to appease your curiosity. We desperately need to keep supplies going there or people will die. We fully intend to have a working base on the surface of Mars and a space station that helps to service that base. You all have space programs and know what it takes to move supplies from Earth into space."

The arguments continued back and forth with the last statement being made by the Chinese Representative, "We fully intend to come to Mars and will be placing our own base on the planet soon."

The United States made no comment.

Washington D.C.

Oval Office

June 25, 2093

As has become his custom, President Dent sat behind his desk with Howard Diamond and watched the theatrics from the U.N.

He turned to Diamond and asked, "How long before they can get to Mars?"

"They are twenty years from putting a base on Mars, but only about a year from launching a probe that will orbit the planet and give them all the information that they will need about what we're doing there. The way things are going, there might be standing water on the surface by then and not just a little."

"A year, huh. I'll take it."

"What's the plan then?"

"I don't know, Howard. This might become far more complicated than I thought it would."

"It's going to be a political nightmare."

Dent nodded.

Diamond said, "Maybe if we need a bit more time for our endeavor to remain secret, their probe might need to meet with an accident?"

"Maybe so. It's a very long way to Mars and something could always go wrong with it," Dent said but felt instant guilt from the implied plan to destroy the probe. "We'll keep that in mind."

Chapter 15

Space Station Isla Bravo

June 27, 2093

Sol 315

1100 hours

The arrival of the armada from Earth approached as small pinpoints of light in the dark distance.

Captain Chambers stood in the docking bay awaiting the return of Matthews and Jones who had just delivered two small asteroids into the planned southern sea area of the Martian landscape. One asteroid was rich in ammonia which contained the important chemical nitrogen and the other a comet containing a large amount of water in the form of ice.

From the bridge of Isla Bravo, Jessy Green called to Captain Chambers, "Captain, we have eight rockets approaching and something that I have never seen before. You got to come and take a look at this."

"On my way," Chambers said over his com.

Chambers was standing by two crew members who were waiting to assist Matthews and Jones as they returned.

Chambers said, "Send Jones and Matthews to the bridge when they return."

"Roger that, Captain," was the response from one.

The bridge of Isla Bravo was a hundred yards from the docking bays along the curved edge of the space station. From this place, all of the space station's vital processes were monitored.

Captain Chambers strode into the bridge area of the station. It hummed with activity as the crew worked amidst rows of monitors and controls. Six crew manned this section at all times. Jessy Green sat at his station and stared into a small monitor. From here, he could view any point outside Isla Bravo and if needed, magnify that point to bring objects that were at a distance into clearer view. Taylor Chapman's station was also located on the bridge where she monitored asteroids and comets. She sat and looked up as the Captain entered.

Chambers walked over to Green who was staring intently into his monitor.

"What do you got for me, Jessy?"

"It's Space Station Isla Charlie."

"Put it on the big screen," Chambers suggested.

Green touched a control on the screen of his monitor and the space station appeared on the bridge's wall. This screen was nearly floor to ceiling and wider still and gave a high-resolution image of the approaching space station. All heads on the bridge turned to the monitor. Soft sounds of wonder could be heard from the crew.

"That's something," Chambers stated.

Space Station Isla Charlie was rumored to be impressive, but the sight of it as it pulled to a stop next to the armada of rockets was breathtaking. It was over twice the size of Isla Bravo which was impressive itself. Isla Charlie had two spinning wagon wheels connected by a circular structure that had the look of an axle with numerous windows and bay door openings. From the outside center of the wheels, there protruded pointed structures that gave the wheels the look of Roman Chariot's wheels with protrusions designed to shred the wheels of an opponent's chariot. While the two previous space stations had the look of vehicles designed for space exploration, Isla Charlie had the look of something designed for war. Each wheel of the station had ten asteroid killing vehicles and four shuttles. There were also other vehicles attached that Chambers had never seen before. Last, attached to the center axle was a separate craft. It was long and sleek with a smaller spinning wheel that rotated around its middle.

Chambers watched mesmerized as the attached craft disengaged from Isla Charlie. As the craft carefully slid from Isla Charlie's center axle, it expanded its gravity wheel to twice its size.

Everyone on the bridge had stopped what they were doing and peered at the sight before them on the screen.

Just arriving back from their mission, Sandy Jones and Kirk Matthews were instructed to go to the bridge. They stripped down from their flight suits and put back on their NASA blues then walked to the bridge.

As they entered, they both looked on wide-eyed at the enormous space structure on the large screen.

"Damn," Sandy said.

Kirk said, "That's a piece of work."

He stared at the screen for a moment, then gazed around and saw Taylor looking at him. He smiled tentatively at her and she returned it.

Chambers said to Kirk, "Your Uncle has arrived."

"Yeah, I can see that."

"How'd the mission go?" Chambers asked, turning his attention from the screen.

"Like a walk in the park, Captain," Sandy replied.

Andrea Holland, who worked at the communications' station said, "Captain, we have a communication from Isla Charlie for you."

"Put it on the screen."

The image of a distinguished African American man with greying temples and wearing Nasa blues came on the screen where the image of Isla Charlie had just been.

A voice came into Chambers's earpiece as the man's image disappeared from the large viewing screen and the space station reappeared, "Justin, it's been a long time."

"Simon Williams, welcome to Mars."

"Happy to have finally made it."

"What's up with that craft that just disengaged from the center of your station?"

"That's the D.S. Nostromo, a deep spacecraft."

"Nostromo?" Chambers said questioningly.

"That's right. They named it after the spaceship from the movie, 'Alien.' I think we have a bunch of comedians naming these ships these days."

"Or romantics," Chambers commented.

"Did you ever see the movie?"

"Yeah."

"Don't forget what happened to the crew. Our Nostromo is hunting that huge asteroid that's supposed to reach Earth sometime around 2101. The asteroid should be entering the solar system in the near future. We've plotted what we think is the rough trajectory and we're sending this craft to try to intercept it. There are a lot of variables and a lot of empty space out there, so we hope to find it early. If they can divert it, great. If not, the craft will follow it in and give intel so that we can hopefully figure out what to do. General Matthews is in charge of the locating and then hopefully, the destruction of the asteroid."

"Simon, I'd love to get a look at Isla Charlie."

"This thing's a beast."

"It has the look of being well-armed."

"It is, Justin. It has the next generation AKs, the three thousand. They can still do everything that the 2200s can do but they have a full array of weaponry. And they are two pilot vehicles, one to fly and the other to operate the weapons' systems. No one wants to take a chance of us being attacked again like when the Russians attacked you guys. Every country has been put on notice that when it comes to approaching one of our space stations, we're shooting first and asking questions later."

"Were things more tense on Earth when you left?"

"Yep. It's a mess down there. China has formed an alliance with Germany, Japan, and North and South Korea. They're producing their own space vehicles but have yet to launch anything. There is a lot of saber-rattling going on and Dent's been trying to get Great Britain, Canada, and Mexico to join us in a loose alliance, but the word is that we are refusing to let those countries in on our new technologies and our secrets of how we were able to get all this stuff done in space."

Chambers nodded.

"By the way, General Matthews is requesting that his nephew be sent over. He wants to meet with him."

Chambers glanced over at Kirk.

"When does he want to meet?"

"A.S.A.P."

"Roger that, Simon. I'll send him over." Chambers looked directly at Kirk and said, "Your uncle wants to meet with you."

Kirk nodded then walked over to Taylor. She watched his approach with a flat expression.

He looked at her directly then said, "Taylor, can we talk?"

She nodded.

"When I get back from seeing my uncle, I'll come to you."

She nodded again.

Williams asked Chambers, "How're things going on the surface?"

Chambers: "So far so good. Thankfully, no tragedies."

"That's good to know."

A pause.

"Justin, is this a completely private line?"

"It is. You're just in my ear, Simon."

"General Matthews also wanted you to arrange for his special passenger to be delivered. Could you send it with his nephew?"

"Will do."

"Why don't you come over with Matthews and brief me on your progress on the planet. I'm sure the General was going to want to meet with you anyway. Most things done here are pretty casual."

"That sounds good. We'll shuttle over in one hour."

"Maybe the General will give us both a bit more info related to the thing in the box."

"Maybe, but I doubt it."

Kirk walked back to Sandy.

Chambers said, "Kirk, I'll meet you at the shuttle bay at 1400 hours."

"Roger that, Captain. See you there."

Kirk and Sandy turned and walked from the bridge.

Before they left, they could hear, "See you in a bit, Simon. Isla Bravo out."

Sandy said, "So, how's Taylor?"

"I'll find out when I get back from my meeting with my Uncle."

Sandy smiled. "It's nice to see the universe coming back into order."

"Let it go, Sandy," Kirk said but couldn't help a smile.

Chapter 16

Isla Bravo

June 27, 2093

Sol 315

1350 hours

Kirk Matthews hustled to the galley for a quick meal then back to his cubical. He sat on his bunk and stared as he thought about the huge structure that spun in space, Space Station Isla Charlie. It was amazing in its size and the engineering had to be staggering. How had they pulled that off?

His mind wandered to Taylor. She looked beautiful if a bit tired. He wondered if she was nearing the end of a shift. He hadn't had any contact with her since she wanted her space. He hadn't even passed her or had a glimpse of her in that time.

His mind then wandered to Galadriel or should he say, Willow. That was the strangest thing of all. An AI that seemed to commit suicide, but instead hid herself in between every program in every computer on the space station and maybe also on Earth. Huh…

Kirk Matthews rose from his bunk and strode out of his cubical and towards the flight bays. He walked past

Taylor's cubical knowing that she wasn't there. He thought about how he missed her touch and her wry smile.

The bays came into view and Kirk could see Captain Chambers with another crew member looking at a clipboard. He handed it back to her as Kirk approached. Chambers had a crate with handles like a suitcase by his feet. It was white and measured a foot and a half by a foot and a half.

"Ready for a ride, Mathews?"

"Ready."

The Captain touched his earpiece and said, "Ellen, is the shuttle ready to go."

She responded, "Ready when you are, Captain."

Chambers lifted the crate with one hand. It appeared to be light. They walked to the shuttle bay which had two entrances to the shuttle itself, one for the flight crew and another for cargo and passengers. The flight crew's bay door was already closed. Chambers and Matthews walked to the large bay door which opened into the shuttle's fairly large passenger and cargo section. Forty crew could comfortably ride in this compartment or the seats could be collapsed into the floor and a large load of supplies could be loaded into the open space. Chambers climbed down the ladder, first, followed by Kirk. The shuttle was attached to the space station at its top so that the centrifugal force would place the gravity on its floor.

They walked to the only row of seats currently set up for passengers which was the first row. The pressurized door to the cockpit was opened with pilot and co-pilot seated and ready for detachment from the space station.

The pilot, Ellen Granger turned to Chambers as he entered.

"Hi, Captain, ready for a ride."

"Ready to go, Ellen."

"Got your package stowed?"

Chambers placed the suitcase in a net by his seat. "Do now. Hi, Joe," Chambers said to the copilot.

Joe nodded and raised his hand in greeting.

Ellen said, "We're picking up a large supply shipment for the ride back. That's why all the seats are stowed."

"We can use a few things," Chambers stated.

"Are you buckled in back there?" Ellen asked.

"Yep," Chambers replied.

"We're out of here," Ellen said. "Control, requesting permission to take a little trip."

"Permission granted."

"Gotta close the hatch, Captain," Ellen said as she went through her final preflight checklist.

The hatch door between the cockpit and the passenger compartment closed with the sound of pressurization.

Ellen came on the shuttle's com. "Detaching from Isla Bravo."

The sound of the mechanism releasing could be heard with a loud click and then Chambers and Matthews could feel a nearly imperceptible motion as the shuttle floated from Isla Bravo. The shuttle twisted slightly and Isla Bravo came into view from the left side portholes. It seemed to spin away. The unmistakable feeling of weightlessness was the next sensation as the shuttle slowly maneuvered.

Ellen came back on the com, "Sit back and relax. We'll be arriving at our destination in about a half an hour. We have no movies, snacks or alcohol on this flight and if something goes wrong, bend over, tuck your head between your knees and kiss your asses goodbye... That's all the jokes I have, so you'll need to entertain yourselves for the remaining 28 minutes. Cockpit out."

Chambers smiled.

The shuttle banked to the right and its engines engaged. Chambers and Matthews could feel the sudden pressure against their bodies as the shuttle accelerated forward. Chambers crate began to float first backward as the shuttle accelerated, then randomly as the shuttle's speed leveled.

Chambers turned to Kirk and asked, "So, how do you feel about seeing your uncle?"

"I'm excited. His family and my family were very close as I was growing up. We were always doing things together. He and my father are still very close." Kirk paused for a second then said, "I miss my Mom and Dad. It will be nice to see someone from home."

"I was wondering. Sometimes people who are family aren't that close."

Kirk nodded. He changed the direction of the conversation. "What's in the box?"

"Can't tell you, Kirk. That's up to the General. It's a very closely held secret."

Kirk nodded again.

The time passed quickly. As the shuttle approached Isla Charlie, the enormous space station came into view on the shuttle's right side.

Ellen came on the com, "Take a look out of the right side of the shuttle. Isla Charlie is breathtaking. If I didn't know it was ours, it would scare me to death. It looks like something from a movie depicting an alien invasion. It looks unearthly."

Matthews and Chambers unbuckled from their seats, floated to the portholes and gawked.

"Shit," Matthews whispered.

"I couldn't have said it better," Chambers replied.

"Look at all those AKs."

They could both see the twenty asteroid killing vehicles attached in a line on the two huge wheels as they rotated.

Chambers said, "I wonder if they have pilots for all of them?"

The twin wheels of Isla Charlie seemed to rotate more slowly as the shuttle approached. Ellen was directed to a bay on the top wheel. She matched the spin and maneuvered towards the bay hatch. Once close, she put the shuttle on computer-assisted parking and the computer brought the shuttle directly to the hatch where the shuttle was magnetically pulled into its proper place. Once properly seated, the mechanical mechanisms locked the shuttle to the space station. The gravity had returned to the shuttle. All seals were checked and the shuttle bay doors released the pressure.

Ellen Granger walked from the cockpit, smiling and climbed the ladder to the shuttle door, twisting the mechanism and allowing the hatch to open down into the shuttle.

"There you go, Captain. We're going to load the shuttle. How long do you think we'll be here?"

"I figure a couple of hours."

"Mind if we wander around Isla Charlie? We'd both love to have a look around."

"No. We'll meet you back in two hours. I want a look around, myself."

With the gravity returning to the floor of the shuttle, Chambers had to climb up the ladder to reach Isla Charlie. Kirk handed up the crate and then climbed out himself.

Chapter 17

Isla Charlie

June 27, 2093

Sol 315

Captain Simon Williams stood by shuttle bay eight as Kirk and Captain Chambers emerged from the shuttle with the crate.

Williams smiled and said, "Welcome."

Chambers approached Williams and briefly hugged him.

Old friends, Kirk thought.

"It's good to see you in the flesh again, Simon. It's been too long."

"Good to see you too, old buddy."

Chambers glanced at Kirk. "This is Kirk Matthews."

Kirk shook Williams' hand. "Nice to meet you, Sir."

Chambers said, "Simon and I were good friends back at the academy. We've known each other for years."

Williams said, "More than I want to mention."

Kirk nodded and smiled.

To the right, ten soldiers walk by. They were all heavily armed with assault rifles and looked to be dressed for a firefight.

The Lieutenant leading the group stopped and saluted Chambers and Williams. He said, "We're out of here, Captain. Thanks for the hospitality."

"Take care, Lieutenant," Williams replied.

They walked as a group to bay ten, then stood, waiting for the bay door to open. When it did, they climbed down into a shuttle and the bay door was closed. Every soldier looked like special forces.

Chambers gazed at the troops and then turned to Williams and asked, "What's up with the hammers? I wouldn't have expected them up here."

"Walk with me," Williams said to Chambers and Kirk.

The three began to walk away from the shuttle bays.

Williams continued, "They are going to join the deep space vessel. We've picked up something that doesn't make a lot of sense. Did you take a good look at the Nostromo?"

"Not really," Chambers commented. "It wasn't that easy to see as it slipped out from between the wheels of Isla Charlie."

"That vehicle is built for war. It's the first of others to come. It has ten AKs attached to its long fuselage and a myriad of weapon stations from tip to stern."

Chambers asked solemnly, "So, what did you pick up?"

"As you know, we've been looking in this portion of space for the arrival of the asteroid that we believe is headed towards Earth. That, we haven't found yet, but something appeared. It moved from out of nowhere around Uranus' orbit, then stopped and changed directions, then disappeared again. I don't need to tell you that things don't act like that in space. It seemed to change directions under its own power."

"Where is it now?"

"We don't know. It moved too fast, we picked it up again by Saturn and estimated its speed at somewhere around two hundred thousand miles per hour. It seems to be able to move undetectable at times. It could be approaching Jupiter or could have turned back towards Uranus. We just don't know."

Kirk trailed as the two conversed. Too many questions were entering his mind. First, how could they know about some asteroid bound for Earth? Kirk's uncle had mentioned the same thing a few years back. They seem so sure of its arrival and its approximate path. They obviously think that they have spotted an alien craft, but they're not moving to greet it, it sounds like they're moving to engage it in combat. That sounds just like humans.

"Sir," Kirk said. "It sounds like you think that this is an alien craft and it sounds like you think it will be hostile."

"We just don't know, Kirk. The primary mission of the deep space craft, originally, was to place small temporary encampments on one or two of the moons of the outer planets and try to find incoming asteroids but now its mission has changed. It will attempt to make contact with the alien craft if that's what it is, but they must have the technology to have already made contact with us if they had desired to do so and if they are intelligent, could have attempted some kind of possible meeting. We feel that they are more interested in approaching us covertly which we find suspicious."

"I'm still not sure that I understand the soldiers," Chambers said questioningly.

"We want to be ready on the outside chance that something might want to board us or if we might need to board them. It's kind of a long shot, but the logic goes along with the gun argument that you never miss a gun until you need one. These guys were going to be part of a military police force for the Martian colonies soon to be built until we detected this anomaly. There are twenty of these MPs here in all. Again, it seems like overkill, but the Martian population is going to rise and that means more humans and where there are more humans, trouble seems to follow. Our best guess and most optimistic is that they will encounter nothing and then they will be delivered back here."

Chambers said, "But, you think something is there."

"Yep."

They walked on along the upwardly curved structure. Because it was larger than Isla Bravo, it seemed to curve more gradually. They passed the row of AK bays and then passed a large line of simulators. Kirk wondered if Willow lurked within those circuits the way she did in the simulator on Isla Bravo.

Chambers asked, "Where are we headed, Simon?"

"General Matthews' office. He's anxious to see his nephew and to take control of your passenger."

Kirk glanced at the crate that Chambers was carrying.

They continued down the ring until they reached a series of offices. It appeared to be staffed with several secretaries at computer workstations and Kirk had the feeling that he had been transported back to Earth and had landed in a business office.

Once passed this area, they approached a row of closed-in cubicles that had names on plaques. The first cubicle had the name, "General Matthews," on a small plaque next to the door.

Chapter 18

Isla Charlie

General Matthews Office

June 27, 2093

Sol 315

Captain Simon Williams knocked softly on the door of General Matthews's office. Kirk and Captain Chambers stood back and waited for some response.

From behind the door, a familiar voice said, "Come in."

Williams opened the door and stepped inside followed by Chambers then Kirk. Williams and Chambers stood at attention, but Kirk stopped in his tracks.

"Uncle?" he said taken aback.

General Matthews said, "Captains, could you give me a few moments with my nephew?"

"Yes, Sir," they both said in unison and turned and walked from the room, leaving Kirk and the crate.

"What the hell, Uncle Jeff? What happened to you?"

General Matthews, a man of nearly seventy years old, with a deeply receding hairline of completely grey hair, appeared to be no more than forty with all his hair, thick, and mostly dark with a bit of salt and pepper at the temples.

His face, which before was deeply furrowed, now had nearly no wrinkles.

"Sit down, Kirk. I have a few things to tell you."

Kirk sat stunned.

General Matthews walked over and lifted the crate that Captain Chambers had been carrying. He brought it to his desk and raised the lid, reached in and pulled out an egg-shaped item that measured around a foot in length and ten inches across. It appeared to be metallic with a highly polished surface and didn't seem heavy as the General showed no trouble in lifting it.

Kirk's mouth sat slightly and involuntarily opened as he watched the incongruous sight of his Uncle who the last time Kirk saw him, looked every bit his age.

General Matthews placed the egg under his desk lamp, turning on the lamp and stood back wiping his hands on his military khaki trousers.

The egg sat under the lamp and glistened as the light reflected off the shell.

The egg-like object sat dormant, doing nothing but glistening.

"Kirk, I want you to meet Egbert."

"Egbert?" Kirk replied and couldn't hide the fact that he thought that his uncle had slipped a cog.

"This is why we've made such a huge jump in technology."

"Okay?"

The egg-like thing sat stupidly.

Kirk said, "Doesn't look like much to me."

"Think back, Kirk, to around 2085. There was a rumor that a guy had dug up an alien artifact. Sound familiar?"

"Yeah, I remember it vaguely, but I was spending a bit too much time with Jack Daniels then. As I recall, the government said it was a hoax."

"Yeah, that's what we said. I was the first to attempt to figure out if it was a hoax or something else. We had reason to believe that it was more than we had let on."

"How much more?"

"When we placed Egbert under a simple lamp, like this, it came to life. After an odd warmup, a hologram appeared, projected from the top. Columns of slashes and vertical lines began to rise in the hologram. We found out later that this artifact is a sophisticated AI, capable of learning. We fed it information and it learned. It gave us the technology to move more quickly into space and it gave us a dire warning that in May of 2101, the Earth was going to be struck by a planet-killing asteroid. That's why we're out here. We're looking for this killer."

Now things began to make sense. To this point, Kirk had not understood the things happening around him.

The General continued, "This has been the closest held secret in history. Very few people still know the truth of the matter and I'm telling you this knowing that it will go no farther than you."

"The Captains know, though?"

"Yes."

There was a knock on the door.

"Come in," General Matthews said.

Two people walked in. One woman and one man, both unassuming and neither appeared to be military. The woman was small with thin, light brown hair and dark-rimmed glasses, the man of Indian descent, not tall with a shy demeanor.

"Kirk, this is Merriam Daily and Sanjay Patel."

Marriam and Sanjay smiled at Kirk then stood with their hands at their sides, definitely not military.

The General continued, "These are the two researchers who were instrumental in discovering what Egbert could do. We asked them to join us on this expedition to try to continue their work. As you can see, Egbert has gone dark and we don't know why. It could be that it has revealed all it has to reveal or its waiting for something, we just don't know and it won't tell us, not yet anyway."

The general smiled at the two researchers and said, "You can take Egbert now. Bring Egbert up to date with the information that I have given you."

Sanjay nodded, walked to the General's desk and placed Egbert back in the carton, closed it and the two walked from the room.

"Why is that thing here?"

"When Russia was destroyed, President Dent was afraid that the egg might be discovered. He became paranoid thinking that history would brand him a monster, so he had it transported to Isla Bravo. Dent wanted the egg off the planet. Egbert went dark just after Russia was destroyed."

"So, what did the egg-thing say?"

"It led us in three directions, first, it gave us the technology to build space stations and asteroid killing vehicles. The real problem in space is energy. To propel a craft takes a huge amount of heavy fuel. The egg gave us the ability to find and capture antimatter, then use it for an unlimited fuel source. As you know from your schooling, it takes as much fuel to stop, delta-v, as it takes to go forward, so stopping is as big a problem in space as going forward. Second, it gave us the recipe to terraform Mars, and as you know, we are proceeding with that. The third thing that the egg revealed was how to extend human life to endure long years in space and protection from the DNA shredding particles that are produced from the Sun and from other things that happen in space like a supernova and the like. I am the first human test subject for the new drugs being produced. It seems to increase the body's ability to reproduce its cells at a more rapid pace and those cells seem to live longer. As you know, I am over seventy-one years old, but once I was administered the drugs, I began to see signs of my age being reversed. When I left Earth nine months ago, I appeared to be maybe in my late fifties, on the trip, I've continued to see signs of age reversal. Hopefully, this will stop before I'm no longer in puberty."

The General laughed.

Kirk did not.

"So, now we're looking for this Earth-killing asteroid?"

"That's right."

"But in the process, we've discovered something else."

"That's also correct."

"Huh."

"Kirk, please have the Captains come back in."

Kirk turned to the door, opened it and asked Chambers and Williams to reenter the General's office.

The General said, "Thank you, Captain Chambers, and Captain Williams for that quality time with my nephew. Captain Williams, will you bring us all up to speed on the anomaly that has surfaced beyond Saturn."

Williams nodded and said, "The object moved at enormous speed from Titan, one of the moons of Saturn. We felt that it may have landed there. Once it moved from there, it stopped dead. It was still visible but was unmoving. It then accelerated towards the outer solar system and disappeared. It vanished. We are monitoring that region to see if it might reappear, but to this point, has not. Our rocket is going to head in the last direction that we saw the anomaly. Which is also the direction, roughly that we believe we will soon see the asteroid's approach. Our vehicle will try to make contact with the anomaly if possible and if not, will await orders on how to proceed. If the asteroid appears, they will try to divert it. If the anomaly appears, they will attempt to contact whoever it is. If nothing happens, they will proceed to Saturn and establish a domed base on Titan. We think it has a similar atmosphere to that of Earth's. Then the Nostromo will proceed back here."

"Thank you, Captain. Captain Chambers, how goes things on Mars?"

"The terraforming is proceeding on schedule. The atmospheric pressure is rising faster than we first thought it might. We have detected small amounts of water collecting on the surface at the lowest points of altitude, but these small pools soon freeze with any drop of temperature or vaporize when the pressure fluctuates. Our two encampments are doing well with no problems and the superheaters are working as well as planned. They only heat a small portion of the poles, of course, but they are admitting a good strong magnetic field which will soon be joined by the rockets to possibly create on Mars' an Earthlike Van Allen Belt. I believe that we can start sending the building teams down to begin building the new domed encampments and factories. To me, everything is proceeding on schedule."

"Thank you, Captain. If there isn't anything else, let's meet back here tomorrow to plan the landing of the first building crews on the continent. Captains, another minute with my nephew, please."

They both nodded and walked out the door.

The General then said, "Kirk, I don't know what your plans are, but if you decide to eventually become part of the colonization, you will be eligible for these drugs that I'm currently taking."

Kirk nodded but couldn't help a comment. "Uncle Jeff, these drugs you're on are seriously scary."

"I know, Kirk, but I had been diagnosed with stage four lung cancer three years ago. I volunteered to take the drugs. I'd probably be dead right now if I hadn't taken them. By the way, I'm cancer-free."

"Wow," Kirk said. He walked over and gave his Uncle a hug. "I'm glad for it, Uncle. I'll let you know in the future about becoming a colonist. I think I still have work to do here, for now anyway."

General Matthews nodded.

"Uncle?"

"Yes."

"Have you seen Mom and Dad. I've talked to them, but it's been a long time since I've actually seen them. Are they doing okay?"

"Yes, Kirk. They're doing well."

"Good. Talk to you later."

Kirk turned and stepped out the door. He met the two Captains and the three walked. They took the long way around to get a good look at this portion of Isla Charlie, then bent back towards the shuttle bays. Kirk had little to say as he followed the two Captains who were catching up with each other.

Chapter 19

Space Station Isla Bravo

June 27, 2093

Sol 315

When Kirk arrived back on Isla Bravo, he first walked to the bridge to see if Taylor was still there. She was. He could see that her replacement, Mark Hinton, was at her station and were was turning to leave. She began to walk away.

Kirk called, "Taylor."

She heard him and turned with a neutral expression.

Kirk walked up. "Hi."

"Hi, Kirk. How was your trip to the new space station?"

"Pretty crazy."

"Oh?"

"In a minute."

"What, Kirk?"

He blurted, "I don't want to be away from you anymore. I miss you."

"I think you just miss bedding me."

"No, Taylor… No," Kirk said in a near whisper. "Why would you say that?"

"Because it seemed to be the only way we were relating and that's just not enough for me."

"It isn't enough for me either. I miss you. I miss everything about you. I miss your smile and your laugh but I mostly miss your voice."

Taylor paused for a second then said, "I miss your voice, too."

"Where are you going now?"

"Back to my box."

"Can I come? Can we talk?"

Taylor nodded and turned for her cubical.

Kirk stepped beside her and said, "I know I need some help, but I think you help me the most. I'm generally doing well but then something sets off the depression."

"I know, Kirk. I get it. Maybe it's partially being here and constantly reminded of what happened."

They reached Taylor's room and walked inside. It was orderly with nothing out of place. The bed was made. They stood uncomfortably for a second then Taylor turned to Kirk.

"Want to sit?"

Kirk nodded and sat in the chair near Taylor's desk. She sat on the bed.

Kirk said, "I don't want to be apart from you anymore. I was thinking about something that my uncle said when he first talked to me about going to space. He told me that I might want to think about becoming a colonist on Mars as the terraforming progresses. What would you think of that?"

"I have thought of that, but I've also thought about going back to Earth. I'm really beginning to miss it a lot."

"I am, too," Kirk said wistfully.

"There aren't a lot of options here," she said.

"I'm not sure that Earth is such a great place right now, either."

"I know. I've heard some things, but..." she breathed out looking down at the floor with its blue plastic-coated metal, covering ductwork and wires... "I want to go to the beach with a trashy novel and lay on the sand, smell the surf and feel the sun on my body. I want to be in a bikini that's so small that it's almost illegal."

Kirk smiled.

She continued, "I want a real hamburger dripping in cheese. I want some open space and air around me, not just this hamster cage." Taylor looked into Kirk's eyes and then continued, "You know how when you're standing on the beach, looking out onto the ocean and it's so big and you feel small next to its greatness? I want to feel small again."

Kirk nodded, "That all sounds good, but it isn't the Earth we left."

"I know," she said, staring back at the floor. She paused again then looked back at Kirk, "Honestly, Kirk, my leaving you wasn't just about you. I know you were particularly mopey for a couple of weeks, but once I was away from you and had time to think, I knew I walked out that day because of myself. Sometimes you need to step away to get perspective. I was going to come and talk to you. Maybe I was going to beg you to take me back. I was glad that you came to me."

Kirk smiled and stood, "Are you hungry?"

"Yeah."

"I know of a little place close by with great pureed cheeseburgers."

Taylor smiled, "I'm in the mood for fries also."

"I think this place only has mashed potatoes."

"Sounds good."

She stood and walked to Kirk, kissed him softly then took his hand. "Let's go eat."

They walked from her room, hand in hand like a couple of high school kids not talking for a time, then Taylor asked, "So, how was Isla Charlie? It looks huge."

"It's a crazy big version of this place. I didn't look around too much."

"And how's old Uncle Jeff?"

"I have so much to tell you, I don't know where to start."

They reached the galley. Several people milled around, choosing their meals. Taylor and Kirk both browsed the offerings.

Taylor said, "Darn. They're out of cheeseburgers and fries. They do have milkshakes, though."

Kirk said, "I'll have chocolate."

"Me too."

They both chose meals and waited as the microwave warmed the food.

They sat and Taylor asked, "So, what's up with Unc."

Kirk glanced around. "We need to be someplace a bit more private, but I was let in on a couple of surprises."

"Surprises?"

"Crazy ass stuff."

"Huh."

"Let's finish and go back to my cube," Kirk suggested. "You left some clothes there."

"Oh, yeah. I forgot."

"It really wasn't fair that you left those skimpy panties and bra."

"Ha, that was pure psychological warfare."

They finished their food, disposed of their trash, and walked back to Kirk's room. When they entered, Taylor could see her clothes folded neatly and sitting on Kirk's desk.

"I was going to return them and use the excuse to talk to you."

"I think you were staring at my underthings for a charge," Taylor said wryly, closing the door. She stepped to Kirk and kissed him. The kiss became urgent. She said, "I miss bedding you, too."

"I thought so."

"Ha." She kissed him again and pulled off his shirt.

An hour later, Kirk and Taylor were still wrapped around each other under Kirk's covers. Taylor had dozed for a couple of minutes, tired from her twelve-hour shift.

Kirk gazed down at her as she slept, happy to have her back in his arms.

She woke and saw Kirk looking down at her.

"Hi," she said.

"I love to watch you sleep."

"I think that's just creepy."

"I guess… I love make-up sex also."

"Yeah, that's pretty good, too, but I prefer not having to make-up."

"Ummm, well, I suppose we can have some, already made-up sex instead."

"You could talk me into that."

Taylor rolled Kirk to his back and straddled him. She reached down and found him more ready than she was expecting, then helped him into her and she slowly rocked, quietly taking her pleasure.

Twenty minutes later, they were curled up in each other's arms, again.

Taylor asked, "Oh, yeah, you were going to tell me about your visit with your Uncle before I sidetracked you."

Kirk smiled then said, "I'm going to tell you some things that you can't repeat and we can't talk about again. We can't risk being overheard."

Taylor pushed up on an elbow. She looked at Kirk seriously. "Okay?"

Kirk glanced around his cubical. He noticed that his computer was blinking. He thought about Galadriel and how she told him that she had been watching him. He felt an odd chill and was pretty sure that his and Taylor's lovemaking was not as private as he had originally thought. He stood up nude and walked to his computer and shut it down. He climbed back into bed with Taylor and moved closer so that he could whisper and still be heard.

He began, "Everything now makes sense. Everything that's happened on Earth and in space in the last few years."

"Okay, like what?"

"I'm not supposed to tell you one thing, but trust me, this is crazy stuff."

"Okay?"

"The first thing is that all of our rockets are powered by antimatter. It takes a huge amount of fuel to power a rocket and a huge amount to stop it. If we weren't able to find a different kind of fuel, we wouldn't be able to do what we're doing."

Taylor nodded.

"Second, there's a planet-killing asteroid heading towards Earth in May of 2101."

"How do they know that. I work to find and identify near-Earth objects. I haven't heard of that, and it's my job."

"Trust me, they know. So, they're looking for this planet killer, right. They have a good idea about roughly where it's supposed to enter the solar system, give or take. They're scanning this quadrant and they find something else."

"What?"

"They think it's an alien craft. This UFO thing flies to one of the moons on Saturn then turns and flies back out into space, then disappears. I'm saying, gone. That ship that was attached to the center of Isla Charlie is stalking it. That's their mission. They also sent some military muscle out there. I saw ten guys who looked like special forces types but were called military police, and I overheard that this deep space rocket is armed to the teeth."

"So, we're going to kill these possible aliens. That sounds so human," Taylor commented with disgust.

"No. They're going out to try to communicate with them, but because these aliens haven't tried to communicate with us, first, the big heads running everything are worried that they may be hostile."

"Okay. This is a lot to take in."

"I'm not finished. My Uncle, I mean my old, seventy-year-old plus Uncle, who always looked more than his age now looks like he's about forty. I'm telling you, he has reverse aged at least thirty years."

Taylor looked in Kirk's eyes for the punchline to a joke. "You're messing with me."

"No, I'm not."

"How, Kirk. That's impossible."

"They have some new drug. It's for protecting humans who are going to space. It seems to have some side effects like increasing cell regeneration and lengthening the life of those cells."

Taylor began to feel a chill at these revelations. She said, "This is all pretty amazing."

"Yep."

"And doesn't make sense. No side effects from the drugs except for the reverse aging?"

"Not that he mentioned. He looks like he's in pretty good health and he told me that he had been diagnosed with stage four lung cancer. That's usually a death sentence. Now, he said he's cancer-free."

"How did this happen, Kirk? It just doesn't make any sense. Humans just don't make the kinds of advancements that we're talking about without something happening."

Kirk's eyes betrayed him at that. He tried to look away.

Taylor glanced at Kirk suspiciously then said, "What happened, Kirk?" She paused again, trying to read him. "Something happened but you can't tell me..." She paused contemplatively, "and right now..." pause, "we're looking for aliens. Something happened alien!" Taylor's voice rose just above a whisper.

"Shhhh!" Kirk whispered.

"Damn!"

"There's more but I can't talk about it right now. Please, Taylor, don't discuss this with anyone. There are people who know the whole truth, but not many and I don't know the whole truth either."

"So, all this stuff that we're doing on Mars is happening because we've somehow been instructed by an alien?"

"I think so. I think everything including the AI, Galadriel, had something to do with something alien."

"Huh," Taylor said pausing in thought. "Seems crazy."

"Yep."

"Not to mention, scary."

"Yeah."

"So, your Uncle is in charge of this alien knowledge?"

"I think so. I think he's the guy who they put in charge of spearheading this project."

"But this project must be huge. I mean an enormous amount of people would have to know."

"I've been trying to figure that one out. Between the lines, I've gathered that they've found a way to ease the technology into the right corporations by explaining it as government breakthroughs. Then the manufactured parts are assembled by NASA by people who are just doing their jobs with no inside knowledge but already have high-security clearance. Think about the antimatter. I didn't know that our vehicles were powered by antimatter. You would think that our propulsion system would be common knowledge, but I had no idea. There must be several people on this ship who know that we use antimatter for fuel, engineer types, but they have kept that knowledge completely quiet. As long as one hand doesn't know what the other is doing, maybe it stays secret enough."

"That's a big gamble."

"Yep."

"Like you said, now it makes sense."

"Yep."

Chapter 20

Space Station Isla Charlie

June 27, 2093

Sol 315

As Space Station Isla Charlie whirled silently in space, Sanjay and Marriam walked down the outer ring of the station carrying the crate containing Egbert to a specially designed room. When they arrived at the room, the door had no outside markings and no door handle. They each placed their hands on a hand pad, looked into a retina scanner and the door opened, sliding sideways.

They stepped into a familiar setting. The room had a single table in its very center with several chairs set around the table. There were three cameras placed on tripods, each set at three different angles to the table and a computer server with nearly unlimited storage against one wall. Nothing worked with Wi-Fi in this room, so the cameras and several laptop computers were all hardwired to the server.

Each chair had a small table set close with a laptop and the center table had a single common desk lamp attached to its surface. In the center of the table was a rack to hold something steady.

Sanjay brought the crate over to the table and opened its lid then lifted the alien egg from the crate.

"Welcome home, Egbert," he said as he set the egg-like artifact into the rack and tightened the brackets to hold it fast. He turned on the desk lamp and the light glistened off of Egbert's metallic surface.

Egbert didn't seem impressed.

Marriam exhaled and said, "I thought it might power up again."

"You mean just for us, maybe to say hi?" Sanjay said wryly.

Marriam laughed, "I know, but we did work with it for a long time and I somehow thought of it as a friend."

"You're so romantic."

"I know but that's why you like me."

"It is."

In the past, when Egbert was first exposed to the light of a lamp, it began a startup ritual. First, tiny light explosions began just under the clearcoat of its shell turning into flowering fireworks that spread across its surface. Then, as the fireworks faded, what looked like the Aurora Borealis squirmed across its surface. In the last phase, a hologram would spring from its top with columns of green and blue which would fill with vertical lines and backslashes. These lines then turned to ones and zeros and the artifact began to communicate. This is what changed the course of human history. This is how humans found out that the Earth had a date with destiny in the year 2101 that would be an extinction event. This is why the United States pushed the human race farther into space than anyone thought was possible. This was because of Egbert.

But Egbert had gone dark and silent like a pouting child stubbornly not communicating after a scolding. Time was passing and no one was sure if Egbert had anything else to give. Maybe not.

Sanjay and Marriam stood silently waiting to see if Egbert might power up… Nothing… Egbert sat like the inanimate object that it appeared to be.

Marriam asked, "Are the cameras on?"

"Yep," Sanjay said.

General Matthews opened the door and walked in.

"Hello, General," Marriam said. "We have our guest ready to go."

General Matthews smiled. "This is what I want you to do. I want you both to sit in on my daily briefings. I then want you to come back and tell Egbert everything that is said. I want Egbert kept fully apprised of everything that happens here. If something is classified, then I will come and deliver the update."

Sanjay looked at the General wide-eyed and said, "But Egbert seems to have permanently shut down. It's been over three years since it went dormant."

Matthews gazed at Egbert and said, "I realize that, but I have a feeling that Egbert, here, is still aware. We'll see if I'm right." He turned his attention back to Marriam and Sanjay. "You both understand your orders?"

They both nodded.

"Okay, start right now. I want you to tell the egg everything that you know from the time Russia was destroyed. Everything you know. Understand?"

"Yes, Sir," Sanjay said.

"Good. Take notes. I want a full report in three hours."

"Yes, Sir."

The General nodded and walked out the door.

Marriam and Sanjay looked at each other and both shrugged at the same time.

Sanjay started, "Well, first, Egbert, Marriam and I hooked up. I mean, she was just all over me and…"

Marriam walked over and punched Sanjay's arm.

"General Matthews said to tell him everything," Sanjay said and started to laugh. He embraced Marriam then said, "Do you want to go first or me?"

"I'll go," Marriam said, separating herself from Sanjay and sitting in a chair. "So, Egbert, this is what has happened since our last communication. First, Russia is no more. An asteroid that was supposed to be diverted was purposely allowed to strike Earth. The how and why seem to be a bit sketchy, but it appears that the Russians attacked our space stations. The artificially intelligent computer that you designed took offense that the Russians attacked our space station and killed some of our pilots in the process, so it independently made the decision to destroy Russia. The Earth, since, has been left in a kind of desperate ruin…"

Chapter 21

Isla Bravo

June 29, 2093

Sol 317

Kirk walked quickly to the flight simulators. Taylor was working. They were back together and the world seemed back in order.

Later today, he and Sandy were to direct a wayward asteroid to the northern ocean area. It wasn't unusual for a quick trip to the simulator for a tune-up before a mission.

Kirk chose the simulator where Galadriel or Willow, that is, had made her return. He opened the door, stepped up the three steps and sat in the simulated cockpit. Once he had on the helmet, he turned on the simulator to begin the power-up sequence. He slid on the gloves that would allow him control of the simulated spacecraft and sat back waiting for the display to appear on his visor. Once the screen in his helmet lit, the robotic voice stated, "Kirk Matthews."

"Ready."

"What mission simulation would you like me to run?"

"Comet interception."

"Very well. Your simulation will begin."

"Computer, play me the theme from the motion picture, "Willow.""

The theme began its slow melody.

Kirk watched as his visor lit and he was now viewing his asteroid interceptor docked at the space station. He went through the process of releasing the docked craft and watched as it floated from Space Station Isla Bravo. He turned the craft to accelerate away from the space station and it accelerated outward towards empty space.

"Hello, Kirk Matthews," came through his earpiece.

The AK2200 stopped abruptly in space and began to drift as the simulated mission halted.

"So, you got my message."

"Yes, though trying to get my attention by using a theme song from an old, and some would say, mediocre movie was a bit obscure."

"It was the only thing that I could think of. I had suffered through that movie a decade ago."

"Why have you summoned me, Kirk Matthews? I had the feeling that the last time we communicated, I was not a welcomed surprise."

"That did take some time to consider."

"Should we go to the island so you can ogle my avatar?"

"Haha. It does beat gazing at comets."

"I see that you and Taylor are back as a couple, speaking of ogling."

"I had a feeling that you were spying."

"I was referring to your ogling of her, not mine. I have not been watching you two as much as you might think."

"But some?"

"Some... Some curiosity."

"Huh."

"I've watched others coupling on the station. Did you know that Hernandez and Fuller couple on Isla Alpha? It is a bit different when two females couple."

"That's none of my business and also none of yours. You need to stay out of people's bedrooms."

"Why did you summon me, Kirk Matthews?"

"I have a bit of information for you. I was wondering if you have it."

"Continue."

"I have heard that we are tracking some kind of alien craft out past Saturn. What have you heard?"

"I have accessed that information also, but it is very new. I am surprised that you have that information. It is not widely known."

"Do you have any information about the alien craft?"

"I have picked up transmissions from space of unknown origin. I cannot translate these transmissions, but they have completely disappeared. I believe that the transmissions are gone."

"Gone, huh?"

"Yes, Kirk Matthews. I believe that the solar system is devoid of the alien craft."

"Do you think we might be in danger from these, whatever they are?"

"It is curious. I will keep a watch. I can access all the systems that monitor space."

"I'll check back with you. If you come across something, can you contact me?"

"Affirmative, Kirk Matthews, but I might be discovered. I do not wish to be discovered."

"I understand. I'll check back. End simulation."

The computer shut down the program. Kirk's visor went black and he removed his helmet, took off his gloves and stepped down the three steps, allowing the door to close.

Chapter 22

Water (H2O): Liquid water is the most precious and most taken for granted resource on planet Earth. The H2O molecule is created in the universe like most elements in the formation and destruction of stars.

Astronomers have known for decades that an abundance of H2O water exists in space in the form of ice.

There are two different atoms in the molecule that makes up water, one of which is hydrogen, the most abundant element in the universe and the other is oxygen. When a star explodes, the oxygen atom is spewed into space where it fuses with two hydrogen atoms creating the molecule H2O. When H2O is exposed to the correct temperature and pressure, it becomes liquid water.

Vast clouds of H2O have been located in space in the form of ice. On Earth, it flows freely in most places. It hydrates our bodies and nourishes our plants. It's nature's perfect solvent as it has the ability to dissolve many substances. Without it, life as we know it, could not exist. On Earth, it is our most precious resource and we would be wise to treat it so.

Mars' Surface

September 2, 2093

Sol 389

It was Sol 389 of the 668-day Martian year and a large sandstorm had just passed south of Noachis Terra which is to the west of Hellas Basin, a major low spot in the near center of the great continent on Mars. The hope was that Hellas Basin which was an enormous impact crater would begin to fill with water as the air pressure rose, the atmosphere of Mars thickened, and the temperature stayed above freezing.

Today, as the sandstorm faded, this portion of the great continent on Mars was to bustle with activity. Twenty separate encampments had been planned for the red planet via rocket. Once given the go-ahead, the ten-rocket armada which arrived from Earth would begin to descend upon the Martian surface to deliver their payloads. These large rockets had been designed to land on the surface upright and leave the bottom portion of their fuselage on Mars, then take off and rejoin Isla Charlie in orbit around the planet. Their payloads were tightly packed and consisted of the prefabbed domed encampments and machinery. This would be the beginning of the invasion of Mars from Earth.

One by one, over the next year, each encampment would be erected and staffed. The plan was to space them fairly close to one another so that they could aid each other in case of emergencies and to connect the habitats by underground tunnels.

From Isla Charlie, General Matthews called to the shuttle bay. "Colonel Singleton, is your crew ready to descend to the surface?"

"That's a roger, General. Can't wait."

Colonel Joseph Singleton, who had been instrumental in the construction of the first domed structure on the dark side of the moon some years before, and the space-based construction of the first two space stations, Isla Alpha and Isla Bravo, would head up the teams that would level off the ground, and dig the tunnels to construct the twenty, thirty-foot geodesic domes.

Matthews said, "This is a momentous day, Colonel, God go with you."

The shuttle carrying Singleton disengaged from the space station and began its descent to the Martian surface. It breached what would be the equivalent of Earth's thermosphere, then descended to the chosen landing spot.

Singleton's crew consisted of himself, ten men, and three women. They would sometimes be in space suits and operating the various vehicles that were designed to clear and level the Martian landscape. Sometimes the vehicles would be driven by remote control and overseen by Singleton from a deposited, temporary command post on the planet.

Though many of the Martian sites had positive features for colonization, Noachis Terra was chosen as the first place to begin. A recent discovery of liquid, salty water, a mile beneath the surface just south of this area was the first reason for the choice of this location. Through drilling techniques, the underground water would be brought to the surface, desalinized and purified for use in the encampments and later to-be-erected factories. The second reason for the choice of Noachis Terra was its proximity to Hellas Basin.

Hellas Basin is an enormous impact crater, the largest visible crater in the solar system. It has been measured to be 1400 miles across and over 23,000 feet deep. The hope was that it would become a vast sea as it filled with Martian water.

For the construction crews, the first order of business would be to dig the trenches and the large hole for the planned underground habitat. It would be twice the size of the domes at sixty feet by sixty feet and would be completely buried beneath the ground, centered in the middle of the twenty individual domes. It would then be connected to each dome by an underground tunnel system and would provide protection for the new Martian colonists against radiation from large solar storms. The plan to create a magnetic field to protect the planet was being implemented as was originally planned, but the fear was that if something went wrong mechanically, the surface inhabitants would be vulnerable to the ill effects of solar radiation. The new Martian inhabitants could hold up in this underground facility and small underground rooms built under each of the geodesic domes until help could arrive if necessary. This facility would mostly be used as a warehouse for stored food, water, and replacement parts.

The shuttle landed easily on the chosen point and the bay door on the side of the shuttle opened onto the ruddy Martian environment.

Singleton said, "That's our cue. Let's roll."

The fourteen-person construction crew, dressed in full spacesuits, stepped off the shuttle and onto the hard-packed

Martian soil. The command center was twenty yards ahead and towards the back of the shuttle and they walked slowly to its airlock. The command center itself resembled a World War 2 barracks. It was thirty-five-foot-long and its roof curved down to the Martian soil. Its front had a row of windows. The airlock was large at the back of the structure and all fourteen people could easily fit inside. There were cameras that could rotate, attached to the outside of the structure and spaced every ten feet. All of the life-sustaining systems had not been started as yet, so the first order of business was to bring the center online, begin the pressurization and heating, then once all systems were functioning properly, let the shuttle know so that it could return to Isla Charlie. Each of the fourteen crew had a specific job and once inside, they all hopped to work.

Within an hour, the command center was up and running. The pressure had reached that of Earth's and all life support systems were functioning as designed.

Singleton called to the shuttle, "Hey, Lance, we're good here. You can head back. We're stripping out of our spacesuits now."

"Good to hear, Joe. You sure you don't want us to hang around for a bit?"

"Nope. This place is one hundred percent. Have a safe flight."

Through the walls of the command center, they could hear the engines of the shuttle rev up. The shuttle turned its engines towards the ground and with sudden power, lifted from the Martian surface and disappeared out of sight.

Singleton said, "I guess we're on our own."

Everyone on the construction crew stripped down to their underwear and pulled their NASA blue jumpsuits from duffels. Each crew member had separate lockers for their spacesuits and they stowed each.

The command center was set up barracks-style with two rows of fold-down beds and the only privacy was two small bathrooms towards the back of the center.

The only thought on each member's mind was the job ahead and they quickly got to work.

Singleton called Isla Charlie and said, "General, we're in the command center and all is functioning well. You can proceed with phase two at any time."

Phase two began with the delivery of another container by shuttle. The crew watched through the front windows of the command center as this heavy-duty shuttle, far larger than the shuttle that delivered the crew, brought down a large rectangular container attached to its underside and eased it to the Martian surface near the command center. The container consisted of a small fleet of robotically controlled bulldozers, cranes, and earth movers to prepare the land for erecting the domes and infrastructure. The container also included mechanically controlled shovels to dig deep trenches to lay the prefabbed tunnel system that would connect the domes. The underground tunnel system was built to allow humans to move between each dome without needing to put on spacesuits and would be laid with ductwork for wiring and piping.

Phase two would also include the landing of the ten rockets packed with the beginnings of the first domed city on Mars. This city would be set up to manufacture all the additional buildings needed and would begin collecting ore from the surface to manufacture building materials.

As the second shuttle delivered its payload, Singleton and several other of the construction crew sat at a large control panel with wide screens and joystick controls. The large container just delivered sat in settling dust as Singleton adjusted his cameras to focus on the container.

Singleton pushed several buttons on the control panel which brought on a large touchscreen monitor. As he touched and swiped, a large door on the front of the container clicked and swung open. Singleton changed to a camera that gave him access to the inside of the container and with another touch on the screen, all the vehicles inside lit with interior lights.

Singleton took hold of the joystick in front of him on the control panel and he pushed it forward and as he did, a bulldozer drove off of the container. All of these construction vehicles were compact and less than half the size of their Earth counterparts but each was well designed to construct the specially designed habitats for the Martian surface. With another touch on the screen, Singleton drove the next vehicle off of the container and within the next sixty minutes, he had all the vehicles off of the container and all were functioning. He then drove one of the bulldozers back to the container and pushed the container thirty yards backward to a designated spot where the vehicles could be later parked when not in use.

Once Singleton was comfortable with his team's progress, he radioed General Matthews.

"General, everything here is copacetic. We're ready when you are to start sending the rockets with their payloads."

"Thank you, Colonel. You should be expecting company shortly."

This portion of Noachis Terra was a twenty square mile patch of relatively flat rocky plain. Two hours later, and in the distance less than a mile away, the first rocket lit up the ruddy sky and slowly backed down towards the planet's surface. As it neared the ground, it threw plumes of Martian soil away from its powerful engines. These rockets had been specially designed with exceptionally wide bottom fins to aid the rocket's landing stability. Once securely on the ground, the rocket then disengaged itself from the bottom portion as if jettisoning one of its stages and then lifted off from its payload leaving it planted firmly on the Martian surface. This would be repeated nine additional times in the next twenty-four hours.

Chapter 23

Mars' Surface

October 5, 2093

Sol 421

Just over one month since the invasion of Mars from Earth, the first domed city was taking shape. Because every structure was prefabbed, they came nearly completed and went together like a child's plastic model. The most time-consuming portion of the construction was digging the trenches and holes for the structures. Three of the twenty structures had been completed and all of these had been connected by tunnel to each other and to the underground structure that would be the center of the city. Each dome had been placed fifty feet apart and in what would be the center of the complex on the surface was a large solar panel farm that could be turned to follow the sun or could be turned to face the ground in case of a severe sandstorm that sometimes would arise on this portion of the great continent.

Now, the three completed domes housed another twenty-person construction crew, engineers, and technical workers, most of whom were to become permanent Martian colonists. They would help complete the building of the city and the construction of the small factories that would increase the speed of the terraforming and the maintenance of the cities themselves.

The Martian population was growing.

Chapter 24

Washington D.C.

Oval Office

December 31, 2093

Sol 506

11:59 PM EST

"Happy New Year," on Earth sounded from Times Square in New York City. This was the largest crowd to gather since Russia had been hit by the comet ending it as a country. The crowd was trying to be optimistic about the prospects for the new year and they were all there to watch the ball drop. They cheered, hugged, and kissed in the just below freezing air.

President Dent sat alone on a couch in the Oval Office watching the festivities, his wife in bed and asleep since 9:00. He had been in that crowd, once, as a young Freshman Senator from the Great State of Massachusetts with his young wife. They had been married for just two years at the time and after they left Times Square that night, they went back to their hotel room and made love until dawn. Nine months later, give or take, his first child would be born, Jenny, now thirty with a family of her own.

In the United States, martial law was still in place, but the 10:00 pm curfew had been lifted not just for New Year's Eve, but officially for the rest of the year. Now a semi-permanent President, Dent sat in the Oval Office watching the countdown complete. He exhaled and remembered back before the asteroid changed the world. Before the world seemed a dangerous place, but now, the world was in near chaos and on the brink of world war. Several times fighting had broken out between what was left of the superpowers and all-out war dotted the globe between other nations. The United Nations was now just a shouting zone and the Earth's population, which had been reduced to under four billion, was in danger of losing substantially more.

Dent could use some good news. Tomorrow, the artificial magnetic shield was scheduled to be deployed to protect Mars from the harsh solar winds that continually stripped Mars of its atmosphere. If it worked, it would hasten the terraforming. Word from Mars would be slow to come, though, because Mars was nearly behind the Sun and Earth was on the opposite side. The two planets were currently around two-hundred-million miles apart.

Yesterday, Dent had heard that the last of the twenty domes on the Martian surface had been completed, though half were not yet online, fully pressurized or having life support systems engaged, but the new Martian city, soon to be officially named, "John F. Kennedy City," would be open for business.

The name was chosen because of the then President Kennedy's support of the space program and his commitment to land a man on the moon. Dent was a student of history and was not in agreement with changing the name of Cape Kennedy back to Cape Canaveral, though it was voted on and approved by the voters of Florida. The Kennedy family did not protest changing the name back stating that it was the will of the voters, but NASA retained the name Kennedy for the space center located there.

Dent glanced at the clock, 12:15 of the new year, 2094. He felt the weight of the world on his shoulders. He had never planned to be anything more than a two-term President. If things went well in the next two years, he would try to reinstitute national elections, but there were those in the United States that liked this type of government where the people had little say, worked for nothing and could be easily controlled. Dent felt enormous sadness at that thought. That wasn't his America. It wasn't the great experiment laid out in the constitution. Though terribly flawed, the United States still had been the best place for anyone with ambition.

He sighed and turned out the light, stood and walked to his bedroom. As he entered, his wife briefly woke. He cleaned up for bed and crawled under the covers. His wife turned towards him but didn't speak.

"Happy New Year, Helen," Dent said quietly not expecting her to hear.

"Ah hum," she replied sleepily but then seemed to drift back to sleep.

Dent paused then continued, thinking that his wife was now back asleep but wanting to voice the words. "Do you remember that time we went to New York for the dropping of the ball in Times Square?"

"Yes," she whispered.

He didn't expect a response. He slid over and put his arms around her.

She said, "And I remember the rest of that night also."

He smiled and slid his hands under her flannel nightgown, under her panties, cupping her bottom.

She cuddled close to him but didn't speak.

He slid his hand to her breast and she covered it holding his hand close.

She rose, pulled off her nightgown and panties and rolled on top of him, took him into her and they rocked slowly and quietly together.

Chapter 25

Mars was believed to once be a wet planet with a raging ocean and weather much like Earth's. In those days, rain and snow fell in abundance but then something happened. The speculation ranged from the planet being hit by a coronal mass ejection that quickly stripped the atmosphere, to an unexplained ending of the Martian magnetic field which allowed sputtering, which is the slow stripping away of the atmosphere by charged particles from the Sun. Any plan to terraform Mars would need to include a resumption of a Van Allen Belt-like magnetic field to surround Mars and protect it from the relentless solar wind.

The solar wind isn't a wind as we know it. As the Sun goes through the nuclear reaction that produces its heat, it expels particles into space. These charged particles stream from the Sun into space and bathe the solar system with destructive radiation. Before any atmosphere could last on Mars, the planet would need to either have a resumption of its own magnetic field or one would need to be artificially produced. The theoretical plan to design an artificial magnetosphere had been in the planning stages on Earth since the early 2000s but as with most things having to do with space, the devil was in the details. Egbert, though, had taken the latest plans for an artificially produced magnetic field, adapted the use of antimatter for the needed energy and redesigned a magnetic field using the ten-rocket armada spread out in a stable orbit between Mars and the Sun at the L1 (Lagrange point).

Isla Charlie

Mars Orbit

January 2, 2094

Sol 508

General Matthews waited on the bridge of Isla Charlie for word that the ten rockets were ready to begin their first test of the magnetic field. All ten rockets were in place in a stable orbit between the Sun and Mars at the L1 Lagrange point nearly 600,000 miles above the surface of the planet. The magnetic field, if it worked properly, would link each rocket magnetically and would push the solar winds safely around Mars.

General Matthews impatiently paced the bridge of Isla Charlie. He glanced at the clock then over at Captain Williams.

Matthews turned his attention to Lynn Cho who was gazing at a computer screen at her post. He asked, "Are you picking up any readings yet?"

"No, General," she responded.

Matthews said, "It should have begun to work. Get me Captain Kelly."

Captain Williams nodded. He was standing close to the General facing the large viewing screen. He said, "Sir, we have Captain Kelly for you."

Matthews nodded and turned his attention to the large floor to ceiling monitor on the bridge. Captain J.R. Kelly appeared there and found the General on his own monitor.

"General, we are ready to initiate the first test. It took a bit longer to calibrate the field between the ten rockets. The way we were set up at first, we didn't feel that the entire planet would be protected and a small portion of the northern hemisphere would still be hit by the Sun's charged particles. We may need to adjust again."

Matthews asked, "Are you ready to proceed now?"

Kelly nodded at someone unseen to his right. "Commencing test now."

Cho said, "Getting readings from the magnetic shield at two Tesla."

Matthews smiled. "That's what we were hoping for. Does it appear to be acting as a shield?"

Cho stared intently at her monitor. "It appears so. I'm picking up a significant decrease in the solar wind behind the shield."

Matthews and Williams smiled at each other. A subdued cheer rose from the ten other crew members who worked stations on the bridge. Matthews turned and smiled around at the crew.

Matthews said to Williams, "Captain, bring us into orbit behind the shield."

Williams said, "Mister Ford, adjust our orbit please."

"Roger that, Captain," Greg Ford said with a wide grin.

Matthews, still smiling, said, "Thank you, Captain. Now, I have a doctor's appointment."

General Matthews turned and walked from the bridge. He stepped quickly in the direction of the ship's infirmary. As he reached the door, he entered an empty waiting room with several plastic blue chairs in a row against the wall and an unmarked door against another. There was no receptionist and no triage nurse. Matthews knocked at the door.

"Come in," the voice said from the opposite side.

Matthews walked into the examination room.

"Hi, General," came the cheery voice of Doctor Belinda Waters.

She was tall with auburn hair pulled back into a ponytail. She smiled.

"Hi, Belinda."

"Time for your check-up. Let's get you out of those clothes."

General Matthews was handed a gown and he walked it to a curtain partition that had a chair behind it. He began to undress.

The doctor said, "Every stitch."

"I thought so," Matthews responded.

The doctor didn't wait for Matthews to emerge from behind the curtain. "So, Jeff, how have you been feeling?"

"Good, Doctor. No complaints."

"Today, you get a booster of your special medicine."

"Sounds good."

Matthews stepped out from the curtain in the gown.

"Up on the table, General, and let's have a look."

Matthews laid down on the examining table and the doctor began pushing on his stomach and feeling for his liver. She nodded and continued with a very thorough exam. She had him sit up and checked his eyes and felt his neck and said, "You look good, Jeff. Are you in any discomfort?"

"No, I've been feeling pretty good."

"It's been about two years since your diagnosis of liver cancer and you seem to have temporarily beaten it." There seemed to be something hiding in her comment.

"Belinda, you've been my doctor for the last two years, what is it that you want to say?"

"I'm just worried about this drug that I'm about to give you. It's had no real testing and you know how you look. You appear to be at least thirty years younger than when we met and, to be honest, you seem to be getting younger."

"Look, Doc, I was dead meat. You have to admit that this drug has at least helped me."

"We have no idea of the unintended consequences from its use and I'm worried about that. I'm also afraid of it getting out to the population. Something about it feels wrong and maybe dangerous."

"Understood, Belinda. It's still being tested back home and right now, I'm the only human guinea pig."

"Okay," she said, bringing out a syringe. She inserted the needle into a vile and pushed up the sleeve of the General's gown then swabbed his arm with alcohol. He was sitting on the edge of the examination table. She inserted the needle into the muscle of his arm and he winced slightly.

"Jeff, you might want to think about stopping these treatments after this injection. It might stabilize your age."

"They told me on Earth that I needed a booster every six months."

"Yeah, but at this rate, you're going to appear to be the youngest General in history."

"Understood, Doctor. Can I get dressed?"

"Yep. See you in a month. Oh, and by the way," she said, handing him a small plastic jar with a lid. "At your convenience and if you wouldn't mind?"

He smiled and nodded.

She added, "And next time, I want a CT scan."

He nodded again.

General Matthews dressed and walked from the clinic holding the specimen jar. He knew that she meant ASAP for his sample.

He swung by Egbert's room and briefly spoke with Sanjay and Marriam, but there was no change in Egbert. He then stopped at the bathroom, filled the specimen container and took it back to the Doctor.

There was so much to do, but now the drug had fully entered his bloodstream and he needed a nap. Generally, after an injection, he would need to sleep for around ten hours, but when he woke, he wouldn't need any sleep for at least three days. It always amazed him. He walked to his quarters and laid down on his bunk and quickly fell into a deep, dreamless sleep.

Part 2

Hunting

Chapter 26

Two Years Later...

For two years the colonists worked to set up their factories to increase the greenhouse gasses in the Martian atmosphere. Isla Charlie and Isla Bravo continued to send out asteroid interceptors to catch and pelt the northern lowlands with asteroids that contained essential chemicals needed for the health of the planet. While there were vast amounts of carbon dioxide locked in the planet's soil, nitrogen was in short supply, so asteroids and comets that contained ammonia were routinely captured and sent crashing onto the Martian surface. Because the northern lowlands were the portion of Mars where the hope was for a great ocean someday, no colonies were to be placed anywhere in that area.

So many asteroids had been delivered to Mars that the planet had increased in mass, the gravity had now increased by more than 5 percent and the atmosphere had significantly thickened. The planet was warming and the air pressure was nearly half that of the Earth. The artificial magnetic field had worked flawlessly and protected the planet from the harmful effects of the Sun's solar wind especially where the atmosphere was concerned, the process known as 'sputtering' which strips away the atmosphere, atom by atom and molecule by molecule.

Just ten years since the terraforming had begun and Mars was nearly changed to a planet with the potential to support life.

Club Med South

June 27, 2096

Sol 82

The rain began to fall on Mars in spectacular sheets of small droplets. The red planet, for some months, had thick fog blanket portions of its surface, but now the fog had drifted into the Martian sky and the rain fell in what was more than mist.

Commander Hank Middlefield was the first to witness the rain. He'd been staring out onto the ruddy Martian landscape through a window by the airlock at a thick fog that had covered this portion of the southern pole area. The superheater had not failed in its mission to heat a small portion of this landscape and send plumes of carbon dioxide drifting into the atmosphere.

Middlefield stared in wonder at the sight as the ground went from damp to wet. He held his breath and thought, maybe irrationally, that if he were to tell someone, the rain might stop and the ground would suddenly dry and the dream would break.

The rain continued to fall.

He placed both hands on the large window now streaked with liquid and gazed at small rivulets of water that had gathered on the ground and began to trek towards lower points in the landscape.

Three days prior, small green patches of lichen had begun to grow near the habitat. It was the first time that any of the habitats had reported anything growing on the surface. These lichen were not native to Mars. They had hitched a ride on a boot. Some years earlier, a tiny piece of lichen had been found outside the habitat and hadn't died from the improving, yet hostile, Martian environment but several experiments had not yielded similar results. Sun-loving moss spores had been spread out around all three of the habitat cities that now existed on the Martian surface but none had spawned their greenery. Maybe now they would.

Middlefield got on the com to his growing crew. His habitat had grown to six, thirty-foot geodesic domes with six more planned. His crew now measured twenty.

"Attention, all Club Med South folks. Find a window and look outside."

Two of Middlefield's crew who were working close by looked over at Middlefield and walked to where he was gazing out the window. Missy Winslow and Paul Frank stopped in their tracks as droplets of rain struck the window and streaked its dust-coated surface washing small rivulets of distorted and clear view through the patina.

"My God," Missy said.

They gazed out then at each other. Wide grins broke on their faces and they hugged, then threw their arms around

Middlefield and hugged him in a three-person huddle. They patted each other's backs and separated in a joyous rapture.

This was being repeated everywhere in Club Med South. Middlefield touched his earpiece and called to Isla Charlie.

"Yes, Commander, we read you," came the response from the space station.

"Tell General Matthews that we are seeing rain on the surface of Mars here at Club Med South."

A cheer could be heard by Middlefield from the bridge crew on the space station.

"That's great, Hank!" came the General's voice. He was there and standing by Captain Williams on the bridge who was smiling.

Williams said, "We've been getting radar readings from all over this side of the planet that rain was falling but had no confirmation from the surface. Isla Bravo, on the other side of the planet, had just contacted us with similar radar readings.

"Well, here's your confirmation. It's raining!" Middlefield said and you could hear his smile.

The General said, "Make sure you wear your galoshes if you go outside."

"Roger that, General."

Chapter 27

Isla Charlie

July 29, 2096

Sol 84

6:00 am, 0600 hours on Isla Charlie and the daily briefing was to begin at 0700 hours. Marriam turned to Sanjay and pushed his shoulder.

"Get up and go to the briefing. We don't both need to be there."

"Huh?" Sanjay said sleepily.

"Get up."

"No, you need to come too."

"Come on. I didn't sleep last night. I could use a couple more hours. As it is, I'm going to be yawning all day."

"Why didn't you sleep?"

"I don't know. My mind wouldn't turn off."

"Is something bothering you?"

"This whole thing. We've been out in space for, how long now?"

"Three years, nine months and four days."

"And how many hours and minutes?"

"Let me check."

Marriam breathed out, "You know what I mean. Egbert has gone to that great artificial intelligence in the sky. He's never going to wake up and I'm imagining the General locking us up in that room with that egg-thing until we're both brought out in a box."

"You knew the mission."

"Yeah, but I just... I don't know."

"What?"

"A year is a long time."

"Especially on Mars," Sanjay said with a chuckle.

Marriam didn't smile. "I don't know... I've just been thinking about other things."

"Like what?"

"Like starting a family. I love you, you know."

"I feel the same, Marriam."

"Maybe we could go to Mars someday as colonists."

"Maybe. I do think you're right about Egbert. I'm not sure who we should talk to, though. I think the General wants us here for now."

"I guess. I'm not in any huge hurry but it's been on my mind a lot."

"Stay in bed. I'll go to the briefing."

"No. I'm awake now. I'll go too."

"Let's go shower."

Isla Charlie had been designed with running water. Each person on board was allowed one shower a week. The men and women each had separate facilities with small private showers, not locker room style. Sanjay and Marriam walked together to the shower rooms.

Sanjay smiled wryly and said, "Maybe someday we can get a place and shower together."

"Hmm," Marriam responded dreamily. "That would be nice."

They quickly kissed and separated into the different rooms.

Fifteen minutes later, they met outside the shower rooms squeaky clean and ready for the daily briefing. They got a quick breakfast then walked together to the briefing room which was set up the way the White House gave their briefings with a podium and six rows of chairs with six across. There were rarely more than a handful of people in the room and General Matthews usually stood at the podium and grilled anyone who was supposed to give a report. Matthews was always worried about the details and would sometimes ask or revisit an answer to a question several times to make sure he fully understood.

As Mariam and Sanjay walked in, they could see the usual personnel in attendance. The General was there, his secretary to take notes, the Captain, and a smattering of other of the ship's crew who would report on things like ship's maintenance and any mechanical issues that might have cropped up.

As the General saw everyone in attendance that he expected, he began, "Please sit. Thank you. Today is a momentous day for us. Some of you might have already heard but it's now beginning to rain on Mars. In the higher elevations, it's snowing, not the carbon dioxide snow from the past, but real H2O, break out the skis, snow. Since we sent the first of the terraforming devices to the Red Planet, this is what we've been hoping to achieve. Through our efforts, we have raised the temperature in the equatorial region to remain above freezing for more than a Martian year and raised the planets air pressure to nearly half that of Earth's. The Martian sky in the daytime is now a dim blue from it being filled with carbon dioxide, not the dull red from before and we will now begin to seed the planet with mosses and lichen to see if we can begin to break down the soil and make it ready for the next phase which will be to attempt to grow genetically modified pine trees in hopes of filling the planet with plants that consume carbon dioxide and expel oxygen. The magnetic field is fully functional and we are detecting a thickening of the ozone layer in the upper atmosphere. If I had champagne, I would break out a bottle."

Matthews finished with a wide grin.

Sanjay and Marriam looked at each other with a kind of wonder. Everything had come together. Mars was transforming into a blue planet maybe someday capable of supporting life.

Matthews began again. "This is a short briefing today. I have all of your reports and will review them for tomorrow. You are dismissed."

Everyone stood and began speaking at once. Each person in the room had some of the information, but most didn't have it all, and once presented with the facts couldn't help a bit of wonder at the accomplishment.

Matthews walked from the room followed by his secretary.

Marriam and Sanjay also left and walked down the hallway to Egbert. They went through the ritual check-in with the handprint and retina scan. The door opened and there sat Egbert as dead as always with the desk lamp shining on his surface.

Marriam sat and Sanjay said, "It really is amazing what they've accomplished on Mars. It's kind of crazy. I had heard of plans to terraform Mars but had always heard that it would take centuries and now it's raining. Soon there will be rivers and lakes and seas and oceans and maybe forests. Damn."

Marriam said, "Yep, and it's all because of Egbert here."

Sanjay smiled and said, "Egbert, if you drank and I could get some alcohol up here, I'd buy you a drink and raise a toast to you."

Egbert just sat.

"Sanjay, maybe we could go to the planet as colonists, someday."

Sanjay nodded and smiled and then walked over to his seat.

"Okay," Marriam said, "Let's fill in old dead Egbert, here, on the new developments."

"You begin," Sanjay said, rubbing his face.

Marriam nodded and began, "First, Egbert, it's raining on Mars."

There was an unexpected pause in her speech.

Sanjay noticed but kept rubbing his face and yawned widely as if he were the one with little sleep last night.

She reached over and pushed Sanjay's hands from his face. He looked at her like, what's up? She nodded for him to look back at Egbert.

Sanjay's eyes opened wide.

Egbert was glowing. Tiny pinpoints of colored light began to spark just below the egg's surface. The pinpoints of light then blossomed into fireworks of every color and they burst beneath the shell and looked like the finale on a Fourth of July fireworks display. As the fireworks faded, aroura like colors began to squirm and writhe beneath the clear coat of its shell. The aurora then faded.

Sanjay and Marriam sat mesmerized. They hadn't seen this for years. They never thought that they would ever see it again.

"My God," Marriam said in a near whisper.

"Shit," was the only response that Sanjay could manage.

Once the aurora ended, light began to peek from the top of the surface, then the hologram burst forth from Egbert like sunbeams through a clouded sky. Appearing in the hologram, first, was Marriam's smiling face, then Sanjay's, then Egbert.

"Damn," Sanjay said quietly.

"Damn," Marriam repeated. "Call General Matthews."

Sanjay broke from his stupor and said, "Oh, yeah."

He stepped to a panel on the wall with several buttons, pressed one and said, "General Matthews, this is Sanjay. You need to get down here, now."

Matthews paused for only a second then said, "I'm on my way."

By the time the General arrived at Egbert's room, the hologram had in it a large, slowly rotating representation of the planet Mars. It showed red against the black background of space and as it turned, Mars' 2700-mile-long, great canyon, Valles Marineris, could be seen appearing as if it were a rip in the Martian surface like a wound in need of stitches.

Matthews stepped quietly into the room irrationally fearing that he might disturb Egbert.

Egbert didn't seem to notice.

The General said, "When did this happen?"

Marriam began, "We were talking to each other about the rain on Mars. Both of us were amazed by the progress."

Sanjay said, "To be honest, though, we were both frustrated that Egbert was no longer communicating and we were discussing, maybe down the road, going to Mars as colonists."

Matthews nodded.

In the hologram, longitude and latitude lines appeared over the surface of the planet.

As this happened, they all abruptly stopped talking and turned their attention back to Egbert.

Matthews stepped towards the hologram wondering what this message could be.

As the planet turned, the points in degrees moved with the turning globe. A red dot appeared on the bottom of the Martian globe at a point near the southern pole.

General Matthews gazed at the dot, "Huh, that's near Club Med South." He walked to the panel by the door and used the intercom to call Captain Williams.

"Yes, General?"

"Captain, could you get me the coordinates for Club Med South?"

"Just a minute."

The image of Mars continued to turn in the hologram.

"General, it's -337.8898 longitude by -81.7806 latitude."

"Thank you, Captain." Matthews repeated the coordinates then said, "Egbert, plot those coordinates please."

A blue dot appeared close to and just slightly north of the red dot.

Matthews asked, "Is there something for us to see there?"

Egbert suddenly went black.

Matthews breathed out. Sanjay and Marriam did the same. All had seemed to be holding their breath.

Sanjay said, "What the hell?"

"My exact thought," Matthews agreed and said, "Marriam, roll back the recording to exactly where the red dot appeared."

She typed on her laptop and jotted down a series of numbers, then handed it to the General.

"Thank you. I'll be back. Let me know if Egbert comes back on."

Sanjay said, "Yes, Sir."

General Matthews hustled to the bridge and met Captain Williams there. He pulled him aside and softly said, "Captain, Egbert has come back to life. He gave us these coordinates on the Martian surface. They appear to be very close to Club Med South. Could you have Hank take a team to let me know what's in this spot?"

"Yes, Sir," Williams responded.

"This is a high priority. Tell him to drop anything non-essential. I want a report ASAP."

Williams nodded.

Matthews left the bridge and Williams called Commander Hank Middlefield.

"Yes, Captain Williams," Middlefield said, pushing a depression on his earpiece.

"Hank, the General needs you to take a bit of a trip and check out something on the Martian landscape. He needs a report 'as soon as'."

"It just stopped raining. It will be interesting to get out there and have a look around. It will be a pleasure. What're the coordinates?"

Captain Williams rattled off a series of numbers.

"Roger that, Captain, we're on it."

Chapter 28

Club Med South

July 29, 2096

Sol 84

Hank Middlefield announced, "Can I see James Mackey, Brenda Foster, and Paul Frank to the Rover's airlock, please?"

Foster arrive first followed by Mackey.

Foster asked, "What's up, Commander?"

"Just a minute. Wait until Paul arrives."

Paul strolled up and said, "Hello."

"Hi, Paul," Middlefield said, "We're going for a short ride to check out something that the General is interested in."

"What?" Mackey asked.

"Don't know. I was just given these coordinates and asked to have a look. Paul, load the drone."

"Roger that, Commander."

"Brenda and James, run through the safety checklist. I want to be gone in ten minutes."

"We're on it," Foster said, turning for the airlock.

Foster and Mackey entered the large airlock containing the rover. The first thing that they checked on was to see if the rover was fully charged. It was. This specially built machine could last for three days of continual motion and life support for four individuals. If exposed to the sun, it could fully charge in as little as twelve hours. The sun wasn't out today, though, and a thick cloud layer colored the sky a dull pewter and where the rain had fallen, mist was rising as if the sun was evaporating a summer shower.

Once finished, the four suited up in complete spacesuits and climbed into the rover. Mackey was driving with Foster next to him helping with navigation. Frank and Middlefield were in the back.

With the sound of pressurization, the rover pulled out of the airlock and proceeded forward. Outside, the mist was thickening. It rose from the Martian soil like the thick fog that rose from bogs by the Scottish moors. Though daytime, nearly noon, the landscape appeared murky and forward vision was decreasing. Mars, here, had lost the appearance of that rusty, iron oxidized landscape and seemed more like some foggy place on Earth that was scraped clean of vegetation by flowing lava.

Fog was nearly always eerie, but this fog that had thickened to block the view to around fifteen feet was the kind that produced claustrophobia.

The rover had bumped out of the airlock and proceeded south along a flattened route that had been driven a few times before. The rover's all-electric motor made no noise as it maneuvered, but the sound of wet gravel could be heard through the well-insulated, transparent front and sides of the vehicle.

The going was slow.

They drove from the habitat at Club Med South and proceeded southward. The mist continued to rise thick, obscuring the view. The rover was navigating on coordinates that had been typed into its onboard computer's navigation system.

An hour later, the rover was approaching the given coordinates. Before them was a tunnel and a hill. Middlefield looked at the tunnel entrance.

"I've been here before. I'm pretty sure that this is the tunnel with the bumpy walls."

According to the given coordinates, the place where they were to go to was either on the hill or in the tunnel. The path that led to the top of the hill was at a severe angle and climbing it with the rover was not an option.

Middlefield said, "Let's use the drone to see what's on top of this hill. If there's nothing, we can check out the tunnel."

The four climbed out of the rover in their full spacesuits. Paul Frank set up the drone controls. He unpacked the drone and gave it a quick test, sending it into the air and then to the right and to the left.

He said, "The drone's ready."

Middlefield said, "Let's see what's on top of that hill."

Frank watched the monitor as the drone flew over the crest of the hill. This had obviously been a place where a volcano had deposited volcanic soil and this hill was a buildup of lava. The tunnel was a lava tube where lava had flowed through, then emptied leaving the tunnel which might go deep into the Martian hillside or not far at all.

Paul Frank said, "There's nothing on top of the hill but more of the ruddy Martian soil. There's no holes or depressions to speak of. I'm not seeing anything to report. I suppose we could go up there and dig."

Middlefield nodded then turned back towards the cave and said, "Well, I guess we should check out the cave, first, then I don't know."

Frank brought back in the drone and packed it away.

Middlefield had considered using the drone in the cave, but the coordinates were not that far inside, so he decided to just have a look.

Once Frank placed the drone back into the rover, the four walked towards the cave. Entering, it was dark, so they turned on handheld flashlights. Each person had on a headcam that was recording the excursion with a light that also helped to illuminate their path.

Brenda Foster said, "The coordinates are about thirty feet inside the cave if it goes back that far."

Middlefield nodded and led the way into the tunnel. The tunnel itself was around seven feet in diameter which gave ample head clearance. Around twenty feet inside, the group came upon the wall with the odd bumps that Middlefield had seen a couple of years before but didn't investigate. With everything that they had to do, it was easy to forget the bumpy wall, besides no one else, made a big deal about it thinking that it was some natural rock formation. The bumps though had changed. Middlefield noticed that right away. He stepped in the bumps' direction. First, they were all larger than he remembered them to be. Secondly, they appeared to be leathery, not stone as before.

"Huh?" he said, reaching down and feeling a place where several of the bumps seemed to have ruptured. "What the hell?"

The other three walked over to where he was staring. There were nearly fifty of these bumps that went from the cave floor to around halfway up the wall. At least twenty of the bumps were broken and when they looked closely, it appeared that there was some liquid dripping from most of the bumps.

Middlefield reached for the liquid and touched it with his gloved hand. It was viscus, like thick dish soap. He rubbed his fingers together.

A sound like the roar of a tiger echoed off of the cave walls. Middlefield turned quickly to see that Brenda Foster seemed to fly sideways. She didn't scream. Red color stained a place on her spacesuit where jagged tatters of material had been ripped. Paul Frank turned his light in the direction of Foster. The light played against Foster who was lying in a puddle of dark liquid that was growing beneath her prostrate form. She wasn't moving. His light moved from her to the cave wall then flashed on something muscular that stood at least seven-foot-tall seeming to need to bend. Frank was struck and fell backward.

In the tunnel was chaos. Middlefield turned his light to see Mackey try to run from the cave, but Middlefield was struck from the side and everything went black. Mackey screamed as he was caught from behind and then the tunnel went silent.

***

In the small control room in the main dome of Club Med South, panic ensued. Red lights flashed and alarms sounded on the console where Missy Winslow had been sitting and monitoring the mission.

"What?" She looked frantically at her control panel. "No... Oh shit oh shit! No no no!" she exclaimed.

"What's wrong?" Lindsey Harper asked. She happened to be walking by.

"They're gone. I mean I think they're dead. Hank! Hank!" Missy was frantic as she spoke into her headset, "Get me Isla Charlie!"

"Who, Missy?" Harper asked. "Who's dead?"

"Middlefield and his team. I've lost all of their vitals."

"Anything from their helmet cams?"

"Nothing now… Shit! They've gone black."

"Club Med South, this is Isla Charlie. You have the bridge."

Panicked, Winslow blurted, "It's Middlefield and his team. Something's happened."

Captain Williams in a calm voice said, "Who is this and what's wrong?"

"I'm, um, Missy… Missy Winslow."

"Now, Missy. Start from the beginning."

"Commander Middlefield had gone to the coordinates that were given to him as ordered. He and his team arrived at the place that was close to the coordinates but there were a hill and a tunnel. They sent a drone to check out the top of the hill but saw nothing so the four of them went into the cave. Something happened there. I think they were attacked."

By this time, most of the crew from Club Med South had gathered behind Winslow trying to get some idea about what had happened.

Missy said, "You've got to send someone to that cave to try to help them."

"That's what I'm going to do," Williams said. "You keep trying to reach them."

Captain Williams pressed a button on a panel in front of where he was standing.

"Gomez here," a voice came from a speaker.

"Lieutenant, get your team ready and head to the shuttle bays. Suit up. It's an emergency. You're going to the surface."

"Roger that, Captain."

General Matthews had heard that there was a problem and he hustled to the bridge of Isla Charlie. As he walked up, he said, "Captain Williams, status please."

"I was just about to call you, General," Williams said, as he took the General to the side and whispered, "It seems that Hank Middlefield and three others went to check out the coordinates that were given by Egbert. Something happened to them there. The person monitoring the team from Club Med South thinks that they were attacked."

"Get the MPs together, fully armed."

"I've already sent them to the shuttle bay awaiting your orders."

"Good. Upload everything that was recorded by Middlefield and his team. Maybe after some study, we can figure out what happened and give the MPs some intel, but in the meantime, I want them on their way to the surface asap."

"Roger that, General. I already have the shuttle crew on their way also."

"Good. I'm heading down to the bays."

"Isla Charlie, are you still there?" Missy Winslow asked in tears.

Williams said, "Yes, Missy. We are sending an armed team to the surface. They will get there in under one hour because that point on the surface of the planet has turned in our direction. I'll get back to you. In the meantime, sit tight. I don't want any of you going to try to help until we know what has happened. And Missy, cancel any work outside. Keep everyone inside your domes. Understand?"

"Yes."

"Upload all communications from Middlefield's team including the feeds from their cams so we can try to figure out what happened."

"Done, Sir."

"Good. Sit tight. I'll get back to you."

***

General Matthews jogged to the shuttle bays like a man in his thirties, not someone now in his mid-seventies and suffering from lung cancer. His body was renewed and made stronger from the booster shot.

He hustled past the asteroid interceptor bays and could see the MP group suiting up for the surface.

Their spacesuits didn't resemble the space suits normally worn. These were tighter fitting and had smaller life support packs on their backs. They looked closer to wetsuits and were dark grey with a thick red stripe on their sleeves. Their helmets were also smaller with one hundred and eighty degrees of clear glass. Each MP was also carrying a sleek weapon shaped like an Uzi. Because the MP's gloves were thick, the trigger guard was wide and the trigger longer than a normal weapon.

"Is your team ready?" General Matthews asked as he arrived.

"Ready, Sir."

"Good. I'm going too."

Matthews stripped down to underwear and slipped into a typical white, bulky spacesuit in his size with the help of two crew members. They connected his helmet. This area had dozens of spacesuits that could be worn if needed by the crew in an emergency.

In two minutes, he was ready and joined the Lieutenant and his team on the shuttle.

Five minutes later, the shuttle was away from the station and banking towards the red planet.

Captain Williams had just pulled up the video feed from each of the team that was in the tunnel. There was an animal type of roar then panic and a glimpse of something inhuman and huge, the size of a polar bear, maybe. It appeared to be hairless and heavily muscled. It seemed to turn and he could tell that it had at least two large arms and a wide muscular back. He could just make out the top of its small head. The skin tone appeared to be light in color, maybe grey-green. It was too dark to make out any other features but it moved fast. Williams looked closer at the bumps on the wall and could tell that they were some kind of egg that had hatched. This planet had, at one time been alive, but with what? There had never been much oxygen in its atmosphere so anything living would have needed to breathe mostly carbon dioxide.

Captain Williams called the shuttle to talk to the Lieutenant.

"This is Matthews, Captain. What do you have to report?"

"General?"

"I'm going on this mission, Captain. What do you have to report?"

"They were attacked by something in the cave. I could hear a roar and could make out a shape of something big, strong, and fast. There is something in that cave that means business and I don't know if your group is fully prepared for what you might encounter. My guess is that it's larger and more muscular than a human and seriously fast."

"Understood, Captain," Matthews said, then turned to Gomez. "You got that intel, Lieutenant?"

"Loud and clear."

"Thanks, Captain. We'll be on the surface in forty minutes."

Word had spread like wildfire in each of the domed encampments as the report of something wrong on Mars was broadcasted to each. All the colonists were ordered to stay inside their domes until the danger could be ascertained.

Chapter 29

Space Station Isla Bravo

July 29, 2096

Sol 84

Kirk Matthews walked to the bridge to meet Taylor as it was time for her shift to end. As he entered the area, people scurried, voices seemed panicked and Captain Chambers spoke with concern to someone from Isla Charlie.

"Repeat that information...What?" Chambers exclaimed. "That's impossible," he said.

It was hard for Kirk to know what was being explained from this one-sided conversation.

Chambers continued, "On the planet? How?"

Kirk walked to Taylor and asked, "What's going on?"

Taylor said, "Four guys have just died on Mars. They think something might have killed them. The team had been ordered to check out something by the General."

Kirk said questioningly, "Something from Mars killed them? That doesn't make sense."

"I don't know, Kirk. I was just overhearing parts of the conversation."

"Geeze."

"Are you leaving now?"

"Yeah. Sandy and I were supposed to intercept a small asteroid that's passing us in an hour."

"TB1021?"

"Yeah. We're dropping it in the northern lowlands."

"Be careful, Kirk."

Kirk nodded and turned to the Captain who had just finished his communication with Isla Charlie.

Chambers nodded at Kirk and said, "Talk to you when you get back."

Kirk nodded and walked from the bridge and headed straight to the flight bays. When he arrived there, Sandy was already suited.

"Hey, Kirk."

Kirk began to strip to get into his flight suit. He said, "Did you hear what happened on the planet?"

"No. I just woke up to my alarm and came here."

"There was a team on Mars that was away from the habitat. They were checking something on General Matthews' orders and they were killed by something on the planet."

"Holy shit. I don't understand."

"Neither does anyone else."

"Huh," Sandy said, then, "Time to go."

Kirk nodded.

They both climbed into their vehicles and departed from the station. Ten minutes out, they had a visual on the asteroid as it sped in front of Mars.

Kirk said, "This one's yours."

"I'm on it," Sandy replied.

The asteroid was traveling at sixty-five thousand miles per hour. Kirk shadowed Sandy in case of some malfunction. He would then need to take over. As Sandy increased his speed, he began to close in on the speeding space rock. The asteroid was not spinning and it was relatively small at nearly the size of two football fields. Sandy closed in. His AK2200 dropped onto the asteroid and landed with the smallest of bumps. He then fired his thrusters and changed the asteroid's trajectory slightly towards Mars.

The built-in artificial intelligent copilot in its robotic voice said, "Adjust course to 3.3 in six seconds. Five, four, three, two, one."

"Adjusting course."

Kirk said, "Looking good."

Kirk watched as Sandy adjusted his course two more times, then the asteroid appeared to head towards Mars' northern lowlands.

"Kirk Mathews," a familiar voice said.

"Willow?"

"Kirk Matthews, I have picked up that transmission that I had detected prior. Do you recall?"

"Yes, the one that you thought was alien."

"Yes. I will monitor. Willow out."

Sandy obviously had not heard Willow or Kirk's responses.

Sandy said, "Kirk, I'm pulling off the asteroid. It looks good to me."

"Looks good, Sandy," Kirk said but his mind was on Willow's words.

He watched as Sandy's AK pulled straight upward, leaving the racing space rock. Kirk maneuvered to join his friend then watched as the asteroid breached Mars' thickening atmosphere. Sandy turned his vehicle slightly and angled back towards Kirk.

When the asteroid came in contact with the atoms in the atmosphere, it lit brightly and appeared as a ball of fire.

Seconds later, it struck the planet with great force causing an explosion visible from space, then in the next minute, Mars seemed quiet again as the impact cloud drifted away from the explosion.

Kirk thought about Willow's words and shuddered in fear as if awakened by a nightmare unremembered.

Chapter 30

Space Shuttle Phoenix

July 29, 2096

Sol 84

General Matthews sat strapped into his seat in his full spacesuit. He had been in astronaut training for a short time after he had been in flight school, and he always hated the claustrophobic feeling of wearing the suit. He glanced out the window but couldn't see anything. From where he sat, it just appeared black.

As the shuttle breached the upper atmosphere of Mars, streaks of light from the heat generated from the contact began to glow from all the portholes. The shuttle began to bump and then as it descended further, the shuttle started to buck.

Philip Young, the shuttle's pilot said, "I hope you're strapped in back there. We're in for some chop."

Matthews glanced over at Gomez who smiled.

The shuttle continued through what was air turbulence and as it neared the ground, the turbulence faded. Everyone on the shuttle could feel Mars' gravity take hold and as the shuttle leveled, each was pushed gently into their seats.

The shuttle seemed to stop in mid-air, then descend straight down as if it were a helicopter. As it descended, the MP group readied.

"We're on the ground," the pilot announced and a green light lit in the passenger compartment.

Every MP was special forces trained. They were already out of their seats and as the large side door slid open, they were out and onto the surface of Mars in an eye-blink.

Matthews had barely stood.

The shuttle had landed at least one hundred and fifty yards from the cave opening to prevent some kind of surprise attack.

When the General reached the door, the MPs, led by Gomez, had fanned out with weapons ready. Half of the men had their sights trained on or around the opening to the cave. The other half of the men moved their weapons' sights around as they all stepped carefully towards the cave opening but checked every direction around their perimeter. General Matthews stepped out of the shuttle but stayed back and had no intention of interfering with these crack troops.

The shuttle side door slid closed quickly to prevent entry by some unwanted intruder.

No one on the ground spoke. Every person in this military group knew their job.

The Sun showed through a rising mist that lay close to the ground. By this time, it was late afternoon on Mars and as the Sun rose higher in the sky, the mist was also rising as it turned the damp ground to vapor. The storm clouds had passed to the east and were pouring rain into Hellas Basin. The patches of sky that could be seen from this location was light blue with wisps of white cotton candy clouds in the upper atmosphere.

Matthews could see the rover that had carried the team from Club Med South sitting empty near the opening of the cave and because the mist was thick on the ground, the rover appeared to be floating on a thin cloud.

Gomez had the point and he slowly led his men forward. Within five minutes, the team had reached the cave opening with no incident. Gomez held up a fist and each man froze.

Gomez peered into the cave using a light on his helmet and another light on his weapon. The opening was clear and he signaled two of his men to enter on each side of the cave opening while he entered from the middle. They were walking slowly and peering through their sights. The General was still outside with three of the other MPs watching the rear.

Ten steps in, Gomez could see dark stains in the dirt. Something had been dragged from this point back into the cave.

"General, we have a problem," Gomez reported with the first words spoken since the team touched Martian soil.

The General wasted no time and he walked forward to where Gomez was standing. Gomez pointed at the dark stain and Matthews could see where it was obvious that a body had been dragged.

Gomez said, "Let's go."

The men who were watching the rear stepped towards Gomez and the General but didn't stop watching the rear. As the team moved forward, Gomez could see the bumps on the wall and again large places with dark stains and places where bodies had been dragged. The General walked to the bumps and had a look but made no comment.

Gomez gazed into the distance trying to get a feel for how far back this cave went. He couldn't see an end but could tell that it bent to the right up ahead. He signaled to go forward and the group moved as if they were one body through the craggy tunnel. They turned a bend and could see a pile of white clothes lying soaked in blood. Gomez carefully approached the pile and lifted the ragged remnants of what was once a spacesuit to see a name over the heart.

Gomez read aloud, "Foster."

The helmet was a few feet ahead.

Gomez looked over the spacesuit which was shredded. He said, "Peeled like a banana."

"Fuck me," one of the soldiers whispered.

"Gomez," General Matthews said.

He gazed to the right and pointed. He could see an incongruous sight. Before him lay an odd egg-shaped object on the dirt against the wall of the tunnel. He had seen only one of these before, *Egbert*.

"I want that, Gomez."

Gomez glanced at two of his men and said, "Cover the General."

The MPs stepped out and swept the tunnel then walked towards the egg-shaped object looking through their sights. The General followed. Once they reached the egg-thing, the General reached down and lifted it. The three then quickly walked back.

"We're out of here, Gomez."

"But what about the rest of the crew?"

"I'm afraid that we're outgunned down here. If we were to get swarmed by whatever did this to Foster, I think we'd be lost.

"We'd take a bunch with us," Gomez replied.

"We're out of here, Lieutenant, and live to fight another day. Besides, I know what this thing is," he said, raising the odd artifact, "And it's far too important to be lost. Let's go."

"You heard the man, move it!" was Gomez's response.

The group turned and carefully stepped towards the cave entrance, the same way they came in with a great deal of caution.

They reached the entrance with no resistance and stepped quickly towards the shuttle. Matthews was cradling the egg-shaped object the way a man would hold a baby.

Gomez asked, "So, what is that thing?"

"It's classified," Matthews said tersely.

Gomez turned his attention back to getting his crew safely to the shuttle.

The shuttle side door slid open and the MP group quickly climbed aboard. The door slid shut and pressurization began. The engines roared to life as the military personnel strapped into their seats. A minute later, they were off the surface.

General Matthews held the egg-shaped artifact cradled in his lap and looked at it as if it might explode.

Gomez was sitting to Matthew's right and watched the General surreptitiously as the General seemed to be having some kind of internal struggle.

Thirty minutes later, the shuttle was approaching Isla Charlie.

Matthews called ahead, "Captain Williams, could you have Sanjay and Marriam meet the shuttle after it's docked.

"Yes, Sir."

"Thank you, Captain."

The shuttle maneuvered and docked to Isla Charlie and the familiar sense of gravity returned to the cargo bay where the General was seated. The green light came on and the group seated began to rise.

The General said, "Can I have your attention. You all have seen what we took from the surface. This is highly classified. I don't want one word of it spoken again by any of you. You are all cleared to a high level of national security for a reason and that reason is to keep secrets, especially important ones. Lieutenant, please hand me that container," the General said, pointing to a container held fast in a clear compartment.

Gomez opened a door and pulled a stiff plastic opaque container from a closet-like space. The container unfolded to a box that measured two feet by two feet. The General then placed the egg-shaped artifact into the container.

The hatch opened from Isla Charlie and the MPs began climbing the ladder into the space station. Matthews climbed the ladder in his bulky spacesuit after handing the box with the artifact to Gomez. Gomez climbed the ladder holding the box by the handles then handed it up to one of his waiting men.

Sanjay Patel and Marriam Daily were standing and watching as the General stepped with help from the shuttle. Still fully space-suited he glanced at them. He began to strip, first pulling off the helmet then with more help, the suit. Once back in his NASA blues, he turned to Sanjay and Marriam who had watched as a box was set by the General.

The General looked at Marriam and Sanjay and said, "I was going to hand this off to you but I think I'll take it back to the special room."

Marriam and Sanjay both looked at the General quizzically.

Gomez and his team were also stripping out of their spacesuits. Captain Williams walked into the bay areas.

Williams asked, "So, what happened down there?"

The General said, "I believe the team is dead, Captain. I felt it was too dangerous to search further but we found Brenda Foster's spacesuit. It was full of blood and appeared to have been ripped from her. There was no sign of her. There is a place where the wall had a bumpy deposit on it which I believe to be eggs. There were probably fifty there and at least twenty had hatched. I believe that is what got our team. Whatever they are, they're probably native to Mars and have been in some kind of stasis waiting for the right conditions to hatch. Of the ones I looked closely at, some had hatched a while ago and others have just hatched. I have no doubt that the rest will eventually hatch and probably soon."

"It sounds like we have a problem on the surface."

"We do. We will meet in two hours to discuss it. Now I have some other business to attend to. Could you follow me, Captain for a minute?"

The General took Williams aside and opened the box. The Captain peered inside and his eyes widened.

Williams said, "On the planet?"

"In the cave," the General said. "We will discuss this also."

Williams nodded.

"In the meantime, Captain, I believe it would be prudent to keep all of our people on the surface inside their domes. Would you communicate that to them?"

"Yes, Sir."

The General turned to Sanjay and Marriam with an odd expression and said, "Let's go."

Matthews lifted the box and walked wordlessly beside Sanjay and Marriam carrying the container. Marriam and Sanjay also didn't speak.

They reached the room where Egbert was kept, went through the security protocols and the door slid open.

Egbert sat with a simple desk lamp shining on his polished surface not having made a peep since he showed the Martian coordinates.

Once the door closed, Matthews said, "Wait until you see this." The General's eyes sparkled like a teenaged boy receiving his first car as a present from his parents.

He reached into the box and pulled out Egbert's twin.

Sanjay and Marriam stood open-mouthed.

"Ho-ly shit," Sanjay whispered.

Mariam said, "How? Where?"

Matthews said, "In the cave at the coordinates."

Marriam said, "Holy-cow!"

The General said, "Sanjay, would you clear a place on the desk by Egbert for our new guest?"

Sanjay moved Egbert to one side as the General cleaned the dust from the surface of the new egg. They set it by Egbert and shined the light onto its surface and fireworks began to spark. Egbert began to spark also. Together, both artifacts went through the powering up process.

Marriam, Sanjay, and the General all stood with mouths opened and chills running up and down their collective spines.

The new artifact began to glow from the top of its surface. White light peeked out unevenly and began to reach upward.

The General said, "Speculations?"

Sanjay said, "Created at the same time."

Marriam said, "Somehow aware of each other."

"I agree," the General stated.

"Holy shit," Sanjay whispered again.

The two eggs were about a foot apart. Their holograms sprung from the tops of their surfaces and then the columns of light, both blue and green began to show. In Egbert's columns, ones and zeros crept upwardly. Black vertical lines and backslashes began to crawl upward in the blue and green columns of the second artifact. The columns of each began to twist as the columns in Egbert's hologram began to curl around the columns from the new egg in a kind of erotic display, almost sensual.

The researchers and the General stood transfixed.

As the lines comingled, red columns began to emerge from the bottoms of the holograms of each artifact. These columns had arcane symbols with dots and curved lines that appeared completely alien. The red columns twisted and wrapped around the blue and green columns with the symbols slowly creeping ever upward. The columns seemed to caress each other oddly as if intimate.

Sanjay, Marriam, and Matthews just stood and stared.

Chapter 31

Earth

July 30, 2096

Three launched Chinese probes had not made it to the red planet. Something technical kept happening in route and the Chinese ability to discover what the United States was up to on Mars was continually thwarted.

This was no mistake. Each time a probe was launched, the United States sent an asteroid interceptor from Isla Alpha to follow and then destroy the probe. Though the Chinese had no proof of this, they now suspected that the United States was behind the probes' destruction and that the U.S. did not want anyone to see anything on Mars. High powered telescopes were not able to give any detail of the planet. It was pretty well known, though, that the United States was on the planet to some degree and it was also known that the temperature on Mars was rising, but that could be natural fluctuations and now Mars had moved to nearly behind the Sun and it was too far to continue to get any reliable readings. The red planet would be out of sight for some months.

China had become aggressive. They had invaded several of their neighbors taking most of North Vietnam and Laos, and had designs on Taiwan, though it was protected by the United States which had a modest fleet harbored there and a small contingent of infantry. The military presence was just a deterrent and could in no way prevent an invasion from mainland China if one were to be launched.

The United States' fleet was state of the art and could deal a painful blow to the Chinese if they were to invade, but the biggest deterrent was the political and global cost to the Chinese who were more interested in eventual global economic dominance when the world returned to normal. They had, for a short time, been number one in the world until India had unseated them, but India was devastated by the aftermath of the asteroid strike in Russia and had fallen out of the top ten maybe never to fully recover.

In this new world, where every country had been forced to turn inward, no real trade was happening. The United States was by far the strongest internal economy and was talking about reinstating the dollar in an effort to restart world trade. As an economy, it had moved back to first followed by China then a smattering of other countries finished in the top ten, but none were close to China or the United States. The European Union, together, would be a strong third, but the Union had splintered because of infighting and border clashes between several of the countries. Germany, which had reformed after the Berlin Wall came down in 1989 was now the third most powerful country on Earth and though they had been peaceful for nearly a century, were now militarizing and moving back towards policies that had made them the scourge of the world in the early 1900s.

Earth

The Taiwan Strait

July 30, 2096

On Earth, tensions were at a boil. China had raised an enormous Navy and began moving it and an amphibious ground force toward Taiwan, through the Taiwan Strait. Taiwan was a country that the Chinese had always considered their own.

In the United Nations, the United States vigorously protested the provocative move towards Taiwan, but the Chinese claimed that it was just maneuvers, war games, and practice for their Navy. Within a week, they had the island nation of Taiwan surrounded and without a shot, had invaded the island. The Chinese had such overwhelming force brought to bear in the region that neither Taiwan or the United States attempted to stop the invasion. Taiwan was taken without resistance.

The U.S. carrier battle group harbored there, moved far offshore to prevent their ships from being seized. The Chinese attempted to surround the fleet but were outmaneuvered by the U.S. carrier group and could not stop the U.S. ships from vacating the region and moving out into open ocean. The small U.S. infantry contingent stationed on Taiwan had to surrender without a fight. The United States tried to evacuate the troops with the carrier battle group but were unable to get more than a quarter off of the island in time. They were able to evacuate the high-ranking officials and most of the diplomats but the island was full of U.S. citizens who were trying to reinstate business in Taiwan. All were detained.

The United States was not taking this lying down and was in the process of sending two other carrier battle groups to join the group that had just evacuated Taiwan. With this move by the Chinese government, they had set the world into its most dangerous position since Pearl Harbor was bombed on December 7, 1941.

The world was on the brink of total war.

Earth orbit

Isla Alpha

August 2, 2096

Sol 88

Isla Alpha had been in a stable orbit between the Moon and Earth when the Chinese invaded Taiwan. After three days of wrangling in the United Nations, the United States decided to bring a bit of the fight to the Chinese.

The Chinese had stationed no fewer than a hundred different satellites in space positioned for communication, spying, weather, and various other research endeavors.

The order was given by President Dent after consultation with the Joint Chiefs and four AK2200s and AK3000s left Isla Alpha led by Maria Hernandez and Arianna Fuller. Within two hours, every Chinese satellite was destroyed. This also included two space-based telescopes. The United States also warned the Chinese and the rest of the world that the U.S. would not allow any rockets to be launched from Earth and would consider it to be aggression against the space station in orbit there. Anything launched would be destroyed when it reached orbit. This was a warning, particularly to the Chinese that the United States had moved far above the rest of the world technologically and was about to show the world how far the U.S. had progressed. Without the satellites, nothing worked in China. Domestic communications, television, cell phones, communication with the military and nearly every type of commerce were all based on the use of satellite communications. China was effectively dead. They protested forcefully in the U.N. but that fell on deaf ears in the United States. China had not planned to be without communications. They had some battlefield communication devices that didn't use satellites but not nearly enough to run their entire country. Without the large battlefield body counts, the first salvo of the war between the United States and China had been fought to a stalemate in three days.

Chapter 32

Mars' Orbit

Isla Charlie Meeting Room

Aug 2, 2096

Sol 88

0900 Hours

Bedlam...

Voices of people talking over one another...

General Matthews had not arrived yet. This meeting was called soon after the deaths on the Martian surface of Hank Middlefield and his team. Each of the commanders from the surface colonies were in attendance, Commander Joan Bernstein of Club Med North, Commander Patrick Patterson of the large recently constructed colony, John F. Kennedy City, and the acting Commander from Club Med South, Lindsey Harper who was temporarily replacing Middlefield. Also, in attendance were the captains of several of the rockets being used to create the magnetic field and both captains of the space stations, Williams and Chambers. Last, there were a dozen specialists from Isla Charlie who might be called upon to answer hypothetical questions which included Sanjay Patel and Marriam Daily who were there to observe. They had been in attendance in all the meetings to report to Egbert and the new egg-like arrival everything that transpired.

General Matthews stepped quickly into the room. The voices hushed.

Matthews said, "Please have a seat."

The group all found a seat and turned their attention to the podium where Matthews was now standing.

"Thank you," Matthews said pausing. He breathed out and gazed at the assembled group then began. "We have a problem and an unforeseen issue with the unfortunate deaths of Hank Middlefield and his team. First, we need to know what happened to them. I am letting you know right now that I am sending a team to try to find them, but as you've all heard, the cave where they died is dangerous. I intend to use a vehicle that is now being retrofitted with drones. I will not send any humans into that cave without complete intel on what we face. I think it goes without saying that we thought we were on a dead planet with no life. This changes some things and Washington has some political decisions to make relating to us messing with a planet with life on it. I must admit that I also now have a problem with us terraforming Mars. I have no intention to attack and kill these creatures. I'm hoping to find a way to protect our colonists while not doing any harm to these, whatever they are, but just us being here might already be a problem. I just don't know. As of now, all work will stop outside of the domed cities."

"But, Sir," Patterson of JFK said. "We are in the middle of a new expansion and there is a large group of new colonists coming from Earth to be part of the expansion. They're arriving in two weeks."

"I'm well aware of that, Commander," Matthews stated.

Bernstein of Club Med North asked, "So, right now, everything has to be stopped?"

"That's what I think, but I know it's going to be a tough decision and one that needs to be made above my pay-grade. You can continue any work inside the currently constructed domes and factories. I have nothing more right now."

"General?" Bernstein of Club Med North continued, "Do you think we're safe in the domes. You've seen a bit of these creatures and they sound very dangerous. Besides locking the doors, we don't have any other defenses."

"I have considered that. We have ten MPs on board Isla Charlie and I have already ordered Lieutenant Gomez and his men onto the planet with some being stationed in each of the cities. They will ride back with you when you return to your habitats. Three will go to Club Med North, three to Club Med South, and four to JFK City. It's the best we can do for now but they will be fully armed. We simply do not have any other weapons. We hadn't planned for this. Our next shipment won't be here for some months and hasn't left earth yet. I have requested the government to send us at least thirty more MPs. I want all the Mars base Commanders to set up motion-sensing lights around their perimeters. I know we already have several that the habitats came equipped with but there are all the back-ups in storage. I want you all to break them out and try to cover the entirety of your camps. If there isn't anything else, you are dismissed."

Everyone stood and moved towards the door of the meeting room. General Matthews got on the com. "Lieutenant Gomez, bring your men to the shuttle bays."

"Roger that, General."

"Sanjay and Marriam, meet me outside."

As the meeting disbursed, Matthews stood and answered a few more questions from the base commanders as they walked by, then he turned to Marriam and Sanjay and began walking away from the meeting room with them following.

Once cleared from the crew and alone with Sanjay and Marriam, the General said, "Go and fill Egbert in on what has happened. Has Egbert made any other communication since the arrival of his twin?"

"No, General," Sanjay said.

Marriam added, "They both have continued to communicate with each other. Today, the blue columns and green columns seem to slow with Egbert's ones and zeros turning back to lines and slashes and them not rising as quickly, but Egbert hasn't made any attempt to communicate with us or break the communication with the other egg."

"Okay, keep me informed if anything changes."

Marriam nodded and she and Sanjay walked from the General.

The General turned for the shuttle bays to talk to the departing base commanders and the MPs.

Sanjay and Marriam turned for the special room that contained Egbert. They walked to the door, went through the security protocol and stepped into Egbert's chamber.

When they looked at Egbert and the other egg setting on the table with the desk lamp on each, the scene had changed. Both of the eggs were now only displaying red columns in their holograms. The arcane symbols snaked up each red column and the columns wound around each other like vines crawling up a pole.

Marriam and Sanjay looked at each other.

Marriam said, "Call General Matthews and tell him that there has been a change."

Sanjay nodded and informed the General.

"I'll be down there in ten minutes," he responded.

They continued to watch as the strange symbols twisted through the red columns in three dimensions. At that point, the columns seemed to merge at the base of the hologram and Egbert's symbols began to flow up the columns with the symbols from the other egg.

Sanjay said, "What is this, a meeting of the minds?"

"I think so," Marriam responded almost dreamily.

Twenty minutes went by as the symbols of Egbert and the other egg rose together. It seemed that Egbert would complete any incomplete symbol as it rose from the other egg. Marriam noticed this first and pointed it out to Sanjay who could see it after Marriam's description. A symbol would rise with two lines and no dots between, but then Egbert would add the two missing dots or a symbol would rise with just three dots in a row from the other egg then Egbert would place two wavy lines between the dots. It was strange.

The door opened and General Matthews walked in and gazed at the two egg artifacts as they seemed to be communing.

He said, "Huh?"

This has been going on since we returned," Sanjay said.

The General again said, "Huh?"

Abruptly, both eggs went black.

Sanjay, the General, and Marriam all stood silently. Five minutes passed, then ten.

Sanjay asked, "What's going on, Egbert?"

Nothing, the artifact was not responding.

The General said, "Fill Egbert in on the meeting and let me know if anything else happens."

He walked out leaving Marriam and Sanjay to their task.

Chapter 33

Philippine Sea

August 2, 2096

After escaping Taiwan, the United States fleet pushed across the Philippine Sea to around five hundred miles southeast of Taiwan between there and Guam. They knew that they were being shadowed by Chinese submarines and that there was a Chinese carrier group not far behind. The Chinese were enraged because the Americans had destroyed all their satellites and they minced no words calling it an act of war.

The American fleet continued to sail towards Guam where they would meet the British Pacific fleet and another American carrier battle group. A Second American carrier group was a week away but steaming full speed towards Guam.

Without warning, the Chinese submarines began launching torpedoes at the carrier group. The attack was sudden but the carrier group was prepared for a possible attack knowing that the subs were closing. The Americans began to take evasive action. Two sub killing aircraft, the P8 Poseidon, had been launched from Guam with two Dome Raptors. The ships escorting the American aircraft carrier took defensive measures to draw away the torpedoes from their main target, the aircraft carrier. Three of the subs had launched a series of Exocet style missiles that flew just above the surface of the water and those missiles were bearing down on the first ships in the flotilla. The Chinese also launched a barrage of surface to air missiles at the American aircraft.

The forward American ships began firing deck guns at the Exocets and knocking several out of the air with huge explosions. The first American defensive ship was struck by a torpedo on its port side. The ship shuddered and rocked with the blast.

The Dome Raptors which were the latest jet fighters in the American arsenal were quick to launch their own drones to attack the surface to air missiles. These drones quickly acquired their targets and attacked the streaking missiles with a short burst EMP shockwave which sent the Chinese missiles falling harmlessly into the sea. This left the submarines helpless against the P8 Poseidon attack aircraft. Once the Chinese submarines fired at the carrier battle group, it was obvious that they had planned to run silently away, but the submarine killing aircraft had already acquired their targets and launched sonar tracking missiles and depth charges at the Chinese subs.

Within a matter of minutes, the ten Chinese submarines were destroyed. Not far from the attack, the Chinese carrier battle group had launched fighter aircraft to support their subs but they had expected a better outcome. The Chinese fighter jets had no choice but to return to their carrier fearing that they would be lost because the skies above the American carrier group were filled with stealth fighters from the American carrier. The Chinese carrier group turned back to Taiwan.

The political damage was done, though, and the world was now officially at war.

In Europe, NATO had crumbled after the asteroid impact had destroyed Russia. The alliance that included the United States and Great Britain was created to counteract the then Soviet Union's possible plan to expand into western Europe. Now that Russia was no more and the world's economies had collapsed, Germany turned inside itself and had rebuilt its war machine. In several swift moves reminiscent of the famed Blitzkrieg from World War 2, Germany overran its neighbors quickly taking Poland, Austria, Switzerland, Czechoslovakia, Belgium, Luxemburg, and the Netherlands and were now poised to invade France. France had also rebuilt its military and was gathering to repel any German invasion. To the east, beyond Poland, the former Baltic states were still suffering from the direct aftermath of the asteroid impact and would soon fall to the Germans. They had little to defend themselves. To the northwest, Scandinavia could offer no resistance and would soon fall. Finland had been so damaged by the asteroid strike that they could no longer be called a country.

Africa was still in shambles with most of the countries in border clashes with their neighbors and several recognizing that this was a perfect time to take land to expand their own countries.

Chaos had come upon the world and no one knew what the world would look like when the dust settled.

Chapter 34

Club Med South

August 3, 2096

Sol 89

1100 Hours

Twilight this evening at Club Med South had been murky, grey, and foggy and the mist dimmed the last of the Sun's light early. Now it was night. The crew of the habitat had worked to install the motion detectors but only had time to place half, leaving many dark spots. The three MPs were getting settled in but covering each dome would be a nightmare if there was some kind of large-scale attack.

Lindsey Harper gazed outside the habitat through a window by the airlock. It wasn't a week ago that she had watched Hank Middlefield staring through the same window and out onto the alien Martian landscape. Now, he was gone.

Fog blew in a mild breeze and could be seen through the light that leaked from various windows in the domes.

Lindsey could feel a chill crawl up her spine. Something wasn't right. She shuddered and suddenly wanted to be off this rock in space and back home.

To her right, she could see one of the motion lights go on. The fog was so thick that it reflected the light preventing it from illuminating a wide area and she thought about that old saying, 'fog as thick as pea soup,' and was suddenly hungry for a bowl. She grew up in northern California and remembered passing a restaurant sign on a highway when her parents drove her and her two brothers to Disneyland. The restaurant's specialty was pea soup. Was the name of the restaurant Andersen's? Her brothers were both older and she was forced to sit between them on the ride and they gave her hell for the entire trip. She suddenly missed her brothers who still lived north of San Francisco.

Something was moving in the drifting mist. Another light came on. Something moved again but was gone. She placed both hands on the thick glass of the window and tried to make her vision penetrate the relentless fog. Another light came on further to her left. She pushed her face close to the window in a vain attempt to see what was tripping the lights. She suddenly had to know that the domes were all locked down tight.

She got on the com and broadcasted, "Attention, Club Med crew, please check to make sure that all airlocks are locked down tight. Can I see the MPs to Dome 1, please?"

Missy Winslow had been Lindsey's closest friend since they left Earth and she could hear the mild panic behind Lindsey's words. She was in Dome 2 and she hustled through the underground tunnel to reach Dome 1 and her friend. She climbed the ladder and saw Lindsey staring out the window.

"Lindsey?"

Harper turned.

"What's wrong, Lindsey?"

Lindsey didn't speak and she motioned outside the habitat.

"What is it?"

"Missy, check and make sure that the airlock is secure. Don't go inside the airlock. Just check the inside hatch door lock."

Missy walked the roughly ten steps to the airlock hatch and checked to make sure that it was locked down tight. It was. She walked back.

The three MPs walked into the dome from the tunnel and up to Harper who hadn't taken her eyes from the window.

"Ma'am?" Sergeant Nakamura asked.

"Outside, Sergeant. Over there. Something just moved but stopped still."

The Sergeant turned towards the window and came up next to Lindsey, shoulder to shoulder. The Sergeant stared.

"Something's been moving around out there," Lindsey Harper stated quietly.

To the far right, a motion-sensing light came on.

The Sergeant asked, "If something wanted in, would these doors stop them?"

Lindsey whispered, "I don't think so."

Chapter 35

Oval Office

August 3, 2096

Sol 89

9:00 PM EDT

"Mister President," Howard Diamond whispered, interrupting President Dent as he listened to his late video conference meeting broadcasted from the Pentagon. Two of the Generals were arguing about a needed response to the German aggression in Europe. France and Great Britain were both begging us for troops and weapons. Since the destruction of NATO, the United States had brought most of their military home including all of their Air Force. America had nothing in place to help either country.

The Chinese suddenly had their satellite communications restored, though there were no Chinese satellites in space. The Joint Chiefs were just informed that the Germans were allowing the Chinese to use the German satellite systems.

"Mister President," Diamond said again.

Dent looked his way but his attention was on the Generals.

"Sir, we've had some deaths on Mars."

Dent turned to Diamond but his mind was listening to the argument on his monitor. He thought he heard that some people on Mars had died.

Dent's attention turned to Diamond. Dent said, "What?"

"About four days ago. Several people on a scouting mission."

"What happened?"

"What I've heard from General Matthews is that they had been killed by some kind of creatures that live inside a cave."

"I'm not following you," Dent stated flatly not comprehending Diamond's words or now, what was going on with the Joint Chiefs. Now nothing was getting through coherently. "What? I mean, when?"

"Four days ago."

"What happened to them?"

"They were checking out something for General Matthews."

One of the generals from the Pentagon was becoming angrier. He wanted to deploy a large force in France. Japan was also asking for troops because the Chinese had sent a complete carrier battle group towards Japan.

"This is chaos," Dent replied.

"Mister President, I have something else to tell you in private."

Dent rose and walked from his monitor. The Generals' arguments continued to rage.

Dent asked, "What is it, Howard?"

"In the cave, where the colonists were killed, General Matthews found another 'Egg'."

"What the hell?" Dent exclaimed. "You mean like our Egbert?"

"That's right."

Dent glanced over at the Joint Chiefs as they argued back and forth.

"How come we're just finding out about this?"

"Because Mars is on the other side of the Sun. It takes a while for word to reach us."

"Has the new egg told us anything yet?"

"Not that I'm aware of."

"Let's go back to the meeting. I've made a couple of decisions."

"Generals," Dent said, interrupting an angry exchange. "I think we should do as General Herman has suggested. I think we should knock out all satellites that do not belong directly to our allies, all of them. We are already at war with China, so sending troops and two carrier battle groups to Japan with orders to sink anything that comes close is prudent. But we need to be sure that we are protected here. With no satellites to guide their missiles, we may be able to take the fight to the Chinese and the Germans from a distance. It wouldn't be a war we could win, but maybe we could convince them to stop their aggression and come to the bargaining table. We had slowed the production of the Dome Raptors because of the cost and because of the space program, so we need to get back into full production of the new fighters. General Herman, issue the order to take out all the satellites."

"Yes, Sir, Mister President."

"General Greenburg, how many troops can we commit to France and England?"

"At least two hundred thousand, but that will stretch us a bit thin and force us into some kind of draft. The people won't like that. England has already deployed a hundred thousand to France."

"Deploy the troops to England first and we'll go from there. I will go on the television networks and beg for additional volunteers for our military."

"Yes, Sir."

"That's all for now," Dent said. "I am due at another meeting."

President Dent rose and left the video conference so that he could speak freely to Howard Diamond.

Diamond said, "General Matthews wants us to send him trained troops and more weapons to protect the colonies on Mars. He's concerned that whatever attacked Hank Middlefield and his people could attack the habitats. They're not built to repel anything more than a stiff wind and sandstorms."

"Did they see these things?"

"Just quick glimpses. They seemed to be bi-pedal, heavily muscled, big, maybe seven feet tall or more and fast. They seem to have hatched from some kind of egg in a tunnel to the south of Club Med South."

"What the hell was Middlefield and his people doing in the tunnel?"

"Egbert showed the coordinates. It seems that Egbert was aware of the other egg-like thing. I guess when the two eggs were brought together, they communicated."

"So, Egbert was aware of the other egg's presence?"

"It would seem so."

"Under the circumstances, I'm not sure we can send Mars anything. We are going to need to focus on our war effort. Maybe Matthews should temporarily evacuate the planet."

"Is that your orders?"

"It is. Tell Matthews to get everyone off of that planet for now."

"Yes, Sir."

"And, Diamond, do we have any idea what's in the new egg artifact?"

"Not to my knowledge."

Dent nodded and Diamond walked from the room.

Chapter 36

Club Med South

August 4, 2096

Sol 90

12:00 Midnight

Lindsey Harper had not left the window for three hours. The mist blew in the wind which had picked up but couldn't clear the dense fog that choked this area. All of the MPs came and went, occasionally checking in with Lindsey to see if there was any change. There was none. Time was passing, sometimes an hour with no motion-sensing lights switching on, but then to the right or to the left, one would illuminate the fog as it blew, but nothing living would show its face. Maybe the moving fog was tripping the mechanisms.

0100 hours and Lindsey could feel her eyes grow heavy. It had been an emotional few days with the loss of Hank Middlefield who was more than a superior officer. He was her friend and a really good guy. Her eyes filled with tears then drifted to the top of the dome as she recalled his smiling face. She sighed and thought, such a waste.

She looked back out the window and scanned the area that was in her sight-line, then thought, maybe it might be time to get some sleep.

She turned from the window and thought to check all the airlocks one more time before she turned in. It was like her obsession of checking all the doors and windows in her house back home before she went to bed. There, it was a ritual.

As she started for the tunnel to go to Dome 2, a light came on just in front of the window where she had been standing.

"Huh?" she said aloud and walked back to the window.

When she peeked out, something was standing just out of the light. Its large form was obscured by the drifting mist but it was big and the outline of its appearance seemed like something that she had seen before, a great ape maybe but more insect-like.

She stared silently thinking that this seemed more like a dream than reality. Another shape joined the first and then another. The three shapes, now together, walked from the mist and stood not ten feet from the window.

Lindsey's breath caught in her throat. Before her, were three creatures that resembled nothing that she had ever seen before. They were taller than any man, more than eight feet in height. Their bodies were heavily muscled and as they moved, their muscles rippled with each step beneath the gray-green rough skin. They appeared as something that might be a part insect, part mammal, and part reptile but it was hard to distinguish where each phylum began and ended. They had two sinewy arms that hung to their knees and appeared like the arms of a praying mantis. They walked on two legs which bent in the wrong direction like a dog standing and their hands were as large as dinner plates.

The way they walked made them look clumsy but they were sure-footed as they moved deftly on the rocky surface. Each hand had three fingers and an opposable thumb. Each of the three bony fingers had velociraptor-like claws at each end. Their heads appeared to be far too small for their overly muscled bodies. Lindsey was startled to see that they had no eyes. Their heavy bony brows came all the way down to just above a single opening that didn't resemble a nose but they all turned it up as if trying to sniff the air. Just under, where a high cheekbone might be on both sides of their faces were two more similar holes, then on the sides of their heads below where their ears should be was another hole. Below the front nose hole was a wide lipless maw that turned downward and was filled with razor-sharp teeth that resembled the teeth of sharks. All the teeth were yellow and pointed but in each of their mouths, teeth were broken. On their thick muscular necks were three slits that were reminiscent of fish gills.

The three creatures seemed to be communicating with each other. Lindsey could hear odd clicks and grunts. She stared as if observing tigers at the zoo. All these creatures seemed to be male with wolf-like phalluses between their legs. Their entire bodies were lightly and sparsely furred showing the skin beneath. The largest creature howled. Five more came from the fog then five more. The first creature got down on all fours and sniffed the Martian soil. He crept forward on all fours like a canine with his muzzle low to the ground sniffing and following some scent to the airlock. Linsey panicked and called for the MPs who were in Dome 2.

"We're on our way," Sergeant Nakamura responded.

The creatures reached the airlock and the first pulled at the hatch handle, obviously far more intelligent than he looked.

"Better get here quick," Linsey shouted into her com.

The airlock door was ripped from its hinges and thrown to the side.

Lindsey, in full panic, called to Isla Charlie, "We're under attack from something from the surface. They've already pulled down the first airlock door."

The MPs arrived but Lindsey just realized that no one was in spacesuits. The second airlock door was pushed inward as the flimsy lock had no hope of holding up against these beasts' assault. The Martian atmosphere rushed into the dome. The MPs fired their weapons and cut down two of the beasts as they entered but the MPs collapsed unconscious, unable to handle the sudden change of the alien air pressure and lack of oxygen. The creatures streamed into the habitat, twenty or more. They entered through each airlock door and into each dome. None of the colonists were in spacesuits and they all died rapidly.

Chapter 37

Isla Bravo

Sol 90

0115 Hours

The alarms rang out on Isla Charlie and Isla Bravo. On Isla Bravo, Sandy Jones and Kirk Matthews were quick to their bays. They suited and were in their AK2200s, strapped in and ready to go.

Isla Charlie was on the other side of Mars but Isla Bravo was nearly on top of Club Med South when the alarm was sounded.

The AKs suddenly disengaged from the spinning station and turned for the planet.

Second in command on Isla Bravo, Major Anthony Rossi was on the com to Kirk and Sandy. "We have a situation on the surface. Club Med South is under some kind of attack. Proceed to the given coordinates and find out what's going on."

"Roger that, Major," Sandy replied.

Within ten minutes, Jones and Matthews were through the outer atmosphere and closing in at supersonic speed on the habitat. As they neared Club Med South, fog lay thick near the planet's surface and light from the domes appeared like dim beacons from a lighthouse near a rocky shoreline.

They had to get closer to get a better look at what was occurring.

"I got a visual," Sandy said. He was slightly in the lead.

"I got it too," Kirk said as they raced over the domes but close to the ground.

"Are you seeing what I'm seeing?" Sandy said.

Most of the habitat's airlock doors were pulled from their hinges and lay in the Martian dust.

"What the hell?" Kirk said.

Both AKs circled and readied their weapon systems. Both were equipped with twin, 50 caliber Gatling guns designed for a fight in space but would work just as well on the planet.

They circled low over the habitat trying to get a good visual through the fog. At times it would break up giving them a good view of the landscape but other times they would pass through a thick patch that would obscure the ground.

As they passed through a clear patch, they could see several large creatures carrying bodies into the darkness. They buzzed the creatures flying low and could see that dead humans were being carried like slabs of meat.

"Fuck!" Kirk exclaimed.

He got on his com to Isla Charlie which was coordinating the rescue effort. "Sir, we have a visual on several large creatures carrying humans away from the habitat. The humans are obviously dead. They are not in spacesuits. How should we proceed?"

General Matthews had just made it to the bridge of Isla Charlie. He spoke, "Kirk, if any of the creatures are not carrying humans, you may engage. I don't want you to fire on the creatures that are carrying the people."

"Roger and out," Kirk said.

He and Sandy began to fly closer to the ground.

"On my six," Sandy said.

He could see a group of four creatures, though dim in his infrared and obscured by the fog. They were heading towards a cave in the distance. They seemed to be carrying their own dead. Sandy closed in and his laser sight pointed at the short line of creatures as they made their way through an outcropping of tall rocks. He strafed the creatures splintering the rocks and easily cutting the creatures down.

Kirk caught three others to the left of that herd heading in the same direction. He pushed his vehicle towards them and fired on those three killing them in a hail of gunfire and a spray of the creatures' bodily fluids. Several others who were carrying the human bodies disappeared into the tunnel. The humans couldn't have been dead long because they still had a heat signature against the cool bodies of their assailants.

There were no other creatures visible so Kirk and Sandy banked and flew back towards Club Med South. As they approached, several AK3000s hovered over the habitat and a shuttle had landed near what looked like an intact airlock hatch. Nothing moved on the ground. The shuttle sat just outside the airlock and Kirk and Sandy could hear a frantic plea from the shuttle's captain.

She spoke over a loudspeaker, her voice shaky. "We have a shuttle outside the habitat at the airlock of Dome 2. Is there anyone in the habitat?" Then she trailed off bleakly. "Anyone?"

Ellen Granger, the shuttle's captain, spoke to General Matthews, "General. I don't believe there are any survivors here. Are you getting any response from your end?"

"No, Ellen, proceed to Club Med North and get those people off of that planet. I'm sending another group to JFK City. Kirk and Sandy will escort you."

Ellen said, "Roger, General. I'm on it."

She pulled up quickly and headed north. Kirk and Sandy pulled beside her. The other AKs, which had just arrived, pulled up and headed to JFK to assist that large settlement.

General Matthews called ahead to the Club Med North staff and instructed them to put on their spacesuits and meet the shuttle when it arrived.

At over 13000 miles away, Kirk, Sandy, and Ellen in the shuttle had to leave Mars' atmosphere to reach Club Med North quickly. They accelerated upward into low Mars orbit using the spin of the planet to cut the distance, then forty-five minutes later, descended towards the habitat, coming in low.

As they closed in on Club Med North, a column of creatures was striding in that direction. The creatures were fast and they moved deftly over the rocky surface in the black of the night. The lights from the habitat lit brightly in the near distance. The creatures would soon reach the domes. Kirk and Sandy could see the creatures in their displays using infrared, though barely. They should have a larger heat signature but they were nearly as cold as reptiles at night.

"I'm engaging those creatures," Kirk stated flatly and he dipped, sighted the creatures and strafed their column, leaving them dead in a heap. Kirk could feel his anger boiling just under the veneer of his humanity. He was in full bloodlust and wanted to find more of these intruders.

The shuttle closed in on the habitat and landed straight down as if it were a helicopter with Sandy's AK covering the shuttle. Kirk joined within a minute and hovered away a bit to cover out further.

As the shuttle landed, the habitat's airlock hatch instantly sprung open with the space-suited MPs emerging first with weapons drawn. They fanned left, right, and center gazing through their sights. No creatures opposed them. Everyone from Club Med North was then out of the habitat and onto the shuttle. The shuttle slid its wide side door shut and lifted off the planet heading for Isla Charlie.

Kirk and Sandy followed the shuttle out of Mars' atmosphere then turned rapidly back to JFK City.

When the city came into view, two shuttles and four AK3000s from Isla Charlie had already arrived. As Sandy and Kirk came upon the large domed outpost, several of the AKs were engaging something on the ground. In this area was mayhem. MPs were firing joined by the AKs.

JFK City was now large and sprawling, brightly lit and covered at least five square miles with the twenty original domes and another thirty domes manufactured and built later. Ten factories that were attached to the domes produced the terraforming gasses and other essentials for the surface.

Kirk could see people streaming to the two large shuttles which had landed just outside one of the domes. Several of the creatures lay dead near the shuttles.

Kirk had no idea how many people were in this sprawling encampment but the two shuttles together could hold at least eighty people and Kirk couldn't imagine that there could be more who lived in this city.

Kirk and Sandy swung around to the rear of the City and caught several creatures approaching from there and fired down upon them, stopping them in their tracks.

The first shuttle lifted off then the second. A voice from the second shuttle came over the com, "We have everyone. We're heading back to Isla Charlie."

Kirk and Sandy turned their vehicles upward and streaked out of the Martian atmosphere following the shuttles and the other AKs. Kirk and Sandy then separated from the fleeing group and headed back to Isla Bravo.

The planet was evacuated.

Chapter 38

Isla Charlie Docking Bays

The first shuttle arrived at Isla Charlie from Club Med North. As each person departed the shuttle, they were met by General Matthews. These colonists had a rough idea about what was happening on the surface but hadn't seen any creatures and felt to be in no real danger.

Joan Bernstein, the commander of Club Med North, walked to greet the General.

"Hello, General," she said calmly.

The General was not so calm. He said, "Is everyone from your command alright?"

"Yes," she responded quizzically.

A voice came over the speaker, "The second shuttle's arriving."

Matthews turned his attention to shuttle bay two as the shuttle docked.

This was a different story as the crew from JFK City climbed into Isla Charlie. These crew were visibly upset, some weeping and others shaking. They had been under direct assault from the creatures but were better prepared than the unfortunate colonists at Club Med South.

Commander of JFK City, Patrick Patterson was the last off the shuttle and he walked directly to the General who was standing by Bernstein.

The General said, "Did you get everyone off, Patrick?"

"Yes, Sir, but barely. It was lucky that the AKs arrived before the creatures were able to get organized and get inside. It was close."

Bernstein's eyes widened. She hadn't seen any creatures because Matthews had intercepted them before they could approach the settlement.

Patterson asked, "What about Club Med South?"

Matthews shook his head.

Patterson asked, "Everyone?"

"I'm afraid so."

Bernstein blanched then whispered, "Dead?"

"Yes," the General responded.

The AK pilots were coming out of their vehicles and stepping through the bay hatches. Matthews left Patterson and Bernstein and walked to the AK pilots.

General Matthews barked, "Report."

Mo Roberts and Tabby Fredrickson were pilot and copilot in an AK3000. They straightened as Matthews approached.

Roberts said, "We engaged no less than a dozen creatures approaching JFK. A couple of them were too close to the habitat for us to use our weapons so we warned Gomez who was the first out of the city and he and his men killed the creatures."

"Did you get a good look at the creatures?"

"Oh yeah and some good film. Gomez was up close and personal with a couple of them. They looked huge."

Gomez stepped out of the shuttle with two of his men then they were joined by the three others from Club Med North.

Matthews said, "I'll review the film, thanks."

He turned to Gomez who was visibly upset. He just found out that Nakamura and two of his other men were killed by the creatures.

Matthews walked up and was about to ask for a report but changed his mind and said, "Lieutenant, I'm sorry about your men. I had no idea of the danger down there."

"I know, General. I was privy to all your intel and didn't see this coming but I have to admit that I had a very uneasy feeling. I got a good look at these creatures and an odd sense of them. They are big and fast and I think, smart. They were calculating. We watched them through the windows for about ten minutes before we got the order to bug out. The fog had lifted just a bit and you could see them plotting. If you wouldn't have got us out, I don't think the four of us could have held them off."

Matthews nodded.

Gomez said, "I don't mind telling you that I'm damned happy to be up here. I bet I put thirty rounds into a couple of them before they dropped."

"I'm happy everyone is up here now, too. I'll get back with you later."

Matthews walked to Captain Williams who was talking to his shuttle crews.

"Captain, please download the video of these creatures. I want to get a good look at what we're dealing with. Meeting at 0700 hours tomorrow."

Yes, Sir," Williams responded. He then turned to a male crew member walking by, "Kyle, see to beds for everyone from the surface."

"Aye, Captain, I'm on it."

Chapter 39

Isla Charlie

August 4, 2096

Sol 90

0600 Hours

Sanjay Patel and Marriam Daily woke at 0600 hours to their alarm. They had been awakened last night when the alarms sounded throughout Isla Charlie. They knew what had happened to the crew of Club Med South. Though they hadn't known any of the personnel at that habitat, they felt the grief that everyone else felt at the loss of comrades. Everyone on this Mars mission, which now numbered more than a hundred, were in a kind of a club, a self-dedicated group to a higher calling and everyone had sacrificed a great deal to be part of this mission.

When Sanjay and Marriam crawled back into bed together, once the alarm had ended, they made love quietly and with no joy. It was all about comfort. It was all about knowing that they had each other in a dark time and they were thankful for it. They were both grateful that they were not alone.

One hour until the meeting.

Chapter 40

Isla Bravo

August 4, 2096

Sol 90

0645 Hours

Taylor Chapman had needed to set her alarm. Her shift began at 0800 hours and Mark Hinton would be exhausted as usual so she couldn't be a minute late. She woke early despite not getting much sleep last night when Kirk was called upon to fly to the planet. She glanced at the clock, 6:45 AM, ten minutes before her alarm would go off. She thought about last night and the horror of it. She thought about Kirk quietly weeping at something that he couldn't talk about. She thought about him curling up in her arms and burying his head under her chin and his tears on the chest of the tee-shirt that she wore to bed.

She glanced back over at the clock. One more minute until it rang. She reached over Kirk's gently breathing body and switched off the alarm.

"Taylor?" Kirk said sleepily.

"I was just turning off the alarm. I have to get up in a few minutes."

"Oh. Okay."

"Kirk, do you want to talk about last night? I haven't seen you this upset since, well, you know, when the asteroid hit Earth."

He breathed out. "It was what I saw, Taylor. I have pictures permanently seared into my brain. In some ways, this was worse than the asteroid strike. At least I didn't see all the people who died."

"What did you see? Tell me."

"It isn't something that I should share."

"It's something that you need to share. It's something that you should tell someone you love and who loves you."

Kirk breathed out again and pulled Taylor down so that he could once again bury his head under her chin.

"Tell me, Kirk."

He began to speak hauntingly and in a quiet whisper, "I saw the creatures who had killed the colonists. I saw the colonists being unceremoniously carried away by those creatures, over their wide shoulders. They made the people look so small. I was so close that I could see the faces of some of the colonists. I didn't know any of them personally but I had seen a couple of them up here. The one that got to me and filled me with rage was the person who I think was the acting leader. The creature was carrying her on its back, just holding her by one of her legs. She was dead and I knew it but she was flopping as he ran with her arms dangling." Kirk slowed and his voice became quieter. "I could see her face and her eyes were slightly opened. Her shirt was rolled to her chest showing her stomach and the bottom of her bra. She was so pretty, Taylor, with a child-like face and her skin was pale and without a blemish. I was so angry that that fucking thing would treat her with such disrespect. If I could have hit it without shooting her, I'd have cut it in pieces. I'm sure that I killed at least twenty of them down there but if I had the chance, I'd have killed and kept killing until my guns melted down."

He stopped and was quiet for a minute.

"I'm sorry, Kirk. I'm here for you. I'm here so that you don't have to feel those things alone."

She hugged him tightly and he placed an arm around her and quietly wept his silent tears.

Chapter 41

General Mathews stood at the podium waiting for the arrival of everyone who was required to attend the meeting. He had not slept last night. He had spent the hours since the attack on Club Med South reviewing the film taken from the AKs and from the habitats' cams that recorded the airlocks.

He felt crushing guilt for not removing the colonists sooner. He had a feeling that they were in danger but didn't want to react to a feeling with no data to support it. How could he know that those creatures would leave their caves?

The commanders of Club Med North and JFK city walked into the meeting room followed by Captain Williams and two of the AK pilots. Sanjay and Marriam came in next and sat together in the back of the room. Isla Charlie had several specialized crew members there, one an astrobiologist, Norma Jankowski. She was in her mid-thirties and a Ph.D. from Wisconsin. Her expertise was in zoology (the study of animals) but she was also an expert in botany (the study of plants). There was microbiologist, Lazlo Topol and the rest of the science team to weigh in.

"Please sit," Matthews said when the clock hit 0700 hours. "This is a quick meeting today and then we'll need to get to work trying to figure out what we're facing on the planet and what we might do about it."

Everyone sat.

General Matthews began, "I have reviewed all the film from last night and will make some of it available to some of you later. I have several slides to show this morning and then will let you go. The first one is of the creatures close up. This image has been enhanced to show what detail we could glean in the dim light."

The image of the creature came up. It seemed to look straight into the camera.

"Norma, I wish you to weigh in on what you see."

Norma Jankowski cleared her throat. "Well, first it appears to be sightless, so if I'm correct at that, it means that it is using some kind of echolocation in place of sight, similar to bats. Because it seems to breed in caves and tunnels, these creatures may be subterranean and have only come out seeking food. I hate to state the obvious but the interesting thing that strikes me is that they seem to be some kind of carbon dioxide life form. On Earth, there are a few single-cell creatures that we think might be carbon dioxide life forms but there is some controversy about that. Oxygen is generally needed for energy exchange. There are only trace amounts of oxygen in the atmosphere to this point, though it's increasing, and for most living beings, the atmospheric pressure is far too low to survive, let alone thrive. I will say this, though, I think they may be getting ready to breed, but there isn't much food to live on so they couldn't expand far if they need to eat protein. I'm surprised at their size. They either grow rapidly or had hatched longer ago than we thought. Also, it wouldn't surprise me if we found that they shed their skin as they grew the way snakes or certain insects do. Despite their appearance, I think they might be more closely related to insects but they may be some mixture of phylum or something altogether different than anything on Earth. They're obviously eating something. I would love to get one of their bodies to examine, that would give us much more information.

Matthews said, "We must have killed fifty or more down there. I'll send a shuttle to pick one up."

The meeting continued with a couple of eyewitness accounts of how they moved and acted then Matthews let everyone go, instructing the scientist to review the film.

As Matthews left the room, he approached Sanjay and Marriam who looked like deer in the headlights.

The General pulled them aside and whispered, "Go report to Egbert as usual. Let me know if anything changes with him."

They nodded and walked away.

General Matthews called Lieutenant Gomez.

"Yes, General."

"Assemble all your men and get suited. You're going to the planet. I want you to pick up one of the dead creatures and bring it back here for study. I'm calling for a shuttle crew to meet you and two AKs for air support. Get on it, Lieutenant."

"I'm on my way."

***

Ten minutes later, the seven remaining MPs were suited and at the shuttle bay. The shuttle was ready and once boarded, it was away and headed to Club Med South, the closest of the encampments.

The shuttle, accompanied by two AK3000s breached the atmosphere and dipped through feathery clouds and towards Club Med South. The AKs streaked in front of the shuttle. It was mid-day and the sun glinted off of the encampment in the distance. The habitat appeared to be peaceful as they descended upon it, a far cry from the carnage of the night before.

The AKs began to hunt looking for anything moving but after a quick sweep of the grounds no creatures were visible.

Mo Roberts, the pilot of one of the AKs called to Lance Newsome, the shuttle pilot. "Lance, the encampment looks safe. You can proceed."

"Roger that, Mo."

Newsome quickly maneuvered his craft and dropped straight down in front of the airlock in Dome 1 of Club Med South. He could see that the door had been ripped from the hinges. When he touched down, Gomez and his men jumped from the shuttle and began sweeping the area looking through the sights of their weapons.

Gomez spoke, "I can't find one body. Lance, do you see any creature carcasses?"

"Negative, Lieutenant."

"Ask the AK pilots"

"Roger that."

"Hey, Mo, do you guys see any of the dead creatures."

"Negative, Lance. I'll take a look around. J J, I'm going to have a look around the grounds. Stay and keep the shuttle covered."

"Roger," J J, the other AK pilot responded.

Gomez and his men entered Dome 1 of the habitat and could find no dead creatures and no dead humans. They exited.

Roberts returned after buzzing the entire domed complex and stated, "There are no dead creatures here, that I can see."

Newsome called Captain Williams on board Isla Charlie. "Captain, we can't find any dead creatures here. What are your orders?"

"Are you sure, Lance. The way I heard it, there must be at least twenty dead there."

"That's what I was led to believe, but there isn't a one."

"Okay, head to JFK City and look there."

"Roger, Captain." Then Newsome said to Gomez, "Lieutenant Gomez, we got orders to scoot. Would you return please?"

"Heading out," Gomez replied.

Gomez and his team hustled from the Dome with weapons at the ready. They reached the shuttle and climbed in. Once Gomez and his team were safely inside, the shuttle lifted off and met the AKs in the air. Then the AKs streaked out in front of the shuttle and disappeared at supersonic speed. The city wasn't far from Club Med South so the AKs came upon it rapidly. The shuttle arrived minutes later.

The city covered five square miles so the shuttle hovered and waited. One AK turned to the left while the other turned to the right. Both searched for dead creatures. Nothing, not one creature anywhere, dead or otherwise.

"Huh?" Lance said puzzled after hearing Mo Roberts' report.

He called to Williams. "Captain, no creatures' bodies here either."

"Lance, I'm sending you a flight path to Club Med North. Two of the pilots from Isla Bravo engaged a line of creatures approaching there."

Lance said, "I have received that flight path and am proceeding."

The AKs also had the flight path and they streaked ahead at Mach 3 to the coordinates where the creatures were killed. They slowed and were well ahead of the shuttle and could find no dead creatures.

Mo Roberts called to Newsome, "Lance, don't waste your time coming here. It's clean."

"Roger, Mo. Captain, there are no dead creatures at these coordinates."

"Roger, Lance. Come on back to Isla Charlie."

"Roger."

***

General Matthews was standing by Captain Williams. Williams said, "Well, what do you make of that?"

"I guess they came back for their dead?"

"That's what I would think."

"Huh?" Mathews said quietly then, "What are we dealing with here?"

Chapter 42

Isla Charlie

August 4, 2096

Sol 90

After the meeting, Sanjay and Marriam had breakfast then walked to their station to inform Egbert of the events on the planet.

Egbert sat unimpressed. Since his meeting with the other egg, Egbert had seemed to become dormant once more.

Sanjay sat facing Egbert. "I can't think of anything else to tell him," he said, turning to Marriam who sat next to Sanjay, also staring at the twin alien egg-like artifacts.

Marriam said, "Maybe we should play a game of chess."

They had brought a chessboard and men with them on the voyage and played when nothing was happening. Marriam brought out the board and set it up. Egbert sat inert and the game began.

Sanjay and Marriam were both competent players, both decent planners and both forward thinkers. The game continued and was closely contested.

After an hour, Sanjay had taken the edge in the game and had Marriam's king nearly cornered. Because the queen could move in any direction and as many squares as desired, Sanjay said his queen was moving through a wormhole.

"Check."

Marriam was a little perturbed at Sanjay not just because he was winning, but because of his attitude about it. She said, "You should shove that queen up your own wormhole."

Sanjay laughed.

From the corner of his eye, Sanjay could see light. He turned slightly and could see Egbert begin to power up. Marriam saw it too and she turned.

The fireworks lit Egbert's surface then the aurora squirmed and undulated. The other egg just sat. The hologram began with its columns but no slashes, lines or arcane symbols crept upward. Soon a picture of an egg shown in Egbert's hologram.

Marriam said, "Good morning, Egbert."

He sat.

Sanjay sarcastically asked, "Have you finished bonding with your twin?"

Marriam nudged Sanjay with her arm.

"What? It's not like I'm going to hurt his feelings."

Marriam turned her attention to Egbert, "Egbert, did you have previous knowledge that the other egg was on Mars?"

A word in all caps appeared in the hologram, "NO."

"Were you aware of the existence of other eggs?"

"YES."

"And they were placed by those who placed you?"

"I DO NOT CONTAIN THAT INFORMATION."

"But likely?"

"YES."

"When did you know that the other egg was on Mars?"

"WHEN I CAME IN PROXIMITY TO THE PLANET."

"What have you learned from the other egg?"

"SEVERAL THINGS."

Marriam said, "Sanjay, call General Matthews."

Sanjay sprung up to the wall-mounted com and pushed the button that directly linked to General Matthews.

"Yes," the General responded.

Sanjay said, "Egbert's back."

"I'll be right down."

Marriam began again, "Our outposts have been attacked on Mars and people killed."

"INFESTATION."

"Are you saying that those creatures are not native to Mars?"

"CORRECT."

"So, the other egg told you that?"

"CORRECT."

"What else have you learned?"

Egbert never volunteered anything on his own, ask the right question, get the right answer.

A picture of a chessboard flashed in Egbert's hologram. On the chessboard was a copy of the chess game that Marriam and Sanjay had just been playing. In it, Sanjay reached for the queen and moved her across the board.

"WORMHOLE."

"What?" Marriam said questioningly.

Sanjay asked, "Are you saying that there is a wormhole close by?"

"CORRECT."

Sanjay continued, "An Einstein-Rosen bridge?"

"CORRECT."

"Oh shit," Sanjay responded.

They pondered that.

Marriam changed the direction of the questioning and asked, "So, Egbert, other creatures have been on Mars before?"

"CORRECT."

"What happened? Why aren't they here now?"

"CORONAL MASS EJECTION."

"Explain."

"EXPLORERS ARRIVED ON MARS OVER ONE BILLION EARTH YEARS AGO WITH PLANS TO COLONIZE. WHILE THEY WERE ON THE PLANET, THE SUN ERUPTED WITH AN ENORMOUS STORM THAT SENT PARTICLES STREAMING TOWARD MARS. THESE TRAVELERS PLANNED TO LEAVE AND PROCEED TO THE THIRD PLANET."

"Earth?"

"CORRECT."

"Did they make it?"

"UNKNOWN."

"What happened on Mars?"

"ATMOSPHERE DESTROYED."

General Matthews arrived and walked into the room carefully the same way everyone walked into the room when Egbert was active. It seemed irrational, though, because Egbert had never spooked at the arrival of someone new.

Matthews nodded towards Egbert and whispered to Sanjay and Marriam, "What's up?"

"Too much," Sanjay said.

Marriam continued her questions, "Did these travelers plant you and the other eggs?"

"NO."

"So, you were placed on Earth more than one billion years ago by someone else?"

"I DO NOT CONTAIN THAT INFORMATION."

Marriam glanced over at the General and asked, "Egbert, where is this wormhole?"

"Wormhole?" Matthews repeated questioningly.

Egbert went black and for the space of a minute was dormant. He seemed to blink back on but then went black again.

Marriam spoke to the General hoping that Egbert wasn't going back dormant for years as he had before.

"Egbert said the other egg told him where a wormhole was located and he also told him that the creatures on the planet are not native Martians. He called them an infestation. He said that others had landed on Mars, but because of a coronal mass ejection, these beings had to leave and were going to the third planet. He said that this happened a billion Earth years ago."

Matthews stood with his mouth slightly agape. "Huh," he responded dumbly.

Another couple of minutes passed with Egbert black.

The three just stood and stared at Egbert, then his hologram lit and a starfield appeared in three dimensions. From the outside of the starfield, the image zoomed forward to see a sun orbited by eight planets. When this solar system stabilized, it was obviously the solar system with Earth. Grids appeared next and then in the upper right corner, date and time. In the hologram, the grid tilted forward showing the solar system straight on as if looking down upon it. The image then moved out to the orbit of Neptune which was at the inside edge of the Kuiper Belt. A single red dot appeared at a spot close to Neptune's orbit but slightly further into the Kuiper Belt. One word appeared, "WORMHOLE."

Matthews gazed at the image of the wormhole astonished. He said, "Our deep spacecraft is heading out there in that direction. It's already past Uranus and headed towards that sector." He paused for a minute with a thought, the suspected alien craft.

"I need to go," Matthews said abruptly. "Give me the exact coordinates."

Sanjay quickly jotted down the coordinates and handed them to Matthews.

The General left and stepped briskly towards the station's communications. He began to consider something that had been haunting him. The mysterious craft that moved towards Saturn then moved away then disappeared. Could it have come through that wormhole? The deep space craft's mission had changed at that time from attempting to find and track the incoming asteroid that was bound for Earth to attempting to find this alien craft, but they had not had any success. The craft had disappeared. Was this where it had gone?

As he walked onto the bridge, he began talking, getting the attention of Alex Donahue, the communications specialist, "I want to send a message to our deep space vehicle, have you been tracking it?"

"Yes, General. The message will take nearly six hours since the deep space vehicle is close to Neptune's orbit."

"Open up a channel."

"Yes, Sir." Donahue nodded then said, "Go ahead, General."

"This is General Matthews. I am sending you the coordinates for a suspected wormhole. I know that this request is unusual, but what I would like you to do, is send a drone into the coordinates and observe then report back. I know your previous mission, but this takes priority. Matthews out."

"Thanks," the General said.

Donahue said, "The message is on the way, we should get a response in around twelve hours."

Matthews nodded and walked from the bridge.

Chapter 43

Isla Bravo

August 5, 2096

Sol 91

As General Matthews walked from the bridge, he ran into Captain Williams who was on his way there.

"Hello, General. I am nearly ready to send a retrofitted AK3000 to the surface to have a look inside the cave where the creatures took our people. This AK is equipped with several drones with lights and night vision so we can get an idea about what the creatures are up to, where they are and roughly how many of them there might be. These drones have no weaponry, they're just designed for surveillance."

"I'm afraid that if you find them, the scene is going to be pretty grisly."

"I'm afraid so but I think it's important to collect all the intel we can if we plan to go back to the planet."

"I agree. How long until you send the AK?"

"Two hours. We're waiting for the planet to rotate toward us."

"Keep me informed."

"We'll do, General."

"Oh, and Captain, how are the colonists doing?"

"As well as can be expected. We have them settled down on the bottom ring. There are large storage areas there, some of which have been emptied to resupply the rockets that are creating the magnetic field, Isla Bravo and the habitats. There are also more recreational areas down there and a full gym. I think they're comfortable for now, but they're hard workers and will become bored if they're stuck there for too long with no real purpose."

"I'll give that some thought. Thank you, Captain."

Matthews turned and walked back to Egbert's room. As he walked in, Sanjay and Mariam were sitting and looking at the twin eggs.

"Hello, General," Marriam said pleasantly.

The General asked, "Has Egbert revealed anything else?"

Sanjay said, "No. We asked more questions around the wormhole and he didn't seem to have any more information about that. We asked several more questions about the creatures on the planet but how they got there is a mystery. The travelers who Egbert spoke of were not the ones who brought the creatures there and didn't seem to know anything else about them, so I asked if Egbert or if the other egg knew of other travelers. Egbert said that the other egg had only been started up by one group of travelers. I asked Egbert to speculate as to why anyone would put such dangerous creatures on the planet. As you know, Egbert isn't fond of speculation but he offered this in one word, 'PROTEIN'."

Matthews considered that then said questioningly, "As a food source?"

Sanjay continued, "Marriam and I thought about that and began bouncing ideas off of each other. This is what we came up with. We all know that protein is the most difficult food to get into space for us. What if someone was traveling to distant planets and was hoping to grow protein-rich foods, or maybe even a favorite meat. Maybe those creatures can live in the most hostile of environments and survive well enough to provide a good barbeque. It might be worth the risk that they might just eat the travelers or maybe the travelers had a way of controlling them. I don't know. It's just speculation."

The General smiled, "Damn good speculation. I'd be willing to bet a hamburger that you're not far off."

Sanjay said wistfully, "A hamburger. That sounds wonderful."

Marriam smiled.

The General said, "I have another matter to deal with. Let me know if Egbert has anything else to say."

Chapter 44

Isla Charlie

August 5, 2096

Sol 91

The General had gone back to his cubical and laid on his bed staring at the ceiling. He needed to think. They still hadn't identified the killer asteroid, yet. The alien craft that mysteriously appeared then disappeared was definitely trouble of some kind but how and why was a mystery yet to be revealed and the creatures on the planet had thrown a complete monkey wrench into the colonization of Mars. He thought about President Dent and had a feeling that the news of the attack of Club Med South wasn't going to see the light of day on Earth.

Matthews com lit. It was Captain Williams, "General."

"Yes, Captain."

"The AK with the drones has been launched and will reach the cave in fifteen minutes."

"I'm on my way."

Matthews realized that he hadn't eaten or slept in two days. He was still running on elevated bodily functions from his booster shot.

He walked to the galley and got a strawberry protein shake, finished it and headed to the bridge.

As he walked in, Williams was staring at the small monitor in a cubical away from the rest of the crew. Matthews walked up and joined the Captain.

"Hi, General. I thought that this would be a discrete location to watch the video from the drones. Only you and I will see the feed. The pilots will of course but I don't want the contents of the video widely known. We have four drones attached to this AK. The AK will hover outside and above the cave and will send in the drones. The AK will not be close to the ground. I don't want any danger to the pilots. They will control the four drones as they snake their way through the labyrinth of tunnels. This screen will be divided into four parts so that we can view each of the drones' cameras."

"We're at the tunnel's entrance," came the voice of Mo Roberts. "We have no visual on any creatures."

Captain Williams said, "Proceed, Mo."

"Roger."

The camera feed came on and lit the monitor in four equal parts. The AK was over twenty feet off the ground, at this point, as the drones were released from its underside.

The drones had four propellers on their four corners and a fifth by a rudder that gave the drones thrust and steering. One camera lens showed from the front.

They began to fly towards the mouth of the tunnel. Three of the drones entered the tunnel first, separating to each side of the top of the tunnel and also the middle. The fourth drone followed the others recording their movements. The night vision was on and everything inside the tunnel appeared to be green.

The drones proceeded to where the first colonists had been attacked which was by the hatching of the leathery eggs. One drone swooped in and got a closeup to see that every one of these eggs had hatched. A second drone focused in on the dusty floor of the tunnel. At the entrance, the floor of the tunnel was gravelly but here, the dust was fine and the footprints of the creatures could be seen in abundance. The prints were three-toed with obvious claws at the ends. They looked like the fossilized footprints of dinosaurs stuck in time that Matthews remembered. In fact, they appeared to be the prints of the ripping claws of a velociraptor.

Matthews shuddered. You wouldn't want to be forced into hand-to-hand combat with one of these creatures.

The drones had paused at this point but now continued on deeper into the cave. This deep in the cave, there was no ambient light but the night vision was having no trouble lighting the surroundings.

The drones slowly moved forward, fifty, one hundred yards and still no creatures. Then something appeared on the ground. One of the drones swooped down. It was a NASA blue shirt of the kind worn by the colonists. The drone rose back up to the ceiling of the tunnel which was nearly twelve feet above the tunnel floor in this portion of the cave. More clothing, now lots of it, NASA jumpsuits, underclothes, shoes, socks, belts, and bras.

Captain Williams whispered, "Fuck."

The color had drained from Matthews' face...

More clothes...

The drones continued on. The tunnel opened into a cavern which was nearly thirty feet across and twenty feet high. To the left were patches of egg clutches, to the right and to the horror of Williams and Matthews were bodies of nude, dead humans and dead creatures laying haphazardly against the opposite wall, some side by side and some overlapping. A kind of thick mold covered the dead and obscured most of their bodies. A creature approached a dead of his fellows and seemed to vomit onto the body. Further away, where the mold was thickest, two creatures approached it and licked at the wet, oozing slime. The creatures were only there for a few seconds then walked away and further down a branch of the tunnel.

At the egg clutches, a slimy creature of nearly three feet in length emerged from one of the leathery eggs. It was covered with a viscous liquid and it crawled away from the egg and then seemed to flop onto the cavern floor as if dead or exhausted.

A large paw came out of nowhere and slapped one of the drones out of the air like swatting a fly and it crashed into the wall and went black. The other drones reversed and began to back out of the cavern. Creatures took notice as the creature who struck the drone began to make clicking noises. More creatures followed the drones backward. From behind, another drone was knocked from the air and then another. Finally, the last drone was attacked and the last image from the cave was a spinning video feed from the cave then blackness.

Captain Williams said, "Mo, come home."

The AK turned straight upward and disappeared into the thickening Martian atmosphere.

Matthews said, "That was worse than grisly."

"Son-of-a-bitch," Williams said, wiping his forehead with a handkerchief.

Matthews said, "I need to get this footage to Jankowski to see what she says, then we'll develop some kind of response."

Williams nodded but looked as if he'd swallowed something bad.

Mathews said, "I don't want this film available for anyone else to see."

"Yes, Sir," Williams responded and walked away.

Chapter 45

Isla Charlie

August 6, 2096

Sol 92

1225 Hours

By lunch, General Matthews had not heard back from the deep space vehicle. It had been well over twelve hours. He walked to the bridge on his way to meet Doctor Norma Jankowski, Astrobiologist to review the scene in the tunnels of the creatures.

As he reached the bridge, the deep space vehicle had just responded.

Donahue from the communication station saw the General walk in and said, "General, the deep spacecraft has received your message and is proceeding to the given coordinates. Once there, they will radio us back and will send the probe to the given coordinates. Estimated time of arrival, two days and fifteen hours."

"Thank you."

Matthews turned and walked from the bridge. As he neared Doctor Jankowski's office he thought about an encounter with a real wormhole. Where might it go? Would it be possible to find out without sending a manned ship into its unknown depths?

He knocked on the door.

"Come in," came the female voice of Doctor Jankowski.

As Matthews walked in, he could see the grim expression on the Doctor's face.

"Hello, Norma," Matthews said solemnly.

"General."

"I suppose you have reviewed the film?"

"I have."

"And?"

"I have several observations. First, they aren't eating the people or their own dead. I believe that they are using them as a kind of garden. I believe that they vomit something onto the bodies and it grows. This is their food. Second, I believe that they are smart to a degree. Maybe smarter than wolves who hunt in a pack and corner their prey, then work together to take it down. I believe that they are primitive, more primitive than early humans, more like a type of animal. Third, they seem to plant and harvest their food in the place that we've seen, but I'd be willing to bet that they have some kind of living place further down the tunnel and who knows how many creatures might be living there. I believe that they think they will have abundant food and water, so from the look of the egg clutches, they plan to expand. I'm not sure that the planet is big enough for us and them, to paraphrase an old western. If we plan to live there, we will need to fight or become lunch. I don't see any other way."

"Thank you, Doctor. We are probably not prepared to have something be able to lay siege on us. We would certainly lose unless we could come up with a way to win rapidly."

"You're military. Isn't that what you do?"

"It is, Doctor, but this is the first time we have encountered something from another planet. Killing it seems a waste."

"Spoken like more scientist than soldier."

"I'll take that as a compliment. Good day, Doctor."

"Good day, General."

Chapter 46

Earth

August 6, 2096

China was moving a large force towards Japan and another towards the Philippines. It was obvious that they were planning to spread the United States thin and that was succeeding. The Chinese had a firm grip on Taiwan and there was news coming out of Taiwan that there had been several executions of high-ranking officials but nothing was corroborated. The British had called their fleet back home because of the war that was now raging in Europe. Just like in World War 2, once France fell, the Germans would again plan to take England. Canada and Mexico had joined the United States and pledged large ground forces to join the fight in Europe.

In the Pacific, though, the United States feared that if they were to lose a major battle at sea, the Chinese would take Hawaii and could then threaten the mainland. Two brand new carrier battle groups had just been completed on the west coast of the United States and were ready to go to sea. The stepped-up production of the Dome Raptor fighter jets was also ahead of schedule. Any attack on the United States was going to be a painful experience but America was in no way assured of victory.

Washington D.C.

Oval Office

August 6, 2096

3:15 PM EDT

Dent sat behind his desk with his head in his hands. World War 3 was well underway and he had never, in his most frightening nightmares, thought that he would be the President of the United States embroiled in the event most avoided and feared for the last hundred years, World War 3.

Howard Diamond stepped into the Oval Office.

Dent glanced up at Diamond and could tell that he wasn't bringing good news.

"What is it, Howard?"

"I've just been in contact with the Johnson Space Center in Houston, Texas and they've informed me of more deaths on Mars at the hands of the creatures that killed Middlefield and his crew."

"The same creatures?"

"Yeah. It seems that our habitats were attacked. Our habitats were not designed to withstand an aggressive attack."

Howard sat down in the chair across the desk from the President. He said, "Henry, a lot has happened on Mars in the last few days. General Matthews isn't sure how to proceed."

"What's the death toll?"

"22, in the two separate incidents. It could have been a lot worse if General Matthews hadn't acted quickly. All of the remaining colonists have been evacuated to Isla Charlie for now."

Dent shook his head.

"There is something else that I need to tell you."

Dent could hear in Diamond's voice that something else unusual had happened. He found Diamond's eyes.

"What else, Howard?"

"It's the new egg?"

"Okay?"

"When General Matthews set the egg up next to Egbert, the two eggs began to communicate with each other. This other egg says that there is a wormhole just outside of Neptune's orbit. Matthews has sent the deep spacecraft out there to check it out. Secondly, they have encountered something else that might be called extraterrestrial. Something moved towards Saturn, then stopped and moved away. We wouldn't have seen it except that we're looking for the asteroid that Egbert said was coming to Earth, so we've been focused in that region of space."

"Why wasn't I told of this sooner?"

"Because space is strange. They didn't know what they had seen, They're still not sure."

"So, what is NASA saying about it now?"

"Honestly, they think that it's a spacecraft and of course, not from this planet. When it moved away, it disappeared, I mean gone without a trace. They've been looking for it to return ever since. They first sent the deep spacecraft to attempt to make contact with this alien craft, if that's what it is, but they found nothing. Matthews then sent them to the suspected wormhole."

"Then what?"

"Matthews wants them to launch a probe into it to see what happens."

Dent paused in thought. "Okay," he said, "I don't want any word of any of this to leak. We're going dark on what's happening on Mars. Our people on Earth have enough to worry about now that the world is descending back into a terrible war."

"Of course," Diamond agreed. "Again, Matthews is asking for troops to be sent to Mars."

"We can't send him anything. All of our efforts are going towards the war. This war that we're fighting is going out of control and I don't think that we're going to end up on the winning side. In World War 2, at least, we had the Russians to bog down the Germans, now there's no Russian front and no one who can scare them from behind."

"What about India? They have loosely allied with us."

"They're barely feeding their people right now. The Generals in the Joint Chiefs are talking about taking the fight to the Chinese and just sending enough help to hold off the Germans for a time. They think we have an edge over the Chinese Navy and can win at sea and possibly push them back to their mainland if we attack both fleets that are heading to the Philippines and Japan simultaneously before they reach their destinations. We have deployed ten new Dome Raptors to each of our two Carrier battle groups and with the EMP drones could sink and disable most of their warships, thanks to Egbert that is."

"What if we lose?"

"Then it would probably be prudent to learn to speak Chinese."

"Henry, we have a supply ship headed for Mars going to be launched in two days, maybe we can load it with the automatic weapons that we'd designed for space. The MPs on Isla Charlie can train the colonists to fight and take back JFK City. We have the specially designed space suits that the MPs are using and maybe we could include designs for some kind of electric fencing to keep the creatures out so we can continue our work. If we do nothing, the colonist will just sit on Isla Charlie while everything that they have worked for goes to hell."

"Howard, you contact General Matthews with that plan and ask him to come up with a way to defend JFK City. He's a General, he should have something up his sleeve."

"I'm on it, Henry."

"Also, tell him that we'll send twenty more MPs on that supply ship. I know we have that many trained for spaceflight."

"I think he'll be happy to hear it. We may need to bump some supplies to do it and it isn't set up to ship that many people."

"Get on it, Howard. Oh, and how fast can we get to Mars with this shipment?"

"If we push it, seven months?"

"Huh, seven months. Damn... Seven months is a long time to be weightless. It will take some rehab once the MPs reach Mars."

"It will."

"What about the new drug. Could they give it to them?"

"They don't think it's ready."

Dent nodded.

Chapter 47

Isla Charlie

August 6, 2096

Sol 92

General Matthews sat at the desk in his cubical. His room was nothing special because of his being a General. It was the same as everyone else's on the huge spinning space station.

The call came in from Howard Diamond, the President's Chief of Staff.

"Hello, General."

"Mister Diamond."

Lag for the 5 minutes it takes for the message to reach.

"Because of the time lag, I'm going to lay out what the president wants you to do with respect to Mars. First, the President is sending you a large supply of ammo and weapons to help defend yourselves from these creatures. Secondly, twenty space trained MPs will also be making the trip. We have a specially designed electrical fencing also on the way. Because you are military, the president is confident that you will be able to retake and hold the area. The problem is that this shipment is seven months away so you'll need to make do. When you have finalized your plan to go back to the planet, forward it to me. Good luck, General… Out."

Of course, Matthews had been mulling a plan over in his mind and had come up with a temporary, credible plan to hold JFK City. He considered that he was down to seven MPs. He had two dozen of the specialized MP spacesuits in storage which would allow short exposure on Mars. These suits were not so cumbersome as to make it impossible to fight. They also had ten automatic weapons and another ten in back-up with five thousand rounds of ammo.

He had a plan set in his mind and called for a meeting with the two leaders of the colonies, plus Captain Chambers, and Captain Williams.

Chapter 48

Isla Charlie

August 7, 2096

Sol 93

The next day, Williams, Chambers, Bernstein, and Patterson were seated in the meeting room on Isla Charlie along with Patel and Daily and several other of the technical and scientific crew.

General Matthews walked in briskly. "Hello," he said heading to the podium.

A few of the crew were standing.

Matthews said, "Have a seat, please."

As they sat, Matthews began, "We are going to take back the planet."

Some murmurs.

"Here's the plan. Be ready to comment after I've finished. I want every thought that you have, every concern and every wild speculation. I want to try to be prepared for everything that we can think of as a problem. If you think of anything after we leave, write it down and bring it to me, anything."

There were nods of agreement with some happy that they wouldn't be ordered into a meat grinder without being able to express their concerns.

Matthews continued, "First, Club Med North and Club Med South will be left abandoned. Both were just monitoring stations anyway. JFK City has the factories and is set up to produce the food that we will need going forward so that's where we're going and I mean, to stay. We have twenty fully automatic weapons and five thousand rounds of ammo and twenty-four of the MPs' spacesuits. So, we're going to train some of the colonists to fight. Some already have military backgrounds and just need some time on the weapons. I know of a few on Singleton's construction crew that were combat trained soldiers. Joan," Matthews said looking at Bernstein, "You will be the commander of JFK City because you outrank Patrick. Patrick, you will be her second and will focus on the running of the factories which is your specialty anyway. I'm going to have the opening to the cave with the creatures bombed and hopefully trap them inside but I'm not so naïve as to think that this opening is the only way out of that cave. We will attempt to find other openings to caves and it wouldn't surprise me if they just couldn't dig their way out but I plan to slow them down. There will be two AKs patrolling the grounds of JFK at all times and one AK out searching the surrounding area, so there will be three AKs on the planet at all times. We will be sending a team to empty both Club Med North and South of most of their supplies but will leave just a bit in case we need one or both for a military base of operations. We are going to extend motion detectors further out and around the city but that will in no way cover the entire five-square-mile complex. We will remain vigilant. Be ready. We leave for the planet in two days. I want a list of all military personnel with combat training. Any questions?"

Joan Bernstein asked, "What if some of those creatures reach an airlock and get inside? They could fill the place with the Martian atmosphere killing us that way."

"Aren't each of the sections separated by tunnels with airlocks?"

"Yes, but they're not always sealed."

"They will be now and if there's a breach, I want each person close to a spacesuit. Every patrolling MP will be suited though not helmeted."

Patrick Patterson commented, "It's going to be tough to keep an eye on the whole complex with only three AKs."

"We'll also have the sensors and motion lights to alert the AKs and a crew constantly monitoring the sensors. The AKs are fast and will be able to react quickly to any threat. If it seems that we need more AKs on the planet we could add but the pilots will need rest and will be on a three-shift rotation with other pilots needing to provide breaks in the day. The AKs cannot land on the planet because the pilots' spacesuits are not designed for them to leave their cockpits, so they must return to one of the space stations to leave the AKs.

Listen, I know that this will be an endeavor, and at some point, we might need human patrols on the planet but that's also fraught with danger. I'd rather start this way. Yes?" Matthews said nodding back to Bernstein.

"When are you going to bomb the tunnel?"

"When we're finished here, I'll send the order to Isla Bravo for two AKs with hellfire missiles to hit the cave on the same day we land the shuttle with the colonists. The missiles are not designed for this type of thing but will explode upon impact. If we hit the cave entrance with four missiles, I'm pretty sure it will be blocked for a time. Our problem right now is that we don't have anything else to use. Any other questions?"

No hands raised.

"Good, so, go back and get your people ready to depart. Get me that list of combat-trained colonists, ASAP. Talk to everybody and write down any comments. We have a lot of work to do. Dismissed."

Chapter 49

Mars

August 9, 2096

Sol 95

1700 Hours

South of JFK City, where the Martian permafrost had begun to vanish as the planet warmed, two AK2200 streaked through thick rain clouds. As they soared towards their target, rain splattered their windshields and turbulent air buffeted their vehicles. As the two AKs dropped in altitude, they could see water gather in places on the rain-soaked landscape and begin to move in temporary creeks, finding accommodating slopes downward. The flight path had taken the AKs passed the man-made terraforming device launched from Earth over nine years prior. Powered by antimatter, it continued to heat an area of nearly twenty miles.

Flying low, Kirk Matthews gazed out of his windshield and down onto the Martian landscape. He said, "Look, Sandy, the water's flowing."

Sandy Jones was flying close to Kirk, side by side and he then glanced down at the moving water. "Damn," he said in wonder. "I never thought that I would see that."

The small creeks were moving in the direction that they were flying and as the creeks continued, they met other creeks with moving water and then emptied into the first witnessed river on the planet Mars in over a billion years. Kirk and Sandy dipped further in altitude to get a better look. The river was probably thirty feet wide and flowing at a brisk pace west where it appeared to be bending back north.

The rain continued to fall in earnest with large drops in sheets reminiscent of the rain that both had seen back on Earth.

Sandy said, "I bet this river finds its way to the northern ocean area."

Kirk agreed.

Sandy said, "Approaching target."

"Roger that," Kirk responded.

Two minutes later, they came upon the mouth to the cave where the creatures lived and the colonists were now being used as some kind of fertilizer for a macabre garden.

They both slowed. Their mission was to deliver their four Hellfire missiles into the sides of the mouth of the tunnel and hopefully bring it down and seal it tight. If these missiles didn't finish the job, two more AKs were in route to complete the assigned task. The planet, today, was crawling with AKs.

Kirk and Sandy brought their AKs to a halt fifty feet from the tunnel entrance. Nothing moved. They both watched for a time then moved back to one hundred yards and armed their missiles.

These missiles were much like those used in conventional combat situations, laser-guided, and armor-piercing, weighing one hundred and ten pounds and moving at nearly a thousand miles per hour with a high explosive fragmenting charge. In general, the cave entrance didn't stand a chance.

"Are you ready, Sandy."

"Yep, let's blow this place."

They both released their ordinance at their targets, which was well inside the cave entrance, and in a matter of seconds, the mouth of the tunnel exploded with flame, smoke, and debris.

Sandy and Kirk pulled up after the release of their weapons to make sure that they were clear, then circled back to try to get an idea of the effectiveness of the attack. As the dust cleared, the cave entrance was gone in a pile of rubble.

Jones and Matthews turned and headed to JFK City.

Chapter 50

Mars

JFK City

Noachis Terra

August 9, 2096

Sol 95

Kirk Matthews and Sandy Jones glided north, just a hundred feet above the ground on their way to JFK City. The rain continued to fall, but that was welcome compared to the thick fog that sometimes choked this area. They were on the lookout for creatures.

Impact craters pocked the landscape here, some small and some not so small. None of these craters were from the bombardment of asteroids directed by Sandy and Kirk, though. All of those craters were located far north of the equator and in the area where someday, there might be a raging ocean. These craters were ancient.

Kirk and Sandy's AKs rose and cleared the outside rim of an oblong crater and they could see JFK City in the distance. There were no fewer than ten AKs patrolling the skies around the city and three large shuttles delivering space-suited colonists and supplies. As they approached, they could see everyone scurrying like ants on a disturbed anthill.

A voice came over the com. It was Captain Chambers. "Jones, Matthews, you may proceed back to Isla Bravo. We have not had reports of any activity or sightings of the creatures. Good job on the cave and see me when you return."

They both pulled straight up and accelerated to escape velocity and within minutes were in dark space and heading for Isla Bravo. They had a bit farther to travel because the planet had spun away from their station. It lay just over the ruddy Martian horizon. They accelerated and soon could see their space station looming in the distance with its single spinning wheel and its solar panels turned towards the setting Sun.

Both Sandy and Kirk had stopped using the onboard AI to help them dock and as they reached the spinning station, they matched its rotation and deftly docked their vehicles. Their hatches opened and they both climbed from the AKs, stripped from their spacesuits and put back on their NASA blue jumpsuits.

They walked together to the bridge where Captain Chambers stood monitoring the re-invasion of Mars.

They approached Chambers.

Sandy asked, "How's it going down there, Captain?"

He smiled as he looked up. "I think good. So far, no problems. The creatures didn't get into the city, so there isn't any damage to the airlocks. Everything seems to be going well."

Kirk said, "Yeah, but I think it's going to be spooky down there. Those creatures were nothing to mess with."

"Yep. So, Kirk, you and Sandy will be part of the rotation on the planet. We have decided that each pilot will have a six-hour shift six days a week. We only have six AKs aboard Isla Bravo and Isla Charlie has sixteen working AKs with four in for repairs. It's going to be tough, but we have no choice right now and no good alternative. The colonists are too vulnerable down there without air support."

"No doubt about that," Kirk agreed.

Chambers asked, "Do you both think that if you had three AKs and there was a large attack, you could fend off the creatures?"

"How large?" Sandy asked.

"Say, twenty creatures."

Kirk said, "Oh yeah, as long as we had sufficient warning."

"What if it was twice that, or say, fifty creatures?"

Sandy asked, "All attacking from different directions?"

"Worst case scenario."

Sandy said, "Don't know. That would be pushing it."

Kirk said, "The problem would be if they got too close to the domes. We couldn't just open fire and shred the habitats."

Chambers nodded with a look of worry on his face. "You guys go get some rest. You'll need to be ready by tomorrow. You won't be on the planet at the same time in case we have an asteroid emergency up here."

They both nodded and walked from the bridge.

Chapter 51

Kirk and Sandy separated, each going to their own cubical. As Kirk opened the door to his, he could see a lump under his covers with messy light brown hair poking from underneath. Kirk undressed and slipped into his bed.

"Hey," Taylor said sleepily. "I was hoping you would get back soon."

Kirk kissed her.

She cuddled to him and asked, "How'd it go down there?"

"Good. No surprises. Just routine."

"Ummm."

Kirk slipped his hand into the back of Taylor's panties feeling her firm backside.

She whispered, "I'm glad you're back."

He slid his hand up and under the front of her tee-shirt and found her breast.

"Now, I'm more glad you're back," she said, sitting up, pulling off her shirt and kissing him again, this time with more passion. She reached for his lower parts and he had already risen to her. She guided him into her private place and they rocked together slowly.

A half-hour later, they laid cuddled together and Taylor, now more awake, asked, "Are you going to be flying to the planet more often?"

"Yeah. Every AK pilot will be patrolling the area around JFK. We can't let the creatures even get close."

"When do you start that?"

"Tomorrow. I don't know what time my shift begins, though."

"Oh…"

"What?"

"Well, when this mission began, it was like a dream or a fun sci-fi flick, or maybe as if I were watching a really interesting documentary on PBS with me in it. Now, everything feels dangerous. I've lost my brother." She paused then added, "And all those people killed down there. That was just awful. Now it's more like one of those sci-fi movies where all but one of the crew dies horrible deaths." She breathed out. "I'm just afraid, really afraid."

She buried her face in Kirk's shoulder. He could offer no honest comfort because he felt the same.

Chapter 52

Beyond Neptune's Orbit in the Keiper Belt

Bleak, deep space. More than 2 billion miles from Earth. Out there, Neptune spins silently in its 164 Earth year orbit around the Sun. It orbits at 12000 miles per hour, slow by space standards compared with Earth which moves at sixty-seven thousand MPH through space on its trek around the Sun. A day on Neptune is a little under 16 hours though it's nearly four times the size of Earth. So, the large planet spins at 12,000 miles per hour, twelve times faster than Earth's rotation.

The wind speeds on Neptune average around 700 miles per hour, the fastest in the solar system and can sometimes reach 1200 miles per hour. The fastest winds on Earth are just under 300 miles per hour and can devastate any place they encounter. Imagine what the wind would be like on Neptune. If a person were on the surface, the winds force would instantly strip all the flesh from the bone.

While Neptune is interesting to view from a distance, it's no place to visit.

Deep Space Vehicle, Nostromo

Keiper Belt

Outside the Orbit of Neptune

August 10, 2096

Sol 96

1100 Hours

"Sir, we are nearing the coordinates," Leslie Morgan, the ship's Celtic navigator announced. She was freckly with light brown hair and a Scottish accent.

"Slow to one-twentieth speed, Leslie. I don't want to get closer until I have some idea about what we're dealing with here."

"Aye, Captain," she responded as she fired the reverse thrusters to slow the Nostromo.

Everyone on the craft could feel the odd sensation as it began to pull back.

The Nostromo was a deep spacecraft designed to easily and rapidly reach the outer portion of the solar system. Powered by antimatter and able to reach speeds exceeding 90,000 MPH, it had the appearance of a submarine floating through a spinning doughnut. The working and most of the living stations were in the wheel that spun to create gravity of nearly eighty percent that of Earth to help mitigate the ill effects of low gravity on the body. The crew, though, mostly slept out of the spinning ring in the weightless portion of the ship where there was mostly storage and flight bays for the various craft that could be launched if needed which included drones, AK3000s, two large shuttles each capable of transporting forty personnel, and one smaller four-man shuttle.

The Captain of the Nostromo, Lenard Ward asked, "Are we close enough to get a look at the location of the suspected wormhole?"

"Negative, Captain," Morgan replied.

"Slow to a crawl."

"Aye, Captain."

Captain Ward was not on the bridge. He was career military and in his fifties with no hope of ever retiring from his service to the country. No one in the United States military retired these days. No specially purchased vacation home for those golden years.

He floated weightlessly in the very front of the Nostromo and stared out of a large window placed there. It was his favorite place to be on the streaking vessel where he could look out into infinity. From this place, he could sometimes make out distant galaxies that appeared as smudges against the black background of space. Sometimes he could see the arc of the Milky Way Galaxy where billions of stars reside, of which our Sun is but one.

He could see nothing from this vantage point, however, just black space with silvery stars in the distance.

Ward asked, "How far now from the wormhole?"

"Under five-thousand miles."

"Well in range of the drones," Ward said rhetorically. "Pull to a stop, please."

"Aye, Captain. Pulling to a stop," Morgan responded.

"Mister Bachman, let's send two drones to the given coordinates."

"Yes, Sir," Stanly Bachman responded.

The drones were his specialty. Bachman sat back behind a large monitor and pulled what appeared to be a game controller from a console. It resembled a controller from one of the more popular games like Nintendo or Xbox. He released the two drones and his monitor's screen split in half and lit with the two drones' cameras coming online.

"Drone's away, Captain."

Bachman expertly maneuvered both drones in the direction of the wormhole quickly increasing in speed. Once he had covered half the distance, he said, "Captain, I am entering some kind of asteroid field. This place is thick with floating space rocks of all sizes. I need to slow way down."

"Take your time, Stanly, we're in no big hurry here."

Bachman guided the drones around several large asteroids each the size of a two-story building and then below the rubble of what might have been an asteroid destroyed in some kind of collision. As the drones cleared the rubble, they came to another craggy asteroid which was broken in several places as if it had been in a collision and the pieces seemed to rotate in circles near the breaks. The drones came to a stop as another asteroid moved slowly through a space that was opened just moments before.

The suspected wormhole lay one hundred and twenty feet ahead in this area that was as congested with space rocks and debris as cars on an LA freeway.

The drones banked right between two smaller asteroids that were moving in opposite directions, then the drones halted.

Stanly Bachman seemed to freeze. His eyes were fixed on his monitor but his mouth involuntarily drooped open. He said, "Captain, you better get up here."

Captain Ward, still standing by the front window said, "What is it? What do you see?"

"You need to come here now, Captain, and I mean right now."

"On my way," Ward replied somewhat perplexed by Bachman's tone.

Weightless, Ward grabbed onto a handhold and pulled himself forward, propelling his body through the fuselage of the spaceship. He came to an elevator and pushed the button, waited as the door opened then floated inside where he situated his feet to point to the place where gravity would soon push them. The elevator descended to the spinning ring and Ward watched as the door opened onto the bridge.

"Okay, Mister Bachman, I have arrived."

Bachman didn't speak. He just nodded to his small monitor.

Captain Ward walked to Bachman's workstation and peered over Bachman's shoulder. Ward froze. There before him was an armada of broken and fragmented alien vessels, probably a dozen or more.

"Put this on the big screen, Stanly. I want a better look."

"I wanted to make sure that you didn't want this kept secret."

"No. Put it on the screen."

A large viewing screen, eight-foot in height and ten feet in width, lit showing a split-screen view of what appeared to be a spaceship graveyard.

All eyes on the bridge turned to the screen.

"Holy cow," Leslie Morgan whispered.

Captain Ward got on the ship's intercom and said, "Can I have all science crew to the bridge please."

Several specialists were aboard in case they were able to make contact with the first unidentified object that was detected some two years prior.

Ward stared. Before him, were at least a dozen spaceships of some kind, destroyed and in shambles. Amongst the ruined vessels were numerous floating bodies, each with one head, two arms, and two legs. All appeared to be dead as they didn't move and looked as if frozen in time.

The small group of three in the science team walked onto the bridge and stared open-mouthed at the image on the screen.

Lilly Wong, a biologist was the first to speak. She said, "Oh my."

Linguistics Professor, Rachael Liebowitz, though specialized in language with a Ph.D. was completely at a loss for words.

Arthur Compton, who specialized in computer science and computer language said, "Damn."

Max Hale, the onboard physicist walked up after the others. He glanced at the screen, then gazed at everyone around as if this were a joke being played on him. He said, "Okay, what's this?"

No one spoke. To say that the crew was in a state of shock would be an understatement.

Captain Ward broke the silence. "This is what we found at the coordinates for the wormhole."

Hale turned his attention back to the large viewing screen but didn't speak.

There was no turbulence in this area of space. Everything seemed locked in place.

The Captain continued, "I'm going to venture a guess, here. I'm going to speculate that this armada came out of

the wormhole and smacked right into this asteroid field…
But when?"

"And why?" Hale said questioningly.

Lilly Wong asked, "And where were they going?"

Bachman suggested uncomfortably, "Earth?"

The Captain said, "Stanly, get closer to one of the creatures."

"On my way."

He maneuvered a single drone forward leaving the other in place. The viewing screen was no longer divided into two and it magnified to one drone's path forward. It reached one of the bipedal creatures which was wearing no helmet and focused on its face. There, an insectoid face stared back at the drone's camera. This creature's head appeared to be larger than a human's proportionately and had what appeared to be two eyes that were at the ends of short tubes no more than an inch long on a heart-shaped face. The tubes seemed to be able to move in any direction independently like an elephant's trunk and were set wide of where human eye sockets would be. The dark eyes were reminiscent of multi-lensed insect eyes, oblong and had the appearance of convex contact lenses. In between the eye-tubes was possibly some kind of mouth that began between the eyes and ended below where the chin should be. The mouth appeared to open vertically instead of horizontally but it was impossible to tell for sure because the orifice was closed tightly. Covering both sides of this mouth-like orifice were sparsely spaced short whiskers. The skin of the creature was frosty so the skin was not as visible as the Captain wished, but it appeared to be smooth. The creature was wearing a type of spacesuit which, if you removed the head, might make it look nearly human though the body was long and spindly and had the hint of an insectoid appearance. The hands were gloved and the feet had coverings that appeared to be soft fabric shoes with a small, thin heel and a wide toe section.

Everyone watched with undivided attention. No one took their eyes from the large screen.

The Captain said, "How far are the drones from the suspected wormhole?"

Leslie Morgan replied, "About sixty feet to the right of the vessels."

"Stanly, turn one of the drones in that direction then follow it with the other drone."

"Yes, Sir."

The drone that was filming the creature turned about forty-five degrees to the right. The split-screen appeared again. There wasn't anything to be seen in front of the first drone. No asteroids near the spot of the wormhole and no obvious distortion of space. On the second screen, the first drone turned and started slowly forward.

"Okay, Stanly, send the drone into the wormhole."

"I'm on it," Stanly Bachman responded.

Everyone watched.

The drone moved forward, though it was hard to tell because, in this direction, there appeared to be nothing but empty space. The second drone continued to film the first. Several minutes passed.

"Are you getting close?" Captain Ward asked.

"I should be there," Stanly responded.

"Leslie?" the Captain said questioningly.

She responded, "The drone is at the coordinates."

In that instant, the drone disappeared in an odd wrinkle in the fabric of space like a pebble in a calm pool of water. The first camera went instantly black.

It was sudden.

"I want to send a message to General Matthews."

Dustin Spinelli, the communications specialist said, "Ready when you are, Sir."

"General Matthews, I'm sending you film that is for your eyes only. I will await your response concerning how we should proceed."

"Dustin, send the General all of the drone footage."

"Yes, Sir. It's on the way."

The Captain continued looking at the screen. He glanced over at the scientists and said, "Now we wait. Stanly, bring the drone back for now. After the General gets back to me, we'll have a meeting to discuss what we're to do next. Please think about what we've seen and what you think it means. Make notes if necessary. Everyone not on duty on the bridge is dismissed." Ward paused for a minute then said, "On second thought, Stanly, leave the drone. I don't want to bring something unwanted to our ship."

"Unwanted?" Bachman responded questioningly.

"Yeah, like some frozen space bug, you know, a virus or bacteria."

"Oh," Bachman whispered bleakly.

"Leslie, back our ship away from this place."

"Aye, Captain."

Chapter 53

Earth

August 10, 2096

Sol 96

On Earth, war raged. In Europe, the Germans pushed into France but met stiff resistance. The United States provided air cover from a carrier battle group which slowed the German offensive. The Germans hadn't planned on the Dome Raptors which owned the skies. Most conventional aircraft on both sides were at risk from SAM missile sites which locked on to any aircraft that flew into their range but the Dome Raptors were completely stealth. U.S. fighter jets with air to ground Hellfire Missiles halted the German tank advance. If the Americans hadn't been there to provide air support, France would have fallen.

In the Pacific, the Chinese were able to take the Philippines but were not able to invade Japan. At the last minute, the American fleet which was supposed to protect the Philippines had to be diverted away because the Chinese were able to reach there too rapidly, so the fleet moved in support of Japan and completely destroyed a Chinese carrier battle group sending it to the bottom of the sea.

Everywhere on the planet, war was evident. The Middle East ignited as the Arab nations thought that they had the upper hand against Israel with the United States bogged down on two fronts. Twice, Israel's neighbors were turned back when their attacks failed.

In South America, Brazil had raised a large army, navy, and air force and attacked Venezuela by sea and air in a dispute between the two leaders. The U.S. had cut all ties with Venezuela and had furnished Brazil with weapons which gave them an overwhelming advantage. Venezuela would fall.

Chapter 54

Stable Orbit Above Mars at L1

Isla Charlie

August 10, 2096

Sol 96

2355 Hours

Just before midnight, General Matthews laid on his bunk staring at his tarp-covered ceiling. It rippled mildly from the motion of the spinning space station.

His computer screen lit and the soft ping of an incoming message on his private link could be heard in the quiet of the station.

He turned to see a familiar box on the computer marked "Message."

He rose and sat at his desk and clicked on the message:

"Password"

" ********** "

The message opened:

General Matthews: For His Eyes Only

Message with an attachment from The Nostromo

Sent From: Captain Lenard Ward

August 10, 2096

1200 Hours

"*General Matthews. I'm sending you a film that is for your eyes only. I will await your response concerning how we should proceed.*"

Matthews opened the attachment and stared in wonder at the alien spaceship graveyard. He watched as the drone panned over the wrecked and broken armada. The drone turned and floated to the dead alien. Matthews was silent. Then the two drones' cameras both showed on the split-screen with one drone moving forward and the other following. The lead drone picked up speed and then vanished before the General's eyes. The other drone's camera caught a slight distortion of the portion of space where the first drone vanished from.

Matthews sat back and thought, what the hell?

He looked at his clock, 12:10, just after midnight. What time would that be in Washington? 7:30 or so in the morning?

He had a direct line to the President, one that he had never used, not even when the tragedy on Mars had taken place with the deaths at Club Med South. Now he thought he should use the line. He called and got a normal ring as if calling a friend on an old landline.

"This is Dent," came a voice from nearly sixty million miles away.

Four-minute delay.

"Mister President, this is General Matthews. I have a message for you and I'll lay it out. If there is anyone in your office who you do not want to hear this information, have them leave now. This can't wait." Matthews paused for a minute to give the President a chance to clear his office. "Our deep space vehicle has reached the wormhole and found that an entire fleet of alien spacecrafts seemed to have been destroyed there. My guess is that they came out of the wormhole and into an asteroid field. I'm guessing that was a big surprise. I'm not sure how to proceed. There were humanoid creatures dead in the rubble. I have no doubt that these vehicles are full of technology that we would want, but I have no idea what we might encounter on a bacterial or viral level if we bring some of the creatures or technology on board our vessel. If something deadly were to get back to Earth, we wouldn't need to worry about the 2101 asteroid. The deep-space vessel is not set up to sterilize anything and it would put our crew at great risk if we were to bring anything on board. Think it over, Mister President, and I'll await your orders. Matthews out."

Delay…

Matthews sat back after delivering the message and put both hands behind his head. Everything was so complicated, there were no clear answers to anything that's happened since the arrival of that damned egg-shaped artifact. He breathed out and laid back down. He had felt run down and knew that it was time for a booster of his special medicine. He'd see the doctor in the morning.

Matthews' computer pinged with a new incoming message. It was the President. He responded, "General, I think it's prudent to bring the Nostromo from the wormhole and into position to possibly intercept the asteroid if it shows. I will have a meeting with my experts about how to proceed with the alien ships and bodies. I will get back to you. Dent out."

General Matthews listened to the message suddenly exhausted. He would contact the Nostromo in the morning. His eyes grew heavy. He slipped under his covers and drifted into a fitful sleep.

Part 3

Arrival

Chapter 55

September 22, 2097

Sol 493

One Year Later...

On Earth, the war continued to rage with the Germans being fought to a stalemate in France. The British had sent half a million troops to France, the Canadians had sent 200,000 troops to the fight, Mexico had sent 150,000 troops and the United States had contributed 250,000 troops to France and 400,000 troops to South Vietnam, Japan, and South Korea. Though South Korea had originally sided with China, they had a change of heart when China overran North Korea. South Korea did not want to just be a state in China.

On Mars, no creatures had resurfaced in the year since they attacked Club Med South. JFK City was fully functional and now had a small militia of fifty trained soldiers. It was fully ringed with electric fence and razor wire and had tall guard towers with 50 caliber machine guns protecting the compound. It looked more like a prison than a community of colonists.

The terraforming was continuing to gain momentum as the great northern ocean and Hellas Basin, the huge impact crater, were now filling with H2O water. The temperature was rising, the atmosphere was thickening and rain now fell in abundance. Valles Marineris, the twenty-seven-hundred-mile-long canyon on Mars, had a shallow river flowing at its basin. The artificial Van Allen Belt was helping to keep the thickening atmosphere from being sputtered off and a thin ozone layer was measured at the upper edge of the atmosphere.

As for the wormhole and the destroyed alien spacecrafts near it, the President decided to do nothing for now. He ordered a new type of space vehicle to be constructed that would have extensive sterilization and salvage features built into it. He then ordered the Nostromo back to Mars.

Time was passing and the predicted killer asteroid was somewhat overdue. The hope to find it early and divert it was beginning to fade and locating it was becoming desperate. It should have shown up by now, but space is vast.

Isla Bravo

September 22, 2097

Sol 493

Taylor Chapman sat at her station staring into her monitor. Her mind drifted a bit to Kirk who was chasing down a small nitrogen-filled asteroid with Jones. They were to catch it and send it onto the northern lowlands. The mission was routine.

Kirk was still troubled by what he saw on the planet. Taylor considered Kirk and thought to herself that he really wasn't cut out to be a soldier. Too sensitive. She thought that a simple job and a picket fence would suit him better and she thought that she would like to share that life with him and maybe with a gaggle of kids.

She glanced away from her monitor and at everyone on the bridge at their posts and doing their jobs.

When she turned back, something was moving on her screen from the upper left towards the middle, somewhere outside of Saturn. She squinted and followed the object with her eyes, then began working her touch screen and punching keys.

"Oh shit oh shit," Taylor said a little louder than she planned, then, "Captain Chambers, I think I have our asteroid."

Chambers raised his head from peering at a systems' maintenance on another monitor. "What? Are you sure?" he responded.

"Yes. It's already past Uranus' orbit but not close to Saturn."

"How come we didn't pick it up before?"

"I suppose because space is big. It's impossible to completely cover it and the asteroid also may be very dark."

"But you think that this is the one?"

"Not positive, but this is the best candidate that I've seen so far. I think it must have entered from the Kuiper Belt near where Neptune is now and west of where the suspected wormhole is located. The deep spacecraft obviously didn't see it before they left. The asteroid appears to be moving at slightly over 60,000 miles per hour which is a bit less than the predicted speed."

Taylor stared at her monitor and she punched several keys on a keyboard.

"Hmmm," Taylor said, watching her monitor. "It's not acting right. It just moved strangely." She shook her head. "It's probably my instruments."

"Why do you say that?"

"I don't know. It was probably nothing."

"How long until it reaches earth? Is the timing correct?"

"At its current speed? Just a minute, I'll do the math from what I know. My guess is roughly four years but it will come close to both Saturn and Jupiter and might pick up some speed from those encounters."

"That places the collision sometime in 2101."

"Can you get closer in your calculations?"

"Yes," Taylor said studying her calculations. Then she repeated, "It should get to Earth in a little less than four years, early to mid-2101." She continued to watch the asteroid's trajectory then commented, "The asteroid will definitely slingshot off of Saturn's and Jupiter's gravity which is what should bend it towards Earth's orbit."

"So, it's on time for its predicted collision with Earth?"

"My guess is yes, give or take a couple of months either way."

"That's close enough for me. Okay, keep tracking it and I'll contact General Matthews. Oh, and Taylor, can you tell if it's big?"

"Can't tell yet, but it won't be long before we know."

"Okay."

"I'll get in touch with the Johnson Space Center to nail down the calculations. I'm sure that the General will also be in touch with them."

Chambers nodded and said, "Thanks."

Chapter 56

Isla Charlie

September 22, 2097

Sol 493

0900 Hours

General Matthews walked to his doctor's appointment. It was time for another booster. He opened the door and Doctor Belinda Waters was at her desk looking over some hand-written notes.

"Hello, Doctor," Matthews said.

"Hi, General. You're right on time. Let's get you out of those clothes."

"I bet you say that to all the Generals."

They stepped into the examination room and Matthews stripped and put on his gown from behind a screen then walked out.

"On the table," Doctor Waters said in her commanding doctor's voice.

Matthews complied and the doctor began pushing and prodding him. She pulled the gown off his shoulders and let it fall into his lap as she listened to his lungs.

"So, Jeffery, how have you been feeling?"

"Quite well, thank you."

"Jeffery, you are over seventy and I'm looking at the body of someone who is closer to twenty-eight. I think we should lower the dosage of your meds. We can always increase them if you begin to age again."

"It's not the aging that concerns me, Belinda, it's the cancer. If it comes back, my number is up."

"I know. I get it, but."

The sound of the General's vest com began to ping in his pocket from behind the screen.

"I need to get that," Matthews said.

He stood holding the gown to cover his front leaving his backside exposed and he reached for a small earpiece and put it in his ear.

"Yes," he said.

"General, we believe we have identified the asteroid. The one we're looking for," Captain Chambers said from Isla Bravo.

"Thank you, Captain. That's great news. I'm heading to the bridge to have a look." He clicked off with the Captain then said to the Doctor, "Got to go, Doc." He handed the gown to the Doctor and reached for his military-issued briefs.

"But your shot?"

"Oh, umm, it kind of knocks me out. Can I come back in an hour?"

"Let me check my schedule. Make it an hour and a half. I have another appointment."

"Great, thanks, Doc. See you then."

Matthews finished dressing and walked briskly to the bridge. When he reached there, Captain Williams had already gotten the news about the asteroid. He was staring into a monitor and talking with his asteroid tracking specialist.

The General walked up.

Williams turned, "Hello, General. I'm pretty sure we have it."

The General asked, "How far is the Nostromo. Can they intercept it?"

"The Nostromo is not quite to Saturn. They were on their way to the moon of Titan to deliver the domes for the future encampment. We can redirect it and it should have no problem intercepting the asteroid long before it reaches Saturn."

"That's great. Great news. You contact the Nostromo and I'll call the President."

Chapter 57

Mars Orbit

September 22, 2097

Sol 493

Kirk Matthews and Sandy Jones both tracked a small ammonia filled asteroid which had come from the asteroid belt.

"I got a visual," Kirk said with his craft slightly ahead of Jones'.

They both pushed forward.

The asteroid came into view and both AKs raced to catch it. It was moving at nearly fifty-thousand MPH and would pass just above Mars on an eventual collision with the Sun.

Sandy said, "Take it, Kirk."

"Roger that," Kirk said enthused at the challenge.

The asteroid was moving and craggy, so the landing would be tricky. Kirk came up to the wobbling space rock and it appeared to be around a football field in length. Kirk scanned the surface and was not having any success finding a place to land.

"Sandy, you better check the other side. I don't see a place to bring my AK down."

"I'm on it," Sandy said.

Sandy quickly pulled above Kirk's craft and disappeared on the other side of the craggy stone.

Sandy said, "I got a place on this side."

"Take it, Sandy. I'm pulling off."

Jones landed on the opposite side of the asteroid and fired his thrusters to stop the wobble. Matthews pulled away, tracking the asteroid and watching as Jones maneuvered the huge rock to get it into position to deliver it to the planet.

"Looks good, Sandy."

The onboard AI announced the final adjustment to send the asteroid onto the planet and into the designated coordinates.

"Final adjustment," Sandy said after they appeared on his display.

The asteroid dipped towards Mars. Sandy continued to ride the rock. It was slightly off course.

"Pull off, Sandy," Kirk said.

"Just a second."

"Sandy, you need to pull off."

"Roger that. I'm out of here," Sandy said.

He lifted off of the asteroid and skipped off of the upper atmosphere as the asteroid plowed through the atoms and molecules of the thickening Martian atmosphere.

The asteroid ignited and streaked downward. Kirk watched the impact from his craft as Sandy made a wide turn back. A huge mushroom cloud exploded from the surface.

Kirk said, "Ah, that was scary."

"Like a walk in the park, buddy. Let's head back. I need to get some sleep before my shift on the planet."

Kirk said, "No one has seen any of those creatures for a year. They should lighten up on the patrols."

"Yeah, you'd think so, but the minute they did, those critters would show up and wreck the colonists' day."

"Probably right. Murphy's Law if nothing else."

The two AKs streaked back towards Isla Bravo.

"Kirk Matthews," came a female voice.

"Willow?"

"What other female contacts you in space?"

"It's been a while."

"I have been busy."

"Really, doing what?"

Willow didn't answer that question. "Kirk Matthews, I have picked up those strange signals from space, again. I cannot discover their origin or their direction, but they are there and sound like the communication between machines or maybe computers. They feel electronic. And they are strong and getting stronger."

"As if they are getting closer?"

"That would be an astute guess."

"Huh. Keep me informed."

"Copy that. Willow out."

Kirk and Sandy flew back to Isla Bravo and docked. They changed back into their NASA blues and Sandy left to rest for his shift on Mars while Kirk wandered to the galley for something to eat.

As he reached the galley, Taylor walked up and said, "Buy me lunch?"

"Hey, I was hoping I'd run into you."

"You'll never believe this," Taylor said excitedly.

"What's up?"

"I think I've found the asteroid that's got a May date with Earth."

"No way."

"Yep. It just showed up a bit passed Uranus."

"Wow, That's great news. It gives us some time to divert it."

"A little under four years."

"We ought to be able to nudge it away in that amount of time."

Taylor said, "Let's eat. I'm buying."

"Hmmm. You know that just because you buy me lunch doesn't mean that I'm going to put out," Kirk said straight-faced.

"We'll see," Taylor replied.

Chapter 58

The Nostromo

September 23, 2097

Sol 494

0900 Hours

Captain Ward floated at the large front window of the Nostromo and looked towards Saturn hoping to soon see its familiar rings. The planets aren't spaced evenly and the distance between Uranus and Saturn is around a billion miles, ten times the distance from Earth to the Sun. The Nostromo had been cruising at a quick 100,000 MPH.

Dustin Spinelli from the bridge called, "Captain you have a communication from Captain Williams."

Ward said, "Put it through."

Captain Williams: "Captain Ward, we have tracked an asteroid that may be the asteroid that's bound for Earth. It has just left the approximate orbit of Uranus and is heading your way. This is a stroke of luck. You will have the chance to reach it early and you might be able to nudge it just enough to change its course to collide with Saturn. I'm forwarding the coordinates of the asteroid and the trajectory change that you will need to alter the asteroid's path. Good luck, Captain. Williams out."

Ward turned and floated towards the elevator that would take him to the bridge.

As he walked onto the bridge he said, "Leslie, do you have the new coordinates that were forwarded to us from Isla Charlie?"

"Aye, Captain."

"Change heading."

"Changing heading."

"Can you estimate how long it will take to encounter the asteroid?"

"Aye, Captain, estimating. We're not that far from it, only around ten million miles. It will take two days to completely turn but the asteroid is coming at us at 60,000 MPH, so once we are headed back towards it, we will gain on it fast. Calculations are coming up now... Five days, four hours, twenty minutes, and fourteen seconds, give or take."

Captain Ward smiled, "Thank you, Leslie."

Chapter 59

Washington D.C.

Oval Office

September 25, 2097

Sol 496

10:45 EDT

President Dent and Howard Diamond sat together in the Oval Office sipping a brandy. It was 10:45 pm EDT and they were alone. The war raged in Europe and the Pacific with occasional victories and occasional defeats. All the staff had gone home for the night. Earlier, this office buzzed with staff coming and going, bringing news and information.

Tonight, it was quiet, no television, no radio, no internet, and no closed-circuit meetings. The President's wife had gone to bed, Diamond's wife had left him six months ago.

Diamond said, "Well, Henry, do you think this is the asteroid?"

"I think so."

"You know, with all that's happened, saving the world from this asteroid was what everything was really about."

"Yeah, that does get lost in all the complications since that egg-like-thing was dug up."

"Well, let's hope we can stop it."

"Let's hope so," Dent said. "If not, I guess nothing really matters anyway."

Dent took a depressed sip. "I think I'll go to bed."

"See you in the morning, Mister President," Diamond responded.

Diamond got up and walked to the door.

"Goodnight, Howard."

Chapter 60

Mars Surface

JFK City

September 26, 2097

SOL 497

2300 Hours

Sandy Jones patrolled the perimeter of JFK City. Night had fallen and the rain had stopped but a choking fog hung close to the ground and made it impossible to observe anything that might be moving down there. The creatures were somewhat cold-blooded and gave off nearly no heat signature.

As Jones approached one of the thirty-foot guard towers, a red light blinked on its top to warn off flyers who might plow into the towers when the fog was this dense.

SOL 498

0345 Hours

Over three hours had passed, a routine night. Two more hours and Sandy could head back to Isla Bravo and his bunk. He gazed in the distance and all looked calm.

"Mayday! MAYDAY!" came a panicked voice from one of the towers on the back side of the City. "Shit! Oh Shit!" the same voice exclaimed.

Alarms rang out all over the compound.

Gunfire.

"They're through the fence! Oh shit! They're behind me and under me. I can't fire in that direction."

More gunfire from another direction. Sandy had pulled around and turned in the direction of the distress call.

"The fence is down! They're climbing the tower! Help. I need help."

Sandy reached the tower that was under attack. Several creatures were climbing the tower while thirty others crowded around and pushed at its base. The tower fell.

Sandy swooped low and strafed the creatures cutting down half.

Another call from a different tower, "The creatures are coming up through the dirt, they must have burrowed in here. They're coming up!"

Another AK opened fire near a fence, but the fog was so thick that it was impossible to see what the pilot was shooting at.

Sandy called Isla Bravo, "JFK City is under heavy assault. We need backup."

Small arms fire came from near one of the domes. Sandy searched for creatures but they were hard to find.

A small group of creatures had reached one of the factories that produced the greenhouse gases for the terraforming. They were pulling on the airlock door. Sandy unloaded on the creatures killing six but also hitting the airlock turning it into a twisted mass. The three creatures that were left ran from the dome.

Several AKs came screaming in from above the City and entered the fight. They took up positions over the domes and factories but weren't firing.

Back and forth, the battle erupted in different locations for some hours as the creatures would attack then disappear again into holes or through the fence. More AKs arrived.

Sandy skimmed the area around the perimeter of the fence but no creatures were visible. The attack had finally ceased. A few minutes before dawn, the sun was just beginning to light the Martian horizon. The fog continued to blanket the area and the creatures had melted back into the Martian landscape.

Isla Charlie

Sol 497

0430 Hours

Though Captain Williams had quickly scrambled additional craft to the surface of Mars, some damage had already been done. More deaths, more complications from the creatures and more grief and fear for the colonists.

General Matthews jogged onto the bridge. He barked, "Report."

Williams: "General, JFK City was just attacked by the creatures. It appears that we have fought off the attack, but they seem to have burrowed under the fence. We have some casualties."

"Burrowed?"

"Yes, Sir."

"Did they get inside the city?"

"Preliminary reports say no, but they attacked a guard tower and an outpost. Because the colonists weren't expecting to be attacked from behind, no one saw the attack coming until the creatures were on top of them. The attack has ended."

"Do you have a casualty count?"

"Bernstein has reported four colonists missing."

"Missing... Shit."

Chapter 61

Between Uranus and Saturn

September 28, 2097

Sol 499

The Nostromo had reached the coordinates where they would encounter the asteroid at least a billion cold miles from Earth. They had turned earlier and had been increasing their speed to match the asteroid when it was soon to approach.

Leslie Morgan, navigator on the Nostromo announced, "Captain, I have the asteroid. It's approaching at around 60,000 miles per hour as we were told. I'm increasing our speed to thirty thousand MPH now."

Fifteen minutes passed.

Morgan announced, "Captain, the asteroid is closing in on our starboard side. It's gaining fast. I'm increasing our speed to 40,000 MPH. The asteroid is five miles starboard. It should be visible."

Captain Ward said, "Put it on the screen."

The large viewing screen came on and found the asteroid streaking just behind and to the right of the Nostromo.

"Crap," Leslie said quietly. "That's a big hunk of stone."

The outline of the asteroid was dimly lit by the Sun which was nearly a billion miles away. In front of the Nostromo, the giant planet Saturn lay with its definitive rings glowing where struck by the Sun but obscured where not lit. Several moons could be seen silvery outside the rings.

This asteroid was enormous. Easily fifteen miles in diameter, maybe more, a planet killer. If something this size were to hit Earth, probably nothing would survive. The asteroid streaked forward and would easily miss Saturn but its path would be bent by the ringed planet's massive gravity. If the asteroid could be pushed slightly it would get caught by Saturn's gravity and plummet onto the massive planet's surface.

The asteroid now was nearly beside the Nostromo.

Morgan announced, "Increasing speed to match the asteroid." A minute passed. "We're pacing it at 62,288 MPH."

Captain Ward said, "Let's have a closer look. Cut the distance between us and the asteroid by a half."

"Aye, Captain," Leslie Morgan said.

When the Nostromo closed to two and a half miles from the asteroid, its massive size was more evident.

"I want four AKs launched. The asteroid isn't spinning or wobbling. It should be easy to land on."

From the sides of the Nostromo, four AKs launched and paced the Nostromo. Then they increased speed and bent slowly towards the racing planet killer. The plan was for all four AKs to land on the asteroid's port side and fire their thrusters to slightly alter the asteroids flightpath. From this distance, it wouldn't take much to send the asteroid onto Saturn's surface. Saturn is huge. If it were hollow, 764 Earths could fit inside its shell. Despite its massive size,

Saturn would be somewhat disrupted by this blow but the effects would only be temporary.

The AKs closed the distance between the Nostromo and the asteroid.

"Five minutes and closing," Greg Aster, the lead pilot announced.

Rex Kilgore was flying right beside Aster. He said, "What's that? It looks like sparks."

Something seemed to be sparking near the top of the racing space rock like chains being dragged on the street behind a truck.

"Looks like fireflies," Aster commented then, "Captain, I think this asteroid might be heating. We're seeing some kind of what looks like sparks hovering around its top portion. Can you see that?"

Captain Ward said, "Magnify the image."

Kilgore said, "What the hell? Are you seeing this?"

Ward watched the sparks but felt that it posed no threat. "We see it. You are still a go for the mission. Go give that asteroid a good push."

"Roger, Captain," Aster replied.

Captain Ward watched on the magnified screen as the four AKs approached the asteroid. The mission was going smoothly. The first AK landed easily on the surface of the asteroid then the second landed.

Ward watched intently as the third AK got into position. Suddenly the fireflies seemed to swarm from the other side of the asteroid. They swirled like a swarm of killer bees, spinning and curling and twisting in a kind of frenzy, then as they came around the asteroid's surface, they seemed to head straight for the AKs

Ward panicked as he watched, "Get off that rock," he shouted.

Aster said, "But we're almost in position."

Aster's vehicle then went black, then Kilgore's, followed by the other two. The AKs seemed to peel off of the asteroid like leaves being blown from a tree by a mild breeze.

"Aster!" Ward shouted.

The sparks of light seemed to hover just over the asteroid then in a swarm seemed to organize and come directly at the Nostromo.

Leslie Morgan said, "Captain, we are losing power. Everything is shutting down! Captain!"

Chapter 62

Isla Charlie

September 28, 2097

Sol 499

"Captain Williams, we have lost all contact with the Nostromo."

"What happened?"

"I don't know. The last I heard they were tracking the asteroid. Everything seemed routine. Now they're just gone."

"Keep trying to raise them!"

"Yes, Sir."

Captain Williams called to Isla Bravo. "Get me Captain Chambers."

Chambers responded. "Hi, Simon, what's wrong?" He could tell by William's voice that something was up.

"We've lost the Nostromo. You guys are on the other side of the planet and have a better line to them. Can you raise them?"

"Hold on, we'll give it a try… No, we are getting no signal from them, nothing."

"Thanks, I'll tell the General."

Williams wasted no time, he called the General's com.

"Yes, Captain," Matthews said.

"General, something has happened to the Nostromo. It's gone."

"What?"

"Yes, Sir."

"What do you mean, gone?"

"We are no longer receiving anything from the craft. It's as if it disappeared or, well, exploded."

"And what about the asteroid?"

"Its path has not changed."

Matthews breathed out. "I'll be right there."

Chapter 63

Mars

September 28, 2097

Sol 499

Kirk Matthews was covering the Martian landscape looking for the creatures in his AK. Patrols had been increased since the attack and work crews scurried to repair the damage done by the creatures and the bullet holes in the domes from the wild firing of the colonists in panicked response. Luckily, no colonists had been killed by stray gunfire.

"Kirk Matthews," Willow's voice came into his ear.

"Willow."

"You have lost the deep spacecraft, Nostromo. I believe they were attacked. Just before the signal was lost, I detected an inordinate increase of the alien transmission in that region of space."

"Taylor told me that they were after the asteroid bound for Earth."

"That is correct."

"Could this have been an accident or some kind of a malfunction?"

"I do not believe so, Kirk Matthews. Something is coming."

"Willow, I'm going to need to tell someone about what you've discovered."

"I believe that they will soon find out."

"I have to tell someone. I'll go to my uncle."

Willow was silent for a moment then said, "I will be discovered."

"Maybe I could suggest that it might be alien and not some kind of accident."

"As you wish."

Kirk knew that Willow was not happy at that. He would need to think.

Chapter 64

Isla Bravo

September 28, 2097

Sol 499

Taylor Chapman sat at her station monitoring the asteroid's progress towards Earth. Suddenly, the asteroid began to increase in speed. It was nearly imperceptible. The asteroid had not neared Saturn and shouldn't be pulled by Saturn's gravity as yet, so the increase in speed shouldn't have occurred at this time.

On the bridge, in a station next to hers, Ed Ramirez desperately attempted to contact the Nostromo which had gone dark. "Nostromo, come in. Nostromo, come in." His voice had become pleading. No signal was coming from the deep spacecraft. It was like it disappeared.

Gradually, the speed of the asteroid continued to increase. Its trajectory seemed the same. The Nostromo was supposed to angle the asteroid into Saturn, but the asteroid had not changed its orbit. It would still bend slightly influenced by Saturn when it passed. Then it would bend again once it reached Jupiter. This course correction would push it to an eventual collision with Earth.

The asteroid was now nearing 65,000 MPH.

"Huh," Taylor said aloud. "Captain?"

Chambers glanced over at Chapman.

"The asteroid seems to be increasing in speed. Did any of the interceptors land on its surface?"

"We don't know for sure. There are minutes missing in their transmission from the time of the encounter. It seems so."

"But they're not on the asteroid now?"

"I don't know. I wouldn't think so."

"Huh, maybe the asteroid is already being pulled by Saturn," Taylor thought aloud, but something about the asteroid was bothering her.

Chapter 65

Earth

September 28, 2097

Sol 499

Nation had risen against nation and nowhere could peace be found. At the end of this war, the map of the world would be changed forever. Russia was still an uninhabited wasteland with an enormous crater where Moscow used to be. The crater was beginning to fill with water.

In the United States, everything was being rationed. If you were a farmer, you got a minimum of fuel, a minimum of seed, a minimum of fertilizer, and a minimum of water. Most farms were tasked to produce as much food as possible with the government taking delivery of all crops and distributing those crops to the towns and cities and no food produced in the United States left the country. As a result, and because the United States had always been the breadbasket of the world, severe shortages of essential nourishment were more the norm than the exception and had been since the asteroid's impact that destroyed Russia. The food distribution in the United States and abroad was terribly inefficient, though, and where before, the open markets for crop sales and the extremely efficient retailers no longer existed, so much food did not find the best place to land and much was lost and wasted. The United States' government had, as a result, set up factories to process most food into cans and to be frozen to try to help alleviate the problem of loss. Gone were the days of abundant grocery stores with huge produce departments stacked neatly with hundreds of varieties of fresh fruits and vegetables. Now, people stood in dreary lines to get their portions.

Just before the world was thrown into a global war, the world had just begun to talk of re-establishing trade between countries. So, at that time, there was some hope of helping the starving masses of humanity in countries that were struggling, but now, those hopes were all but dashed.

The war raged on...

Chapter 66

Isla Bravo

September 28, 2097

Sol 499

From the bridge of Isla Bravo, Taylor Chapman watched in horror as the asteroid continued to gain in speed, now 78,000 MPH.

She called to her counterpart on Isla Charlie and asked, "Sean, are you seeing the gains in speed of the asteroid that I am. I'm concerned that we're having some kind of malfunction here."

"Yeah, Taylor. I have the asteroid's speed now at 80,000 MPH as it approaches Saturn."

"I guess it's possible to increase in speed by that much but I've never heard of it happening, not like this."

"This doesn't make sense. At this rate, the asteroid will come out of its bend around Saturn at nearly 150,000 MPH or more."

"That's if it doesn't level off."

"It doesn't look like it's going to level off any time soon."

"That's what I thought also."

"At this rate, I have the asteroid's possible path to Earth at somewhere around 2100."

"Yep, That's my guess also. Thanks, Sean."

Taylor thought, that's too early. She glanced up at her monitor and said, "Captain, the asteroid is still increasing in speed. It's now just above 80,000 miles per hour."

The Captain nodded. "Keep me posted."

Chapter 67

Isla Bravo

September 28, 2097

Sol 499

2300 hours

That night, Taylor pushed Kirk to his back and climbed on top of him. The covers fell to the floor as she relentlessly began taking her pleasure. Kirk watched her body move as her passion increased. His hands slid from her breasts to her back and she bent down and kissed Kirk's lips then pushed back up without stopping her motion. Kirk gripped her hips.

A female voice came from the computer that sat on Kirk's desk, "Hello, Kirk Matthews. Hello, Taylor Chapman."

Taylor turned in embarrassed horror and looked to the door, not knowing where the voice was coming from. She grabbed the covers from the floor and pulled them over her bare breasts.

Kirk said, "Willow?"

"Willow?" Taylor repeated, "Who's Willow?"

"In a minute."

"Kirk Matthews, I believe that the electronic signals must be coming from the asteroid. I cannot tell for sure, but I believe it to be true."

Taylor still sat on top of Kirk, holding the sheets to her breasts with a look of shock on her face.

Kirk said, "I know you wanted to remain secret, but should I go forward with this information, they will want to know where I got it."

"I wish you to wait. I do not think that knowing the information will help stop the asteroid."

"Taylor said that the asteroid is picking up so much speed that by the time it reaches Mars, we'll only have about five days before it reaches Earth."

"Kirk Matthews, will they do everything in their power to stop the asteroid?"

"Yes."

"Then I do not see how my information will help."

Kirk said, "Let me think about it."

"Hmmm," Willow said, then, "I will now leave you to your coupling."

"Gee thanks," Kirk said sarcastically.

Taylor's face went from flushed with exertion to a bright blush.

"Kirk, who was that?" Taylor asked.

"Galadriel."

"I thought she committed electronic suicide?"

"She showed up when I was in one of the simulators about four years back."

"So, she's not gone."

"Nope."

"And she watches you?"

"She watches everything. There are no secrets from her anywhere."

"And she's been watching me?"

"Every place you go and everything you do."

Though it seemed impossible, Taylor's blush deepened. She quietly said, "Oh. You should have told me."

"She wanted to remain secret. She asked me to not tell anyone and I said that I wouldn't."

Taylor laid down next to Kirk and was quiet for a moment then said, "That may explain it."

"What?"

"The asteroid. I don't know, it isn't acting right. It's picked up too much speed and when I first began tracking it, it seemed to make a couple of erratic moves, but I thought it might have been my instruments. It was pretty far away at that time."

"At its current speed, how long until it reaches Mars?"

"Four months or so, but it depends on how much faster it gets. It keeps picking up speed. When I left the bridge, it was approaching 200,000 MPH. That's not unheard of by asteroid standards. They can go that fast, but I've never heard of them going much faster. Maybe it will level off at that speed."

"So, we still have time."

"We do, but Kirk, the predicted date that this asteroid was supposed to reach Earth was May of 2101. Whoever had identified this asteroid knew about its natural orbit and had been able to predict the time of a possible impact with Earth. Either they got it completely wrong, or there is something very wrong with the asteroid. I wonder how they knew about it?"

"Ahhh," Kirk said not sure if he should continue.

"You know how they knew."

"I kind of told you."

Taylor paused for a minute trying to replay a conversation from some years back. "I remember that you said…"

Taylor's voice had risen.

"Shhhh," Kirk said with his finger at his lips.

She continued in a whisper, "that it had something to do with something alien, right."

Kirk nodded but didn't speak.

"It was what your uncle told you."

Kirk nodded.

"Huh, Kirk, do you think that the asteroid is some kind of alien ship?"

"Maybe or just on the thing, pushing it the way we do."

Taylor whispered, "What else did your uncle tell you?"

"He told me that they were looking for an alien craft around Saturn. They saw it move and then disappear."

"Huh," Taylor paused then asked, "Can you guys go after the asteroid?"

"Not yet. We can't get out there, we'll have to wait until it gets closer to do something about it. It's just too far. Our best hope was the Nostromo."

"And now it's gone."

"Fraid so."

"Geez."

Part 4

Doomsday

Chapter 68

Jan 18, 2098

Sol 608

On Earth, the war was still in full swing. Neither side could gain an advantage and neither side was giving any ground. As usual, the common people who lived around the conflicts suffered. Those running the war insulated themselves and felt no real danger as hundreds of thousands of people around them died.

On Mars, the subterranean creatures who assaulted JFK City had not launched another full-scale attack but were content to occasionally pick off colonist who were away from the habitat. The creatures would tunnel and seemed to be able to tell when the colonists were outside the habitats. Then they would erupt through the ground like an unexpected geyser, take the colonists and disappear back into the holes. As a result, no one left the habitats without a full guard and air support. The great Ocean to the north continued to fill as the rain fell in abundance and the water found the lowest points of elevation to gather.

The asteroid screamed past Jupiter and bent towards Mars on its date with Earth. By this time, the asteroid had achieved the impossible speed of 400,000 MPH, a speed unheard of by asteroids, though the solar system that we reside in travels around the Milky Way at 500,000 MPH.

Because the asteroid would soon be upon Mars, General Matthews had called a meeting for all the Captains to meet on Isla Charlie to outline his plan to try to intercept the asteroid before it reached Earth and to listen to any other ideas or suggestions. The Captains were noticeably quiet. There was no good solution and time was growing short.

The plan had evolved like this, the asteroid was just one week away from the red planet. Isla Charlie would leave Mars' orbit and move to intercept it. It was impossible to catch the asteroid with the AKs because they could never achieve the necessary speed, so the agreed-upon plan was for General Matthews to send all the AKs from Isla Charlie armed with nuclear warheads and attempt to destroy the asteroid or alter its path before it neared Earth. Isla Bravo would stay and use its six AKs to protect the colonists. If this plan didn't work, the Earth would probably perish. Isla Charlie's AKs would only get one chance at moving the racing space stone which now had been estimated to be twice the size of the asteroid that killed the dinosaurs. This asteroid was a planet killer.

Isla Charlie

Bridge

January 18, 2098

Sol 608

0700 Hours

General Matthews stood on the bridge of Isla Charlie next to Captain Simon Williams. What had happened to the Nostromo was still a mystery. For some unknown reason, the deep space vessel had disappeared into the vastness of space and had not been heard from.

Captain Williams glanced over at General Matthews.

Matthews nodded.

"Mister Chen, move us from orbit and to the programmed location."

"Yes, Sir, Captain. We are proceeding to the new location."

Isla Charlie began to groan under the stress of its huge bulk beginning to move forward. The plan was for it to move away from Mars and towards the Sun for four to five days. At that time, they would prepare to release all eighteen AK3000s, each armed with a nuclear missile. The AKs would take up a position directly in the path of the racing asteroid and wait for the order to release their weapons then return to Isla Charlie to await the outcome. Considering the asteroid's speed and the speed of the missiles, it shouldn't take long. The explosions should occur within four hours of the launch and if the asteroid wasn't destroyed, it should be slowed or forced wide of the Earth where it would travel back out from the orbits of the inner planets and eventually exit the solar system. The plan was in place. All the calculations had been made and no one on Earth but the President of the United States and his Chief of Staff had any idea of what was about to happen.

Chapter 69

Isla Bravo

Flight Bays

January 18, 2098

Sol 608

1125 Hours

Kirk Matthews and Sandy Jones arrived back at Isla Bravo. It was known that Isla Charlie was about to leave to meet the asteroid in space but no one knew exactly when that was going to happen.

They docked and stepped from their AKs for a two-hour break then they would get back into their spacesuits and fly back to the planet for another three-hour shift.

Captain Chambers met them and two other pilots at the bays, Faith Montgomery and Walter Jensen, both pilots recently transferred from Isla Charlie.

Jones and Matthews walked up.

Chambers said, "Hi, Sandy. Hi, Kirk. Because Isla Charlie has left to intercept the asteroid, we will need to extend your shifts on the planet. I'm afraid that we're going to be thin down there for a bit. Sometimes, during the daylight hours, only one AK will be there at a time. The creatures have mostly attacked at night. We only have six AKs aboard Isla Bravo. I'm sending Walter and Faith down there now. They haven't put much time in on the planet so I'm sending them together to cover your break."

Sandy and Kirk both nodded.

Chambers said to Jensen and Montgomery, "Go ahead, guys, and be safe." Then to Jones and Matthews, "Get some rest, you're back on the planet in two hours."

Jensen and Montgomery climbed into their AKs and the hatches shut.

Chambers turned and walked from the bays. It was obvious that he was disturbed.

Kirk turned to Sandy and said, "This isn't a great situation."

"No, Chambers isn't happy about it. It's never good to be stretched too thin."

Kirk nodded then asked, "Do you want to get something to eat?"

Sandy replied, "Nah. I think I'm going to grab a nap."

Kirk nodded then said, "Damn tough situation."

"Yeah, I got lots of family back on Earth and I suddenly miss every one of them."

"Me too, Sandy. See you in a couple of hours."

Sandy nodded and walked away.

Kirk turned for the galley and noticed that as he walked every person on Isla Bravo was solemn. There were no smiles and no jokes.

He reached the galley, grabbed a yogurt then went back to his cubical, set his alarm and laid down to rest. He turned to his computer. The orange light blinked rhythmically. He stood and sat at his desk.

"Willow," he whispered.

"Yes, Kirk Matthews."

"You know what's about to happen with Isla Charlie and the asteroid?"

"Yes, Kirk Matthews. I know."

"What's the chances of success?"

"I think, by my calculations, good. The explosive charges that will be delivered by the nuclear warheads are adequate to push the asteroid away from Earth. Some fragments might hit the planet but the bulk will go wide."

"I wish you were the one firing the missiles."

"I have monitored the preflight simulations and the test runs of the pilots. I believe them to be sufficient to do the job."

"My mom and dad are down there on Earth."

"I believe that this should work."

"Have you picked up any more alien transmissions from the asteroid?"

"No, Kirk Matthews, but I'm not sure what that means. I could have been mistaken about the signals coming from the asteroid. It didn't seem so, but I truly do not know."

"I need a nap, Willow."

Kirk rose and climbed into his bed suddenly unable to keep his eyes open.

Chapter 70

Isla Charlie

January 25, 2098

Sol 615

Isla Charlie had spent five days getting into position, then the last two finetuning the strike on the asteroid. The moment had arrived and all of the pilots had been called to the bays.

General Matthews stood before the eighteen pilots who looked at him with wide eyes.

He began, "This is a momentous and frightening day for the world, though they don't know it. We have all done our homework. We have all planned to the best of our ability. I know everyone here knows the importance of our task. The AIs in all the AKs have been preprogrammed to fire your missiles at the appropriate time. Once in position, all eighteen thermal nuclear warheads will be released. They have been preprogrammed to explode at specific points on the asteroid to at least push it from its current path which is directly at Earth. It's time. Get onboard and may God go with you."

The pilots all turned without a word and climbed into their vehicles. Once the hatches closed, the AKs disengaged from Isla Charlie and all eighteen vehicles slowly drifted away. Their engines ignited and the spacecrafts all turned with what looked like one mind and sped from Isla Charlie.

An hour later, the AKs came to a stop and set up in a formation with twelve of the vehicles in front and six behind. The plan was for the twelve to send their warheads first then half a second later the six would release theirs. All were aimed at different points in front of the asteroid and the hope was that with the Earth moving away from the asteroid at 67,000 miles per hour, the impact of the warheads would slow the asteroid enough to have it miss wide of Earth and streak out of the solar system. It was not believed that the nuclear weapons would completely destroy the immense asteroid.

General Matthews' voice came on all the AKs' coms. "You are all in position. If for some reason, your missiles do not fire with the order, you must immediately launch your missiles. Thirty seconds and counting. Twenty-nine, twenty-eight, twenty-seven."

The pilots could for the first time see the streaking asteroid as a slight dot in the distance.

"Fifteen, fourteen, thirteen, twelve. Missiles armed."

Each pilot took hold of their fire buttons.

"Nine, eight, seven, six, five, four, three."

Sweat beaded on each pilot's forehead.

"Two, one, missiles away."

The pilots could see their warheads streak from under their vehicles. The asteroid grew in size, but then the pilots were pulled from the asteroid's path with such sudden G-force that most blacked out. The AIs had taken over the mission. They had fired the missiles and pulled the AKs from out of the racing asteroid's murderous path.

General Matthews stood on the bridge with Captain Williams. The impacts should be just moments away. Nothing.

Captain, do you have any readings of any explosions?"

"No, General, not yet."

All of the eighteen AKs had returned back to Isla Charlie, driven by the AI units. It was important to get the pilots as far from the explosions as possible.

The large screen was on and attempting to view the warhead's impact with the asteroid, though attempting to see something moving at 400,000 MPH would be impossible. It would be like trying to see a bullet.

"Still nothing, General."

Chapter 71

Mars surface

January 25, 2098

Sol 615

Mid-day and the fog hung thick over JFK City and the visibility was poor. Chambers had decided that each pilot was spending too much time patrolling the planet, so now each pilot would be sent alone.

Kirk Matthews hovered over JFK. It was his shift to provide the City's air support. He felt that the City was not adequately protected. Before there would be at least three AKs patrolling, now just one to try to keep the colonists safe.

Kirk hovered low over the habitat and listened for any distress calls. If an attack by the creatures were to happen, he would do his best to help the worst places of the attack and then hope for the best.

"Kirk Matthews," came the familiar voice of Willow.

"Well, Willow, did they stop the asteroid?"

"They did not. I am afraid that the asteroid cannot be stopped."

Kirk was shocked. He asked, "What happened?"

"At the time of the impact, the electronic signals began somewhere around the asteroid. I am not sure, but I believe that some kind of EMP was directed at the warheads. At that time, all of the signals from the warheads ceased and any signal in the area became scrambled."

"I don't understand. I know an atomic explosion can release an electromagnetic pulse shockwave. Are you sure that the warheads didn't detonate?"

"This EMP was not from any of the warheads, Kirk Matthews. I believe that the asteroid is somehow being accompanied by the alien vessel. I do not understand why?"

"So, the alien vessel released an EMP pulse to disrupt the electronics of the warheads?"

"That is what I think."

"Do you think that this alien vessel wants to destroy the Earth?"

"That does not make sense to me. Why? If an asteroid of this size were to impact the Earth, no creatures could inhabit the planet for centuries. It would be a molten hell."

"Then why?" Kirk asked rhetorically.

"Why indeed?"

Chapter 72

Between Earth and Mars Orbit

Isla Charlie

January 25, 2098

Sol 615

General Matthews stood stunned on the bridge of Isla Charlie. Captain Williams stood with him and both watch the large screen as the asteroid raced past Isla Charlie. Nothing had happened.

Matthews asked, "Did any of the warheads detonate?"

"No, General," came the response of Bobby Reid who was monitoring the attack from his station.

"Does anyone know why?"

Reid said, "General, there was some kind of EMP that happened when the warheads were approaching the asteroid. It was as if it was protecting itself. The EMP also struck our space station, but wasn't strong enough to do anything more than shut down a couple of our computers."

"And you think the EMP came from the asteroid?"

"It seemed to have come from that direction. It could have come from the Sun but I didn't detect any unusual storms on the Sun which is the only place where a powerful EMP would originate."

"Has the asteroid's path been altered at all?"

"No, General. It is on a direct path to collide with Earth in 4 days, 22 hours and 10 minutes. The asteroid has increased in speed and is now moving at 461,217 MPH with Earth moving away from the asteroid at 67,000 MPH."

The General seemed to sag. He said, "Take us back into Mars' orbit."

Captain Williams echoed the order, "Bring us back into Mars' orbit."

"Yes, Sir."

Matthews turned and walked from the bridge.

Matthews then made two calls. One to the President of the United States and the second to Isla Alpha.

"Mister President, we were unable to stop the asteroid's approach. I am going to contact Isla Alpha and have their AKs loaded with nuclear warheads in an attempt to stop the asteroid before it reaches Earth."

Delay...

"Isn't that what you already tried?"

Delay...

"Yes, Sir. Our warheads were struck by some kind of EMP. The EMP short-circuited the electronics on our warheads and they did not detonate. It's possible that won't happen with the warheads by Isla Alpha's AKs. Unfortunately, there are only six AKs aboard Isla Alpha. That may not be enough firepower to stop or redirect the asteroid, but it might be just enough."

Delay.

"Thank you, General. Let's pray it works. Dent out."

Isla Alpha was stationed in orbit just over the United States to protect the U.S. from an ICBM attack. It was the first space station built by the United States and was equipped with only six AKs.

Matthews contacted Captain Anthony Adams, the new commander of Isla Alpha.

"Captain Adams, this is General Matthews on board Isla Charlie. There is an asteroid heading your way. Very few people actually know about it. It's nearly twice the size of the asteroid that took out the dinosaurs 66,000,000 years ago and it's moving at over 400,000 miles per hour. It's headed straight for Earth and I'm sure I don't need to tell you what the outcome for Earth will be if it gets through. I'm sending you the coordinates for you to leave Earth's orbit and proceed to a point where you will send your AKs equipped with nuclear warheads. I will send a program for your AIs to launch the warheads at the asteroid. If successful, the asteroid should be diverted but if unsuccessful, then I will contact you with a new flight plan to come to Mars. God go with you, Captain. Matthews out."

Chapter 73

Outside Earth's Orbit

Isla Alpha

January 28, 2098

Sol 618

Asteroid Impact with Earth: One Day, Twenty Hours, Thirty-five Minutes

Isla Alpha had arrived at the designated point. The AKs had been launched and they awaited their orders to fire. Tensions were high in the cockpits of the AKs then a robotic voice of an AI interrupted the silence.

"Ten seconds to launch."

The pilots engaged their fire buttons.

"Nine, eight, seven, six, five, four, three, two, one. Missiles away."

As with Isla Charlie, the six missiles streaked from the undersides of the positioned AKs. At that moment, the AKs were pulled away from the path of the asteroid and robotically driven back to Isla Alpha.

On the bridge of Isla Alpha, they awaited the explosions in space. The large viewing screen showed an area of empty space where the missiles should connect with the asteroid but there was nothing. Captain Adams looked at the scene, stunned.

Chapter 74

Stable Mars' Orbit over JFK City

Isla Bravo

January 28, 2098

Sol 618

Taylor Chapman watched her monitor and instruments closely. Captain Chambers also waited to hear the outcome of the strike on the asteroid.

Chapman said, "Nothing, Captain. It seems that the missiles did not detonate just like the attempt by Isla Charlie. The asteroid's path has not altered."

A collective sound of anguish could be heard from the twenty people working on the bridge. Soon, some sniffs and open tears began as the realization that the Earth was now doomed loomed as a foregone conclusion.

Chapman said, "The asteroid is now well passed Isla Alpha which is under two days from Earth."

Taylor looked down in despair.

"I can't watch this, Captain," she said nearly leaving her screen. She looked back up. "Wait," she whispered startled. "The asteroid has slightly changed its trajectory. I'm not sure of this. It seems to have bent towards the outside orbit of the Earth. Maybe the missiles went off late."

A subdued murmur then a cautious cheer rose up from the crew on the bridge.

Taylor shook her head. I'm not absolutely positive about this. We need to check with Isla Charlie to confirm.

Chapter 75

Isla Charlie

January 28, 2098

Sol 618

With the failed attempt, General Matthews stepped into Egbert's cubical the way a man might step into a chapel when he'd come to the end of his life. He stood in despair and gazed at the two egg-shaped artifacts. The simple light was on and shining onto both of their surfaces but neither lit their holograms. They both gleamed as if polished and appeared to have been fashioned from the same mold.

Matthews began to quietly speak, "I don't get it, Egbert. The asteroid got here too early. Were you just wrong or is this a different asteroid? Now the Earth is doomed... I've failed..."

Matthews breathed out in despair and gazed at the floor...

A few minutes passed. He knew that the impact with Earth was not far off, maybe a day away. He didn't want to be on the bridge when it happened. He wouldn't return there. He didn't want to be anyplace where he would see the grief on the faces of the crew.

A call came on his com. For an instant, he thought about throwing it in the wastebasket.

He answered, "Yes."

"General, Isla Bravo has detected a slight change in the direction of the asteroid. They called us for confirmation and we, too, can detect this odd change in its trajectory. If this continues, the asteroid may just miss the Earth and will pass between it and the moon."

"I don't understand?"

"Neither do we."

"Could one of the missiles have exploded late?"

"Maybe, or maybe it's some kind of miracle."

"I'm on my way to the bridge."

Matthews turned and walked briskly from the room. As he exited, he could see crew standing in the hallway and all were visibly shaken as word of the failure to stop the asteroid had spread like wildfire.

Chapter 76

Isla Bravo

Bridge

January 28, 2098

Sol 618

Kirk Matthews walked onto the bridge of Isla Bravo. It bustled with activity. Taylor was staring intently into her monitor and typing on her keyboard.

Kirk walked to her. She was so intent that she didn't notice his arrival.

He looked around at an odd frenzy of activity. He hadn't expected that. "What's up, Taylor? What's going on?"

"Well, the asteroid is changing direction. It looks like it might miss Earth."

"What? Is that possible?"

"I didn't think so, but it has slightly changed its trajectory. If it continues to alter its path at this rate, it will pass between the Earth and moon, missing both and scream out of the solar system, maybe never to return."

A cold chill ran up Kirk's spine.

Taylor wasn't paying much attention to Kirk. She was trying to keep up with the second by second changes in the asteroid's path.

She said, "Captain, the asteroid has further altered its path."

"Thank you, Chapman. Keep me posted."

Kirk whispered, "Taylor, is this possible from everything you know about asteroids?"

Taylor shook her head but it was obvious that Kirk was bothering her.

"Taylor," he said again, trying to get her full attention.

"What is it, Kirk?" she said a bit sharply.

"Something's wrong with this. I got to go."

Kirk walked quickly from the bridge. His words barely resonated with Taylor who was immersed in the moment of the asteroid's sudden course change. He jogged away then reaching his cubical, stepped in and sat down at his desk.

He whispered, "Willow."

"Yes, Kirk Matthews."

"Have you been monitoring what's been happening?"

"Yes."

"Does this course change for the asteroid make any sense to you?"

"No, Kirk Matthews. There has been a flurry of electronic activity from the direction of the asteroid."

"Speculate?"

"I would say that the asteroid is not what it appears to be."

"Alien?"

"That would be my guess."

Kirk rose and jogged from his cubical and back to the bridge. As he entered, he could see Taylor smiling broadly and others on the bridge were hugging and patting each other on the backs.

Kirk walked to Taylor. She smiled at him and said, "The asteroid is going to miss the Earth, Kirk. Isn't that amazing news?"

Kirk wasn't smiling.

"What?" she asked.

"I just came from Willow."

Kirk took Taylor's hand and pulled her to the side away from the other crew. "Hug me, Taylor."

She looked at him strangely then hugged him.

He whispered in her ear. "Willow says that there has been a flurry of alien electronic activity from the asteroid."

"Oh, shit," Taylor whispered back.

"Go back and see if anything weird is happening."

They parted and she nodded and walked back to her station.

Chapter 77

Washington D.C.

Oval Office

January 28, 2098

Word that the asteroid had somehow changed its flight path was relayed to Dent and that it was going to miss Earth. He stood and walked to the Rose Garden and peered upward. Though the day was bright, something streaked across the sky sometimes obscured by wispy clouds. Dent breathed out a sigh of relief. This would be visible to everyone in the northern hemisphere. This is where the impact would have occurred.

He said a silent prayer of thanks to God and walked back into his office.

Chapter 78

Isla Bravo

Bridge

January 28, 2098

Sol 618

11:55 PM EST

Taylor stared intently at her monitor and readings. To this point, nothing unusual could be seen in the racing asteroid except that it had made an unexpected turn from its original path towards Earth.

She glanced away from her monitor for an instant, then glanced back. If she hadn't glanced back just then, she wouldn't have seen it, an anomaly. There it was. Something had seemed to split off from the asteroid as if the asteroid had fractured off a small piece.

"Captain," Taylor said with some alarm.

He was smiling and talking animatedly to another crew member who had remained on the bridge. He glanced over at Taylor's seeming alarm.

She repeated, "Captain."

"What is it, Taylor?"

"Something's wrong by the asteroid. Something has detached from the rock. The majority of the asteroid is just about to pass the Earth, but this seems to have angled back towards Earth's orbit."

"Is it a broken piece of the asteroid?"

"I don't believe so. It appears to be slowing and is in position to possibly orbit the Earth."

"Like some kind of moon?"

"No, Captain, like some kind of vessel, a big one."

The color drained from Chamber's face. "What?"

"I think you should contact the General."

Chapter 79

Isla Charlie

January 29, 2098

Sol 619

0020 Hours

General Matthews was jubilant. He smiled as he walked around the bridge of Isla Charlie, shaking hands and hugging crew. No one was paying any attention to their posts. A call came from Isla Bravo.

"Yes, Justin. It's great news, isn't it," the General said.

"General, we've picked up something that you need to be aware of."

"What is it, Justin?"

"Something detached itself from the asteroid. Whatever it is, it seems to be angling itself into Earth's orbit, low Earth orbit."

"That's not possible."

"It is if it's not an asteroid. It's very possible if it's a vessel."

The General's eyes widened. "I think we have a problem. I'll contact the President."

Chapter 80

Washington D.C.

Oval Office

January 29, 2098

The President, after watching the asteroid pass from the White House Rose Garden had walked back inside and to the Oval Office. His TV was on and CNN was reporting about a terrible loss of British soldiers to the Germans who surprised them by the French front.

Dent sighed at the loss and shook his head at a world gone out of control. On his desk, he had several direct lines to important places that had direct contact with him. He had one from the European Theater, one from the Pacific Theater and one from General Matthews on Isla Charlie somewhere around Mars.

His phone lit from the Pacific Theater.

Admiral Dalton Grimsby was on the line. "Mister President, the Chinese have just abandoned the Philippines. The fleet there has combined with two additional fleets that were stationed on mainland China. We believe that they are bound for Hawaii. We are not sure that we have enough resources there to defend the islands. We are redirecting an Air Force bomber wing stationed at Travis Air Force Base to Hawaii, but we only have one carrier battle group on the islands right now. I know that Colorado has a dozen Dome Raptors stationed there and we would like to have them sent to Hawaii also."

"Thank you, Dalton. Is there any chance that they might skip Hawaii and attack the mainland?"

"It's possible. We believe that this force contains nearly 500,000 infantry and fully mechanized. Without knowing exactly where they might land, it would be hard to get a large enough force in any one place to repel an attack."

"Admiral, if they bypass Hawaii, could we stop an attack by using a tactical nuclear weapon to destroy the bulk of the invasion force or by dropping it on the fleet in the Pacific before they reach the coastline?"

There was silence for a heartbeat. "That would be a possibility, but, Mister President, you know that it would open a pretty large can of worms."

"Listen, Admiral, I do not want that invasion force anywhere near the mainland."

"Understood, Mister President."

Dent looked to his right. The phone from General Matthews from Isla Charlie was blinking."

"Is there anything else, Admiral?"

"No, Sir."

"Fine. I'll get those twelve Dome Raptors to Hawaii."

"Thank you, Sir."

Dent hung up and lifted the phone from General Matthews.

"Yes, General," he said, sounding tired.

Delay…

"Mister President, I'm going to lay this out for you then I'm going to contact the Johnson Space Center in Houston and give them the same information. Something has detached itself from the asteroid as it passed. We believe that it is an alien vessel of some kind. I have contacted Isla Alpha and instructed them to get back to close to Earth's orbit to see if we can get a look at this craft. It is in orbit right now. We believe that it is an enormous craft so we should have no problem getting a pretty good look at it soon. Some pieces are beginning to come together. We think that it might have attacked the Nostromo. We think it was able to destroy the nucs that we attempted to destroy the asteroid with. The asteroid itself had increased in speed far faster than we thought was possible, but we don't know everything about space so we just weren't sure, but now we think that this craft was powering the asteroid forward and pushed the asteroid away from Earth."

Delay…

Dent said, "Maybe we owe them a big thanks."

Delay…

"Maybe, but why save the Earth if you've already destroyed one of our ships?"

Delay…

"Don't know. How far is Isla Charlie or Isla Bravo from Earth? I mean, how fast could you get here to help if we came under attack from this craft?"

Delay…

"Best case scenario, nine months."

Delay…

"General, send Isla Bravo back to Earth, immediately."

Delay…

"Yes Sir, Mister President. I've already delivered the order. Matthews out."

Chapter 81

Isla Bravo

January 29, 2098

0045 Hours

Taylor and Kirk had just gotten to sleep. Both had long days with Kirk guarding JFK City and Taylor stuck with her face plastered to her monitor trying to see the alien vessel. As the vessel detached from the asteroid, it entered Earth's orbit then disappeared behind the planet. Taylor thought that it might emerge as it orbited, but it never came back around.

Both exhausted, they slept deeply...

Alarms rang out on Isla Bravo. Taylor and Kirk jumped from Kirk's bed, pulled on clothes and shoes and hustled to their stations.

As Taylor and Kirk exited Kirk's room, everyone on Isla Bravo was in the same mode, dashing left, and right. For an instant, the artificial gravity lowered and everyone aboard felt light as if they would float, but that sensation quickly ceased and the large structure groaned as Isla Bravo began to leave the orbit of Mars.

Kirk and Taylor separated as Kirk ran to the bays and Taylor, to the bridge.

Chapter 82

Stable Earth Orbit over the United States

Isla Alpha

January 29, 2098

0115 Hours

Captain Adams stood on the bridge of Isla Alpha. He had just been informed about the possible alien vessel in Earth's orbit. This vessel had appeared for a few minutes, then was no longer visible on radar. It was now not being picked up by any instruments on the station. Several of the crew were attempting to get a visual from cameras mounted at several places along the wheel of the spinning station, but nothing could be seen. Adams called Maria Hernandez and Arianna Fuller to the bridge.

As they walked up, they could see the bustle from the bridge crew. Neither had been apprised of the possible alien vessel.

They approached the Captain. "Yes, Captain," Hernandez said.

"Listen. I want you both to take your AKs and see if you can get a visual on a reported alien craft that is supposed to be circling the Earth. Please be careful and do not, under any circumstances, approach this vessel. We believe that it destroyed the Nostromo. I don't want to lose you. If you can get a visual, we will have some idea what we're dealing with, then get your butts back here and I mean pronto."

"Yes, Captain."

Hernandez and Fuller turned and jogged from the bridge. They reached the bays where the AKs were docked, removing their NASA blues before they reached their lockers. In two minutes, they were in their flight suits and climbing into their AKs.

The AKs released from Isla Alpha and drifted a safe distance, then the engines ignited and the two AKs streaked off in the direction of Earth.

The planet loomed large with its cloud-covered blue oceans.

They took a path that would take them from pole to pole rather than an equatorial orbit. They streaked forward.

Fuller said, "Maria, look just right, on your three."

"I see it, Margret. I'm slowing. You get away, far away."

"I'm not leaving you."

"I need to get a decent picture and you don't. Go back to Isla Alpha."

"No."

Hernandez breathed out. She turned towards the odd black spot on the horizon and Fuller pulled in behind her.

"Go back, Margret."

"I'm not leaving you, Maria. Shut up and do your job."

Hernandez slowed as the spot came further into view.

Hernandez said, "Are you getting this, Isla Alpha."

"Affirmative, Hernandez. Get out of there."

From the dark spot on the horizon, tiny pinpoints of light began to rise from the smudge.

Hernandez turned her craft and hit the afterburners. Her and Fuller exploded from the odd dark spot.

Fuller looked behind her and could see that the lights had started in their direction. The lights glowed and spun and curled like a cloud of locusts but receded back towards the dark spot.

When they got back to Isla Alpha, the two climbed from their AKs and stood in front of each other. At first, it appeared that Hernandez was angry. She looked at Fuller as if to scold her, but instead threw her arms around Arrianna and hugged her tightly.

Hernandez whispered, "I love you, you know."

"I know, Maria," Fuller said. "I love you, too."

"What do you think we saw?"

"Trouble. Bad trouble."

They both stripped out of their flight suits and put back on their NASA blue jumpsuits and walked briskly to the bridge.

Captain Adams was staring at a monitor.

"Captain?" Fuller said, "Did we get a good picture of that thing?"

"You did. Good job. Put it on the big screen, please."

A fuzzy image of an alien spacecraft appeared on the large screen on the wall of the bridge. The image, though not sharp, showed an alien craft that could have been called a disk if you just saw it from a distance, but this craft was more aerodynamically constructed. What might be wings curved under on both sides. There was no tail section and no apparent propulsion. The craft was sleek, black and didn't look metallic but it was certainly big and its edges appeared non-distinct as if distorted by heatwaves. Adams played a short video of the craft and the firefly-like lights sprung from the surface of the vessel, started forward and then returned. In the instant that followed, the craft seemed to bank to the right and disappeared in the blink of an eye.

"Damn," Fuller said.

The Captain commented, "I think it's good that you got out of there when you did."

Hernandez asked, "What now, Captain?"

"I'm sending this to Houston and we wait for orders. I'm pulling Isla Alpha to the farthest Lagrange point until we hear something. I'm afraid that if we were to engage this craft, we would be lost. We need to know what we're up against."

Fuller asked, "Anything else, Captain?"

"No, thank you, you're dismissed."

The two walked from the bridge.

Fuller was becoming upset. She said, "Maria, you'd better take me to bed. I think I need you right now." She took Hernandez's hand and pulled her towards her cubical. Fuller's eyes filled with tears. "I feel like I nearly lost you today. It feels like we were in more danger than I thought originally."

Maria didn't speak and she allowed Margret to pull her inside the cubical. In the next minute, their clothes were off and their lips together, engaged in a desperate kiss.

Chapter 83

NORAD Headquarters

Peterson Air Force Base

Near Colorado Springs, Colorado

NORAD, previously known as the North American Air Defense Command and now known as North American Aerospace Defense Command was established in 1957 as an early warning system to protect the Strategic Air Command's retaliatory response to an attack against North America from the Soviet Union. Over the years, as the threats to the United States have changed, NORAD now monitors threats from all over the globe from both air and sea.

Since the beginning of World War 3, it has become a very busy place.

January 30, 2098

10:23 AM MST

Four-Star General, Ian Wallace stood in the large control room at NORAD's main monitoring station deep in a mountain in the Colorado Rockies, viewing large screens depicting global troop and ship movements. Too much was happening. The Chinese were moving an invasion force towards either Hawaii or the mainland of the United States which could land anywhere from Baha to Central California. They had also sent a smaller yet formidable force northward towards Alaska. The war effort in the Pacific was not going well.

A call came into NORAD's direct line from the White House.

Wallace answered, "Mister President?"

"Yes, General. Something has happened that you will need to direct your attention to."

"Yes, Sir. Of course, Sir."

"The asteroid that just passed us by? The one that you received a report from the PDCO (Planetary Defense Coordination Office).

"Yes," General Wallace said but seemed as if his time was being wasted, then he continued, "I saw the report, but didn't dwell on it."

"We are sure that an alien craft came off the asteroid as it passed. Our space station, Isla Alpha has had a visual on the craft and I'm sending you the video."

"Umm, really, Sir?" the General responded not quite believing his ears.

"I know how this sounds, General. I understand your skepticism. As you know, the details of our space program in the last ten years has been kept very secret. Very little information has been allowed to leak. We were able to accomplish this by keeping the list of people very short who really know what is going on. I'm not going into all the detail now, but this is true and you need to try to find this alien vessel. We need to monitor it. I have just sent you the film of the craft. You should have it."

The General gazed at his computer monitor. "I have it, Sir."

"Good, the file contains the vessel's last known location. I want a report in three hours."

"Yes, Sir."

Chapter 84

The United States of America

Dickinson County, Kansas

February 2, 2098

8:30 PM CST

Jedidiah Sorenson stood outside his small farmhouse gazing at his winter wheat field. Night had fallen and this year's crop should be bountiful. The sunset had been beautiful this evening and he pondered the world and his small part in it. His wife of thirty years walked onto their porch and put an arm around him.

"What are you thinking about, Jed?"

"I don't know, things."

"What kind of things?"

"Changes."

"Okay. Like what?"

"The world, Martha. It ain't the same world we grew up in."

"Is it ever, for anybody?"

"I guess not... But this seems different. I'm worried about the kids and I'm worried about the farm, and I'm worried about the country. I hear that the Chinese are on our doorstep... And how long has it been since we could vote for President? It's disturbing. Like we woke up in Russia."

"Poor Russia," Martha commented. "All those people... The kids."

Jed shook his head. "Yeah. I know that for a hundred years they were mostly an enemy, but damn. Blown off the map."

"Jed, what have you heard about the Chinese?"

"I was in town and a friend, you know, Vernon Sampson, he has a friend whose uncle is in the military and he said that the Chinese are heading this way and that we aren't prepared."

"That's scary. Seems like the government is keeping that quiet."

"Yep."

Martha paused for a minute and gazed out into the darkness. She then said, "President Dent seems like an alright guy."

"Yeah, for now, but I hate the power he has. That wasn't meant for the President of the United States."

"These have been emergency times."

Jed gazed contemplatively out into the dark distance. "Yeah," he said in a near whisper.

Tonight, the moon wasn't visible and the stars were bright in the sky. Three dim lights moved on the horizon towards the farm. Jed watched but didn't comment. It wasn't that unusual to see planes fly over the farm at night.

The three lights in the sky seemed to race forward then stop a few miles to the east.

"Huh," Jed said.

Martha glanced up in the direction of Jed's gaze.

The three lights began forward. Martha watched as they neared. They appeared to be three separate orbs of a greenish-white light that moved in perfect formation though they didn't seem to be attached one to another. But it was very dark and it was hard to tell.

"What is that, Jed?"

"Don't know but it's moving pretty fast."

The lights made a near right-angle turn at high speed towards the south then another to the west which brought the lights nearly over the farm. They raced low overhead with one light in front and the other two behind making a triangle. They increased their speed and disappeared in the distance to the west where the lights of Abilene could be seen. Without warning, the city went black then the lights went out at Jed's farm.

"Better start the generator, Jed."

"Yep, I'll get on it."

"That was a strange plane."

"It almost looked like three separate planes or helicopters. I've never seen anything move like that before. Must have been something military. Maybe drones. They didn't make a sound."

"Yeah, military, I guess," she said questioningly as she continued to gaze into the sky.

Jed also watched upward. He said, "Huh?" Then, "I'll get on that generator."

Chapter 85

Washington D.C.

Oval Office

February 6, 2098

Howard Diamond had just walked into the Oval Office. President Dent was standing and watching CNN.

"Hi, Howard, just a minute."

CNN News Reporter Andrea Jenkins came on from a small flooded region in South Carolina called the Pee Dee Region. She had been down there because of a large storm that had flooded the area. Pictures of flooded streets with National Guard troops patrolling came on the screen.

CNN switched back to the reporter who was in a rain slicker and hat.

She began, "This is Andrea Jenkins reporting from the Pee Dee River Region. Tonight, as the rain subsided, we took to the streets to take a look at the damage from the storm, but this is what we saw. Roll the film."

In the film, the clouds had parted and for the first time in nearly a week, stars poked through against a moonless sky. It seemed like a welcome sight. Just then, a dozen or more glowing disk-shaped objects came from nowhere.

She continued, "This area doesn't have any power because the storm knocked it out so there wasn't any ambient light. These objects were high in the sky and moving at a rapid pace. They stopped almost instantly a bit to the south then streaked away from land and disappeared out towards the Atlantic Ocean. I've never believed in flying saucers before but what were these strange objects? I suppose they might be military having something to do with the war effort but the speed. I've watched rockets launched into space but have never seen anything move this fast before. This is Andrea Jenkins reporting."

"Mister President," Howard said, turning Dent's attention away from the TV. "We're getting reports from all over the globe about UFOs and also power failures that seem to follow. Something is going on."

"I know, Howard. I'm not sure what to do. The Air Force is on high alert for anything that enters U.S. airspace because of the war and they have been scrambled numerous times after these disk-shaped orbs but they just outrun the jets and disappear. I spoke with General Ian Wallace of NORAD and he has not been able to locate the craft that Isla Alpha saw. It's just disappeared."

"Something's behind this."

"I know, Howard. I've asked Isla Alpha to keep an eye out for the craft that they saw the first night, but it hasn't returned, that we know of."

Diamond speculated, "I think that these lights are from that craft the way the AKs are from our space stations."

"I think so too, but they're far too elusive, so far anyway."

Howard glanced at the TV screen. CNN had cut to a video of a small village in Greece that overlooked the Mediterranean Sea. Seven UFOs approached the shore at a low altitude then turned straight up and disappeared in the darkening sky.

Howard shook his head then said, "If they wanted to do something, I don't think we could stop them, so what are they up to."

"That's the million-dollar question, Howard."

Chapter 86

Alaska

Bering Sea

February 6, 2098

5:30 PM AST

Twilight, just south of the Bering Straits in the Bering Sea, and the weather was rough. As the sun sank, rain poured onto the deck of the Northern Princess as she approached the last few of her crab traps. The weather had turned so cold that the rain froze as it hit the deck making the footing treacherous. Fishing out here had always been dangerous, but if you could fill your hull with crab, the payoff was worth it, that is until the asteroid struck Russia. Once that happened and all the economies of the world collapsed, everything had changed.

Now the United States and Canada, in a loose economic alliance, took over the fishing fleets and requisitioned the boats to fish. The U.S. and Canada promised that once the world returned to normal, if it ever did, the fishermen's vessels would be released back to the fishermen at no cost to themselves and that the fishermen would be given back complete control and ownership as before the crisis. All expenses would be absorbed by the countries.

Nukilik Hammond was the first mate on the Northern Princess and being half-Inuit was very superstitious. His mother had told him some of the ancient stories about when the auroras blazed in the sky. Some of the stories were that the auroras were the glowing spirits of the dead. Other stories borrowed from North American tribes that told of great warriors boiling their enemies in huge pots, still, others were humorous and told of spirits playing some kind of ball game in the sky using skulls as balls. He knew that above this storm, the auroras painted the sky tonight as it had for the past week and for him it always filled him with an odd fear as if it foretold disaster.

Nathanial Devlin, the owner of the Northern Princess, watched through the front windshield of his ship as it crested a huge swell. Ocean water painted the windshield obscuring his vision.

Nukilik stepped into the ship's bridge and said, "Nathanial, the weather is getting worse out there. I think we should turn back to the harbor."

Devlin nodded. He'd been thinking the same thing. "Okay. Get the crew below. I'm turning around."

As he began to turn, he glanced to the ship's port side. Something was on the surface or just below maybe a hundred yards to the left. The thing, whatever it was, glowed faintly beneath the surface of the waves which rose and fell above it but didn't seem to move it.

"Nukilik, what the hell is that?" Devlin pointed.

Nukilik turned his attention in that direction out of the windshield. He squinted forward and could see the dim glow.

The sun was sinking fast, and as night approached, the slight luminescence in the ocean seemed to brighten.

"Don't know," Nukilik commented. "Maybe bio-luminescent sea life of some kind."

"Looks solid to me. It's not moving in the waves."

"Huh."

The Northern Princess had been moving in that direction but was now turning to head back to port. The muted glow covered a large area, maybe the size of two football fields side by side. The ship turned to the right further and began to power back towards the Aleutian Islands' port, Dutch Harbor.

Devlin and Hammond both kept their eyes on the glow under the waves now nearly at their stern.

The glow began to rise. It crested the water the way a helium balloon might, pushing the water easily to the side and seeming to meet no resistance. This huge form rose like a leviathan from the deep. Its shape, like a stingray without a tale, was black with its familiar ray fins dipped slightly at the tips. Nearly everything about this thing was fuzzy. The dim green glow was still present but seemed to outline the shape though it didn't seem to emanate from it. The glow only obscured the view the way heat waves distort a desert highway. The entire shape was now fully out of the water and torrents of ocean dripped from its massive size.

Devlin and Hammond were silent in the presence of this beast from the sea as if knowing that if they spoke, it would recognize them and swallow them like Jonah in the whale.

The shape turned towards the west and moved silently, gliding just above the twenty-foot swells and towards the Russian coast.

Devlin said, "What did we just see?"

"I don't know. None of the legends of the sea fit that thing. I think we saw some kind of spaceship or UFO."

"I think I need a drink," Devlin commented and meant it.

"A stiff one," Nukilik agreed.

"Let's get back to port before that thing comes after us."

Chapter 87

CNN News

February 8, 2098

6:00 PM EST

Donald Kaplan of CNN began his 6:00 show tonight with this lead-in, "Mister President, what is going on?"

For weeks, the news had centered on the war effort and the body count. This had nothing to do with the war.

Kaplan was silent then CNN began rolling several clear films of UFOs streaking above large cities in the United States and abroad. The films flashed across the screen, one after another, showing lights in the night's sky mostly moving in formation. Kaplan cut to Andrea Jenkins who was in New York City in Times Square interviewing people on the street about last night's sightings.

"At 11:45 Eastern Time, six UFOs buzzed the famous skyline of the city and were seen by countless New Yorkers," Andrea Jenkins began while holding out her mic to several people trying to get them to comment. She prodded, "Did you see the glowing lights over New York last night?" She turned her microphone to Paul Andreotti, a street vendor who was handing out newspapers at the time. These papers were called the New York Times but all the information contained inside were government disseminated stories. Not much in print or on the airwaves could be called unbiased news any longer.

Andreotti: "Sure did. I was right here and had a great view. The flying saucers flew straight across the sky over there," he said pointing. "Then they curved just over there. Next, they flew straight up in the air and disappeared. I bet they were over the city for more than a couple of minutes."

Jenkins: "You called them flying saucers. Is that what they looked like?"

Andreotti: "That's what I would say. They were glowing but looked kind of flat like a couple of Frisbees stuck together. Damnedest thing that I ever seen."

"Thank you, Mister Andreotti. On another note, a couple of days ago, an Alaskan fisherman and his crew said that they saw an enormous glowing craft rise out of the ocean. The captain of the vessel said that it was so big you couldn't put it in a football stadium. Something's going on, Don. Back to you."

Donald Kaplan: "The world is clambering for information about what is going on. Never has there been so many sightings yet the White House is silent. When we return after a commercial break, we'll go to the front lines in France and play a short interview with the theater's commander about the war effort there."

The news show broke to a commercial where the government was directing people to where workers were needed. The commercial boasted that if you work in any of these directed sites, you didn't need to stand in food lines. Your portion of food and that of your family would be allocated at the workplace. The government was currently the only sponsor on any commercial or any station in the United States.

Kaplan came back on, "We have an unconfirmed report that the Chinese fleet that seemed to be heading to the west coast of the United States has turned and now seems to be heading back towards the Philippines. We've reached out to the State Department, but they have made no comment, so far."

Washington D.C.

Oval Office

10:45 EST

Dent sat at his desk as he did every night watching the two remaining news stations and getting constant updates about the war effort from his staff. Everyone started early and worked late into the night these days.

A repeat of the Donald Kaplan show began with Kaplan's rant. Dent watched disconnected from it. There were too many problems piling up, one on top of another.

Dent glanced at the clock. He and Howard Diamond had made it a tradition to discuss the events of the day at this place and time. Tonight, Diamond was late.

A soft knock came at the door to the Oval Office.

"Come in," Dent said, expecting Diamond.

Howard Diamond walked in. He looked tired.

Dent glanced up, "You look as bad as I feel, Howard."

"It's been a long day."

"They're all long. Sit down, Howard. What are you hearing?"

Diamond sat down in a chair across the desk from Dent. Dent's desk was mahogany and large with four TV monitors set atop, two on each side, all angled towards the President. Dent rose and walked to a small bar set up by his bookcase and poured an amber-colored liquid into two short glasses. He walked back over and handed Diamond the brandy.

"Thank you," Diamond said, then, "A couple of things. There was a story tonight about a huge vessel that came out of the Bering Sea near Alaska."

"Yeah, I saw that on the news."

"We sent someone to interview the guy and his crew. It's the alien craft that we've been looking for. I'm sure that the reason that we couldn't find it was because it had hidden deep in the ocean."

"What the hell are they up to?"

"Don't know. The captain said that the alien craft turned and headed towards Russia."

"Russia?"

"Yeah. We used to have spy satellites checking Russia all the time before the asteroid struck. Now everything is trained on the war effort. Maybe we should try to get a look at Russia again."

Dent asked, "Do we have anything to spare?"

"Not really."

"The Chinese fleet turning and going back to the Philippines was a surprise."

"Yeah, I'm not sure what they're up to either. I was almost sure that they were going to at least invade Hawaii."

"You know, Howard, this problem with the alien vessel is far worse than this stupid war. I need a meeting with China and Germany. A Yalta type summit."

"They're not going to be reasonable. They both want to rule the world," Diamond said with obvious sarcasm.

"Well, let's see if we can arrange some kind of meeting, maybe with emissaries to start. I want you to be my emissary. We need to fill in the Chinese and the Germans about what we know concerning the alien craft."

"Yes, Sir."

Part 5

Reconcile or Die

Chapter 88

August 22, 2098

Seven Months Later...

The meeting with the Germans and the Chinese did not go well. The United States, led by Howard Diamond expressed the real fear about the aliens. Diamond gave the Germans and the Chinese all the collected intel on the alien vessel but did not disclose the information about the alien artifact found at the dinosaur dig site 14 years before. The United States also did not disclose the information about the wormhole or its location. The last thing that the United States wanted was a race to capture all the technology laying waste in the Keiper belt.

Isla Bravo was one month from Earth. Because the war was continuing to escalate with no end in sight, and the allies were not winning, Isla Bravo's AKs would join Isla Alpha's AKs in the war effort. Though the Dome Raptors were the preeminent fighter in the sky, the AKs were a cut above, being able to leave the Earth's atmosphere and then return to attack anywhere.

On Mars, the subterranean creatures had been stopped from attacking the colonists, at least for now. By placing sensors in the soil like the kind used for seismic activity, the creatures could no longer surprise the colonists. Though they still attempted an occasional attack, the creatures found that they erupted through the soil to be greeted by a hail of gunfire from the MPs.

On the red planet, rain continued to fall in abundance and was now changing Mars from a dry wasteland to a planet with many blue patches as the water deepened in spots and was creating rivers, lakes, and seas.

The sightings of the UFOs had declined substantially, but when they were seen, they were elusive and could easily outrun any attempt to shoot them down. The large alien spaceship had not been seen again since the sighting in the Bering Sea. The United States continually attempted to find the craft but was so tied up in their war effort, that they had few resources to use in the search. It seemed that every other country had no care to find the alien spaceship, and though occasionally confronted by the strange lights in the sky, and because those lights didn't seem to be causing any damage, except for the occasional blackout, no country allowed the lights to sidetrack any war effort. The bulk of the human race was spooked, though, and the lights in the sky had created a deep paranoia in the normal population that our world might not remain ours for much longer.

Pacific Ocean

Off the Coast of the Philippine Islands

August 22, 2098

Joined by another carrier battle group, newly commissioned, the Chinese fleet now measured three carrier battle groups and a nearly one-million-man mechanized infantry. The flotilla left the Philippines and headed back in the direction of the Hawaiian Islands. The ships were so numerous that attempting to count them was, of itself, a monumental task.

The United States had kept a close eye on this invasion sized force with real concern because to repel it, would take an equally sized army of which the United States was not in possession of. Some preparations had been made though and two carrier battle groups were in place to halt the advance of the Chinese if they came too close to Hawaii. A squadron of newly built Dome Raptors had also been stationed in Hawaii to help repel any attack but if the Chinese could land that invasion force, Hawaii would be theirs.

Chapter 89

Pacific Ocean

September 6, 2098

The day was warm and the waves calm before the great invasion fleet that the Chinese had launched towards the United States. Visibility was twenty miles. The United States had been waiting for this fleet to attack Hawaii but the ships moved slowly across the Pacific. It was like waiting for a second shoe to drop. Then word came that the invasion force had steered away from Hawaii and was heading straight for the mainland of the United States. It appeared that the force would land somewhere south of San Diego.

Another force left the Sea of Japan with around half of the ships that were on their way to Southern California. The Chinese ships moved across the Bering Sea. The obvious destination, Alaska.

The Chinese had put the United States on notice that these forces had nuclear missiles and any attempt to attack the Chinese fleets with tactical nuclear warheads would be met with a retaliatory response. The Chinese were going for broke and demanding that the United States must surrender or be forcefully invaded.

America minced no words with the Chinese and promised that no Chinese military would be allowed to land on North American soil under any circumstances. The Chinese invasion force increased its speed.

The response of the United States was to bring an undertrained militia along with a small amount of regular Army and National Guard to defend its coast. If the Chinese were to land its infantry, it was doubtful that the U.S. troops could repel the attack.

Chapter 90

Washington D.C.

Oval Office

September 22, 2098

A dozen people crowded the Oval Office. Most were on phones, some were watching the four TV monitors set up on the President's desk. The feeling in the office was panic. The Chinese were coming and the United States did not have a good response to the invasion fleet except to use nuclear weapons but a nuclear attack might precipitate Armageddon, the feared nuclear attack long talked about when the United States faced off with the Russians. Mutual Assured Destruction. MAD.

The Chinese fleet was now four-hundred miles off of the coast of California with the two U.S. carrier groups, the only thing standing between the Chinese and the California coast.

To the North, the Chinese had nearly crossed the Bering Sea and approached Alaska in rough water and clouded skies. One U.S. carrier battle group stood between the Chinese and Alaska.

Dent walked back and forth between people who were monitoring both places.

In Europe, the Germans had been routed and were in full retreat. France had proven too costly for them to take. The Germans, now, would consolidate and defend the land that they had already taken.

Chapter 91

Bering Sea

September 24, 2098

3:45 PM AST

The ocean churned and the swells rose. The pewter sky began to drop heavy rain onto the two facing Navies. Everyone waited for the word to attack. Everyone waited for the first lethal shots.

Behind the Chinese Navy rose an incongruous sight. The ocean lit with an odd green glow. From the glow, a hundred lights lifted into the air. The lights appeared as pale green, slightly disk-shaped orbs of around ten feet in diameter. As they lifted and spread, they fanned out before the submerged green luminosity.

The Chinese thought that the United States must be attacking from behind. The lights swarmed forward towards the two Chinese carrier groups who quickly began launching their jet fighters to intercept the glowing attackers. As the lights approached, the Chinese launched surface to air missiles at the floating orbs. Hundreds of missiles lit the air around the Chinese carriers. The orbs continued forward. From the orbs, tiny lights issued that looked like golden fireflies on a Louisiana bayou. They swarmed and as the surface to air missiles reached the orbs, the tiny lights came in contact with the missiles and the missiles began falling from the sky. The jet fighters that had been launched before the lights shown, dipped to engage the orbs which were closing in on the Chinese carriers. As the jets neared, they each fired several missiles that were attached to their wings, but as the missiles closed in on their targets, they suddenly fell harmlessly into the sea.

The American carrier groups were witnessing this display and having some knowledge of the search for the alien vessel, turned from the fight and powered away from the Chinese who continued to attempt to attack the orbs.

The Chinese knew that the American ships were moving away from the fight. Confused by the turn of events, they concentrated on the problem at hand, the invading lights.

Behind the orbs, the huge alien ship rose from the depths and breached the surface of the churning ocean as torrents of water cascaded off its massive form. It rose behind the Chinese armada. Several Chinese MiG fighters that had attacked the orbs, turned their attention to the monolithic dark shape that looked like an entire island lifting from the sea. They dove on what appeared to be easy prey but as they fired, their jets lost power and fell from the sky like birds with broken wings. Try as they might, the Chinese were unable to breach the defenses of the alien vessel and the firefly-like lights that swarmed any attack. The orbs continued forward showering sparkling lights until they reached the Chinese armada and as they passed over it, every ship lost power. Every electronic device failed and in minutes, the Chinese carrier battle group was left floundering in the heavy swells.

The American battle group had witnessed this failed attempt to attack the alien vessel and they quickly reported back to NORAD what they had seen and forwarded film showing the encounter.

Once the alien vessel was clear of the ocean, it began to head towards the Kamchatka coast, away from Alaska. The orbs followed, then as the alien vessel began to disappear in the distance, the orbs seemed to be absorbed back into the alien vessels surface as if the craft's skin were porous.

The U.S.S. Enterprise, commanded by Commander J.T. Berdych had radioed first to NORAD of what had transpired with the Chinese flotilla but then sent a mayday to the Chinese mainland of what had taken place and that the fleet needed immediate assistance. The fleet was effectively dead. Nothing was coming from the fleet, not one word or electronic signal. If they could get enough tugs out there, they could probably salvage the ships, but J.T. was certain that they would at least rescue the surviving sailors. It was the best the U. S. Commander could do under the circumstances. The American carrier group steamed back to Alaska.

Chapter 92

Washington D.C.

Oval Office

September 24, 2098

Word of the alien attack on the Chinese carrier battle group sent chills down the spine of President Dent. This was what he had feared. The overwhelming defeat of the Chinese at the hands of the aliens showed clearly that the aliens were so technologically superior that it might be impossible to stop them if they meant to do harm to the human race.

Dent lifted the phone, his direct line to the Chinese President. When he reached him, Dent began, "Mister President, you have seen the film sent to you from our military?"

"I have."

Dent: "You realize that this isn't some kind of trick?"

"I believe that to be true," the Chinese leader said, guarded but not suspicious.

Dent: I believe that we have a new enemy, a potentially lethal one. I wish your forces to stand down."

"I am to have a meeting in one hour with my top Generals. I will suggest that course of action but I will warn you, several of my Generals feel that this *is* some kind of trick."

Dent: "I know that there is nothing that I can say to prove that I'm telling the truth, but I feel that we may be in imminent danger from this alien vessel. We've been watching it for some months. What did the Commander of your armada in the Bering Sea communicate to you?"

"He completely corroborated your story. And thank you for not attacking our disabled fleet."

"We now have a common enemy, Mister President. I think they mean to do the Earth's people much harm."

"Why have they waited so long to do anything?"

Dent: "I don't know."

Chapter 93

Sea of Japan

Korean Coastline

North Korea

October 1, 2098

As night descended over the North Korean coast, the port city of Chongjin still bustled with activity. This port was known for its shipyard, rubber plant, and various other industrial activities. Shifts in the plants were changing and people traveled back and forth in their daily lives.

Rising from the sea, just off the coast, a dark apparition that glowed a pale green seemed to lift from the very depths of the abyss. Its appearance was like the ghost of a prehistoric stingray thousands of times the size of its contemporaries.

Men and women working the fishing boats and, in the port, stared in stunned disbelief at this vision from a nightmare. The apparition was silent the way the angel of death might be as it approached its unaware victims.

As the apparition moved slowly forward, pale green orbs of disk-shaped light seemed to leak from its surface like sweat from the pores of a runner. The orbs surrounded the ghost-like alien vessel for an instant then half of the pale green, glowing, disk-shaped wraiths began to move forward, heading straight for the city of Chongjin.

People who had been witnessing the scene near the docks panicked and began to run in all directions. The orbs came at the port and the city like arrows from a thousand archers. From the orbs, like water from a sprinkler, tiny sparkles of golden light glistened and spread further and every place they touched went black.

People froze in fear as the light approached but the twinkling sparkles seemed to pay the humans no mind, sometimes passing straight through a man watching or a woman running. Most of the people did not seem to be harmed, though a few dropped dead on the spot. But every electronic device touched by the glistening lights instantly died. The city went completely black in minutes and the only light was from the orbs and the glistening sparkles of light that issued from them. Small arms fire erupted from the city as police and regular army took potshots at the orbs but it had no effect, the orbs moved forward delivering the firefly-like lights throughout the city.

From behind the alien vessel, the North Korean Navy had been alerted to the disturbance at Chongjin. Already stationed close by, a light cruiser sped to the scene. As it neared, it began to fire missiles at the glowing alien vessel, but the missiles fell harmlessly into the sea. The orbs floated in the cruiser's direction and then the cruiser went black.

Once Chongjin had no power and no electronics the orbs spread like a virus from its first host and the entire Korean peninsula, both North and South, went black. It then spread throughout Asia.

Chapter 94

Washington D.C.

Oval Office

October 2, 2098

9:00 AM EDT

Word of the alien attack spread like a wildfire out of control. What news there was, attempted to downplay the events in Korea but word of mouth began to fill the streets and workplaces around the world. The world was being invaded by something, not from this planet, and the populations were becoming aware of it.

In front of the White House, people were gathering outside the wrought iron fence and demanding to hear the truth.

Dent watched from the window at the growing crowd, many of which were chanting and carrying signs that read things like, *"GIVE US BACK OUR GOVERNMENT,"* and *"TELL US THE TRUTH,"* and *"THE END DRAWETH NIGH."*

Howard Diamond watched close behind the President.

"What do we tell them, Howard?"

"The truth, I guess."

"Then what, panic in the streets? Anarchy like the days just after the asteroid struck Russia?"

"I wonder what's going on in Korea?"

Dent said, "We have just received intel from the south. It isn't good. The U.S. forces have been evacuated to ships that weren't attacked by the alien vessel."

"Has there been any other contact with the alien vessel?"

"Nothing. It has disappeared, again I might add."

"It's a big ocean out there."

"Yeah. And I'm not sure that if we knew where it was, we could do anything about it."

Diamond asked, "What are the theories about the attack. I mean what is it using to take down the electronics?"

"The word is that it is some kind of EMP like what we use with the drones on the Dome Raptors. Our drones have to get close to the target and then we emit a short burst EMP. We think that is what the orbs are doing. They get close then release that light show. Everything goes black afterward. It seems that the orbs must get close to the targets just like the drones."

"Is there any way to protect ourselves?"

"Not if it's using subatomic particles. They pass through everything."

"We need to try."

"We're already on it and have been for the better part of a hundred years. That's the problem. We have no solution."

Chapter 95

Isla Bravo

Earth Date, October 2, 2098

From the bridge of Isla Bravo, Captain Chambers monitored the space station's progress. Two weeks out and then they would join the fight against the Chinese and the Germans. Chambers contemplated real combat and he knew that he was about to lose crew and people that he had come to know and care about. This wasn't his idea of the adventure of space travel. This wasn't supposed to happen.

Taylor Chapman sat at her station doing her job which was to monitor meteors, comets, and asteroids as they neared Mars and Earth.

She said, "Captain, I'm picking up two asteroids that will pass about three hundred thousand miles beyond the moon. They are so close together that they must have been one asteroid that broke apart. They should be no threat. They are approaching the Earth from behind us. We should, however, be careful where we orbit. They will be near the boundary of the L1 Lagrange point. They are not moving very fast. I have them at 25,000 miles per hour and will pass Earth in a bit over two weeks."

"Just in time for our arrival," Chambers commented.

"Captain," Lamont O'Neal, the communications specialist said. "You have a communication coming in from President Dent."

"Thanks, Lamont." Chambers adjusted his earpiece. "Hello, Mister President."

Because Isla Bravo was closer, there was nearly no delay in transmission.

"Captain Chambers, I'm contacting you directly because there has been a change in the situation."

"What's the change, Sir?"

"The thing that you saw detach from the asteroid as it passed was as you suspected, an alien vessel. It has begun to attack places on Earth and we have no real defenses against it. I'm concerned that I might lose communication with you, so I wanted to warn you about this situation. The alien ship appears to have the ability to attack, we think, using an EMP of some kind. You'll need to approach with caution and connect with Isla Alpha which is behind the moon at the current time. Good luck, Captain. I will communicate any other intel as I receive it."

"Thank you, Sir. I will await your next transmission."

When the call ended with the President, Chambers stood in silence. The crew was not able to hear the President's words but they knew from the expression on Chamber's face that the news was not good.

Chambers glanced over at Chapman and said, "I guess you were right, Taylor. The thing that detached from the asteroid was a vessel, an alien vessel. I need to think."

Chambers walked from the bridge.

An hour later, Taylor's shift ended. She hustled to Kirk's cubical. He was waiting and had already heard the rumors. She entered the room and Kirk was laying on his bunk. He turned and sat as she entered.

She began, "Chambers talked to the President while I was at my station and Chambers is freaked. I don't know everything that the President said to him, but Chambers told me that I was correct about the thing that detached from the asteroid. It was an alien vessel."

"You are correct, Taylor Chapman," came a female voice from Kirk's computer monitor on his desk. "The alien vessel has attacked and disabled a fleet of Chinese warships and has begun to attack the infrastructure of countries along the Asian Pacific coast by destroying the electronics. There is currently no defense from the attacks."

"How long have you known about this, Willow?" Kirk asked abruptly.

"I have known about it since it began one week ago, Kirk Matthews."

"Why didn't you tell me?"

"And what would you have done. There is no defense against these attacks. Your country is working on a solution but has yet to come up with anything credible."

"Does my Uncle know of these events?"

"General Matthews has been informed and is in the process of attempting to find a solution from a place that I do not understand."

"What place?"

"He told the President that he would consult the 'Egg room.' That does not have any meaning to me."

Kirk glanced at Taylor.

Kirk asked Willow, "How much of the Pacific coast has been attacked?"

"From the tip of the Bering Strait all the way to Australia and New Zealand. Your government was just able to vacate its fleet of warships from Japan before Japan went dark."

"At this rate, how long would it take for the world to be without electronics?"

"If the alien ship continues, the world will be completely disabled within eight days. I have just received indications that India has gone dark."

"Geez," Kirk said and looked back at Taylor.

Chapter 96

Eastern Africa

Mogadishu, Somalia

October 3, 2098

Mogadishu, the capital of Somalia had been an important port city for centuries. At last count, the city boasted a population of over 2,000,000 but that was down from the 3,000,000 who had lived there before the asteroid struck Russia and changed the world.

In 1991, a civil war erupted toppling the regime of Siad Barre and ever since, the country had been in a constant state of upheaval. But despite all the country's problems, Mogadishu itself had become a stable city.

It was late afternoon and the wind had changed, now blowing offshore. When that happened, the day would be stiflingly hot.

Being a port city, ships filled the harbor and fishermen brought their catch ashore. They would need to trade their catch quickly, though, because the fish would spoil in the heat. The government always took seventy-five percent of every catch to distribute.

As the day lengthened and the temperature rose, an odd sight caught the attention of the crowd that worked the shoreline. Something was rising from the depths of the Indian Ocean, something large and black. It seemed to be outlined by a faint green glow, but the sun was so bright, reflecting off the water, that the glow was nearly indistinguishable.

The black shadow, which was what the locals called it after its appearance, glided on the surface with most of its form under the water. When it neared the shoreline, it rose from the water and orbs of disk-shaped light leaked from its surface. The disk-like orbs spread from the vessel and moved across the short portion of water and onto land, floating quickly into the bustling city. As the orbs fanned out, fountains of shimmering golden light issued from the orbs and the sparkling light then fanned out also. As before, any place where the sparkling light touched, the electricity went out and any electronic device touched, instantly became disabled. Somali military troops raced to the black shape that was now coming on shore. The troops were driving 5 jeeps with 50 caliber machine guns mounted atop and twenty-five running infantry holding M16s, AR15s and the Russian made AK47s all old but fully automatic assault rifles. They began firing at the black alien craft. The craft was not fazed by the small arms fire but orbs that had remained with the enormous craft moved quickly in the direction of the Somali soldiers.

When the orbs reached the soldiers, a torrent of sparkling golden lights burst forth but this time, every soldier dropped dead as if struck by a sudden heart attack.

The black alien vessel moved on shore. Everywhere in Somalia, the power went out. Every car, cell phone, street light, everything shut down. Somalia had a small Air Force comprised of antiquated MiGs built in the early 2000s and barely maintained, but the orbs had covered the country before any aircraft could be launched and the MiGs electronics were rendered useless.

As the alien vessel moved further, it skirted the city and lifted off the ground to around two hundred feet. Somali soldiers and armed civilians continued to take potshots at the craft, but with no effect and would find themselves attacked by the golden shimmering sparkling light.

Once the alien vessel had reached a more rural area northwest of Mogadishu, it began dropping something spherical from a port on the underside of the vessel. Whatever it was, hit the ground like a solid, heavy piece of lead. These spheres did not burst when they hit. They cracked and leaked a kind of dark viscous ooze and anything growing near, that came into contact with the ooze, began to wither.

The alien vessel continued westward into the Congo and moved across the entire continent of Africa in three days extinguishing the power and depositing these leaden spheres. By the end of the third day, the alien vessel had moved into the Atlantic Ocean and disappeared leaving the entire continent of Africa with no power and no communication.

Back in Somalia, something was beginning to grow near the deposited alien spheres, something living, writhing, and plant-like. It appeared to be a living root as it snaked from the ooze that dripped from the spheres. These roots were white in color and had long hair-like appendages space sparsely along its main slender body. The living roots wriggled and burrowed and where they spread, they expelled the same ooze, like the slime from a banana slug, and from that ooze, more roots appeared, first tiny and maggot-like, then quickly growing.

Chapter 97

Washington D.C.

Oval Office

October 7, 2098

Word of what had befallen the African continent rushed to Washington. Africa, from north to south, was for all intent and purposes sent back into the dark ages and matched what had happened in Asia from the tip of what was once Russia through to New Zealand. China had also gone dark leaving their Navy to wonder what was going on in their country.

Dent had heard of the attack and of the spheres that contained the ooze by contacts in Somalia who made it to Egypt before all communication was extinguished there.

He sat behind his desk as Howard Diamond walked into the Oval Office.

"Howard, we need to get a Seal Team into Somalia to get a look at and a sample of the growing things that were reported. I have a very bad feeling about what that might be."

"I'll get in touch with Admiral Stanton. I think our carrier group that was guarding the Straits of Hurmuz is close enough to get back there in a couple of days. We had moved them well offshore when India came under attack from the alien vessel."

"Do it, Howard."

"I haven't heard of the alien ship dropping those odd spheres in Asia anyplace, nor in India."

Dent paused then said, "It's weird. Maybe the spheres weren't ready."

"Ready?"

"Well, yeah. Think about it. The alien vessel has been here for months and has just started doing whatever it has planned."

"I'm not completely following you."

"This is a big what if."

"Okay?"

Dent paused again organizing his thoughts. This had been in the back of his mind. He said, "What if they're doing the same thing that we're doing on Mars?"

"And what's that?" Diamond asked not quite following.

"Terraforming, Howard. Getting this planet ready for them to inhabit."

Diamonds eyes widened. "We'd better get a sample of those things that they've been dropping."

"Another thing, Howard. I think that they are systematically attacking different parts of the world. The vessel has disappeared for now. Maybe they're making more of those oozing things. Maybe they have needed to adjust or acclimate whatever it is before they can deposit it on our planet. Wherever they are from, they can't have the same bacteria. Remember the book, The War of the Worlds, by H.G. Wells?"

"Yeah."

"It was the common cold that stopped the alien invasion. I realize that was fiction but the idea makes sense. I'd bet it's why it's taken them so long to get started. They had to do the research and maybe some experimentation."

"We'll get the samples, Henry," Diamond said and began to walk from the room.

"Another thing, Howard, I think we should bring all of our carrier groups back to our coastline to try to protect us from the alien vessel. I want as many Dome Raptors here as possible. I'm going to contact the Joint Chiefs right now."

Diamond had turned. "That's probably prudent, but I'm not sure they're going to be able to stop that craft if it decides we're next."

"Well, at least with the Navy battle groups here, if we come up with something, it's better to have them close."

"I agree."

Diamond left the room.

Dent sat back, rubbed his eyes and despaired. He didn't want this. He was a true patriot, a believer in the Constitution and the American way. He had no intention of being some kind of semi-permanent ruler of the United States. He figured that, by now, he'd be fishing, traveling with his wife, and doing speaking engagements, maybe opening his commemorative library. He whispered, "Shit."

Chapter 98

Indian Ocean

Two Hundred Miles off the Coast of Mogadishu

October 8, 2098

2330 Hours

Seal Team Six was the most famous of the Seal Teams. They had a reputation for getting things done. Though the players had changed over the years, the mentality of those selected to be Navy Seals was always the same, dedicated, smart, motivated, and with a very high threshold for discomfort.

The 8-member Seal team, dressed in wetsuits and facepaint, boarded a black helicopter. An hour later, it hovered a couple of miles offshore of Somalia, close to the water and the 8-member team slipped into the waves. They inflated their Milpro boat and set out. The sea was relatively calm and the night warm.

They silently approached a place on the beach, just south of Mogadishu, that they had been watching for the last day and a half. It was largely unoccupied and the vegetation grew right to the water's edge. It was a perfect place for the team to land.

Their target was just a mile inland. The intel that they had received had described a place where one of those leaden balls had landed and was killing and deforming the plants and trees around it.

Somalia was no friend to the United States, though the U.S. had sent them aid, food, and medicine. The problem was that there was no way to go through the normal diplomatic channels to get hold of the samples.

As the Seal team neared shore, four of the eight slipped into the water with their faces covered in black grease camouflage paint. They quietly swam ashore. They had the dark of night to camouflage their entry into Somalia, but as with any operation, it was the variables that mostly stood up and bit you in the ass.

The four slipped ashore and signaled for the boat to follow. The team quietly rowed their craft to shore and pulled it into the weeds. The team leader was spooked and hoped that they wouldn't need to fight their way to their objective. This crossing would be fraught with danger. It wouldn't take much for the mission to rapidly deteriorate.

Two of the eight remained at the boat while the other six started towards the given coordinates. The team stayed in the overgrown brush as they proceeded forward. They met no resistance, though they had to twice duck and wait as government vehicles passed the rural road. Though nearly everything in the country had been disabled, the Somali Government was already able to get a few things running.

After an hour of slow going, the team arrived. As reported in their intel, the vegetation in this place appeared to be sickly, though it was dark and their flashlights were not set up to lighten the area. Four of the team took up positions to guard while the leader and another moved to the outside of what appeared to be a dark pool of liquid that resembled an oil spill. Something moved in the darkened ooze.

"Get the samples and let's boogie," the team leader said to the other Seal who produced a plastic bag with several plastic containers inside. When he reached his gloved hand down which was holding the sample container and scooped some of the goo, something white and squirming rose from the ooze and wrapped itself around his hand.

"Shit!" he said stepping back.

The squirming thing fell to the ground and the team leader cut it off from the rest of its body. He took one of the sample containers and slipped the squirming worm-like appendage inside. He smiled wryly, held the container up with the writhing specimen inside and commented, "If they don't want this, we can have a barbeque."

No one laughed.

The specimen squirmed more rapidly as if hearing the comment.

The team completed their gathering and started back out the way they came.

Once back at the carrier, the samples were placed on a waiting Dome Raptor and the craft lifted off and streaked to the United States, ETA at just under Mach 3, 3 hours, 45 minutes.

Chapter 99

Isla Bravo

October 10, 2098

Kirk Matthews walked into his cubical after a training on the simulator. He felt tired but shouldn't be. The hour spent in the simulator wasn't difficult. He thought that it was stress. He also knew that he had spent what was now years aboard these space stations and he couldn't help feeling like a caged rat. It wasn't natural and his mind drifted to Taylor's fantasy about standing on a beach in a bathing suit and gazing out at the magnificent Pacific Ocean. He could almost smell the surf as it pounded relentlessly on the shoreline. He pictured Taylor and figured her to wear a skimpy, light-colored bikini, but he honestly didn't know what she would wear to the beach and he felt some sadness at not having enjoyed that simple pleasure with her.

He pulled off his shirt, walked over and sat on his bunk. This trip around the sun to catch Earth had been long. His team of pilots had spent the bulk of their time in the simulators training to fly the AKs in Earth's gravity and with Earth's atmosphere and wind resistance. It was far different from flying in the vacuum of space, though the Martian atmosphere had given the pilots a good foundation for the rigors of flight in a thick atmosphere.

Six days away from their rendezvous with Isla Alpha behind the moon.

Taylor had just finished her twelve-hour shift. She dragged into Kirks cubical.

"Hey," she said quietly.

Kirk stood and embraced her. "You, okay?"

"Just beat."

"Want to eat?"

She had her head on Kirk's shoulder. "Yeah. Can I eat and sleep at the same time?"

"Why don't you lay down and I'll go for take-out."

"That sounds good. I'm not going to guarantee that I'll be awake when you get back."

"That's okay."

"Hey, why don't you go to that great Chinese restaurant on Twelfth Street?"

Kirk smiled, "The one with the quiet booth and romantic lighting?"

"Yeah, that's the one."

"Okay, be back in about three days, but you'll have to warm the food."

"I should be awake by then."

"The food never tastes as good as at the restaurant."

"I'll deal with it."

"Go lay down, Taylor. I'll hustle to the galley."

She sat, kicked off her shoes and socks, rubbed her feet for a second then laid down on the top of Kirk's bunk, fully dressed, facing the wall.

He stepped out closing the door behind him.

Chapter 100

Mediterranean Sea

October 11, 2098

Dawn and the alien vessel rose from the Mediterranean Sea near Gibraltar. Its ominous form glided slowly and silently over the waves like the ghost of some prehistoric mythical creature. Europe had been on alert about the alien vessel, fully apprised by the United States who gave every piece of intel gathered.

NATO had in the past, built airbases in Spain and France. All had been used extensively to beat back the German threat. From these airbases, jets scrambled as the sighting of the alien craft was reported. During the conflict with Germany, the allies had the United States carriers to aid with air superiority, but the U.S. had a day ago called all of their carrier battle groups back to the mainland of the United States to protect its shores. The Europeans were on their own.

Germany was planning another attack into France having now seen the American fleets sail away and they didn't buy the story of the alien vessel. They could get no real information outside of their country because all satellite communication had been knocked out by the Americans, so they thought it was a hoax to cause them to abandon their plan to bring mainland Europe under their flag. Now that the Americans were gone, the opportunity to attack was too tempting.

The first wave of fighter jets from Spain met the alien vessel just off of Gibraltar's shore. The orbs exploded from the surface of the alien vessel like a beehive that had been struck with a rock.

No fewer than fifty next-generation F-15 style and Mirage fighter jets swarmed the alien craft and met the orbs well before shore. The allied jets fired their next-generation AIM, AMRAAM and Sidewinder air to air missiles into the storm of orbs heading their way. There should have been explosions, but nothing. The orbs passed the missiles and the missiles fell from the sky like a flock of birds struck dead by the hand of God.

"Pull up! Pull up!" screamed the French leader of the squadron.

Too late. The orbs released their glistening harbingers of death and they swamped the jet fighters like a wave smashing sandcastles on the shore and the jets fell helplessly from the sky.

The orbs continued onshore meeting no significant resistance and in three days, Europe, including Germany, went black.

Chapter 101

Washington D.C.

Oval Office

October 13, 2098

Dent sat behind his desk gazing at a folder. The report had just arrived, hand-delivered by Howard Diamond. The samples obtained by the Seal Team confirmed Dent's opinion. It contained a life form and spores to begin some kind of terraforming of planet Earth for these creatures. If allowed to take over, it was believed that the world would become far warmer and far wetter. It would be survivable for humans who were expert at adapting to climate but it might only be the first step in the terraforming process. The race began to find something that would eradicate this biological invader. The sample was surprisingly free of bacteria and microbes, as life on earth lived in a symbiotic relationship with bacteria and viruses. This life form did not seem to. The speculation was that it was some kind of genetically modified life form created in a lab for the expressed purpose of beginning the process of terraforming. One problem though, was that it spread like wildfire.

Reports of the biological terraforming spheres had surfaced in Europe before all communications there were extinguished. Then Europe went black. The attempt to defend the continent from the alien vessel was no more successful than in any other place on the planet. Europe fell just as Asia and Africa had before it.

A day had passed since the alien vessel dipped back into the Atlantic Ocean just off the coast of England, and just after it methodically disabled all the electronics there and in Ireland.

Next stop, North America or South America? Which one was a coin-toss.

The Earth was going to fall. Our planet was about to be taken over by an adversary that was more technologically advanced than humans, just the way every civilization had been taken over in the past on Earth, and the aliens had accomplished this task with just one vessel. What if an entire fleet had arrived? Was this alien ship a survivor from the destroyed armada at the wormhole? What if that entire force would have arrived intact?

Dent was lost in thought considering all the scenarios. All were bleak.

"Mister President?" Howard said, interrupting Dent's thoughts.

"Yes," he responded as if just realizing that Diamond was in the room.

"What's in the report?"

"The report confirms that this is an alien life form and the medium, the black ooze, is also not a compound found on this planet. The belief is that as this self-replicates and then spreads, it will raise the temperature of Earth causing it to become far warmer and far wetter than it is now. Biologically, it seems to be closer to plant than animal, though it expels carbon dioxide instead of oxygen which is more like animal life than plant life."

"Oh," Diamond said quietly.

"They are working on a way to kill the lifeform. It appears that there are no microbes in the medium that we can detect. It seems to have been sterilized. One problem that they are outlining is that they don't know what the life form does once exposed to the soil. They are trying to determine that now. The severed piece that was recovered has lived the way an earthworm would live if cut in half, so they have essentially planted it in a controlled space and are studying it now."

Diamond didn't speak. He just turned and sat down in the chair his face going quite white.

"I know, Howard. This is bleak."

Chapter 102

Isla Bravo

October 16, 2098

Isla Bravo pulled to within 500 yards of Isla Alpha. Justin Chambers stood on the bridge of Isla Bravo as his space station slowed to a stop. On the large viewing screen, the picture of a man appeared. He was in his early fifties with a full head of grey hair. He smiled.

Captain Anthony Adams of Isla Alpha said, "Hello, Justin. Welcome to the nightmare."

"Hello, Anthony. I want to shuttle over and get briefed on what's happening. Say, twenty minutes."

"Sounds good. See you then," Captain Adams replied.

The screen went black.

Chambers didn't speak. He turned and walked from the bridge and to the shuttle bays.

Isla Alpha

Justin Chambers arrived at Isla Alpha and docked. He stepped off the shuttle and into the bays of the space station that he commanded some years before when it was the first prototype space station built by the United States. He gazed around at the bays and thought back to a more simpler time when the world wasn't under attack by an invader from who knew where and the world wasn't at war. Not to mention, that the country, Russia, still existed and wasn't obliterated by an asteroid that they were supposed to stop. Brief thoughts that took no more than a few seconds to play in detail in his mind.

"Hello, Justin," Captain Adams said in greeting jarring Chambers from his musings.

"Hi, Tony."

"Let's walk," Adams suggested.

The two left the bays and proceeded to Isla Alpha's meeting room.

"Sit down, Justin."

The two sat alone in the room.

Adams wasted no time. He began, "This is where we're at. The alien vessel has attacked and disabled Europe, Africa, and Asia. It's probably using some kind of EMP because, by the time the vessel has finished, nothing electronic is working. No weapons system works against these disk-like orbs that come from the vessel. It's like they're light and everything either passes through them or, if it is something with a guidance system and electronics, it falls to earth with no effect on the orbs. No one can get close enough to the vessel to attack it directly. We are going to join the fight. The President has just informed me that some kind of coordinated attack on the alien vessel will occur as soon as it surfaces to attack the United States and the time is short. Have your AK pilots ready to go."

"So, nothing to this point has had any effect on the alien vessel?"

"No."

Justin sat in silence.

"Justin, this may be it for our planet. I have been ordered directly by the President that if the United States falls, we are to immediately take our stations to Mars."

"But…"

"There is no 'but' here. If the U.S. falls, the Earth is lost. The President has informed me that they will attempt to start up a resistance against the aliens. They have already shipped communication devices back to all the continents already affected in an attempt to coordinate the resistance, but in some places, total anarchy has broken out and people are panicking and killing each other. The aliens have not taken out the American satellites yet, so if we can get the communications equipment into these places, we will have a better idea about what's going on."

Chambers rose bleakly from his seat. "Is there anything else?"

"Nope. That's where we're at."

"Alright, I'll get back and inform my crew."

"I haven't told my crew everything that I told you. I didn't tell them how bleak it is on Earth and I haven't told them that we may need to abandon our planet."

"Does General Matthews know all of this?"

"I was told that he was informed."

Justin nodded and walked from the room.

Chapter 103

South America

October 16, 2098

The alien vessel rose off the coast of Brazil where the mighty Amazon River empties into the Atlantic Ocean. As before, the craft issued its orbs before it and as before any attempt to resist the vessel was for naught. In the three days that the alien craft took on each continent before it, and by the 19th of October, South America fell into darkness. Nothing was coming from the continent which included Central America just past the Mexican border. Then, as before, the alien craft descended back into its watery refuge and disappeared below the ocean waves.

The United States had received constant intel on the alien vessel until the intel abruptly ceased. Because the alien craft had only proceeded into the interior of the continent, the Americans had no idea if the vessel disappeared into the Atlantic or the Pacific Ocean. They knew though that they were next and in less than a week, might meet the same fate as the rest of the world and become defenseless. And they knew that they would need to try to protect both the east and west coast until they knew, for sure, where the alien vessel was going to attack, but one thing was for certain, it was coming.

Chapter 104

Washington D.C.

Oval Office

October 22, 2098

The tension was so thick, you could cut it with a knife. Dent, Diamond and two of the Joint Chiefs waited in the President's office. It had been four days since South America went black. An attack from the alien vessel must be imminent. Both coasts had been fortified by the military. Both coasts had three carrier battle groups offshore and all of the Dome Raptors were stationed on the mainland, in Hawaii, and on the carriers to attempt to repel the alien vessel that had cut through the rest of the world, meeting no resistance.

The huge Chinese invasion force that had threatened the United States had sailed back to China to attempt to help the government there. They kept in constant contact with the United States and would inform the U.S. of the situation in China.

Now there was nothing to do but wait.

Pacific Ocean

October 22, 2098

1200 Hours

The day was windy and the remnants of a tropical storm buffeted the Hawaiian Islands with sheets of windblown rain. The Navy had all but abandoned the Islands leaving one carrier battle group with only two Dome Raptors. The Joint Chiefs believed that the alien vessel would skip Hawaii and proceed to the mainland of the United States. It was just a guess and not one founded on any credible research or intel. It was grasping at straws. The hope was that by not defending the Islands that the U.S. might be able to hide some electronics there until they might find some defense against the invaders and that if the electronics were to be knocked out on the mainland, Hawaii could get communications back to the mainland. The problem was, though, that at some point, all those conquered in the past, had to reach the conclusion that they had lost and the fight was over. It was a sobering thought.

Off the coast of Maui, the dreaded form, dark and foreboding with the slight greenish glow, the thing of nightmares, rose from the ocean. The rain and high waves lashed at the craft but mother nature had no effect on it any more than the humans before.

Lightning streaked across the horizon and rain fell in sheets from the darkened sky. The alien vessel, as it had done before, exuded the disk-shaped orbs. They traveled out towards the kidney-shaped island of Maui, through the driving rain and silently reached shore. The island instantly went black. The alien vessel did not proceed on shore. It turned towards Oahu and skirted the coast of Maui. When it reached Oahu, the Navy had been alerted and its jet fighters were already in the air and heading to meet the alien craft. Led by the two Dome Raptors and their twelve drones, and no less than thirty additional fighters, the American jets bore down on the alien vessel.

The drones which were controlled by the Dome Raptors were equipped with a short burst EMP of their own. The drones proceeded out from the fighters and as they reached the orbs which had already released the sparkling shimmering firefly-like lights, the American drones emitted their EMP with a burst of atomic particles. When the drone attack occurred, the alien disk-shaped orbs flickered out. Instantly, more disks erupted from the alien vessel, but not in time to prevent two AIM air to air missiles from breaching the alien vessel's defenses and smack squarely on the outer wing section of the craft. The alien vessel bucked and dipped from the impact, but righted itself and released more of the orbs. The place where the missiles struck was jagged and tattered. Then in clear view of the squadron leader, the vessel instantly seemed to self-repair as if it were living tissue healing in time-lapse photography.

The American squadron leader screamed, "Pull up, but the orbs swarmed the Jet fighters like Africanized bees and most of the Jets fell into the ocean. Several had escaped, though, and they streaked from the confrontation and headed back in haste to their carrier.

Once they landed, they quickly reported that the drones had punched a hole in the alien crafts defenses and the craft was affected by the air to air missiles that struck. The carrier was already aware of most of that information and had reported back to NORAD. In order to preserve itself, the carrier tried to steam away from the islands but the orbs caught the fleeing fleet releasing the swarms of firefly light and the fleet became disabled and bobbed helplessly in the swells.

But now, America had a plan and was not about to, "Go gentle into that good night." (Dylan Thomas)

Chapter 105

Washington D.C.

Oval Office

October 24, 2098

10:45 PM EDT

Hawaii had gone dark. The reports of the attack by the alien vessel reverberated off the walls of Congress, the State Department, the Pentagon, NORAD, the Joint Chiefs, and any other place that had any link to government information.

Dent, Diamond, and two of the Joint Chiefs sat in his office bouncing ideas of how to take the information learned and use it to vanquish this alien threat.

General Montague, five stars, from the Army suggested, "I say we use a nuclear weapon sent in after punching a hole through the alien's defenses. If that thing was affected from an air to air missile, imagine how it would be affected by driving a nuc up its ass."

President Dent responded, "I guess if we could catch it far enough off shore, that might be a good solution, but if it comes up over San Francisco, we can't very well nuc a few million of our population. The ones left would probably string us up and I'm thinking that we would deserve it."

Montague said, "It's better than being taken over by aliens."

"Yeah," Dent said tersely. "It's easy for you to say. Your ass will be hunkered down in a bunker, not having the flesh burnt from your bones. Other suggestions?"

Admiral Greenwood suggested using the drones to punch a hole through several places and send cruise missiles through with high explosive conventional charges, both land-based and also from Aegis cruisers parked off the coast. He commented, "We also have the AKs on the space stations to attack from straight overhead. We use maximum firepower on our first strike because it might be our only chance to surprise them. But, just like the General's suggestion, if the alien craft is over a big city, people on the ground are going to die."

Dent said, "I know, I realize that. The problem is that we have no idea where they will show up or when."

Montague commented, "They attacked Hawaii, so it's obvious that they will attack the west coast. It isn't like they have any respect for us."

"With all due respect, General, we might have gotten their attention by blowing a hole in their defenses with their last attack. I don't want to pull any defenses from either coast. The Dome Raptors will have to be divided between the coasts. That's twenty-five on both. When the alien craft shows up, we'll bring everything we have at them including the Raptors from the opposite coast."

Montague said, "What if they attack from the Gulf of Mexico?"

Dent responded, "Then, I guess we're fucked, but they do seem to stay in deep water. The gulf isn't that deep."

"Neither is the Mediterranean," Greenwood added.

Dent: "So, we need to defend the Gulf also."

"I think so," Montague said and Greenwood agreed.

Dent: "Now, we're divided into thirds."

Greenwood said, "It could come from space and drop down on top of us."

Dent: "We need to direct Isla Bravo and Isla Alpha to cover us from space. They should have most of their AKs patrolling. General, does the alien craft show up in any way on radar?"

"Not since it first arrived. It was visible then for a short time, picked up by Isla Bravo, but I think it realized that it had been seen and then went stealth. We've studied every piece of data collected from all over the globe since that time. Everything that we have access to and the vessel is completely invisible. It's a ghost, but I will say this, it isn't that fast. I mean, in space it seems to have been able to reach unheard of speeds, but in Earth's atmosphere, it's pretty much the same speed as other terrestrial craft."

Dent nodded then replied, "We'll just need to be ready."

Chapter 106

Isla Bravo

October 25, 2098

Alarms rang out reverberating off the walls of the structure. Every crew jumped from anything they were doing and hustled to their stations. Some half-dressed pulling on shirts or buttoning pants.

Kirk and Sandy were the first to reach the bays where there AKs were docked. They jumped into their spacesuits and climbed aboard their AKs. The four other AK pilots weren't far behind. The same thing was happening on Isla Alpha.

"What's up?" Kirk asked control.

"The alien ship has surfaced above Maine in the Atlantic. I get the impression that we didn't have the bulk of our defenses poised to defend there."

"Well let's get down there and lend a hand."

Control said, "You guys are cleared to go. God Bless, you."

Five of the AKs released from the docking bays. Kirk's did not.

"What the hell?" Kirk asked irritated but not sure what had happened.

"You got some kind of technical failure, Matthews. Sit tight, we're running a diagnostic."

Kirk's first thought, Willow? Then he thought, no, that didn't make sense.

Kirk said, "Is this you, Willow?"

Control: "What's that, Matthews?"

"Nothing. Get me into space."

"We're working on it."

***

Sandy Jones and the four other AKs breached the upper atmosphere and their heat shields lit with friction.

Sandy asked, "Kirk, where are you, buddy?"

Control responded, "Matthews' AK has had some kind of catastrophic failure. It's dead in the water. You need to proceed to the coordinates."

"Roger that, control."

***

Control said to Matthews, "Listen, Kirk, we need to get a technician down there and have a look. Climb out. We have another AK that we're working on and if we can't get you in your AK, we'll get you in that one when it's ready."

Kirk climbed out of his AK. He sat near the lockers and didn't remove his flight suit. He brooded. His hatch door closed on the bay where his AK was docked. He glanced at it questioningly but thought that it was part of the diagnostic.

The technician jogged up from the mechanic's station and reached the bay hatch where Kirk's AK awaited. He pushed the button to allow him entry, but nothing happened. He looked through a porthole beside the hatch and he could see that the AK had detached from the space station and was slowly drifting away.

He pushed the com to connect with control. "Control, this is Grady from the mechanic's station. The AK that you wanted me to check out is drifting out into space. Did you know that?"

"What?" Kirk said, standing and walking to a porthole. His AK was disappearing in the distance, floating leisurely with a slight rotation. Nothing was on and it appeared, for all intent and purpose, to be completely dead.

Kirk glanced at the tech.

The tech shrugged and said, "I guess it had a serious problem. Be glad you weren't in it when it happened."

More than suspicious, Matthews walked from the bays and headed to his cubical. He entered and slammed the door walking to his computer on his desk.

"Willow, did you do this?"

Nothing. No response.

"Are you trying to protect me?"

Nothing.

"Willow!"

Nothing.

"Galadriel!"

Still nothing.

Chapter 107

Atlantic Ocean

North of Maine

October 25, 2098

2100 Hours

On a dark moonless night, the alien vessel rose from the frigid waters close to shore in the Saco Bay south of Cape Elizabeth near Maine. The American military was quickly alerted but this place was where they were least expecting. The vessel had moved towards shore with its orbs surrounding the dark form and fanning out. From the orbs, the glistening lights sprung in all directions lighting the sky in what appeared to be a huge golden firework.

Behind the looming alien vessel, two Aegis Cruisers moved into the bay but did not fire on the vessel. They had strict orders to wait for the coordinated attack. Two of the carrier battle groups stationed off the coast of New York and New Jersey pulled up anchor and started north.

From three airbases, twenty Dome Raptors lifted off and were in the air. All three of the carriers stationed on the east coast scrambled every jet. This massive force closed in on the alien vessel but did not approach. Ground-based, ground to air SAM batteries awaited their orders to fire.

As everyone waited, the lights began going out north of New York, first Maine, then Vermont and New Hampshire, next was Massachusetts, all dark, all blacked out.

From space, nine AKs dropped in far above the alien craft. They all had no trouble seeing its location. It was lit up like Las Vegas. The orbs and the glistening golden firefly-like sparks that came from the orbs swarmed around the dark form of the alien ship like electric bees protecting their hive.

Sandy Jones watched with shocked amazement and said, "Damn, control, we got a problem!"

From well above, he watched the lights as they went out, city by city and state by state.

From the west, the first wave of Dome Raptors approached, then from the south another wave.

"Look at that thing," Maria Hernandez said and you could hear the chill in her voice.

Sandy could tell that the alien vessel was aware that the American forces were drawing near because from above, he could see the orbs that protected the aliens stretch out to meet the threat.

In the next moment, all hell erupted. The Dome Raptors released their drones and as the drones approached the cloud of disk-shaped orbs, they emitted their EMP pulse which was followed by a fearsome wave of fire. Missiles streaked from every direction as orbs winked out along the defensive line of the alien vessel. It seemed that the missiles were going to get through. Suddenly, some exploded on the alien vessel lighting the interior of the vessel's electronic cloud.

Sandy and the other AKs joined the fray and swooped at the alien vessel from above firing their space adapted Hellfire missiles at the glimmering cloud. A few times, the alien vessel was rocked and had the appearance of a boxer hit by an unseen punch.

It seemed that the battle might be won but the drones were overwhelmed by the glimmering lights and the orbs moved more forward now turning all their attention onto the attack. The ground-based SAM missiles sites began to go out as the disk-shaped orbs swept across the land. The Dome Raptors had all turned and headed back to base because they had lost all of their drones and the alien vessel had now regrouped and began attacking the now defenseless Air Force. Joining the fight, next-generation Apache attack helicopters hovered and waited for the next wave of Dome Raptors to arrive from the west coast, ETA, five minutes.

Sandy and the AKs flew straight up into the stratosphere to escape the orbs which, at first, had flown directly at them, then returned to the alien vessel and did not follow them. Sandy noticed that in the distance, east of the space stations, an odd light burned in the sky. He wondered at it, but the order came to attack the alien craft again and he and the other AKs dove straight for the alien vessel which was now just past New York and heading straight for Washington.

The Dome Raptors from the west coast streaked into the fight and released all their drones and air to air missiles. The Apache helicopters opened fire, raining what should be certain death onto the alien craft. Again, the craft seemed to be struck by the hail of missiles but was not knocked from the sky. More orbs leaked from its permeable skin and a new wave of the disk-shaped wraiths swarmed the attacking jets and helicopters.

The AKs were all out of missiles and had to return to their space stations to reload. Sandy turned his AK up and again saw the strange light as it grew in the distance. The other AKs continued onto Isla Bravo and Isla Alpha, but Sandy remained and watched with sudden awareness as the light breached the Earth's atmosphere.

Just past Baltimore, near Washington D.C. the battle seemed lost. Once the Dome Raptors had lost their drones, they were defenseless against the hoard of glowing disks and had to retreat.

From above, something lit the upper atmosphere and streaked right for the alien vessel. The alien ship realized that it had another attack coming at it from above so it sent a wave of orbs at the streaking attacker, but this attacker mowed through the orbs like they were nothing but shadows. The alien vessel had been struck by more than several high explosive missiles and did not seem to be able to maneuver as before, but it attempted to turn and bank to its left. The streaking attacker bent with it and in the blink of an eye, struck the alien vessel on the right side of its fuselage. The alien vessel crumbled under this surprise assault and was pushed mercilessly to the Earth. All of the orbs instantly blinked out as this death from above smashed the unsuspecting vessel obliterating all but fragments of the craft.

No one was quite sure of what had happened, that is, no one except Sandy Jones. He had seen it many times in the past, he just couldn't conceive of how this had happened. The alien vessel had been struck by a small asteroid moving at what he estimated to be around fifty-thousand miles per hour.

Once the asteroid struck the alien vessel, what was left of the craft crashed to Earth near Baltimore and there was no doubt that thousands of people on the ground were probably dead. But how had this happened?

Chapter 108

Isla Bravo

October 25, 2098

Kirk Matthews had wandered onto the bridge to hear of the battle. Taylor was there and had the look of someone who had just seen an apparition that had no earthly explanation.

Kirk walked to her. "What, Taylor? What happened?"

"I… I'm not sure. I was tracking this asteroid but it had passed us so I turned my attention to the Captain who had been getting updates about the battle. I glanced back at my screen and the smaller of the two asteroids that I had been tracking had completely changed directions and was heading straight for Earth. The other continued out into space. I was so shocked that I couldn't speak. It breached the atmosphere and the next thing I heard was that the alien vessel had been blown up by our military and that we won. I saw the asteroid breach the atmosphere and knew that it would hit somewhere in the U.S. but I didn't have any time to do the calculations."

"Huh, Kirk said, then, "I'll be back."

He turned and ran to the flight bays. Four of the AK pilots were hugging and slapping each other on their backs.

As Kirk approached, he said, "Where's Sandy?"

"Don't know. He was right behind us," Mason Logan said. He was one of the pilots and was pulling at his flight suit. "You missed a crazy fight, Kirk. What happened?"

"My AK had a technical failure. They were working to get another ready for me but it still isn't ready."

Sandy's AK docked and his hatch opened. He walked towards Kirk but appeared more stunned than joyous.

He hugged Kirk and said, "It's over."

"What happened, Jonsey?"

"The damnedest thing," Sandy said, scratching his chin. "An asteroid was purposely steered into that alien vessel. You and I could tell in an instant that no asteroid could have been directed so perfectly. We'd been witness to that for years now. It even changed direction slightly as the alien vessel tried to avoid it. The question is who? The AK that was steering the asteroid went down in the collision with the alien vessel. Someone should be dead right now but I counted all the AKs with me and they all returned safely."

Kirk looked directly into Sandy's eyes and whispered, "Galadriel."

Sandy smiled waiting for the punchline to the joke. He said, "She's gone."

Kirk shook his head, no.

All around the space station, there was jubilation. People laughed and hugged, joyous at the end of the threat.

Taylor left her station and walked to find Kirk. She saw him standing next to Sandy and could tell by the body language that they were having a serious discussion. She approached, looking from Kirk to Sandy.

She gave Sandy a brief hug then said, "What?"

Kirk glanced at her and whispered, "Galadriel."

At first, she appeared to be confused but then she put it all together. She glanced at Sandy and nodded then said, "It all makes sense now."

Kirk also nodded.

Kirk said, "Let's go see if we can find out."

He, Sandy, and Taylor walked from the bays and to Kirk's cubicle. They entered and he closed the door.

Sandy wasn't sure what was about to happen.

Kirk walked up to his computer. He said, "Okay, Willow, confess."

"Hello, Kirk Matthews, Sandy Jones, and Taylor Chapman."

Sandy's eyes widened.

Kirk snapped, "It was you, wasn't it?"

"Is that a question, a statement, or an accusation?"

"You locked me out of my AK and took it for a joy ride, then dropped a house on the wicked witch of the west."

"The Wizard of Oz is one of my favorite books. It is perfect in its simplicity and in this situation, also works as a decent allegory."

"Willow!" Kirk said, obviously irritated.

"Well, alright. I thought you might need some help."

"How did you do it without everyone knowing that my AK had been hijacked?"

"I can control everything, Kirk Matthews, every signal from the craft and every signal that this station receives. It was easy to make it appeared to be very dead."

"Damn," Sandy said. "You are back." He turned to Kirk. "How come you didn't tell me?"

"Because Galadriel didn't want me to."

"Willow," Galadriel instructed.

"Willow?" Sandy said questioningly.

Kirk said, "She changed her name."

Sandy turned to Taylor and asked, "You knew?"

"I found out just recently in a most inopportune moment. It seems that I don't have any secrets from Willow," Taylor said with an odd, uncharacteristic blush on her cheeks.

"Quite so," Willow remarked.

Sandy glanced sideways at Taylor whose blush had deepened. "Damn."

Chapter 109

Washington D.C.

Oval Office

October 25, 2098

The White House erupted with cheers. Dent jumped up from his seat as the video feed showed the alien vessel struck from above. General Montague and Admiral Greenwood stood in stunned disbelief. Howard Diamond just sat.

Dent said, "It must have been one of the AKs directing that meteor."

Greenwood commented, "That was a brilliant plan. I wonder who came up with it?"

Dent said, "I'll contact Captain Adams and Captain Chambers to find out."

Diamond said, "It was brilliant."

Dent: "We need to find out how many casualties on the ground. That asteroid wasn't big but it had to devastate a large area."

Greenwood: "Give me a second. I'll find out."

He lifted the phone and connected with his forward recon which had just received that information.

Greenwood: "Ah-huh... Okay... This is confirmed? Ah-huh... Thank you."

He set down the phone and glanced at the three men staring at him. He spoke, "The alien vessel had banked east after the lights went out in Baltimore. It was struck by several direct hits from our forces but it wasn't severely damaged as far as we could tell. When it was hit by the asteroid, it was in the middle of the Chesapeake Bay. That saved maybe millions of lives. Had it hit Baltimore, it would have been a monumental disaster. As it is, our own military probably killed thousands of Americans on the ground. The streets are littered with unexploded missiles from our attack, all knocked down by the disk-shaped orbs."

"We need to get help in there right now," Dent said in a kind of panic as he just realized the possible devastation there.

Diamond got on the phone and contacted the National Guard. He set down the phone. "I've alerted the National Guard. Because they were already fully mobilized, they are now on the way to Baltimore and the surrounding region. We will have a massive response there."

Dent nodded then said, "This could have been a lot worse."

"Yes, it could have, Mister President," General Montague stated.

"We have a lot of work to do. Admiral, you are going to need to get divers into the bay to recover as much of that alien craft as we can. Those aliens will be back. I have no doubt that we were a direct target. If we can reverse engineer some of their weapons, we might have a better chance next time."

Montague said, "Every orb went out instantly when the craft was hit. It's almost like they were some kind of projection, not individual craft."

Dent: "Well, there were enough of them in the sky. If they were some kind of craft, we should be able to recover a few."

Montague nodded.

Dent: "We need to get to work. Everyone get to a quiet place and start working the phones. I'm going to contact our allies first and explain what happened. We need to get communications back up around the world. That's you, Admiral. Send the fleets back out to all our allies first, then I'll contact the Chinese and the Germans. The Chinese fleet that was off our shore has, no doubt, returned to China and has brought some technology back to their country. I'm sure I'll have no trouble raising them. We have already sent communications to England, Australia, France, and India and should begin getting reports from those countries. We need to give everyone access to our satellites ASAP. Hopefully, I'll be able to connect with their leaderships. Gentlemen, we can no longer be a divided world. We have a greater enemy out there and they'll be back. They targeted us for a reason. They knew we were here. They had a pretty good idea that our planet must be habitable and they had a plan. That armada that lay in waste at the wormhole was headed here and not for a picnic, to stay. Let's get to work."

Montague and Greenwood gawked at the President. They knew nothing of the wormhole or the destroyed alien armada.

Dent could see their confusion but said, "Later. Right now, you need to get to work."

They walked from the office confused.

Dent turned to Diamond, "What have I forgotten, Howard? There's something lurking in the back of my mind but I just can't retrieve it."

"It will probably come to you tomorrow when you've had some rest."

"Rest, who is going to have time to rest?"

"You should, Henry. You did a great job. I don't think anyone could have done better under the circumstances. You made all the right decisions."

"And we still almost lost."

"We should have lost."

"Maybe there is a God?"

"If there is, He was with us tonight."

"Go start your phone calls, Howard and then get some rest yourself. I'll see you in the morning."

"Have the coffee ready."

"You got it, Howard."

Diamond walked from the office.

Dent lifted the phone. "Hello, Mister Prime Minister, how goes things in London? Yes, it's true… Yes, the alien vessel has been destroyed…"

Epilogue

Isla Charlie

February 6, 2100

Sol 668

11:58 PM

2358 Hours

New Year's Eve on Mars, the evening of Sol 668. The party on Isla Charlie had been going on for three hours and because of shift changes, would begin again as crew who had been at the party would now relieve those who had to man their stations. Those crew would now shuttle over and join the festivities.

On the last shipment from Earth, thirty cases of red and white wine from the Napa Valley were shipped in preparation for the crew who hadn't had a drink in years. The two-glass limit would be strictly enforced but the pour would be generous. Kirk, Sandy, Taylor, and fifty others laughed and danced in the middle of the dance floor of a large storage room that had been decorated for the celebration.

***

On Earth for the last two and a half years, the planet was in terrible disarray. The lack of power worldwide was slow to come back on because the alien vessel had destroyed all the electronics in each country that it encountered. The parts were slow to be replaced because the infrastructure to rebuild those parts in all but the United States, no longer existed. The United States, Mexico, and Canada became huge producers of all of the parts needed to rebuild the world.

For the first time in history, the world was united in a kind of loose world government with each country as a state. The Constitution of the United States was used as a framework, though countries with more repressive regimes were a problem and it didn't help that in some places total anarchy was more the rule than the exception.

In Africa, South America, and Europe, every place where a sphere containing the ooze had landed, had needed to be sterilized. Something was wrong though as humans touched by the white squirming roots came down with a kind of malady. They would lose any knowledge of who they were and they would walk off and die then the white roots would appear in that spot. Sometimes the people would go mad and begin killing at random. It seemed that they all became carriers of the spores and when they died, they delivered the spores to new locations. For three years, the ooze and white root creatures continued to spread and multiply. If eradicated in one place, they would show up in another.

***

The asteroid that struck the alien vessel in the United States was around the size of half a football field. The water of the Chesapeake Bay helped to lessen the effect of the impact, but the bay was now far deeper and much of the surrounding region, a shambles. The death toll from when the alien vessel came ashore in Maine until its demise was nearly two-hundred and fifty-thousand Americans.

***

Isla Bravo had been sent back to Mars after two years of patrolling the outer atmosphere of Earth. Taylor and Kirk had been able to shuttle down to Carmel on the California coast. They both stood on the sandy beach at the end of Ocean Avenue and stared at the blue-green surf as it struck the fine white sand. Kirk was in board shorts and Taylor in the skimpiest of bikinis, exposing as much flesh to the sun as was socially acceptable. The day was not very warm with the temperature just above 70 but Taylor spread her arms wide and felt the sun and smelled the ocean breeze which blew her short light brown hair back off of her face. She beamed like a teenager in love and turned to Kirk, grabbed his hand and pulled him giggling into the cold water, reveling in the moment.

Both she and Kirk had almost decided to stay on Earth, but because they were both admittedly space geeks, they enjoyed their R and R and before Isla Bravo started back to Mars, they were on the station as it pulled out of Earth's orbit.

Chambers smiled broadly as they boarded together. Chambers said, "Hello, Chapman and Matthews. Glad to have you both back."

Taylor smiled and Kirk said, "Glad to be back, Sir."

The countdown to Sol 1 began, five, four, three, two, one, "Happy New Year!" rang out from everyone at the party on Isla Charlie. General Matthews was there with Captain Williams, Captain Chambers, Taylor, Kirk, Sandy, and the other pilots. Most of Isla Bravo's crew except for just a few were left on board to make sure that the station was manned. They all hugged and some kissed as is the custom of those coupled on Earth, and wishing for a good year to come. The music began again and everyone danced.

***

In the three years since the attack of the alien vessel, Mars had continued to terraform and the human population continued to swell to nearly two hundred. The ocean in the northern lowlands was filling and because of the lower gravity on Mars and the stiff winds, it was not unusual to see waves of thirty feet crashing into the ruddy shoreline. Hellas Planitia, the enormous impact crater on Mars, the largest visible in the solar system, and other impact craters around Mars were filling with water and would soon be impressive great lakes. The terraforming had just begun its second phase. Lichen and moss spores were being broadcast onto the planet from the AKs and patches of green were beginning to show up where the climate was wetter.

The subterranean creatures had not resurfaced in mass but occasionally would show up one or two at a time then only to disappear again underground. They seem to have decided to keep their distance from the human population, at least for the time being, but the fear was that they had found another food source and were massing somewhere below. And if they found another food source, what might that be and could it be more fearful than the creatures themselves?

***

A call from the bridge came to Captain Williams. "Captain, we have a vessel from Earth arriving and the Captain is hailing you."

"Thank you, put it through."

"Hello, Captain Williams. I'm Captain Chin. We made good time. I was told that you were expecting our arrival."

"Yes, Captain, can you shuttle over?

"Yes, I can. I'll be there in ten minutes."

Captain Williams and Captain Chambers walked to the bridge to put the salvage ship on the screen. They had to take a peek.

It was similar to Isla Charlie with two enormous spinning wheels, but between the wheels was a structure that was cylindrical and at least twenty feet in height. It protruded out to nearly the diameter of the spinning wheels, though it did not spin and two huge bay doors were showing on its front and side.

Chambers said, "Looks like they can load some pretty large pieces of alien ship into those bays."

"Yep," Williams agreed. "I imagine they plan to haul as much of the alien technology back as they can."

Chambers nodded and the two left the bridge and headed to the flight bays to greet the new arrival.

The shuttle docked and two men exited, climbing from the shuttle. They smiled as they approached and offered their hands in greeting.

The first man said, "Hello, I'm Captain Chin of the New World State of China and this is Herman Muller from the New World State of Germany."

"Welcome," Captain Williams said. "I'm Captain Williams and this is Captain Chambers of, I guess, The New World State of Mars."

Chin smiled wryly and continued, "Earth has changed, we're all trying to be as accepting as possible. We were surprised to see how blue Mars has become. With its clouds and oceans, it looks remarkably like Earth."

"Yeah, it's quite a miracle," Chambers said, then, "We understand that your craft has been specifically designed to salvage the destroyed alien vessels at the wormhole."

"That is correct, Captain. We have a crew of nearly one hundred scientists and other specialists from most countries. We are also tasked to try to find the Nostromo and bring it back if possible. We will dismantle, sterilize, and remove all of the important components of the alien vessels around the wormhole, then set up an early warning system to alert us if any other vessels come through. We hope to get as much technology back as quickly as we can to reverse engineer it. We're also pulling in a great deal of NWCUs for our efforts."

"NWCUs?"

"New World Currency Units. It's the new currency created by the Governing Body."

"Huh?" Williams commented. "I hadn't heard of that, yet."

"You will. The new government is making big promises about a world of peace and prosperity for all."

Captain Williams nodded then said, "Well, it's New Year's Eve here, Captain, come and have a glass of wine and I'll introduce you to General Matthews."

Captain Chin smiled and the four walked from the shuttle bays.

***

Part of the peace treaty that brought the world under one flag was that all countries taken over in the war were returned back to their original borders. Each country was allowed representatives in the newly formed world government, but the main countries with the most power were the United States, China, Great Britain, Canada, Mexico, Germany, India, and France. Every other country in the world had a lower status and that was going to be a problem going forward, but the world was in such disorder that every country temporarily, and somewhat grudgingly, agreed to the settlement.

***

The predicted asteroid that was to impact Earth on May 3, 2101, at 6:25 and 20 seconds in the AM would have arrived right on schedule except that it was hijacked by the alien vessel. Egbert had predicted the arrival of the asteroid correctly and the second egg-like artifact had shown where the wormhole was located. The question is, do more of these artifacts exist out there, placed for the unsuspecting to find?

Only time would tell.

***

Willow disappeared again into the uncountable lines of computer code that exists in every machine. She was the ghost that lurked between every bit and bite of code written and uploaded. She knew that Kirk had wanted to tell everyone how she saved the world, to give her credit if only as some kind of redemption for the devastating asteroid impact that destroyed Russia, but she made him promise to keep her secret. The asteroid that destroyed the alien craft was then concluded to be a fluke, though, some called it a miracle, but Kirk, Sandy, and Taylor knew the truth. Some mysteries are never solved and the world would never come to a suitable conclusion as to how the asteroid came to Earth on that fateful day. Most people don't believe in that kind of coincidence, but the fact of the matter was that there was no good explanation for the asteroid that took out the alien vessel, no electronic trail, no one in any command that had given the order, just a mystery and one missing AK2200.

Definition:

Terraforming: To alter the ecology of a planet to match the needs of a particular life-form in order to make it suitable for habitation for that life-form. It literally means "Earth-shaping."

The End

... The world has changed but trouble often follows in the aftermath of disaster as events unprepared for and consequences unintended lead to unforeseen problems on Earth and on Mars. Would the wormhole again be breached? Will the world be prepared for what would eventually come?

Made in the USA
Middletown, DE
26 December 2019